Undone

Innocence

Thank you!

Best wishes always

Mike Wilson

Undone Innocence

A Novel by Mike Nelson

Edited by Peggy Jo Perry

Author Photo by Alice Nelson

Cover design by Judith S. Design & Creativity

www.judithsdesign.com

Note: *Interrobangs* "‽" have been used in dialogue throughout this manuscript to incorporate questions with exclamatory statements. (See Wikipedia)

To the innocent victims…

Chapter 1

The football arched in a perfect spiral barely above the nearest defender's head. Dave faked left, planted the spikes of his left foot securely in the sod, cut right, and reached above his head. The ball slammed into his hands. Out of the corner of his eye the flash of a blue uniform told him that he hadn't fooled the defender. He yanked the ball into his midsection a microsecond before the defender hit him low and hard.

Excruciating pain ripped through his left knee. In spite of the pain he extended the ball forward and saw it pass over the goal line's white stripe. Off to his right he heard the referee's piercing whistle. He'd done it! He'd caught the winning pass! There was no time remaining now for the other team to make a play!

His joy was short-lived. He pulled the ball against him as he slammed into the turf. A body landed on him. He angrily felt eager arms try unsuccessfully to wrestle the ball away from him. The play was over! What was this jerk doing? More piercing whistles rent the air. He lay still as bodies surrounded him. He could barely hear the referee's command over the roar of the crowd as someone tugged more gently at the ball.

He finally relaxed his grip. Someone pulled on his right arm to lift him to his feet. He tried to plant his left leg beneath him but something was terribly wrong. His leg wouldn't support his weight. He collapsed. Lightning strikes of pain stabbed through his knee. Someone rolled him over on his back.

"Look at his leg!" someone gasped. "It's busted!"

As people thronged around him, Dave fought to remain conscious. He tried to pull his body into a fetal position to relieve the pain but someone thrust him back against the grass.

"Don't move!" came a loud demand, "we've got a gurney coming!"

Dave crushed his flexible rubber mouthpiece between his teeth and thrust both fists into the sides of his facemask as he groaned. Nausea was only moments away. He fought it! He wouldn't allow himself to puke in front of the whole stadium. There were TV cameras everywhere! It was their championship game! He knew at that very moment that the cameras were replaying his winning catch. Other cameras were undoubtedly trained on him, writhing in agony in the end zone surrounded by his coach, the team doctor, and who knew how many of his teammates! If he lost it, tens of thousands of people would see him spew the contents of his stomach through his facemask.

Before he did, mercifully, he lost consciousness.

***

Dave was vaguely aware of extreme, unfathomable pain, voices and sounds as he drifted in and out of consciousness. He knew people were talking – discussing what they were seeing – what was to be done, but he didn't understand a word of what they were saying. He felt a swaying sensation as they moved whatever he was lying on into the darkened interior of an ambulance. Someone wrapped a belt across his chest, strapping his arms to his side. Someone else slipped an oxygen mask over his face. He was somewhat aware of a needle stick in his arm.

***

What seemed to be only moments later, Dave woke up in a sterile, white room. His helmet and the rest of his uniform were gone – replaced by what appeared to be a hospital gown.

"Hello Dave," a person wearing green scrubs, a matching facemask and hat greeted him. "How are you feeling?"

Dave moaned and tried to raise his right arm to swipe away at an itch hovering just beneath his right eye.

The person caught his arm. "Sorry Dave. You've got an IV in that arm. I'm sure you're feeling pretty groggy. We've given you a pretty heavy pain killer."

"What's going on?" Dave mumbled. His tongue felt like it was twice its normal size. His head was spinning.

"We're waiting for the orthopedic surgeon. He's reviewing your x-rays and ultrasounds right now. It looks like you destroyed your knee in that last play. It was pretty grotesque actually. When they brought you to us your leg from the knee down was pointed at a strange angle. We thought you'd broken your leg. The doctor said it would have been better if you had."

"What are they going to do to me?" Dave managed through clenched teeth.

"We'll know when the doctor gets here. Your mom and dad are in the waiting room. The doctor will review his findings with them first and then come and talk to you."

As he lay there waiting, other thoughts raced through his mind. He was here at Colorado State University on a football scholarship and he was in the first half of his junior year. If his knee was as bad as they said it was, it was probably a career-ending injury! He'd never had aspirations for a career in the NFL even though the scouts that he had talked to were interested. He'd been touted to be the best wide receiver in collegiate play that year.

Anguish swept over him. He hadn't read the fine print on his scholarship. What would happen if he couldn't play?

"Hello Dave," a male voice interrupted his thoughts. "I'm Dr. Hooper. I'm the resident orthopedic surgeon. My colleague and I just did an extensive review of the films of your knee and I'm afraid I don't have good news. When you got hit from the side like you did, your cleats were evidently locked into the sod and the force of the impact basically destroyed your knee. In retrospect it's too bad that the bones didn't break below the knee instead. We could have dealt with that. I'm sorry to have to be the one to tell you this, but our only recourse at this point is a full knee replacement. You didn't leave us much to work with."

Torrents of frustration and rage mixed with his pain. He wanted revenge. That player, probably the same one who had tried to steal the ball after the play, hadn't had to hit him that low! He'd seen cheap shots before. The idiot couldn't have stopped the play anyway. Dave was all but across the goal line when got was hit. The jerk had to know that a shot to the knee like that would be devastating. He transferred his agony to that player. He'd find him and somehow make him pay!

Dave drew a deep breath to gain control of his voice. "Do my parents know?"

"Yes. I just reviewed all of our findings with them. I realize you're of legal age and are perfectly capable of giving consent but we really don't have time to let you come down off of all the pain killers we've pumped into you so you can give us legal authorization. Under the circumstances, your parents can sign for you if that's okay?"

Dave gritted his teeth and nodded his head. "Will I ever be able to play ball again?" he asked, knowing before he even posed the question what the answer would be.

"Ever is a long time, Dave. Unfortunately, rehabilitation after a knee replacement like this with all the soft tissue injuries you've sustained will most likely require extensive physical therapy. I understand you're in your junior year at the university. I don't think you'll be able to play your senior year. I do think that given time your knee will heal. Don't get me wrong, though, it'll never be as good as it was but with a lot of work, you should be able to carry on a normal life."

Dave turned his head away as hot tears streaked down his cheeks. He'd been counting on his scholarship to get him through his undergraduate degree. He'd set his sights on an advanced degree in aeronautical engineering. In spite of the time demands of football, he'd been able to maintain a straight 4.0 grade point average.

That thought gave him pause. The current semester ended in a month! If he couldn't attend classes, how would that go? He wondered if it was too late to withdraw and repeat his last semester without it damaging his GPA?

"I know you haven't had any time to consider this," Dr. Hooper interrupted his thoughts, "but we need to get on with this. Do I have your approval?"

Dave nodded dumbly. What other option did he have?

Chapter 2

*P*atti was waiting in the recovery room with Dave's parents when the post-op team finished up and left. Dave's mom and dad stepped alongside his bed and watched for awhile. Patti stood patiently by, watching and waiting. Dave looked like he'd be out of it for awhile yet.

"I think we'll slip down to the cafeteria and grab a sandwich while he's out," Dave's dad, Frank, said. "Do you want to go with us?"

"No, you go ahead. I don't want him to be alone when he comes around," Patti said. "I really don't feel like eating anything right now anyway."

Patti stepped alongside Dave's bed as his parents left and watched him sleep. Thankfully, the pain was no longer skewing up his lightly-stubbled cheeks. The anesthesia was giving him a little break. He looked peaceful – and beautiful. She nearly blushed at the thought. Men weren't beautiful – ordinarily – but in her eyes, Dave was beautiful…

She reached out and swept his dark brown hair off his smooth, lightly-tanned forehead. He'd kept his hair trimmed fairly short, not like several of his teammates who wore theirs long enough that it stuck out from under their football helmets.

Dave's matching eyebrows were normal, neither bushy nor thin. She ran a finger along each in turn loving the feel of the coarse hair under her fingertips. She turned her head to look at his leg. The way they'd elevated his heavily-bandaged, lower leg he didn't look like he was five-eleven. He looked shorter somehow, vulnerable, and hurt.

She smiled as she studied his face and listened to his deep, even breathing. He'd been blessed with good skin, a prominent brow, and chin – and a set of full, soft lips. She resisted the urge to bend over and kiss them. His hospital gown had slid down a little off his muscled right shoulder revealing a coarse matt of dark, brown chest hair. She smiled at a thought. She'd often teased him when they went to the lake about having as much hair on his chest and back as a grizzly bear.

She gently touched his lips with a delicate fingertip and his eyes sprang open.

"Hey, hello hero," she muttered softly, as she watched his dark brown eyes flit from side to side, trying to focus on her, "how are you feeling?"

In spite of the pain grinding away at his lower leg, a warm rush of emotion swept over Dave as his eyes focused on her face. Patti and he had been together since high school – dates, dances, quiet *together* times.

"I'm great," he mumbled through his drug-addled consciousness. "Wanna go dancing?"

The shadow that passed across her face was unmistakable. She obviously wasn't in the mood to tease about his injury. He knew her as well or better than he did anyone – even his parents. He never tired of looking at her. She was beautiful – one of those gifted women who looked great whether he caught her sleepy-eyed first thing in the morning or after she'd just spent an hour getting ready for a date. She stood just shy of five foot six, sported a full head of thick, rich, auburn hair that always carried a soft sheen to it. She was nicely put together, slim but not skinny, full-breasted but not overly large. In short she could be any man's dream – and she was his.

"Sorry," he muttered, "I guess that was rather poor taste."

"No dancing tonight," she recovered quickly, adding a forced smile. "I'll give you a week or two. The Christmas dance is coming up next month and I've already bought a dress. From the looks of what you've got elevated at the foot of your bed, though, you won't be doing much dancing, for awhile anyway."

"And knowing you, I'll bet your dress is fabulous! Maybe I could get one of those scooters for one leg and you could just wheel me around to the beat of the music."

She winced. He could tell she was lying about the dress.

"Course you don't need a dress to look fabulous," he scrambled to keep her from knowing that he'd seen through her. "I'll bet you'd look great in just your underwear."

"You've never seen me that way so how would you know?" she grinned. "My mother hasn't even seen me in my underwear – well not since I was little anyway."

"Maybe not but I've got a great imagination!"

"You shouldn't go there. I think that's the drugs in you talking."

Dave closed his eyes for a few moments and a poignant pause passed between them.

"I was with your folks when the doctor came out of surgery and told them what he'd done to you," she finally continued. "It's late and nobody expected you to be completely out of the anesthetic yet. They went down to the cafeteria to grab a quick sandwich."

"Didn't they invite you to go along?"

"Yes but I was afraid you might come out of the anesthesia early and I didn't want you to be alone when you did."

She bent over him and softly kissed his lips. A familiar adrenaline rush flowed through him in spite of his grogginess.

"I was frantic when I saw the replays on the JumboTron," she said softly, reaching for his hand. "In normal fashion the media was right in there filming all the gore."

"Was there gore?" he asked groggily

"Not in so many words but it was ghastly! Your mom lost it when she saw the screen!"

"I almost puked," Dave moaned. "The only reason I didn't was I passed out before I could."

"That would have been newsworthy," she chuckled. "The camera kept switching from your face to your leg. If you'd blown chunks the whole world would have seen it. I could tell you were in a lot of pain. You were holding onto your helmet like you were afraid if they took it off, your head would come with it."

"I know. I guess it's a good thing that I stuck to a liquid diet before the game. I found out when I was running track in high school that I often got sick after a hard run."

More silence passed between them as he fought the effects of the drugs. It wasn't that they didn't have anything to say; it was just that they'd spent so much time together that verbal communication had slipped beneath the surface of the emotional bond they felt.

"I know you probably haven't had time to think about this yet," she finally broke the silence, "but what do you think you're going to do about school?"

His eyes flew open!

"That was one of the last things I worried about just before they took me into surgery – right after wondering what the status of my scholarship would be. Midterms were three weeks ago. I know I did well but I think it's too late to withdraw from my classes. I'm going to have to talk to the Dean. If under the circumstances I can't go back before finals, I may be able to take an incomplete and try to finish up my classes next term."

She smiled. "That was rather profound. I must have touched a nerve. If you weren't such a celebrity I'll bet I could go to class for you and take notes until you're well enough to gimp in there on your own. Of course I couldn't take your finals for you. As you already know, I'm math challenged."

"I haven't seen the doctor yet," he answered with a faraway look in his eyes. "Maybe I could get some sweet, young thing to push me to class in a wheelchair."

Patti pouted. "You know I'd volunteer but if you remember right, we arranged our classes at the same time so we could spend our non-school time together. I'm not as smart as you are. I'm struggling with a couple of my classes. I can't afford to skip any of my classes."

"I know that. I was just teasing."

"And you already know how I feel about other women," she answered curtly. "I'm sure if you advertised, you'd have a dozen volunteers."

"And now we're going to have *that* discussion again, aren't we?" he answered sullenly.

Patti looked away.

"You already know I can't be tied down right now," he added.

She spun her head back around to glare at him. "Is that what I am to you, chains, shackles?"

He was shocked at the tone of her reply. "You know better than that," he answered meekly.

"Do I?"

"You already know I applied to Purdue. Because of my GPA they've accepted my application to their graduate engineering program. In fact they wanted me to finish my undergraduate studies out there instead of here at Colorado State but my athletic scholarship is paying my bills."

"How long have you known that?" she snapped. "I knew you'd applied, but I didn't know you'd gotten an answer!"

"I got a letter about a week ago. I'd planned to tell you but I didn't get the chance with the big game coming up and all. I'm committed to Colorado State until my scholarship runs out anyway. I have another year before I can leave."

"I was going to ask you about that. Do you think you can play ball as a senior after this has happened?"

He looked away for a few moments. Finally gaining some control, he turned to face her again. "The doctor and I had a chat before I went under the knife. He told me that at best I'll be in rehab and even then I may never be the same. We both think my football career is over. I have to assume that the scholarship ends with my football career."

"What are you going to do then?"

"I don't know, Patti! I simply don't know! There are too many unanswered questions. I know that even though the football season is over for the year, my tuition is supposed to be paid through the end of my junior year. After that, if they drop my scholarship, which they probably will, I'll have to get loans to finish my senior year. If I'm going to have to get student loans to finish my degree anyway, maybe I'll take Purdue up on their offer and move out there to finish my senior year."

"We could get married. I could go with you and work to help put you through school."

"I think that Purdue's tuition is a lot higher than Colorado State's is. Could we afford that? I'll have to get a student loans anyway. Their graduate degree is four more years beyond my undergrad work."

He studied her eyes for a few moments. "I'm facing a five-year commitment, Patti, do you want children?"

"Of course I do but other married couples have done it! How many real couples wait until after school to get married?"

"I don't know if I want the distraction."

"Is that what I am to you – a distraction?"

11

"No! That's not what I'm saying! When I have kids I want to be able to be their dad. I'll want to spend time with them. I can't do that and carry a heavy scholastic load at the same time."

"So that's what's been holding you back – fear of having a family? You know we don't have to have kids right away!"

"No, I…"

"You don't need to explain! You just said it all! I've been hanging on all these years hoping…"

"I thought you were good with this! Your parents have been putting *you* through school. My scholarship has been paying *my* bills. If we'd gotten married all that would have changed!"

"Have you ever heard about economies of scale?" she asked, the anger rising in her voice. "It's almost as cheap for two to live in an apartment as it is for one – except for the food! My parents know what it's like to struggle when we're newlyweds. We've already talked about it. They're willing to keep paying my tuition, leave me on their health and car insurance and help with our living expenses. In fact, us sharing groceries and rent should actually give them a break."

"When did you talk to them about all this?"

A sly smile smoothed the corners of her frown. "Actually, Mom and I talked about all that the first year when I decided to follow you to Colorado State instead of going to school in Colorado Springs. You know how they feel about you. My mom and I have been building a hope chest since I graduated from high school, expecting you to ask me to marry you."

"Is that the only reason you came to Colorado State?"

"Are you totally blind or just selectively so?" she spat. "You can't lie there and tell me that this is the first time this subject has crossed your mind!"

"No it's not! I'm not dumb or blind! I love you, Patti! I want you!"

12

"Then I think it's time for you to make a move! I've been patient! I know your scholarship is limited in what it'll pay but I know we can make it work. Frankly, I'd have said yes if you'd asked me our first summer right out of high school, and I think you know that!"

Tears sprang into her eyes and she looked away.

"This is hardly the time or the place to talk about this," he pleaded quietly. "I'm not thinking too straight right now and I couldn't get down on one knee now even if I had a ring to offer you."

"I don't need a freaking ring this instant if that's what's bugging you! Just a promise would do. Other married students do this all the time!" she argued, unwilling to let the issue slip away unsettled. "I've been sitting here watching you sleep, thinking that maybe this was what it would take for you to finally want to take the next step."

"Can't this wait until I settle my head and get out of the hospital?" he asked. "After nearly four years together do we have to decide this right now?"

She studied his eyes for a few moments without answering, and then more tears traced her cheeks. "I think I already have my answer," she cried softly. "You've got tunnel vision, Dave. You're so focused on where you think you want to go that you can't see anything or anyone standing alongside that gilded highway stretching out in front of you."

She took a deep breath and walked away from his bedside.

She stopped just before she opened the heavy door leading into the hallway. "Thanksgiving is two weeks away. I've got one more week of classes and then I'm going home to be with my family," she said sadly. "You know where I live and you know my phone number. I know you don't like strong-willed women but frankly, I'm feeling like I've wasted the last four years of my life patiently waiting for you to make a commitment. I love you Dave. I've loved you ever since we met. But I'm going to need a little time now to take a hard look at our relationship. I don't want to see you or talk to you before I go home. If you call me before Thanksgiving, I won't answer your call.

You know you're always welcome at my home for Thanksgiving. If you show up then we'll talk about where we go from here. If you don't, it's over."

With that, she was gone…

Chapter 3

The door to Dave's hospital room had barely swung closed when his mom, Karen, pushed through it, followed closely by his dad, Frank.

"We just passed Patti in the hallway!" Karen said anxiously. "I think she was crying! She barely said hi. Did you two have words?"

"I suppose you could say that," Dave admitted sadly, "we started out talking about whether or not the school would cancel my athletic scholarship at the end of the term and the next thing you know she was pressing me for marriage commitments."

His mom walked to his bedside and reached out to touch his hand. "Her timing may not have been the best," Karen said as she smiled softly down at him, "but your father and I have been wondering the same thing for years. You two have been an item since high school. In case you haven't noticed, you're both certainly old enough to get married. She's a vibrant, intelligent, beautiful young woman. Her kind doesn't grow on trees!"

"That's not the issue!" Dave argued. "I'm barely three years into an eight-year college commitment!"

"So what you're telling me is your career is worth more than your relationship with Patti?"

"No Mom, it's not! I'm just trying to be realistic here. I can't afford a wife and a family right now!"

"If your father and I had made that decision, neither you nor your brother would be here. Do you think you're the first to face something like this?"

"You never told me anything like this before." Dave argued.

"You never asked," his dad countered. "We had a rough time of it but we survived and I don't regret it. In fact I think all that we sacrificed is the glue that held us together. I can't believe that you two have been dating for over four years now and you haven't taken your relationship to the next level."

"So now you two are teaming up against me?"

"No, we're not *against* you! We're *for* you!" Karen argued. "I'm telling you that I think you're making a big mistake! She won't wait forever and from what we saw tonight I'm afraid she might already be done. We love Patti. She'd be a great addition to our family. I think she'd make a great mom."

"That's the other side of the issue!" Dave responded. "Do you honestly think we could get married and wait another five years to have kids?"

"Why wait?"

"Because I don't want to be an absentee father!" he argued. "Getting an advanced engineering degree is a huge deal! I've heard people in the field tell me that they think it's as bad as medical school!"

"A busy father is better than no father at all," Frank spoke up. "Do you feel like I cheated you?"

"That's different."

"Why? You don't remember your early years – the years I was working on *my* degree. When you were little your mom filled in for me. By the time you were old enough to be my fishing buddy I was through school. I don't think that either you or Billy got left out of my life, do you? Do you feel cheated in any way?"

Dave held his peace. He was hurting and didn't feel like arguing. His dad was right though. It seemed like Frank had always been there for him. He'd gone to nearly every one of his Little League games. He'd been there to cheer him on at his track meets. When he'd

16

started playing football in high school his dad and his younger brother, Billy, had spent endless hours practicing the finer points of throwing and catching a football.

"I've seen the statistics, Dad!" Dave finally responded. "More than half of all marriages today end in divorce. A lot of the guys I know in school are already divorced. They're all struggling financially and they have horror stories to tell, especially if there are kids involved."

"I won't tell you that a marriage doesn't take a lot of commitment and sacrifice. In fact if you don't think you're capable of giving 110% to make it work, then don't do it! There's no place in a good marriage for selfishness! You've both got to be willing to lose yourself in your partner. If you don't or can't do that, it'll fail."

Dave looked at his mom.

"He's telling you the truth," she said softly. "We're not telling you that it isn't hard. It's the hardest thing you'll ever do in your life – a lot harder than building and surviving a career. But I can tell you all the sacrifice is worth it."

Frank put his hand on Dave's arm. "Sorry, Son, I know you probably feel like crap right now. I used to think that the most important thing in life was the office, my job, and my customers. I can't say they're not important because that's what pays my wages, but what I *can* tell you is at the end of the day there's nothing outside the front door of my own home that's really worth a damn. All that other stuff eventually fades away."

He paused for a moment to gather his thoughts.

"I had a wise boss tell me once," he finally continued, "when I got to thinking that I was irreplaceable, to stick my hand into a bucket of water and then yank it out as fast as I could. The dent I left in the water was how much difference I'd make to the company or to those who came in after me. Do you think you can say that about your family?"

"I need to do this on my own!" Dave argued. The pain was pushing his *angry* buttons.

"No Dave, you don't! Do you think that when you walked out of our front door on your way to the university that we locked the door behind you? You're always welcome in our home as is anyone you bring home with you, whether you stay for a day or a year, or even longer. Don't you think we're proud of what you've accomplished? We are, you know!"

Frank stared at Dave until he looked him in the eyes. "Your getting an athletic scholarship was a huge deal. You know we aren't rich. We can't afford to put you through college the way some of my cohorts have done for their kids, but you can get loans. Loans can be paid back. Sure you'll struggle, but it's doable. That's the way your mom and I got through school. I'll guarantee you that there will be lean years after you graduate because of that debt. Even though a lot of your generation think they need new cars, shiny toys, big vacations, and fancy new homes filled with all the latest gadgets to be happy, they're wrong! All you need is somebody who loves you and who is willing to share whatever comes along, be it a family of your own, economic challenges, or even wealth beyond your wildest dreams. At the end of the day anything you can't hold in your arms eventually rots or rusts away."

"So I guess you told me!" Dave answered, just wanting this all to go away.

"No," Karen argued, "we didn't just *tell* you anything! What we're trying to say is that we've been where you are. We've lived through a few things—enough that we know that like your dad just told you, anything you can't hold in your arms isn't really worth fighting for."

Nobody spoke for a few minutes as their respective emotions calmed.

"Patti told me that she doesn't want to see me or talk to me before Thanksgiving," Dave finally told them, "then she wants a commitment. I won't be told what to do!"

"She's not *telling* you what to do, Son," Frank quietly answered. "She's given you a choice, not an ultimatum. She's sacrificed four years of her life supporting you in every way she can, hoping that you care for her as much as she does for you. I think she's done. You need to carefully consider your next move. We all know Patti well enough to know that there's not a demanding bone in her body. If she's giving you until Thanksgiving to make up your mind, I think she is being more than fair. A lot of others would have ended it today—here and now and you wouldn't have had a choice. You need to do some serious thinking and if you really want her in your life, you need to make some plans. I think she's giving you the only second chance you're ever going to get with her."

"In case you haven't noticed," Karen added, "Patti is not a homely woman, nor is she flawed mentally or emotionally. Any hundred guys you know would move on her in a heartbeat if they got the chance. If you step away I don't think you'll be able to go back."

Chapter 4

The doctor discharged Dave from the hospital Monday at noon and after taking him to his dorm, his parents left for home. He had a pair of crutches, an old-man-style walker with a seat, and two months of rehab appointments. He'd wanted a scooter but he couldn't bend his new knee enough yet to use a scooter – even if he could have stood the pain of kneeling on it. His knee doctor had prescribed enough pain medication to keep him sane but he knew if he used very much of it he wouldn't be able to concentrate in class, and that was all important!

The rest of the week was a struggle in finding out what his limitations were and what his new normal would be. It wasn't easy but he made it to all of his classes on time and was able to spend time in the library studying, after his daily physical therapy appointments. Finals were coming the second week of December. He couldn't afford to slack off.

The most interesting thing about that first week out of the hospital was that only one of his so-called teammates sought him out to offer either congratulations on the win or condolences for his injury.

James caught him in the hallway his second day back and in spite of what Dave knew were his real feelings, James offered his condolences. James and he had competed for the same starting wide receiver position during all three years of his college career. James was at least an inch taller than him, blonde, and more heavily muscled. Dave never told him as much, but he was sure that's what gave him the edge over James. James spent way too much time in the gym buffing up and not as much time on the track building up his wind. An hour-glass physique was more important to James because that's what caught the women's attention. In all fairness, though, when the coach called for short passes in heavy traffic, James would regularly get the ball because that's where brute strength made the difference. When the play called for a hard sprint, that's when Dave got the ball. Dave could out sprint him, and quite frankly a lot of the other teams' defenders as well.

Dave smiled grimly at the thought. The breakaway plays that scored the exciting long-ball passes, and quite often a subsequent touchdown, most often came to him. He hadn't kept score. If he had, James probably had more receptions but Dave had more overall yards, and more passes completed for touchdowns. It quickly became obvious that James was jealous. James had had words with both his coach and with whatever quarterback was running the plays. Dave, on the other hand, didn't really care who carried the ball. He was a team player. James, on the other hand, was a grandstander.

They'd never had a face-to-face confrontation, but James, seldom if ever, congratulated him on a winning catch. That's why, when James approached him in the hallway to offer his condolences on his injury he knew that behind James' eyes the man was exuberant over losing Dave as his only competition.

When Dave began to feel bad about not being approached by any of his other teammates, his thoughts snapped back to Patti and he realized the real truth. Patti had been the only real social life that he'd had outside of the locker room. And now she was conspicuously absent…

In spite of what she'd told him in the hospital, he tried calling. She didn't answer. He left voice messages. She didn't return them. Finally in desperation he sent text messages, assuming that even if she refused to listen to his heart-rending phone messages, she'd at least read his text messages. Nobody ignored text messages. She did.

In all, the two weeks before Thanksgiving were going to be the longest two weeks of his life…

Initially Patti and he had planned on driving home together for Thanksgiving. They had the entire week of Thanksgiving off so on the Friday afternoon prior he sent her a text, offering to drive her home. She finally replied but her reply was simple and heart rending.

"What we need to say can't be said in the car." the message read.

***

"Didn't Patti drive home with you?" Dave's mom asked as he keyed the front door, walked into the formal living room and called out.

"No," he said sullenly as he gave his mom the mandatory hug, "she wouldn't answer my calls or texts. When I offered today after school to drive her home she told me that what we needed to say couldn't be said in a car."

"I can't say that's a good sign," Karen mused. "How do you plan to handle this? What are you going to say?"

"I have to assume now that when she told me she didn't want to talk to me before Thanksgiving that was a firm date. I don't know if that means the day of, or the day after. I'm going nuts, Mom! I don't know what to do!"

"Have you thought about getting her a ring?"

"Of course I have, but I really wanted her to help me pick it out. After all she'll be wearing it for the rest of her life – hopefully. That's a big decision!"

"Maybe you could get her a promise ring for now."

"I think I need to talk to her first. This isn't like her! Maybe, like you told me in the hospital, she's already decided that it's over. Maybe during the silence the past week she's been reinforcing her decision."

"I hope not," Karen said quietly. "After all you two have been through together, I don't think that would be fair."

She studied his eyes for a few moments.

"Has anything changed in your relationship the last couple of months?"

"I don't think so."

"Think hard!" she insisted, "if she's really about to end this, I'd think she'd have shown some warning signs."

"We've done nearly everything together. We arranged our schedules so we could hang out, study and because we live in the dorms we even eat together."

"How much time have you spent with the team?"

He looked down. "A lot," he answered after a few moments. "I spent all summer in training before she ever came out to school. Until the season final we practiced six days a week."

"Did you two study together?"

"Every day, after football practice in the library."

"I don't suppose you did much talking in the library. What about afterward?"

"I'd usually walk her to her dorm. Sometimes we'd grab a drink or a snack but we both had early classes. We couldn't spend many late nights together."

"What about Saturday and Sunday?"

"Saturdays I always met with the team, reviewed films, and had a light practice. That took most of the day. I'd use the rest of the day to study. We always went to church together and if there were any youth activities, we'd go to them. Then we'd mostly try to catch up on homework."

"Were you sexually active?"

"Mom!"

"Just asking."

"No. We both lived in the dorms for Pete's sake!"

She grinned. "That didn't stop your dad and me from making a little *together* time."

"That's awkward."

"I don't mean we were all over each other. We didn't actually do *the deed* until after we got married, but we had some very intimate dates, if you catch my drift."

"We've had those."

"But if that's true, after four years I have a hard time believing you haven't taken it to the next level."

"Don't think for a minute I haven't wanted to."

"How about Patti?"

"We talked about it but…"

"Never mind," Karen chuckled. "That's none of my business. I'm just trying to see your relationship through her eyes. I think she's been more than patient. I'm not her but the way I felt about your father I couldn't have remained celibate that long. We only dated seriously for about nine months and I could hardly keep my hands off him toward the end."

Karen blushed and turned away for a moment.

"I think I can see why it all boiled over that night in the hospital," she finally continued, looking back up at him. "Football has been *your* life from the first time you two met. In fact, if I remember right you asked her to the homecoming dance after the season opener your senior year in high school. She knows that your life is going to change a lot now that you're hurt and I think she's just trying to figure out where she fits,"

Dave looked down at his hands for a few moments before he answered.

"Any advice from a woman of *experience*?" he asked with a half-smile.

She hugged him and then stepped back to look in his eyes. "Do you love her, Dave? I mean do you *really* love her or are you just pals?"

"Yes of course I do!" he answered vehemently.

"Then you need to let *her* know that, and I don't mean just with a few words! You already told me that she wouldn't answer your texts or calls. Have you missed her?"

"I've had a hard time thinking about anything else. For the first time in three years at college I haven't been able to keep my mind on my homework."

"I'd say that's a good thing," Karen smiled. "That's probably the first thing you need to tell her. She needs to know that she means more to you than football, or anything else in your life for that matter."

She studied him for a moment. "When is this monumental meeting supposed to take place?"

"She hasn't said. I wanted her to drive home with me but she wouldn't. I've texted her twice since then but she hasn't responded. All I know for sure is that she told me in the hospital I was always welcome in her home for Thanksgiving."

"We were hoping you'd…"

She stopped and looked away. "Never mind," she muttered softly. "This is way more important."

"No it's not!" he fumed. "I have a family too! She needs to understand that!"

"Maybe she's hoping if you're willing to sacrifice our dinner together that you'll be serious about beginning your own traditions together."

"That's pretty selfish."

"No, actually," Karen said quietly, "I'd say that's pretty desperate on her part. I think she's decided to play hardball. Like some of us old folks used to say: *this is for all the marbles.* I'd follow her lead."

"What if…"

"If she invites you to *her* dinner? Then bring her over to our house afterward for pie," she smiled shrewdly.

***

Dave gave Patti her space until Sunday morning. Then he couldn't stand the suspense another moment.

"Hey Sweetheart," his text read, "it's Thanksgiving week. Can we do church together today?"

"No," came her nearly instant reply. "It's not Thanksgiving until Thursday. Come by for pie about four."

***

Dave was convinced that it took two weeks for the next four days to creep by. He tried to stay upbeat for his brother, Billy, and his folks but from the look on his mom's face, he knew she was seeing right through him. She cornered him in the family room Wednesday night and nodded knowingly at him until he got up and followed her into the other room.

"Have you been practicing your speech?" she asked solemnly.

"I can't do a speech. She'd see right through that."

"Then what are you planning to do?"

"I don't know, Mom. I hope she'll take the lead. This cooling off period was her idea. I assume she'll have plenty to say."

"And if she doesn't?"

"What do you mean by that?"

"She might want you to sweep her off her feet. She may be waiting for you to smother her with apologies even if you don't think you've done anything wrong. I know enough about football from following you and listening to your father explain the game to me to know that there are two inner teams on every team. You have a defensive team and an offensive team. Which are you planning to be?"

"I'm a wide receiver so I guess I play offense."

"A word of advice?"

"Please!"

"You need to be intense but keep in mind that she may want to be swept off her feet, not knocked down."

"I think I understand."

"Did you think to get her flowers?"

Dave swallowed hard. "Crap! It's after six! I'm sure the florist is closed. They won't be open on Thanksgiving Day!"

Karen smiled slyly. "I bought myself some roses. I could share."

"You never buy yourself flowers!"

"Your dad doesn't buy them for me either except on special occasions. I knew you wouldn't think of that so I dropped by Bloomfield's this afternoon. I couldn't decide on red roses or white so I got six of each. They're beautiful, even if I do say so myself!"

Tears brimmed around Dave's eyes as he reached out and pulled his mom into a hug just slightly less crushing than the bro hugs he gave his teammates after a big win.

"You're the best!" he murmured in her ear.

"Thank you, Dave, but you've got to know I didn't do it just for you. I love Patti! I'm hoping I can claim her as a daughter. In case you haven't noticed, I don't have one of those."

***

In normal Thanksgiving fashion, his dad, Billy, and he all plopped themselves on the sofa in front of the game while they waited for the turkey to roast. Karen, of course, busied herself putting together all of the other important parts of their million-course meal! Whenever one of the men drifted through the kitchen with the intent of helping, she firmly ran them off. It wasn't like she had thirty people to cook for! There were just the four of them and she had the meal down to a fine science. Besides, she loved their lavish accolades!

***

"Have you heard anything more from Purdue?" Frank asked over dinner.

"Not recently," Dave answered distractedly, "not since I got their letter of acceptance for my post graduate work."

"I would have thought that if they were serious about you finishing your senior year out there that they would have followed up."

"I doubt they know about my injury. Besides, my scholarship pays through the end of the school year."

"Are you sure about that?"

"I don't know why not! Even if they cut me from the team, this year's season is over. Everyone else on scholarships will be covered."

"In the NFL they have something called injured reserve," his dad explained. "They're required to pay a player out through the end of his contract even if he can't play again. I'm not sure that applies to you and college ball. At the back of my mind I'm thinking they may want those funds to hand over to another scholarship recipient."

"Can they do that?"

"I don't know Son. I don't think either one of us has a copy of the scholarship agreement you signed. You got that scholarship from

Colorado State, not through your high school. I think if I were you, I'd go see the Dean when you get back and get that settled. I don't think Purdue cares if you have to hobble to classes. If they're serious about their offer they may want you out there starting spring semester just after the first of the year."

"I don't think I want to go that soon."

"Oh yeah," Frank mused with a slight smile. "Today's the big day, isn't it? I saw that your mom swept up a nice bouquet of roses for you."

Nobody spoke for a few moments.

"Have you got a big speech ready to go along with those roses?" Frank finally asked.

"He told me that Patti would see right through a speech," Karen interjected.

"You're probably right," Frank agreed as he looked at Dave. "In things of the heart I have to defer to your mom, but if I were to give you a piece of advice, in spite of sounding mushy coming from me, I'd tell you to just tell her what's in your heart. You don't want to tell her what you think she wants to hear. That would be lying! You need to tell her how you feel. Don't sugarcoat it. Just be yourself. You two have been buddies for so long that she'll know if you're lying. Honesty is absolutely essential in a marriage. Without it you have nothing. If she doesn't like what you have to tell her at least she can make her decision based on fact and not on some romantic hope that you might try to snow her with."

Dave studied his plate for a few moments.

"I'm rooting for you, Son," Frank finally added. "I think your mom has already told you that we love the girl but it would be a mistake to continue something based on a lie just because you don't want to hurt her feelings. If you lie to her now, you'll lie to her again and you'll join half of the marriages in the rest of the world that split up."

Frank grinned at Dave's little brother. "So are you paying attention, Billy? You've been seeing a lot of that Brindley girl ever since you graduated from high school. Are you two planning something you haven't told us about yet?"

"No!" Billy laughed, "we're just friends."

"Your dad and I were just friends at first," Karen teased. "If I've been counting the months right, Billy, you haven't dated anybody but her now for going on six months. Just because Dave can't commit to anything doesn't mean that you need to follow in his footsteps."

Billy laughed. "Even though I haven't been seeing anyone else, Linda and I are still in that *seeing other people* mode. We like each other but neither one of us are breathing fire yet like you and Dad did. Besides, I'm a year younger than Dave and I'm not locked into a scholarship. I can still relax at school and play the field."

Chapter 5

Suddenly it was fifteen minutes to four. Karen had been watching the clock nearly as closely as Dave had. She carried the roses to the kitchen table.

"You don't want to be late, especially today!" she urged him. "Promptness denotes eagerness and I think that's one of the things that Patti will be looking for."

The time hadn't really sneaked up on Dave. He'd been fidgeting for the past half hour, hardly able to watch the second football game of the day. He got to his feet and took a deep breath.

Karen giggled. "If I didn't know better, I'd think this was your first Junior Prom or something. Nervousness looks good on you. She'll pick up on that in a heartbeat."

"Is that a good thing?"

"Of course it is. If you showed up all full of testosterone, strutting your stuff, she'd probably slam the door in your face."

The drive to Patti's house took a little over ten minutes. It only seemed like three! He found himself standing awkwardly at her front door, flowers in hand, way before he was ready. He rang the bell and hoped she'd be the one to open the door.

He was disappointed.

"Hello Dave," Patti's mom, Janet, said sweetly as she held the storm door open for him. "That's so very sweet of you to bring me flowers!" she teased. "They are for me, aren't they?"

For the first time since he'd met Patti's mom, he was speechless!

She laughed and pulled him into a quick embrace. "Sorry," she whispered, "that was cruel. She's watching the game with her dad. I'll go get her."

Dave nearly swallowed his tongue when Patti walked into the short entryway! It wasn't like he'd never seen her dressed up before, but today she'd gone way above and beyond. He instantly knew she'd dressed up just for him. Her mom was wearing blue jeans and a cardigan. Patti was wearing a new, red dress he'd never seen before. It clung to her in all of the right places, accenting her already perfect figure! He instantly felt way underdressed.

"I didn't know we were going out," he managed through his fright-restricted vocal cords.

She beamed!

"I assume you approve?" she asked as she quickly did a little flounce and reached for the roses. "Did you bring these for my mom?"

"I swear you two were cut from the same cloth!" he exclaimed. "She asked me the same thing. Can you two give me a little break here! I'm doing the best I can!"

Incredibly her smile broadened. "Give me those and I'll go find a vase."

"Will you hold me first?" he asked pleadingly. "I've been going crazy for you!"

Tears sprang to her eyes and she wrapped him up in an embrace that took what little breath away that he still had.

Neither spoke for long moments as the warmth of their bodies merged.

"Give me those!" Janet interrupted reaching for the flowers. "You're going to make a mess of them!"

Until that moment, Dave hadn't sensed the older woman's presence. All he saw, all he felt was Patti. He didn't want to let her go, but he had to in order to surrender the roses.

For awhile after Janet took the flowers and scurried away, Patti held him against her.

"You're nervous," she finally managed.

"Worse than on our first date!"

She giggled.

"Are we okay?" he asked quietly.

"That's what you're here to talk about."

"I'm ready," he said softly. "I've spent the past two weeks thinking about nothing but us."

"Then we have something in common," she answered, taking his hand. "Mom has already told me it'd be okay if we use my bedroom to talk. Even though you've never seen it before it's downstairs and pretty soundproof. How's your knee? Can you do stairs?"

"My therapist tells me I'm doing better than expected—something about being in great shape before the surgery. I can walk without crutches and I'm wearing what they call an abbreviated brace."

He stopped to look in her eyes. "I've never been in your bedroom before."

"No you haven't. Until now it's been off limits. That's been a cardinal rule around here."

"Should I be afraid?"

"Only if you're afraid of me. Mom said we can have an hour. After that she's going to send my dad down with a big stick to be sure there isn't any hanky-panky going on. I promised not to lock my door."

***

Patti had already prepped her bedroom. Two, padded folding chairs sat closely together facing one another at the foot of her pillow-and-stuffed-animal-covered bed. A box of tissues sat on the foot of the bed between the two chairs.

"Am I going to need those?" he teased as he seated himself gingerly on the chair she motioned him to.

"Probably not, but I think I will. In fact, I already do!"

She snatched a couple of tissues from the box and dabbed the tears off of her flawless cheeks.

"I'm at your mercy," Dave began softly when she seated herself facing him and took a deep breath.

"You blew me away with the flowers!" she began.

"I can't lie to you," he fumbled. "They were kinda my mom's idea. I didn't think about getting you flowers until last night after the florist had already closed. Mom was way ahead of me!"

Patti grinned her approval. "Thank you!" she said. "Somehow I knew that. At least you're man enough to start out our little chat with honesty."

"I've been looking back," he began in a rush. "I owe you a heartfelt apology. You were absolutely right when you told me that I couldn't see anything or anyone beyond that gilded highway I saw stretching out in front of me. I've been totally selfish and completely self-absorbed. I've wanted all of that so badly that I haven't stopped to pay attention to the things that really matter."

"Are you talking about me?"

"I'm talking about us! Who else do you know who has dated for four years without a promise?"

"Nobody."

"Exactly! I'm embarrassed!"

He glanced down at the brace encapsulating his extended left leg. "It's too bad that it took a career-ending injury like this for me to see you."

"You see me all the time or at least you did until the past couple of weeks."

"No, Patti, I don't think I've ever really seen you before, at least not in this light."

"What's wrong with the light?" she teased. "Should I turn on another lamp?"

"You know what I mean!" he countered fervently. "I guess I just got too comfortable around you. It seems like we've known each other forever. You're like family! It wasn't until you walked out of my hospital room that night that I realized how much and how often I've taken you for granted."

"And now?"

"I don't know what to say, Patti. I think I can change. I won't lie to you and tell you that school isn't really important to me, but you and my mom have convinced me that there's room for *us* in those plans."

"How does your mom play into this?"

He smiled. "My mom is the only other important woman in my life. When you left the hospital that night she knew in an instant what was going on and we had a heart-to-heart chat. I guess it took that, and the fear of losing you to wake me up. I can't lose you, Patti! I know I've told you before that I love you, but now when I say *I love you*, it takes on a whole different meaning. I can't imagine my life without you in it!"

Her chin quivered ever so slightly and she dabbed her eyes as she fought for control.

"I'm so sorry I put you through this," she finally managed, "but I'd had it! The last year at school we barely talked."

"We talked!" he interjected.

"No Dave, we didn't talk! We exchanged trivia. We talked all around the elephant in the room – us! I'm not stupid, Dave, I know how much that degree means to you. I was there when you studied. I saw the passion in what you were trying to do – and frankly, I was jealous. I kept wishing I'd see that same passion in your eyes when you looked at me."

"I can change."

"I actually think you can. I've even seen something different in your eyes tonight – something that gives me hope."

"Will you marry me?" Dave blurted. "I don't have a ring. I can't kneel down at your feet and plead for your hand, but I love you, Patti, more than anything else in my life. You've been such a part of me for so long I can't stand the thought of us not being together!"

A look came across her eyes that he didn't quite understand.

"I'm sorry!" he apologized, "what a horrible way to propose! Can we just rewind the past couple of minutes?"

"No," she said thoughtfully. "To coin a phrase: *that arrow has already flown*. I agree you bungled it pretty badly, but I'm not unappreciative. You can't imagine how long I've waited to hear those very words, but they just sort of came spewing out of your mouth."

He tried to look away but she caught his chin between her thumb and forefinger and moved cautiously onto his lap, being careful not to put pressure on his injured knee. Moments later they were locked together in a passionate embrace that took both of their breaths away.

He finally turned his head and pulled her head down against his shoulder.

"I can't breathe!" he gasped.

"You were breathing just fine!"

"Yeah and so loudly that I'm sure your folks could hear me over the football game."

She giggled. "Do you want me to lock the door?"

"Yes!"

She got to her feet but before she stepped away he caught her wrist and pulled her back onto his lap.

"I need the safety of that unlocked door!" he exclaimed softly. "I don't want your dad to feel the need to beat me with a stick, and besides, your mom trusts us."

She pulled him close again. When they finally separated she leaned back and giggled.

"What's wrong?"

"You're wearing my lipstick! You look nice in that color but it's all over your face."

"That's embarrassing!"

"Only if I can't wipe it all off before we go upstairs for pie."

"What if I don't want to go upstairs?"

She glanced at the alarm clock on her bedside table. "We've still got a half hour," she teased.

"I won't last another three minutes like this."

"Me either."

"So what do we do?"

"How about I let you rewind?" she suggested. "Same time about a month from now?"

"Christmas?"

"Exactly."

"Do you want an audience when I propose?"

"No," she whispered, "but I want a ring and a promise. I don't think you'll be able to kneel even by then so maybe I can kneel and you say the words?"

"How about if I kneel on a chair with one knee?"

She suddenly turned serious. "Are you sure this is what you want? I feel like I forced your hand."

"No you didn't force my hand. You opened my eyes! I'm so very sorry it's taken me so long! We could have had two kids by now!"

"Don't jump to conclusions!" she laughed. "We'll talk about all that important stuff after Christmas!"

She took two more tissues from the box on her bed and began wiping his face.

"Don't wipe it all off just yet," he pleaded. "I'm not done, and we've still got a little time."

They wound themselves together for awhile until neither could control their breathing.

"We need to go upstairs!" Dave finally gasped, pulling away, "or I'm going to get up and lock the door."

"You're right," she said as she picked up a couple more tissues. "And if you don't, I will."

***

"Patti, you're glowing," Janet teased as they walked into the family room. "I take it you reconciled your differences?"

"I think we did," Patti answered confidently. "Maybe I finally got his attention."

Patti's dad, Larry, laughed. "I'm sure that dress had something to do with that! I promised not to tell you this, Dave, but she and her mother spent four days shopping for the perfect dress."

"Dad!" Patti exclaimed, "so I suppose your promises don't mean anything?"

"I'm flattered," Dave said softy, taking the time to look Patti up and down – this time unhurried. "You're beautiful!"

Patti blushed a deep red, her face glowing brighter than her auburn hair or her dress. "I feel like a teeny bopper all dressed up for my first date," she stammered, reaching for her flushed cheeks with both hands.

In spite of the fact that her parents were looking on, Dave wrapped his elbow around her neck, pulled her close, and kissed her. She hesitated at first but then already embarrassed, she wrapped her arms around him and returned his kiss with a fervor that left him tingling. Now his face matched hers!

"I'd tell you two to get a room," her dad teased, "but I don't recall being invited to the wedding, yet."

"No, not yet!" Patti laughed, "no ring yet, either, but I have a promise!"

"Did you think to lock the door?" Janet teased.

"Mom!" Patti exclaimed, "that's not what was going on down there!"

"Maybe not, but you didn't wipe all the lipstick off Dave's face, and you're glowing like a newlywed!"

"I think I need some air!" Dave said after taking a deep breath.

"No, you need pie!" Patti exclaimed. "In fact I think we all do! Isn't that the real reason you showed up here?"

"I can't lie," Dave laughed. "I do love your mom's pecan pie!"

"What's not to love?" Larry exclaimed. "I'm partial to that as well, but I especially like it hot with a big scoop of ice cream on top!"

***

"Have you heard anything about your scholarship?" Larry asked as they all settled down in the family room with their pie to watch the last of the game. "You had a couple of NFL scouts talk to you, didn't you?"

"Yes but I didn't really take any of them seriously. I don't have any aspirations for the NFL, especially now."

"Smart man. You could make a lot of money but wide receivers often get hammered pretty good."

"So I found out."

"Where do you want to do your postgraduate work?"

"I don't know if you already know this but I've been accepted at Purdue. In fact, they would like me to transfer out there for my senior year. I haven't done anything serious about it yet, though, because I was planning on finishing out my scholarship at Colorado State."

"Do you think Purdue might offer you a scholastic scholarship to complete your senior year?"

"To be honest, I hadn't really considered that. I mean my grades are good enough but I don't know what sort of pre-graduate scholarships they offer."

"I'd seriously pursue that if I were you," Larry said, turning away from the TV to catch his eye.

"I've had so much on my plate the last two weeks, I haven't even thought about Purdue," Dave confessed.

"I think their engineering school is third or fourth in the nation. You're studying aerospace engineering aren't you? I'll bet some of the big-name companies in that game do some serious recruiting there."

Dave turned to look at Patti. The bright smile and hopeful twinkle in her eye was gone.

"Problem?" he asked, nodding at her.

"Yes. Actually there is," she said quietly. "Where is Purdue located?"

"Lafayette, Indiana," her dad answered.

"Isn't that south of Chicago?"

"It is. It's about 1,100 miles from Fort Collins," Dave added.

"What about me?"

The room filled with silence.

"After spring semester I've still got a year left at Colorado State!" she continued anxiously. "I'm sure I can't afford tuition at Purdue, even if I can get accepted! I'm barely squeaking by financially at Colorado State."

"So do you want me to ask my Christmas question now?" Dave asked. "If we were married that'd at least save you some rent money."

"And we'll keep helping with your tuition," Larry added.

Patti's eyes brimmed over with tears.

"Hey," Dave interrupted everyone's rampaging thoughts. "We've still got spring semester, plus the Christmas holidays to work out all the details. Man, when I give you a ring at Christmas now it's going to be really anticlimactic! I feel bad."

"So ask me now!" Patti insisted. "We've got a month to shop for rings. I kinda wanted a say in that process anyway."

"You said you didn't want an audience."

She grinned through her tears. "Mom and Dad aren't an audience."

Dave pulled himself up off of the sofa and stood in front of her. She grinned and went down on her knees in front of him.

"Patti," he began after he cleared his throat. "I love you more than life itself! You are my everything! Will you make my life complete and marry me?"

She leapt to her feet and threw her arms around him. "Yes I will!" she cried after she kissed him.

Dave turned sheepishly to her parents after they parted. "Sorry," he apologized. "We already decided that because of my knee she'd get down on her knees instead."

Janet hurried over and pulled Patti into an embrace. "I'm so happy that you included us in this special moment," she said, choking back tears. "I love you both! It's not every mom that gets to watch her daughter get engaged!"

Dave turned to Larry. "Dang it!" he exclaimed anxiously. "I got the cart before the horse. Larry is it okay if I ask Patti to marry me?"

Larry laughed. "Even if I said *no* right now, I'd be outvoted three to one."

"Sorry," Dave apologized.

"No apology necessary. I'd be happy to have you as my son-in-law!"

Chapter 6

*A*fter the announcements to Patti's parents, and all the pie and ice cream Dave could eat, they drove to Dave's house to pass along the good news there. At midnight, Dave drove Patti back home and parked in her driveway.

"Maybe you'd better pinch me," Patti said quietly as the engine died. "I'm having a hard time believing this is really happening."

"I'd rather kiss you instead."

"That's a given," she said leaning across the console.

A few minutes later Dave pulled back and took a deep breath. "Now's when I wish I still had my dad's old Ford," he chuckled. "It had a bench seat. This console is a pain!"

"We could get in the back seat," she laughed softly.

"No, actually I'm sort of glad the console is here. Do you know how hard it's going to be for me to keep my hands to myself from here on out?"

"Maybe it's a good thing we're both living in the dorms," she agreed quietly. "That'll make it easier."

Neither spoke for a few moments.

"You know," she finally broke the silence. "We made a promise so I suppose we can announce our engagement but as soon as we do, people are going to want to know when we're getting married. We didn't talk about that."

"We haven't had much time to decide. June seems to be the month for that sort of thing."

"Everybody gets married in June!" she countered, "or on Valentine's Day!"

"What have you got in mind?"

"I love springtime. Maybe April?"

"We could do that if you don't want a lengthy honeymoon until after the term ends."

She turned away.

"Here we go again," he pouted, "letting school dictate our plans. Maybe we should get married over Christmas break."

She chuckled. "I'll bet you'd never forget our anniversary if we did, but that'd be as bad as having my birthday at Christmas. I'd hate that!"

"When then?"

"Can I think about it?" she asked.

"No!" he exclaimed in mock anger, "I want a decision tonight – right now!"

She studied her hands for a few moments. "We've been together four years already; I guess a few more months won't make much difference."

"Except for one thing," he said, pouting, "now that we've spent time in your bedroom I don't know how I'm going to keep my hands off of you!"

"I've created a monster!"

"No, actually, you've just awakened one."

"I knew I shouldn't have bought this dress!" she teased.

"It's not the dress!"

"So do you want me to take it off?"

He grinned. "I'd love that actually, but if you were going to do that, we should have stayed in the house and locked your bedroom door. My back seat is too cramped."

She looked away for a moment. When she turned back the look in her eyes said it all.

"I love you Dave," she murmured. "I wish we could just elope and be done with it. Do you know how hard this is going to be?"

"I do, but you deserve the big wedding, with all the pomp and ceremony. Our respective moms would be devastated if we eloped. Besides, someday our kids are going to want to see our wedding pictures."

"Sorry, I'm having a hard time looking that far ahead. You know they say that you shouldn't be engaged for more than three months, tops, before you get married."

"Why's that?"

"Think about it, Dave. Think about tonight. Do you actually think we can wait that long to – well, you know."

"So it's going to be a Christmas wedding then?" he grinned.

"I couldn't do that to my mom! She goes crazy around Christmastime anyway with all the holiday stuff. Besides, I don't even think I could find a dress on that short of notice."

"When then?"

She leaned across the console for another lengthy kiss.

"Let me sleep on it for a few nights. We both have to leave to drive back to Fort Collins on Sunday night. Maybe once the fever breaks I'll be able to think logically."

"That's a great observation," he chuckled. "When you said that I remembered a Johnny Cash song that goes something like: *We got married in a fever.*"

She laughed. "*Hotter than a pepper sprout!*"

"Yeah," he added. "Then they: *started talking about Jackson, ever since the fire went out!*"

"I don't want to be one of those…"

"Those who?"

"Those who rush off and do something rash and then have it end in a shambles."

"That's not going to happen to us," Dave promised. "We're already family."

"I don't want to be like your little sister!"

"Oh, I'm sure I won't let that happen," he laughed.

***

All too soon the Thanksgiving holiday was over and Dave and Patti climbed into their separate cars to make the 130-mile drive back to Fort Collins. Then they almost slipped into their pre-Thanksgiving rut. Both had finals to study for.

"Let's go for a drive," Dave suggested the next Sunday after church. "I need to clear my head for awhile."

"Where to?" she asked. "In case you haven't noticed, we live in the mountains and it's been snowing off and on for nearly a week."

"I know a great mom and pop place in Greeley. We don't have to go through the mountains and it's only thirty miles or so away."

"Does it have atmosphere?" she smiled.

"Of course! That's why I suggested it. Eating in the school cafeteria doesn't really fit what I'm thinking right now."

***

46

By the time they got to Greeley, the current snowstorm was making a mess out of the roads. The drive was worth it though! They nearly had the smallish dining room to themselves. When they asked the waitress if they could have a table in the corner, she smiled knowingly and led them to a booth by the windows.

Instead of sitting across the table from him, Patti slid around the curved seat and snuggled up at his side.

"We're working on a reduced menu tonight," their middle-aged waitress apologized. "We have a pot roast special, though, for about ten bucks a plate. I'm biased, of course, but I think it's to die for, and there's a ton of it left if you'd be interested."

"That sounds great, actually," Patti answered.

"Make that two," Dave agreed.

The waitress took their drink order and left them alone.

"Do you have enough money?" she asked.

"I'm good."

"I hate having to squeak by all the time," she mused.

"I think we better get used to it," Dave answered softly. "We're going to be living on loans for the next few years."

"I can work when I graduate. That'll help."

"Okay, because the information I got from Purdue strongly suggested that I not work for the first couple of years of my postgraduate work. They tell me I'll be taking so many classes that working would be a mistake."

"Hey," she said, reaching up to touch his chin. "It'll work out. Quit worrying."

"Sorry. I get sorta freaked out when I think about it. We both have a year of undergrad left. I suppose you could work when we go out to Purdue, if that's what I decide to do, but what if you get pregnant?"

"We'll start saving right away for that eventuality. You can probably get loans to cover school and rent. In fact, maybe like Dad said, you can get a scholarship. I should be able to make enough money to cover living expenses and medical insurance. I'll have to have that for sure if we plan to start a family."

He looked at her for a few moments.

"Don't go all crazy on me!" she whispered. "I can see the panic in your eyes. Trust me, Dave, this will work out! It just has to!"

He smiled and put his arm around her. "I'm sorry I have to put you through this. Five years from where we're sitting seems like an eternity!"

"Mom and I talked about this, actually," she said as she snuggled against him. "She told me it'll seem like a long time while we're living it but when we look back it'll be a short blip in our history together."

Neither talked for a few moments.

"Besides," she chuckled, "it's not like either one of us are spoiled little rich kids. I don't need a lot of cool stuff."

"Good thing you bought a new dress when you did," he chuckled. "It may be the last one you'll get in a while."

"I've got a closet full of clothes. I don't have to wear all the latest fashions."

"That's cool if they still fit."

"I'm not planning on gaining a lot of weight! That's not me."

"You don't happen to have any maternity stuff stored away do you?" he hinted.

"I hadn't thought about that. In fact now that you mention it, a lot of the ladies in my church group couldn't get back into their clothes after they had their first baby."

"This is getting depressing," he apologized. "We came here for a romantic night away, and now I've spoiled it!"

"No, actually you haven't. You're asking all the same questions that I've been thinking about ever since Thanksgiving. It's fun knowing that you're going into this with your eyes wide open too. If we're both willing to make the sacrifices I know it'll work!"

He bent over and kissed her lightly on the lips.

"It's scary," she said quietly when they released, "but I promise it'll be worth it."

The waitress brought their meal moments later.

"I hope you're hungry," she said with a smile, "my manager gave you a little extra. He doesn't want it to go to waste and would rather see it go out in a doggy bag if that's what it takes."

"Tell him thanks," Dave replied. "This looks really good!"

"Oh, by the way," their waitress continued, "I assume you kids are going to school at Colorado State? I just heard on the news that I-25 to Fort Collins is closed because of a bad wreck on the icy road. There's a travel advisory on the whole northern end of Colorado because of the snowstorm. There are a lot of secondary roads that'll get you back up there but you might want to think about hurrying your meal a little. I mean I don't want to run you off but the snowplows usually concentrate on the freeways first, leaving pretty much everything else a mess."

Patti sat up straight and glanced out at the parking lot. "Oh my gosh, Dave!" she gasped, "we haven't been here that long and you've already got two inches of snow on your car."

"Yeah," the waitress agreed. "It's dumping a couple of inches an hour. It's not supposed to let up most of the night. We could easily get a foot or more before morning."

"Maybe we should get it to go." Patti suggested.

"Nah," Dave grinned. "I've got studded snow tires. We'll be okay. Besides, this food looks so good I want to eat it hot. It's never the same coming out of a microwave."

***

By the time they finished and walked out to their car, Dave was worried. Now there was at least four inches of snow on their car and from what he could see of the road going past the parking lot, the snowplows hadn't even touched it yet.

"Maybe we should get a room," he suggested as he swept the snow off of the passenger door and opened it for Patti.

He could see mixed emotions in her eyes as he handed her the car keys. "Start the engine while I clean off the car," he said. "We'll talk when I'm done."

***

"You think if we go slow that we can get home tonight?" Patti asked as Dave climbed back in and slammed the car door behind him.

"We can try it. But it's looking really bad out there right now and to make things worse, the wind has picked up. I don't want to get caught on the road in an all-out blizzard. If we get stuck I can't even push to try to get us out."

"And I'm worried about the alternative," she mused. "We don't have luggage. What do we do, sleep in our clothes?"

"We'd be wrinkled but safe," he chuckled. "I'm sorry, I should have known better than suggest a date on a Sunday night. We both have early classes tomorrow."

"I'll bet that with the weather, they'll either cancel or start late."

"That could happen, I suppose. I guess we could try driving and then find something if…"

"I'm not afraid of spending the night with you, if that's what you're getting at. I trust you, Dave."

"I'm not sure I trust myself."

"That could be a bad thing."

Dave backed the car out of the parking stall and drove into the street. There were very few other cars on the road and the ones that were there were driving about ten miles an hour and leaving deep tracks in the snow.

"This looks really bad," Patti whimpered. "I hate driving on slick roads!"

"I don't mind it so much as long as we can take our time."

"At ten miles an hour it's going to take us at least three hours to get back to the campus. It's already nearly ten o'clock, and the snow isn't showing any signs of slowing down."

"Let's go for awhile and see what happens."

***

"I don't feel good about this!" Patti said a few minutes later. "I trust you, but I don't trust this weather, other drivers, or the roads. Let's stop somewhere."

Moments later the wind picked up even more, driving the powdery snow across the road in flowing, headlight-reflecting waves.

"Okay," Dave said. "You're right. If this gets any worse we'll be trying to drive through a whiteout. I don't want to get stranded."

"There's a motel on the right!" Patti exclaimed, pointing. "Its vacancy sign is lit up."

51

***

Fifteen minutes later they closed the world outside the door of a cheap, but clean and warm motel room.

"Okay," Patti said apprehensively, "what now?"

"Luckily there are two double beds," Dave laughed lightly. "You pick one and I'll take the other. Then if you don't want to sleep in your clothes, we'll turn out all of the lights, strip down to our undies, and get into bed."

"I'm going to want to do that anyway," she said, "that wind drove the snow right through my clothes. I'm damp. I don't want to sleep cold."

"Makes sense. I'm glad the office had tooth brushes to sell. That'll help."

"So what do we do in the morning when it gets light?"

"I'll turn my head while you get dressed and then you can hang out in the bathroom while I do."

She laughed. "You know this would be so much easier if we just jumped into one bed and cuddled up. We're both adults here."

"That's what worries me. I was just thinking about that night in your bedroom."

"Me too."

"And?"

"Maybe we should have an early honeymoon. Nobody would know but us."

"You're making this really difficult."

"It doesn't have to be."

"Go brush your teeth," he answered softly. "I'll turn the covers down."

52

The power went out before either of them got their teeth brushed, and a pale-green, battery-powered, exit light over the door dimly lit up their room.

"Now what?" Patti asked apprehensively. "I have to assume that the furnace runs on electricity."

"It's a space heater by the window and yes, even if it runs on natural gas or propane, it won't work without power."

"It's already cool in here," she said. "I say we get into one bed and share the warmth. I can brush my teeth in the morning."

"Turn your back while I get in," she said as she started unbuttoning her blouse. "I should make you get in first, though, the sheets are going to be freezing cold!"

"I can do that," he said as he pulled his long-sleeved sweater off over his head and tossed it on the other bed.

"I'll look away."

"No need," he said, I'm leaving my boxers on. You've seen me in a swimsuit before."

"And you've seen me in a bikini but somehow this seems different."

"Only the color of the fabric is different."

"But in case you haven't noticed we're getting into a bed not a swimming pool."

"Just pretend," he chuckled.

"You just remember that when I snuggle up against your bare back."

Dave quickly shed his clothes, and yanked back the covers. "Maybe we should pull the blankets off the other bed too. If the power stays off very long we're going to need them."

"You get in and warm up the sheets. I'll do it."

"Dang it!" he yelped as he crawled between the sheets. "These things are like ice!"

"I knew they would be," she giggled nervously, "why do you think I sent you in first?"

Dave pulled the covers around him and turned his back. Moments later the other bed's blanket and bedspread landed over him. He instantly became aware of other sounds – the rasp of her jean's zipper, the soft rustling of cloth as she shed her blouse. Then just before she tugged the covers away from his shoulder he heard the soft snap of elasticized material that had to be either her bra or her panties. Moments later she slid into bed behind him, pulled the covers back in place over them and snuggled up to his back.

"Mmm, you're warm," she cooed as she draped an arm over his shoulders and pulled herself against him.

"So are you," he managed, "and I hate to even ask, but it feels to me like you're topless."

She laughed softly. "A bra is so confining. Like you said a few moments ago, just pretend I'm wearing a bikini."

"My imagination won't stretch that far."

"Then just let it run wild."

"If I do that we'll start our honeymoon."

"I don't mind. Like I just told you, nobody will know but us."

"What if you get pregnant?"

"What if?"

"You're making this impossibly hard."

"It doesn't have to be."

"Yes it does, Patti. If we start this now, it won't end. Call me old fashioned, but being celibate before marriage means a lot to me."

"You're right," she answered quietly. "It does to me too. This is going to be really hard."

"Let's put a sheet between us," he suggested. "Then it'll almost be like wearing pajamas."

She threw the covers off, quickly maneuvered a sheet between them, and then pulled the heavy bedding back over them both.

"You're right," she murmured after a few moments. "I'm still warm. Thank you Dave."

"Can I have a goodnight kiss?" he teased.

"No! I'm leaning over the edge of the cliff now! If we do that, it's all over. Maybe you can pretend that I'm your mother."

"Ouch," he laughed, "not that! I love my mother, but that did it!"

She snuggled tightly against him. "Thank you, Dave," she whispered after a few moments. "You can't believe how safe I feel right now."

"I'm glad that's how you feel," he returned. "I'm still dangling over the edge of the cliff."

A loud knock came at the door.

"Who could that be?" Patti asked anxiously.

"I hope it's not your mom!" Dave laughed. "Can you imagine how this would look?"

"You go see who it is!" she hissed. "I'm not getting out of this bed and at least you're partially dressed!"

Dave threw the covers back, leapt out of bed and struggled into his Levi's. "Yeah!" he called out as he walked to the door. "Who is it?"

"It's the manager," a feminine voice called out. "I've got a lantern."

Dave unlocked the door, pulled it open and stepped back. A middle-aged woman he'd never seen before stepped inside.

"I see you've doubled up the covers," she said brightly as she held up a propane lantern. "I'm sure you've already figured out that the heat doesn't work without electricity and I just got off the phone with the power company. A main tower went down over the pass. The power will probably be out for a couple of days. This lantern should probably burn for about six hours on a single bottle. I brought you a spare. It's self-lighting so you won't need matches. The lantern is a lot safer than candles and should keep the room above freezing. You should be warm with double covers. I'm going to ask you to leave the cold water trickling in the bathroom, though, so the pipes don't freeze."

"Thank you," Dave said. "The only reason we stopped was we didn't want to try to drive in this."

"You were wise in doing that. There are whiteout conditions everywhere. I'll leave you my personal phone number. If there's anything else I can do for you folks, please call me. I can bring you extra blankets if things get bad."

"Do you know how long this storm is supposed to last?" Dave asked.

"Until morning, I believe. Even then it'll probably take a while for them to clear the roads. We have a limited kitchen that uses natural gas so we can fix you a hot breakfast in the morning."

"Thank you so much."

"I'll have the desk give you a call about eight in the morning if you'd like. They can give you a weather and road report."

Dave moved the useless electric lamp off the lamp table after the manager left and set the lantern in its place.

"If nothing else," Patti laughed, "that glaring light should do more than warm us up a little, but it's not very romantic."

Chapter 7

Their room phone rang at eight. The desk clerk told them that it had quit snowing about 4 a.m. and the winds had calmed down enough a couple of hours after that so the snowplows had been able to clear the freeways. The power was still out and their room temperature, in spite of the lantern was probably in the 40's. Even though there was hot water, neither of them wanted to brave a shower.

Dave turned his back while Patti got out of bed and got dressed. It took almost every ounce of restraint he had to keep from watching.

"Your turn," she said as he heard her pull her parka around her.

"Are you going to turn your back?"

"Why? I'm dressed and like you told me last night, I've seen you in a swimsuit before. Besides, I'm moving the lantern into the bathroom so I can see to fix my hair a little. If you pull the drapes open you should be able to see to get dressed."

By the time Dave finished dressing, Patti was sitting on the end of a bed. When he walked over to her she stood and took him in her arms.

"That was probably the most romantic night I've ever spent," she purred after he kissed her. "Thank you, Dave, for saving me from myself."

"That goes both ways, Patti. You can't believe how hard it was for me to keep from pulling that sheet out from between us."

She giggled. "Now that's something we can agree on. Let's get out of here while we're both still being strong."

***

They found out over the car radio on the way back to Fort Collins, that the power outage had affected the university and classes had been canceled for the day. They were sure that the dorms hadn't fared any better.

"Too bad it's so far to drive home," Dave said as they drove on trying to decide what to do. "None of the restaurants or grocery stores are going to be open and traffic downtown is going to be a mess because the streetlights will be out."

"Let's drive home then," she suggested. "If we stick to the freeway, it's a straight shot home so we won't have to worry about traffic lights and they just said on the radio that they don't expect to have power restored until tomorrow at the earliest. There isn't any heat in the dorms and I'm sure the cafeteria is closed. We probably won't find any place to eat or stay now until we get to the greater Denver area. That's over sixty miles from here. It'd just cost money to stay there and it's only another seventy miles to drive home. We can spend the day with our folks and drive back tomorrow or the day after. I'll bet the campus will be closed until Tuesday."

"Do you have any regrets?" Dave asked quietly a few minutes later.

"About last night?"

"Yes."

"Yes and no," Patti answered hesitantly. "You can't believe how badly I wanted to pull out that sheet, but I'm sort of blown away knowing I can still wear white at my wedding and not be embarrassed."

"Maybe we ought to stop in Denver and go ring shopping," he suggested.

She looked over at him. "I'd love that," she exclaimed softly. "What a story we'll have to tell our folks!"

"And our kids."

She took hold of his elbow. "Uh huh. I hadn't really thought about that but what an example we just set for them."

"I just hope I can keep it together. You know we still haven't decided when we're going to get married."

"I've been thinking about that, actually," Patti answered. "If we go with the three month engagement thing and go from Thanksgiving, that puts us right after Valentine's Day."

"But you said before you thought that date was too common."

"Only for the rest of the world," she smiled. "This is our wedding. we can't help it if it happened to work out for a couple million other couples too. I really don't want to wait any longer than that. Do you?"

"Hey, I thought Christmas sounded great to me," he countered, "but you moaned about not being able to find a dress by then."

"I was thinking about my poor mom. You know she's going to want everything to be perfect and that takes planning. I think three months will actually go by pretty fast when you think about all the details."

"February 14th then?"

Patti opened her phone. "That's a Tuesday and a school day."

"It is, but it shouldn't interfere with midterms."

"What about a honeymoon?"

"We can just hide away in our apartment until the weekend and then go somewhere."

"That's right. We're going to have to find a place to live. That's going to be hard in Fort Collins with all the students living there."

"I suppose we could stay in the dorms," he teased.

"I don't think my roommate would appreciate that very much," Patti laughed.

"Mine wouldn't mind."

"That's sick!"

"Okay, so I'll start looking for a place to live and see if I can find some used furniture. I'll do that while you and your mom are doing the dress thing."

"And reserving a place to hold the wedding."

"The church is cheap and probably easier to reserve if we do it now."

She looked away for a few moments. "I'd be good with that, I suppose," she finally answered. "You're right. Others have done it. I'll just have to find someone who does wedding decorations and get on their waiting list."

"This is still going to cost your parents a bundle. Maybe…"

"Maybe what?" she countered. "Are you going to suggest that we elope?"

"We could do that right after Christmas and have a few days away before we have to go back to school."

"We could, but like you told me a little while ago, I want photos. I want the big traditional wedding. We only get married once. I know my folks will be good with it. I think eloping would be selfish. I want to be able to share this with our families."

"I don't disagree," he answered softly. "I'm just trying to be practical."

"We can be practical when we're living on ramen noodles and struggling to pay the electric bill. We'll have the rest of our lives to be practical. I'd like to think this is a reward for our parents for putting up with us as teenagers."

He laughed. "You're right. So February 14th is the day then. Look in your smartphone and see if you can find a jeweler in Denver who might give us a good deal."

***

They surprised Patti's parents just after 5 p.m. Patti lead with her left hand after they rang the doorbell and waited for someone to answer the door.

Patti's mom answered and of course instantly knew why they were there. After hugs all around, joined eagerly by her father, Dave let Patti tell their tale. He expected an abbreviated version, but Patti was proud enough about what they hadn't done that she told it all. Dave spotted a tear in Larry's eye as he grabbed Dave's hand and pulled him into an embrace.

"You're an honorable man!" he managed. "I'm so proud of you both!"

"Yes," her mother joked, "now all we have to do is keep a sheet between you two until February."

"Patti thought it was important to give you some time to plan," Dave explained.

"This is the best Christmas present ever!" Janet exclaimed happily. "Have you told Dave's parent's yet?"

"No, I thought you should know first," Dave said. "We'll go tell them in a little while."

"When do you have to be back to campus?" Larry asked.

"Maybe tomorrow, but from what we heard it might be a day or two. We called and got an automated message. We'll just keep checking back."

"I assume you'll be staying with us tonight then?"

"No, actually," Dave laughed. "Patti will stay with you. I'll stay with my folks. I don't want you to think you need to smack me with a stick to get me out of Patti's bedroom."

"Right answer," Larry laughed. "Will you at least come back and eat dinner with us?"

"You're the first to offer, so yes, I'd love to. My folks may want to argue but I'll just tell them that you asked first."

"I don't want to cause issues," Janet insisted.

"There won't be. I'm sure you and my mom will be talking a lot between now and Valentine's Day."

"Wow!" Janet exclaimed softly, "suddenly that doesn't seem to be a long way off. Patti, I think you and I need to go dress shopping when you come home for Christmas. Dave's mom and I can be working on all of the other details while you two are off at school."

"I know this is going to be a financial burden on your part," Dave apologized, "I'm sorry."

"Don't apologize," Larry laughed, "we've only got one daughter and she's only going to get married once – I hope," he said pointedly looking at Dave. "I think we can afford to be a little extravagant."

***

Dave's mom, Karen, cried when Patti showed her the ring. Frank hugged Dave and slapped him on the back a couple of times. Neither Dave nor Patti felt like it was important to tell his folks the whole story, so they simply told them that when the power went out on campus and they didn't have a warm place to stay, they decided to drive home – deciding kind of at the last moment to stop in Denver and shop for rings.

An hour later, they were back in their car headed for Patti's house for dinner.

"I'm so excited!" she exclaimed.

"Sorry this has taken me so long," Dave said quietly. "This should probably have happened before our freshman year. I feel bad that we've wasted so much time."

"And I'm sorry that I sort of gave you an ultimatum."

"I promise to be more attentive from now on," he promised, "but sometimes guys don't learn very quickly. You may have to put me in my place from time to time."

"You wouldn't like that. You told me once you hated demanding women."

"I don't ever see you being demanding."

"What do you call that night in the hospital?"

"Desperation, maybe," he mused. "You probably wondered if I'd ever put you ahead of everything else in my life."

"Is that what you're doing?"

"In a way, yes, but not begrudgingly. I'm actually really excited to be able to share it all with you."

Chapter 8

The campus didn't resume classes until Thursday after the big snowstorm. The Dean called Dave Friday morning.

"We need to chat about your scholarship," he explained on the phone. "I see you have a 2 o'clock class. Please come and see me at 3:15."

Dave couldn't concentrate as he sat through his classes the rest of the day. He had assumed the scholarship would pay for spring semester, now he had a bad feeling about that. Turned out his bad feelings weren't misplaced.

"I'm sorry to be the one to give you this bad news," the Dean began after Dave closed his office door and took a seat, "but as you well know, football practice for next year begins in March. I met with the scholarship committee, your coach, and the team doctor last week and they have decided to release you from the football program. We can't let you play with an artificial knee. I have been in contact with our financial department and because your injury was sustained in a school-sponsored activity, we will continue to pay for your associated medical expenses and physical therapy as long as it's justified, but your scholarship will otherwise be terminated at the end of the calendar year."

Dave had suspected that was coming but the weight of the Dean's words crushed him. He remembered the talk he'd had with his dad about putting his hand in a bucket of water and yanking it out to see how much of a dent he'd leave behind. He was expendable! The sacrifice he'd made to win that championship game had been forgotten. To the school it was simply a matter of money. They needed a replacement for him and they needed the money left from his scholarship to attract someone else to the program.

"What about spring semester and my senior year?" Dave asked, more to put the Dean on the spot than to beg for something he knew wasn't going to happen.

"We have a number of student loan programs," the Dean instantly replied, obviously having already anticipated Dave's response. "When I was talking to our financial department that subject came up. We are anxious to help you succeed scholastically here at Colorado State. If you'll call and talk to Clyde Jeffrey in our Financial Aid Department, he will help walk you through the details. He'll be expecting your call."

After that discussion, the walk to the library to meet Patti was a long one. He had an option. He had Purdue's phone number. They'd already invited him to attend his senior year there. Even though he and Patti had already made plans for a February wedding, he was wondering if Purdue would come up with a scholarship for spring semester. If they would, he'd have to transfer and he and Patti may have to postpone their wedding until late spring.

"What's wrong?" Patti asked after she stood to offer a hug.

"The team just released me."

"Okay, but you were sort of expecting that weren't you?"

"Yes, but the Dean also told me they were terminating my scholarship at the end of the calendar year. I'm going to have to scramble to get financing for spring semester. I'm thinking about calling Purdue."

Patti sat down heavily in her chair and looked away. "What about us?" she asked quietly.

Dave pulled out a chair and sat down next to her. "That shouldn't change anything between us."

"What if they want you to go out there for spring semester?"

"If they offer me a scholarship I'd be stupid to turn it down. I still want to get married but we may have to wait until summer."

He watched her eyes for a few moments before he continued.

"After our talk the other night," Patti said softly, "I called Purdue's admissions department and talked to them about transferring out there. After quickly looking over my transcripts, the lady I talked to told me that some of my credits won't transfer. I'd probably end up having to add nearly another couple of semesters if I transfer – assuming I get accepted. Tuition is another issue. Their tuition is more than double what I'm paying here because I'd have to pay out-of-state tuition."

"How long does it take to obtain residency?"

"A year."

"Maybe you could postpone your degree for a year and work full time in the meantime."

"I suppose that would work. I could help support us until I can go back to school as a resident. Maybe we could save enough money by then to help cover the difference in tuition. I've already talked to Mom and Dad and they're willing to keep paying my tuition even when we're married but I can't stick them with that bigger bill."

Dave took her hand and squeezed it lightly until she looked up at him. "We'll work this out, I promise."

***

Dave called the phone number on the letter from Purdue the next day between classes. When he explained what was happening to him at Colorado State, the lady on the phone seemed pretty excited at the news. She said she'd pull a current transcript even though his grades for fall semester wouldn't have been posted yet, and she'd see what she could do.

James cornered him on the way to his next class.

"Hey Dave, I just heard that the team released you," he began. "I'm really sorry to hear that. I've been looking forward to the competition on the field our senior year – but frankly, that sucks! I assume that means you're losing your scholarship?"

"Unfortunately yes. This whole thing has been a hard pill to swallow."

"Did you know that they ejected that player who creamed you, like it would do any good in the last twenty seconds of the game! I wonder if you might have some recourse against him?"

"I doubt it. It is what it is. I frankly don't have the money or inclination to go after the player of another team. I figure stuff like that happens all the time. I've never seen a player sue another player. I don't know if that's even possible."

"Wow, I don't know what to say. I'm sorry!"

"Thanks James."

"It's finals week. Are you going to come back next semester?" James asked.

"That depends on whether or not I can get financing. I'll have to get a student loan if I do."

"Did the Dean send you to see Clyde Jeffrey? He seems to hold the purse strings for all the athletes. Not all of us were fortunate enough to get a full-ride scholarship like you did. He's kind of a butthead to work with. If I were you, I'd go talk to your bank first. Jeffrey loves lording it over the athletes a little too much if you know what I mean. You may not get a better deal from your bank but you wouldn't have to put up with his crap."

"Thanks James. Purdue sent me a letter of interest a while ago. I'm going to call them first."

"That's amazing! You're an engineering major aren't you?"

"Yes. I applied for their graduate program a few months ago. When they found out I was going to school here on an athletic scholarship, they told me to contact them my senior year. They hinted at that time that a lot of major companies are looking for good engineering students and they often offer internships that might help with school."

"Sounds like you've got that in the basket then. I'm jealous! I just hope I can hang on here until I graduate. A bachelor's degree is as far as I'm going to go. That's been hard enough."

"Aren't you studying accounting?"

"Yes, with a minor in Business Management. My grades aren't anywhere near as good as yours are, but I think they'll do."

"Hey James, I've got to run or I'm going to be late for my next class. Good luck with all that."

***

Dave couldn't get James' conversation off his mind the rest of the afternoon. He wondered what his interest was? Maybe because he was no longer competition, he was safe to talk to now.

Patti was waiting outside his room when class dismissed.

"Didn't you have class?" he asked.

"Only half a class. The professor just went over what we should expect to see on the final and then excused us."

"Are all your finals next week?"

"They are, and yours?"

"Mine too."

"When is your last one?" she asked.

"Thursday."

"Mine too. Are you planning on heading home right after finals?"

"Yes, do you want to ride together?"

"I would but I really want to have my car at home. I haven't done any Christmas shopping yet."

"I need to find you something."

"No you don't. You already got me a ring. That's all I want. Please don't spend any more on me. I'm going to get you an engagement band – so you'll have to act surprised when I give it to you. We need to start watching our pennies if we're going to get married in February. We need to find an apartment as soon as we go back after the holidays. Finding an apartment in a college town isn't going to be easy to do."

He grinned.

"And to answer your devious thoughts," she smiled demurely, "no I won't live with you before our wedding. We've already sort of drawn that line in the sand. Mom and Dad will keep paying my dorm fees until I get married."

"Spoilsport."

"Don't pout. You made that decision last week and the more I think about it, the more I like the idea. Celibacy is a rare thing anymore. I'm quite proud of us actually."

He paused briefly to kiss her. "It's going to be a long two months!"

"Yes, it will be," she agreed, "but I promise you it'll be worth it."

"I have no doubt about that. Hey to change the subject a little, have you and your mom started hatching plans yet?"

"We've been talking on the phone. I've convinced her that I want a reception at the church. That'll save them a ton of money over a wedding hall and she already has a lady lined up to decorate. She and Dad wanted something a little more extravagant but she agreed when I told her about you losing your scholarship and your plans for Purdue. That way if they have to help us a little they won't have a big wedding expense hanging over their heads too."

"That's really mature of you."

"Thank you. I thought so. By the way, my best friend from high school started a photography business, and I've already asked her to do our wedding photos. You don't mind do you?"

"Why should I mind? Is she going to give you her *best friend* discount?"

She laughed. "I didn't ask her that, but I don't really care if she doesn't. She's married and trying to get her business established."

He took her hand and walked beside her for a few moments.

"What else is on your mind?" she prodded.

"Are you reading my mind?"

"No, but your hand is clammy. That only happens when you're nervous. What aren't you telling me?"

"I talked with a lady in the admissions department at Purdue today and explained what was happening here. She told me she'd work the issue and get back to me. I'm afraid now that they're going to offer me something for spring semester."

"Why would you be afraid?"

"Because if they come up with a financial package for my undergrad and want me to go out there, that messes with February."

"Oh!" she exclaimed softly. "I suppose I'd had that thought in the back of my mind, but I hadn't really considered it."

"I'm sure I can skip class long enough to come home and get married."

"What about me? I've already paid tuition for next semester."

"What are you thinking?" he asked.

"Maybe under the circumstances we should think about waiting until summer."

"Well don't do anything rash until I hear from them," he said. "This is really short notice for them too. I don't think they'll be able to work out anything and if I'm going to have to pay tuition anyway, I'd just as soon pay it here where it's cheaper. Then we'll see what develops for next fall. That'll give us time to put our plans together."

"I won't lie to you," she answered, "this is suddenly feeling really rushed and uncertain. Maybe waiting would be the best choice."

"That makes for a long engagement," he mused softly.

"Now I do know what you're thinking and frankly, I agree. I don't know how I'm going to keep my hands off of you for that long."

"You sound like a guy."

"Girls have those feelings too."

"If that's the case, this is really going to be tough!"

He stopped her in the hallway and looked her in the eyes. "Are you sure you don't want to just elope and spend the Christmas holiday hidden away in a honeymoon suite somewhere?"

He could see the dilemma raging in her eyes.

"I can't think about this right now," she finally answered. "Let's get through finals week and then decide. In the meantime, I need some serious study time. Can we call a time-out on us for a few days? I need to be able to concentrate on my schoolwork."

He kissed her lightly. "Thank you," he said. "I was going to suggest the same thing. I haven't felt the best the last few weeks. I need a little undistracted study time."

"I think we were headed for the library. When would you like this distraction-free time to begin?"

"After tonight," he answered as he watched the emotions flashing through her eyes. "I can't just quit seeing you right now. I'm an emotional wreck."

"Guys aren't supposed to be that way. What are you, a little girl?"

"Emotionally I really am," he admitted. "These past few weeks have put me in a real tailspin."

"I'm so happy to hear that," she grinned. "After four years together I finally have hope for our future."

Chapter 9

Finals week was the longest week of Dave's life. Although he tried to keep his mind strictly on school and study, he often found himself daydreaming about Patti. For the first time since they'd met, thoughts about her consumed him. He longed to see her smile, feel the softness of her kiss and the warmth of her body as they embraced. In retrospect it was a good thing that he'd kept up on his studies before that infamous football game or he'd have been in serious academic trouble.

He turned his phone back on after he walked out of his last final on Thursday and saw that Purdue had left him a voice message.

"Dave, this is Brad Williams calling from the admissions office at Purdue University," the message said. "A small team of people have been working your case the last week and I think we have a solution that will interest you. Will you please call me at your earliest convenience?"

Dave looked down at the phone number and hesitated. The man had seemed upbeat on the phone, which probably meant he had good news. Now he worried. If they'd been interested enough in him to put together what Brad had called a "small team" to work his case, he knew it probably meant an offer for spring semester. He wasn't ready to move on that yet. In the few moments aside from school his thoughts had been filled with nothing but Patti and Valentine's Day. He sorely wanted to return Brad's call immediately, but then again he didn't.

He drew a deep breath and punched Patti's number into his phone instead.

"Hi!" she answered brightly. "How did your last final go?"

"I think it went well – no thanks to you!" he exclaimed.

"Why is that suddenly my fault?"

"Because I haven't been able to get you off my mind."

She laughed. "Me either."

"Can I buy you a late lunch?"

"I have another test at four. Sorry but the testing center scheduled my exam late."

"Ouch! I was hoping to talk for awhile before we headed home. You're still leaving this afternoon aren't you?"

"Yes. I really don't want to drive after dark and the weather doesn't look good."

"Maybe we should both wait until tomorrow morning and then caravan home."

"I like that idea. That way if something happens…"

"Misery loves company."

She hesitated for a few moments before she responded.

"Why are you miserable?" she finally managed.

"Purdue left me a phone message while I was in finals."

"Have you called them back yet?"

"No. I wanted to do it when you could hear what they have to say."

"Do you think it's good news or bad?"

"That depends on whether you're talking about school or about us."

"What did they say?"

"Just that they'd had a small team review my case and wanted me to call to discuss the options."

"And that is bad why?"

"Because the guy who called sounded pretty upbeat. They may want me to do something right away."

"Oh."

"Have you given any more thought to eloping over Christmas?"

"It's been on my mind but I have reservations."

"You've already made motel reservations? Where did you book us?" he joked.

"Not funny! I've been thinking about my mom and wedding pictures, and friends – the big wedding – things we already talked about."

"Maybe we're jumping to conclusions."

"And if we're not?"

"Then maybe we'll have a summer wedding instead. If I'm at Purdue and you're here I think we'll be safe. That'll be longer than the three months we were worried about, but it won't be like we're seeing each other every day."

"I can't think about this right now," she said after drawing a deep breath. "I have a final in a half hour. Go make your phone call before their office closes. I think they're in an earlier time zone. We'll do dinner afterward and you can fill me in on the details. I'll plan on spending the night in the dorm and driving home tomorrow."

***

Dave got reservations in Greeley at the small restaurant they'd gone to the night of the storm. He had news and needed some time alone with Patti to discuss their options. She called at ten minutes past five.

"Did you call them then?" she asked as soon as he answered.

"I did."

"And?"

"And we have dinner reservations in Greeley at six thirty."

She didn't answer for a few moments. When she did answer he could sense the tension in her voice. "Should I be afraid?" she finally managed.

"No. Just come with an open mind."

***

The drive to Greeley was filled with light conversation interspersed with long tension-filled pauses. He'd been going over all the options in his mind before he picked her up. In light of what Purdue had offered him he knew what he wanted to do but it was going to take a little salesmanship with Patti to pull it off. He was both excited and terrified. He silently prayed that she'd be open minded about what he needed to ask her. He'd never felt so in love or so conflicted in his life. He had two amazing options lying on his plate. He wanted them both like he'd wanted nothing before in his life. They weren't mutually exclusive choices, but there would have to be a compromise somewhere. Unfortunately, because of what he'd found out on his telephone call, most of the compromise would have to be hers.

"Okay!" Patti finally broke the tension between them after the same waitress they'd had the night of the storm, seated them in the same booth in the corner, took their drink orders and walked away. "You obviously have a lot to tell me and I can tell by the expression on your face that it's probably not going to be good news for me, so let's have it. I've been on the verge of tears for the last hour and a half anyway!"

He reached for her hand and turned in the booth so he could study her eyes. "Purdue wants me for spring semester starting on January 4th. They've worked an internship deal with Raytheon – an internationally prominent Aerospace Engineering Company – and

Raytheon is willing to offer me a full-ride scholarship throughout my college program at Purdue, including summer internship work opportunities every year. If I successfully finish the program it means an immediate position somewhere in their company."

"Okay," she said, allowing a little excitement to creep into her reply, "so what's the bad news?"

"The university wants me out there on Monday, December 19th, for three days so they can get everything put together by the time I have to start classes in January."

"What about Christmas?"

"I'll have Thursday the 22nd through Sunday the 25th off so I can fly home for Christmas but Raytheon wants me at their facility in New Jersey on Monday the 26th, for four days to meet their engineering team and sit through some interviews and indoctrination meetings. This still isn't a done deal so if I don't come off well with the Raytheon team it all goes away."

She was quiet for awhile.

"That's a lot of driving." she finally exclaimed softly.

"Yes it is. It's nearly 1,100 miles just from here to their campus in Indiana. Raytheon will fly me to New Jersey and provide housing and a rental car while I'm out there."

"How can you possibly turn that down?" she asked, trying to control her emotions. Her lower lip quivered.

"I don't see how I can. But that's only slightly bad news for us. We've already talked about doing a summer wedding."

"I thought you just told me that part of that deal they're offering you includes a summer internship."

"It does but we should have time to get married here before we have to drive out there together. It might mean a honeymoon on the road but hey – we need to sleep somewhere, right?"

77

She forced a smile beneath her tear-brimmed eyes. "That's not really bad news. In fact it's exciting when you think about it. You'll get your school paid for and have a great job waiting for you when you graduate. How many students get a deal like that?"

"But what about us?" he asked.

"Well, I can see we won't be eloping over Christmas!" she tried to force a laugh, but failed. "I can't say I'm not disappointed about having to put off our wedding until next summer but we already sort of talked about that. It'll all work out. I don't suppose they'll pay to fly you home over Christmas will they?"

"I didn't dare ask that, but I've got a credit card. I'll make my own arrangements. I can't stand the thoughts of Christmas without you!"

"So what are your plans then? Didn't you tell me it's a thousand miles from here to there, one way?"

"Uh huh."

"Were you planning on leaving from here, or driving to Colorado Springs for the weekend?"

"I'd like to drive home with you but that'll add another three hundred miles to my drive. It's 16 hours one way as it is. I'm sorry…"

"Don't be," she said sadly, "even though I'm crying, I'm actually really excited for you. My dreams for Valentine's Day are temporarily shattered but I think it'll all work out for the better. I can finish my junior year here and then plan on taking a year off while I get residency in Indiana. You'll probably be making enough money with your cool job after you graduate that I won't even need my degree."

"I insist you finish!" he countered. "What if something happens to me? How many women do you know who interrupted their college education to get married never went back?"

"A few – but most of them did that because they started a family."

He watched her eyes as he mulled over several impossible solutions in his mind. He wanted her. He wanted children. He wanted her to finish school. They couldn't have it all. He simply didn't have answers.

She eventually smiled under sad eyes and reached up to pull him against her for a lingering kiss.

"This is actually amazing news." she said after a while. "It's not fairy book, but it's exciting."

She looked down at her hands as tears flooded her eyes. "This is all so sudden! Here I was planning on spending the week before Christmas with you, and then another week with you before New Year's. Now it looks like I'll have to settle for a long weekend with you around the Christmas holiday. You'll have to fly out to Raytheon right after Christmas."

"I'm so sorry!"

She sat up straight in the booth and drew a deep breath. "That's just as well, I suppose. I don't have to be back to school until January 4th. I suppose I'll just spend the time with my folks. Were you going to leave tonight or just wait until morning?"

"I wanted to have dinner with you tonight, so I'll leave tomorrow morning. I don't think I want to drive 16 hours straight through. If I drive eight hours a day that'll put me there late Sunday. I have a phone number for a woman who is supposed to help me find a place to live. With any kind of luck maybe I can find something on Sunday."

"I have a suggestion," she said quietly, "let's get a motel room on the way back to campus tonight and then spend all day together tomorrow. Then we'll both leave Saturday afternoon to drive to wherever."

"I don't think that would be a good idea," he answered tenderly. "We barely made it out of that motel room as virgins last time. The way I feel about you right now, that would never happen again."

"I know," she agreed, "but in view of what's lying ahead of us, maybe that wouldn't be a bad thing. I love you, Dave. I want you. It's not like either one of us would be breaking up a marriage or anything like that."

"You're making this really hard!" he replied, taking a deep breath and watching the expression in her eyes. "You can't believe how badly I want to say yes, but…"

"Yeah, I know!" she said bitterly, "but we've been taught differently."

"Don't be mad."

"I'm not angry. I'm frustrated. I'm afraid. I'm already feeling lonely."

"How can you feel lonely? I'm right here with you."

"Maybe I'm seeing the empty months between now and June. This is going to be so hard!"

"Yes it's going to be hard," he agreed, "but what's another six months when we've already been dating for four years?"

"I hope it's not a deal breaker," she mused. "Ever since your injury I've felt like our relationship was coming to a climax. Now I'm worried."

"Why?"

"Come on, Dave, we're both adults here. Things happen. You're going to be lonely like me. You might meet somebody."

He looked away for a moment suddenly panic-stricken. If anyone were to meet someone new it would be her. She was beautiful, warm, friendly, caring – attributes that made her irresistible to a guy. When he thought about it, he wondered why she'd stuck with him this long. Then that night at the hospital slammed into his conscious thought. She'd been ready to call it quits that night. Even his mom had told him that. After that talk with his mom he'd pulled out all the stops to make Patti his only priority in life. Now he was setting her aside again for something else. What would he do if he lost her?

"Okay," he whispered. "You win. We'll stop."

***

They finished their meal, and ordered a couple of small dishes of ice cream for dessert. From the moment he'd given in, he could think of little else! Simply finishing his meal was torture. He was unprepared. He needed to stop at a drugstore but it was late. He wondered if anything in Greeley would still be open. He fished his phone out of his pocket and did a Google search.

"What are you doing?" she asked as she stopped eating to watch him search.

"Looking for a drugstore."

"Oh."

She sat her spoon down on her napkin and looked away.

"Sorry," he apologized.

"You don't need to be. You're just trying to be responsible."

"This is new ground for me. I don't quite know how to go about it."

She pushed her arm through the crook in his elbow and pulled close to him. "Going to the store is going to take all of the spontaneity out of this, isn't it?"

"I have to face it sooner or later."

"Not really, I was going to see my doctor next week. My mom even made the appointment for me. She said that even though we weren't getting married until February, it would be wise to get on something so my body could adjust."

"There's a CVS Pharmacy about a mile from here."

"No," she said after a few moments, pulling him even closer, "let's wait. If we do this now, it'll just make summer seem that much further away. We'll both have rings to remind us that we're promised. Like you said, what's another six months?"

"Torture."

She giggled, pushed her ice cream aside and got to her feet.

"Let's get out of here and get back to the dorms before we change our minds."

Chapter 10

They spent half a day Friday together doing a little last minute Christmas shopping, then all too soon, it was 4 p.m. and they lingered in her car for awhile before finally saying goodbye so she could make the drive home before dark.

As Dave watched her drive away, he could hardly catch his breath. He suddenly didn't want to drive to Indiana. He began questioning his scholastic dreams. It was as if he was watching her ride off into the sunset knowing they'd never be a couple. What would his degree mean if he didn't have her by his side? It seemed like she'd been a part of him forever!

He drew a deep breath and turned to his own car, telling himself it would only be a week before he was back in her arms again—for Christmas. Then the bitterness of the unknown rose up in his throat. Would summer come for both of them and play out the way they'd dreamed, or would one or the other of them lose their way? He shouldn't have been thinking those thoughts but he couldn't help it. A great foreboding rose up in his heart. Something was telling him that he'd made a grave error.

***

The drive to Indiana was torture. He hadn't slept well the night before—his mind tumbling with thoughts about the things they'd talked about at the restaurant—and later. To make things worse, a snowstorm slowed his progress until finally at 3 a.m. he found a motel room along the road and slept.

For the most part, the roads were the pits all the rest of the way. Dave called the school's housing representative's number he'd been given when he gassed up at Waynetown, Indiana at 5 p.m. The woman he reached told that it was too late in the day to look for a place to stay. She suggested a motel in Lafayette and in fact offered to make reservations for him.

Dave called Patti at about seven local time after he'd checked in and found a nearby McDonalds.

"How did the rest of your drive go?" she asked.

"Okay, I suppose," he said between bites. "The storm added a second motel stop and about six hours to my drive."

"I've been worried about you. I wanted to call but I knew you'd be driving. I didn't want to distract you."

"That's a good term for it, really. I would have been distracted. I miss you already."

She didn't respond for a few moments.

"Mom and I are going ring shopping."

"You already have a ring!"

"For you, silly! What would you like?"

"Something simple."

"Gold or some other color? I know that tungsten or ceramic rings are all the rage nowadays."

"I'll leave that up to you. I like the traditional. I wear a size 11. How is your family?"

"They're fine. Mom saw me crying and has been trying to keep me busy."

"Sorry."

"Don't be. I'm just feeling sorry for myself. Christmas is next Sunday. When are you flying in?"

"I don't dare call for a reservation until I talk to the school on Monday."

"Don't wait too long. You know how busy the airports get at Christmas. You might not get a flight."

"With the weather being such as it is, that might be a problem."

"I hope not. Can you come to Christmas eve dinner with my folks on Saturday night?"

"That should work. I think my mom is planning our dinner for the same day. I'll eat light at our place."

"I feel bad about having to share you. When do you have to be back out there?"

"Raytheon wants to meet with me on the Tuesday after Christmas so I'll have to fly out of Colorado Springs Monday night."

"So, I'm looking at my calendar. You're going to meet with them December 27th through the 30th? You do know that the 31st is New Year's Eve don't you?"

"I do, and then school starts on Tuesday, the 4th of January. It would ordinarily start on Monday but with Sunday being New Year's Day, they pushed it forward a day."

"That's the same as Colorado State. That only leaves us Saturday and Sunday over Christmas," she moaned softly.

"Wanna get a room?"

She laughed softly. "We already talked about that, besides wouldn't that seem rather obvious if we sneaked off from our respective parents' homes to get a motel room?"

"I'm having second thoughts about not stopping last Thursday night."

"So am I, but the more I think about what we didn't do, the better I feel about it. We need to try to squeak out at least a week together after our wedding next summer to have some time to soak each other up."

"That's an interesting term," he laughed, "interesting, but well stated."

She sniffed and he heard it.

"Sorry," she said, her voice breaking. "I'm just so unhappy about this whole affair. I'm being selfish, though, so just ignore me. I'm frankly amazed that they came up with a scholarship for you on such short notice. You must have impressed somebody!"

"I haven't even met anyone yet. All they've seen are my transcripts, and a photo I snapped on my phone."

"Didn't you have to expound all about yourself on your application for admission?"

"Well yes, but…"

"And I'm sure they got your transcripts straight from Colorado State. I'll bet somebody at Purdue called up somebody from Colorado State and had a heart to heart with them to be so willing to offer you what they have."

"I suppose so."

"Dave, you may not realize this yet, but that's really rare. You need to be thanking the fates for that."

"I've been having second thoughts all the way out here."

"We could get married and then have you finish your senior year there at Colorado State," he offered.

"What, and sneak away on break to see each other? No thank you very much! When we finally move in together, I'm not leaving!"

He laughed. "I was just kidding."

"Don't mess with me! I'm already on the verge of tears all the time."

"Sorry."

"Do you have a place to stay tonight?"

"A woman at the university got me reservations for the night."

"Did she pay?"

"Not yet. I don't get student housing assistance until I officially start school."

"How are your finances?"

"Tight but adequate."

"You do have money for a flight home at Christmas don't you? If not I'll buy it."

"No, but I have plastic. I'm good."

"Maybe we ought to get you a money tree for Christmas."

"Please don't. My mom has already been pestering me about finances. She and Dad will help if they need to."

A long pause passed between them.

"Dave," she finally added, "I love you."

"I know. And I love you too."

"No, I really mean it!" she insisted. "I ache all over for you."

"I didn't know I had that effect on women."

"Knock it off! I'm trying to pour my soul out here. Don't make fun of me!"

"Sorry. It's easier to laugh than cry."

"Exactly, but right now I'm in the crying mood. Let me wallow in my self-pity."

"I'll call you when I get back to my room. Maybe we could FaceTime or something."

"I'd like that. Maybe I'll be able to sleep afterward."

"Maybe you could show me something nasty."

"I'm not going there! It's going to be hard enough to go to bed alone as it is!"

Chapter 11

Monday for Dave was one frenetic exercise after another. By the end of the day he had met with his financial advisors, signed the Raytheon contract and scholarship paperwork. In addition he'd met with the Dean of the School of Engineering, agreed upon transferrable school credits, worked out a class schedule for spring semester and opened a financial account. At the end of the day he spent some time with the housing administer that he'd talked to on the phone the night before. She in turn drove him out to meet his new landlady.

Rose, the delightful owner of a century-old, two-story home near campus, seemed delighted to meet him. An old widow lady, she rented furnished rooms to university students. She had two upstairs bedrooms and enjoyed sponsoring college students. It was also a way of supplementing her income. She'd seen all kinds and seemed to have an uncanny knack for sizing a person up in a few moments. When she found out that Dave didn't use alcohol or tobacco, she was that much more delighted. Her two upstairs bedrooms shared a common bathroom. Dave would be one of the two students sharing the upstairs. What she offered was sort of a bed and breakfast experience. She made sure he knew that she provided breakfast and dinner for her guests – included in the monthly rent – and that he'd be expected to help with the dishes. The only issue was, the other upstairs tenant was a female. They'd be expected to work out their own bathroom schedule.

Dave wasn't too happy about the arrangements until he actually met Clarissa. She, bless her heart, was not a raving beauty, but she was as easy to talk to as anyone he'd ever met. Short, rather plump, sporting a multi-colored, boy's haircut and blessed with a ready laugh, Clarissa instantly made him feel at home. If he'd had a sister, he could imagine her being his.

"I think you'll love it here," Clarissa told him as she offered an exuberant handshake. "Rose is a sweetheart and man can she cook! As long as you don't plan on making a lot of noise after ten or having strange ladies up in your room, you'll get along well with her. She's like the cute grandma I never knew."

"I'm pleased to meet you, Clarissa," Dave answered. "I assume you're attending Purdue?"

"Oh yes. I'm majoring in Biochemical Engineering, and you?"

"Aeronautical Engineering."

"Cool! You're a Zoomie!"

"A Zoomie?"

"Yeah, one of those tech heads that build moon rockets. I'm impressed."

"Thank you. What exactly do you do in Biochemical Engineering?"

She laughed. "I could give you the technical explanation but it's long and complicated. In short, my colleagues and I work on things that help the human species live long and prosper."

He laughed. "So you're a pill freak?"

She hesitated and then grinned. "Well spoken. I'll accept that as long as you know it goes infinitely deeper than that."

"That's a deal. Maybe I can teach you how to a build a rocket to the moon and you can teach me how to live to be a thousand years old."

"I like you, Dave. You have a weird grasp of the obvious. Now for the hard stuff. Where we're going to be sharing a bathroom, we need to talk details."

"According to the class schedule I just got today," he explained, "my first class on January 4th starts at 7 a.m."

"Yuck! That's early! I'm sorry about that, but hey, that should help with our bathroom schedule. I don't have to walk out of the house until 8:30 so you should be all cleared out by the time I need the shower. The bathroom is pretty small, though, so you'll have to keep all your toiletries in a basket and stow them in your room. Rose provides and launders the towels, bless her heart, so all we have to team up on is keeping the bathroom clean. I'm sorry, but I'm a bit of a neat freak. There's a list posted on the back of the bathroom door. I think it's pretty self-explanatory. I hope you won't make me get you by the ear if you're not pulling your own weight."

He laughed.

She didn't – at first – and then she grinned. "As you can tell I'm pretty bossy, but don't let that bother you, I cry easily. I think my overt personality is just my way of hiding my tender heart."

"I'll keep that in mind. I played football at Colorado State until I got hurt, but I'm not the typical jock, if you know what I mean."

"You must not have been a lineman. You don't have the build for that. You must have been a quarterback."

"Wide receiver actually. I tried to catch passes."

"I know what a receiver is. My dad is a football freak. That's one of the few things we shared when I was growing up. How did you get injured?"

"I got hit low and hard in the last game of the year. It destroyed my knee. I had to have a total knee replacement."

"I thought I noticed a limp. That steep, old stairway might be a challenge. How long has it been since you had your operation?"

"A couple of months."

"Wow, you're doing well then! Hey Rose just twinkled the dinner bell. Let's defer this discussion until later. She gets a little antsy if we don't come right down for dinner."

Clarissa was right. Rose appeared to be like his kindly, old grandmother but in spite of her smiling demeanor, she was all business when it came to getting dinner on. He didn't dare ask her age but from her heavily wrinkled face, silver hair, and slight stoop he guessed she was in her mid to late eighties.

"This looks great as always!" Clarissa beamed as she hurried to the head of the table to give Rose a quick hug.

"Thank you, dear. I don't know if your flattery is deserved though. It's nothing special."

"It certainly beats McDonalds," Dave offered.

"That's a profanity in this house," Clarissa laughed. "Rose isn't into junk food."

"Sorry," Dave grinned, "I'll try to mind my manners."

"Oh dear!" Rose exclaimed with a sweet laugh, "don't be telling him stories that aren't true! I've eaten my share of fast food. The problem is I don't drive anymore and I really don't think that kind of food is all that good for you."

"Dave," Clarissa pointed, "if you'll take that seat I'll offer grace and we'll dive in before it gets cold. I don't know if you're a praying sort of fellow but this is Rose's home and she is, so you'll be expected to take your turn."

"I come from a good Christian home," he said as he pulled out his chair and took a seat. "I don't have any issues with prayers."

"I knew you looked the part," Rose said with a kindly smile. "I can usually tell."

"Rose has a sort of sixth sense," Clarissa chuckled as she took a seat opposite the table from him. "She's sort of like Santa Claus. She knows if you've been good or bad."

"Oh hush!" Rose laughed. "You do go on, Claire."

"Oh yeah," Clarissa explained, "even though my given name is Clarissa, Rose insists on calling me Claire. I suppose where you're officially part of the family now, I'll allow you the same exception, even though I'm known on campus as Clarissa. I do a lot of research and I prefer to use my formal name among my peers."

"Would you rather I call you Clarissa?" he asked.

"No, not really. By the way is your real name David or Dave?"

"Dave, actually, and don't ask me why. I guess I really don't know."

Although dinner dishes were clearly Dave and Claire's responsibility, Rose pulled up a kitchen chair and instigated a pleasant get-to-know-you discussion as they worked.

"Rose is a widow," Claire explained. "Her husband passed away about twelve years ago. He was a railroad engineer."

"A train driver," Rose interjected, "not to be confused with real engineers like the two of you."

"Was he gone a lot?" Dave asked.

"All of the time! We used to joke about how we don't know how we ever had a son. My husband wasn't home long enough to snuggle, if you catch my drift."

"She lost her son to a drug overdose," Claire added softly, "so she takes a real dim view of any illicit drugs on the property."

"No worries there," Dave said. "I was an athlete. I stay away from drugs and alcohol."

"Dave got hit hard playing college ball a couple of months ago," Claire explained. "They had to replace his knee."

"Oh my!" Rose said. "I'm sorry about the stairs. I do have another bedroom on the main floor. Maybe we should move you downstairs."

"You can't do that!" Claire insisted. "That room is chuck full of your quilting stuff. Besides, from what I've seen he does stairs a lot better than you do."

She turned to look at Dave. "Rose makes quilts and sells them online. She's fabulous! I helped her put a website together."

"And ever since you did, my dear, I can't keep ahead of the orders."

"My mom does a little quilting," Dave interjected, "that's a lot of work. Do you have anyone helping you?"

"Yes, Dear. My old fingers aren't what they used to be and like I already told you, I don't drive so I have a friend who cuts the fabric blocks and I have another who helps with some of the sewing."

"I taught her how to buy her fabric online so they deliver all her supplies right to her door," Claire explained, "but Rose makes the patterns and chooses all the colors. Don't let her tell you otherwise. She's an artist in her own rite."

"You're making me blush!" Rose exclaimed. "I really don't make the patterns. They're just something I picked up from my mother and grandmother. People seem to like the old traditional styles so I figure why should I fix something that's not broken?"

"She's being modest," Claire said quickly. "She entered a monster quilt in the state fair last fall and it won grand champion – best in the show. She even got interviewed on TV!"

"It wasn't a monster!" Rose countered.

"Yes it was Rose! It nearly dwarfed a king-sized bed!"

"I guess I got a little carried away. I've had a few people request quilts for their big beds so I've had to adjust my patterns. When I was younger a big quilt fit nicely on a double bed. Nowadays people don't sleep on double beds anymore – unless they're sleeping by themselves."

"Since then she's even had some Amish women reach out to her for advice and they're touted to be the best."

"We need to change the subject." Rose insisted. "I'm not one to clang my own bell."

"Okay," Claire laughed. "Rose already knows all about me but you don't so I'll go first. Then both of us will tag team you."

"The dishes are all done," Rose interjected, "let's go into the living room where we can be comfortable."

Dave hadn't paid much attention to the rooms or the furnishings when his housing specialist first showed him to Rose's door. Her living room was separated from a hallway leading to the second-story stairway and the kitchen by a graceful, wide archway. Clair took Rose by the elbow and led the way.

"Wow!" Dave gasped softly as he followed behind the two. The smallish room was tastefully packed with rich, overstuffed furniture highlighted by three, hand-crafted, teakwood china hutches. Instead of plates, crystal wear and the like, the cabinets were filled to overflowing with ceramic dolls of all sizes, all dressed in intricate, colorful costumes.

"Cool, aren't they." Claire said as she helped Rose settle into what appeared to be her favorite chair. "Rose sewed every one of their outfits. I think she has a doll from nearly every nation on the face of the earth, all sporting their traditional costumes. She's even got a few boy dolls here and there where she didn't think they'd detract," she chuckled.

"I never got to travel the world," Rose explained, "and my husband let me do with the house as I would, so I tried to bring a little of the world into this room."

"That hand-loomed, Oriental rug on the floor," Claire pointed, "came from Turkey and if the salesman wasn't lying to her, it's nearly 500 years old! The fabric on all the furniture came from France, and the carpet on the floor is hand-dyed wool and was imported from England."

"I've never seen anything like this." Dave mused as he walked from cabinet to cabinet.

"That's because they're all original pieces." Claire explained.

"When I was younger and could still drive," Rose said, "I found a shop in Chicago that imported porcelain dolls. I did some research to come up with the traditional dress. Nobody had what I wanted so I bought the fabric and sewed the costumes by hand."

"I tried to get her to agree to let a lady I know do a feature story on her doll collection, but she wouldn't hear of it," Claire said with a slight frown.

"Why not?"

"Because this room is sort of sacred to me," Rose answered softly. "There's a story behind every piece in here. This represents my life."

For a moment Rose looked out of a nearby window that was covered by crisp, see-through sheers, bracketed by billowy, ornate curtains, and then she turned back to look up at Dave.

"Lots of folks put family pictures on their walls. This *is* my family, such as it is. When I pass on I know whoever gets all this stuff will split it up. It'll go everywhere, possibly admired but unappreciated. I'm a private person, Dave. The last thing I want is for some hoity-toity news lady dragging her cameramen all around in here, tracking a little of the world in here with them."

Dave could clearly sense the passion in Rose's voice. "This is so amazing," he said quietly. "I think I can understand a little of how you feel."

Rose smiled. "Sit down you two. Like Claire already explained, I know her story but I'll sit patiently and listen while she tells it to you. Then both of us are going to grill you unmercifully. I don't watch much television so hearing your stories is about the only entertainment I get. Like it or not, you two are the closest things I've got to family now – besides these dolls – and so far I haven't heard any of *them* talking to me. I figure when I do, somebody will carry my insane self off to one of those so-called senior centers. Frankly, I hope that never happens. I hope they come and carry me feet first out through my front door long before that."

Claire chuckled. "She's already told me that if she starts talking to someone I can't see, to just ignore her. Maybe someone's there, maybe there isn't. In any case it's none of my business."

Dave grinned but didn't respond.

"Okay," Claire changed the subject, "so I'm Clarissa. I'm in the second year of my doctorate degree program at Purdue and I'm studying Biochemical Engineering. You called me a pill freak, and even though I smiled, I was a little insulted. Now that we've talked a little, though, I refuse to hold a grudge. I love my field and do a lot of research. My dad is filthy rich so he pays all my expenses. Like I already told you, I'm his football buddy. He wanted a son and didn't get one but he tells me all the time that I'm the best thing that ever came out of him."

"Sorry," Dave mused. "I didn't…"

"Apology accepted," she cut him off, "but I'm not done yet. You'll get your turn."

Claire grinned, and then incredibly she blushed.

"Oops!" she exclaimed softly as she held her hands up to her cheeks, "there goes my bashful, inner self again."

"Red looks good on you," Dave teased, "you should do that more often."

Her blush deepened.

"I'm all undone," she feigned a horrified look, "maybe you should tell your story now while I recover."

Rose offered a hearty laugh. "Why Claire, in all the years I've known you, that's the first time, I believe, that I've ever seen you blush. You must really like this character!"

Claire abruptly turned away.

"Don't be embarrassed," Dave said softly. "You're delightful! I don't think I've ever met anyone easier to talk to."

"Don't patronize me!" Claire suddenly insisted, turning to face him, "and no I'm not falling in love with you if you think that's what this is!"

"I'm not patronizing you. You *are* delightful. I don't think you give yourself enough credit."

"Look at me!" she fumed. "I'm short, fat, and multicolored!"

"And I can tell that you've got a great heart!"

"That's exactly what I tell her all the time," Rose chimed in.

A long pause passed over them.

"Okay," Rose broke the barrier, "while we give Claire some time to recover, I think I would like to hear a little about you, Dave."

"Like I told Claire, I was going to Colorado State on an athletic scholarship. I got hurt right at the end of our championship game – we won, by the way – and I had to have my knee replaced to fix the damage. They canceled my scholarship because they said they couldn't let me play with an artificial knee. I still had a year and a half left in my undergrad engineering studies but I had already applied to Purdue for my postgraduate work before I got injured. When they found out that Colorado State was going to release me, Purdue offered me a scholastic scholarship, sponsored by Raytheon, that will lead into their graduate program, if I can keep my grades up."

"Any girlfriends?" Rose asked, with a twinkle in her eye.

Dave suddenly didn't want to answer that question. Based on Claire's blushed cheeks she'd obviously had some sort of instant attraction to him. It had to be instant. He'd known her less than four hours. He sadly wasn't attracted to her in the least – other than to her buoyant personality – but he didn't want to be cruel. The problem was, she'd eventually find out about Patti anyway, so it was better to be honest up front.

"Actually," he began hesitantly, "even though I don't have a ring yet, I'm engaged. I'll be wearing an engagement band when I come back after Christmas."

"When do you plan on getting married?" Rose asked kindly.

"Sometime early next summer," he said, sort of stammering his words. "We originally had plans for February but Purdue made me an offer I couldn't refuse so we decided to wait until after spring semester."

"I've never had a married couple living here before," Rose said. "I really don't think you'd have enough room."

"This has all been so sudden!" Dave exclaimed. "I just heard from Purdue a few days ago. I'd initially planned on finishing my senior year at Colorado State. When my head stops spinning, I'll have to make some serious decisions about a lot of things."

"You told me you are studying Aeronautical Engineering," Claire changed the subject. "I've never known a *Zoomie* before. Is that a tough field?"

"I'm sure it's no tougher than Biochemical Engineering. I'm impressed, really. In my opinion what you're doing to help us live long and prosper – as you told me earlier – is actually a lot more important to the masses than sending a rocket ship to Mars is."

Claire grinned.

"This has been really nice," Rose said getting to her feet, "but I have a quilt calling to me that I have to get done for Christmas. If you two youngsters will excuse me, I need to toddle off down the hall. You two feel free to stay here and get acquainted."

Chapter 12

*D*ave and Claire retired to their respective rooms a while after Rose left the living room. Dave needed to unpack and get settled and now that he had his schedule for the rest of the week, he needed to book a flight home for Christmas.

Finding a flight instantly became a nightmare. He had appointments on campus every day that week through Wednesday afternoon so he couldn't leave for home any earlier than that. He finally was able to book the redeye out of Chicago at midnight on Wednesday.

***

Dave's appointments at the university on Tuesday finished before 4 p.m. so he was *home* at Rose's place soon after Claire left for the airport to fly home for the holidays. He could tell by the warm scents drifting through the house that Rose had already started dinner.

"Won't you let me help with dinner?" he asked as he dropped his paperwork on a kitchen chair.

"No Dear!" Rose answered firmly. "That's my job and I don't like anyone cluttering up my kitchen when I'm working. If you've got a little time on your hands, you may want to talk to that sweetheart of yours on the phone. I'm sure she's feeling pretty lonely without you being there for the holidays."

A twinge of foreboding swept over him at Rose's comments. He was planning on spending Christmas at home with Patti but not New Years. Rather than trying to explain, he walked upstairs to phone Patti.

His first phone call to Patti went unanswered. Assuming Patti might be out shopping with her mom, he left a message and then jumped on his laptop to review his new class schedule and look at the class overviews to see what he'd be up against in the coming semester. By the time Rose rang the dinner bell, Patti hadn't returned his call. Rose insisted on helping with the dishes afterward where it was just the two of them, and then she retired to her quilting den, leaving Dave on his own.

***

"Sorry," Patti apologized when she finally called him back at nearly 10 p.m. "Mom and I drove to Denver today to look at wedding dresses and find you a ring. I got your message but Mom and I were having a little *together* time that we haven't had in forever. It was great! I hope you don't mind."

"Not at all," he answered. "I just had a little time on my hands after all of my meetings today and was missing you."

"I know that feeling." she sighed. "Hey, let me call you right back. I want to FaceTime. Holding this phone up to my ear just isn't getting it done."

When he answered her call and arranged his cell phone so they could see each other, he involuntarily drew a deep breath. She was still made up from the day out with her mom but she was sitting cross-legged on her bed dressed in a white, clingy, satin robe. It was obvious that she had little or nothing on under it.

"You're killing me here!" he moaned. "Maybe you should go put on a sweatshirt or something."

She giggled. "Don't you like my robe?"

"What's not to like? The problem is, I'm a thousand miles away and you look fabulous in that!"

"Wanna see more? I'll go lock my bedroom door!"

"I'm beginning to think that Face Timing you was a really bad idea! This is way worse than cuddling up to you in that motel room!"

101

She laughed and then turned the phone over on her bed with the camera facing down. A few moments later she turned the phone back over and this time she was dressed in a bulky, blue sweatshirt and matching pajama bottoms.

"That is so much better!" he exclaimed. "At least now I can breathe."

She laughed. "I'm sorry. Just so you'll know, Mom and I bought that clingy robe when we were in Denver today at a wedding boutique. I just thought it'd be fun to give you a little preview of what our wedding night might look like."

"You're terrible! You're not so naïve that you don't know what that just did to me!"

She grinned naughtily into the camera. "I Just wanted to be sure you hadn't changed your mind."

"Of course I haven't changed my mind. Are you having second thoughts?"

"Not about *my* commitment. I just worry about you being out there in that college environment all alone, surrounded by a thousand lonely coeds. I'm sure it's just a phase I'm going through but I'm jealous and a little insecure right now."

"You've got nothing to worry about. I'm not staying on campus. I'm living with Rose, an eighty-year-old widow and Carissa a frumpy, short, single girl with tri-colored hair."

She laughed. "I think I'd like to see a picture of that—but then maybe you're just telling me that so I won't worry."

"I could wander around and let you see the place over my phone but you wouldn't get to meet Clarissa. She left to go home for the holidays before I got home this afternoon."

"Who is Rose?"

"My landlady."

"Oh. Why is it you're living there and not on campus?"

"It's what the housing administrator could come up with on such short notice. Like I told you, Rose is an old widow lady who rents out her two upstairs bedrooms to students. It's only a couple of miles from campus so I can walk or even catch a bus when the weather is bad. I think she may be giving the college a deal on the rent. I don't know how much they're paying her."

"How are they working your finances?"

"They haven't told me much about that yet, other than to have me sign paperwork for all my classes. They told me that Raytheon is covering everything – tuition, books, lab fees, housing – all that stuff. I even have a meal allowance they pay to me in cash because I'm not living on campus. I'll have to cover clothes and personal incidentals but I've got some savings that should cover that."

"Have they told you anything about your summer internship yet?"

"No. I guess I'll find out about all that the week after Christmas when I fly out to New Jersey."

"Just so you know, I really hate this! It's like you're living in a foreign country."

"I'm sorry, Patti. I'm not happy about this either. At least we'll have Christmas together."

"I'm excited. Do you have plane reservations yet?"

"I do, but I'm not too happy about them. I couldn't get anything earlier than the redeye on Wednesday night. I sent my dad a text. He'll pick me up at the airport."

"You know I would have picked you up."

"I know, but Mom and Dad will want to see me for a few hours while I'm home. Even though I want to spend as much time as I can with you, it's only fair that I share a little time with them, too."

She pouted. "When do you have to leave to fly out to Raytheon?"

"Probably sometime Monday afternoon. I haven't had a chance to call them yet and make those arrangements. I'm sure I'll know more tomorrow afternoon."

"That only gives us five short days together and we have to share some of that time with our parents. I'm already feeling gypped!"

"How about we have breakfast, just the two of us, early Thursday morning?"

"In my room?"

"Don't tempt me! I'm sure your mom would pitch a fit if I cooked up something in her kitchen and then hauled it down to your room."

"Just bring milk and muffins. I'll lock the door."

"Patti! You're not making this any easier."

"Sorry."

She looked away from her phone for a few moments.

"I hung the new calendar on my wall just before I called you," she said. "There are a lot of empty months between Christmas and June."

"Yes there are," he conceded quietly, "it's going to be a long winter."

"*The winter of my discontent*", she quoted solemnly.

"Maybe you should skip spring semester and come with me when I fly back out after Christmas," he suggested.

"That's almost like eloping, and we put a down payment on my gown today."

"Really? Do you have pictures?"

"I do but you don't get to see it until I come strutting down the aisle wearing it."

"Spoilsport."

She laughed. "This coming from a guy who just made me change out of my slinky robe?"

"I did that so I can sleep tonight."

"Speaking of that," she said after a half-stifled yawn, "I've had a big day and it's late. Call me when you get home tomorrow."

"I love you, Patti!" he said earnestly.

A soft look swept over her face. "I love you, too, Dave. Sweet dreams."

Chapter 13

"It's been snowing all night!" Rose called out as Dave carefully trod down the steep stairway to the kitchen the next morning. "I looked at the news on the television a few minutes ago and they're saying there's a polar express bearing down on us. I was hoping for a white Christmas, but this doesn't look good. The last time we had a storm like this we were without electricity for a week."

A shock wave swept through him! He was supposed to fly out of Chicago at midnight.

"I wonder what the roads are going to be like from here to Chicago," he mused as he stepped into her kitchen to watch the newscast on her small TV.

"That's right!" Rose exclaimed. "You're supposed to fly out tonight, aren't you? It's about 150 miles to O'Hare International Airport from here. What time is your flight?"

"Midnight."

"I guess your flying out depends on when the worst of this storm hits. It's snowing hard right now but we haven't seen any strong winds yet. On a good day I think it takes about 2 ½ hours to make that drive. If you're fighting traffic, slick roads, and snowplows, that might be tough. Have you looked to see if they're canceling any flights yet?"

Dave quickly pulled up his phone app. What he saw made him sick to his stomach. *His* flight hadn't been canceled yet, but the information board on his phone was already filled with other canceled flights.

"It doesn't look good!" he grumbled.

"Oh dear, what are you going to do?"

"I don't know! I only have a few days home with my fiancée over Christmas as it is! I have to fly to New Jersey next Tuesday."

"Could you drive home?"

"Not realistically. It's almost 1,100 miles one way and the roads will probably be a nightmare!"

"I'm so sorry, Dear. Does your girlfriend know?"

"I've only been up a few minutes. I haven't called her yet."

"Maybe it'll all work out," she offered hopefully.

Dave's phone rang.

"Hello, this is Kelly at the admissions office," a voice answered. "We've canceled your meetings for today. They're shutting down most of the nonessential services on campus because of the storm and after reviewing the weather forecast we've decided to postpone your meetings until after Christmas."

"I won't be available right after Christmas!" Dave explained anxiously. "I've got a four-day interview process lined up at Raytheon beginning the 27th!"

"Oh, that's right! I was just looking at the notes in your file. We could do most of the rest of our business over the phone, but the people you'll need to talk to most likely won't be on campus now until after Christmas. I'll text our people and explain. I think if nothing else, we can work with you after classes start on the 4th of January."

"Is there anything I can do in the meantime?"

"No Dave. Luckily we completed most of the important business on Monday and Tuesday. If we need anything else after Christmas, we'll phone you. Have a Merry Christmas. Oh, and if we don't see you until later, have a Happy New Year and we'll see you on campus on the 4th."

"Breakfast is ready," Rose announced cheerily. "I'm sorry things aren't working out for you but I find things always look better on a full stomach."

"Thank you, Rose. I'm sure you already know this, but you're a sweetheart."

"I'm flattered but you needn't waste all those flowery words on an old woman like me. Eat your breakfast, give things a while to settle down, and then call up your girl and show *her* your charm."

***

The wind rattled the windows in Rose's old home and veiled the streets out front in billowing waves of white by about ten. Just after breakfast, Dave called Patti on FaceTime with the bad news. She hung up after his initial pronouncement and called him back. She didn't want him to watch her cry.

For the next full hour he stared blankly out at the storm while they talked on the phone. All the while, he kept beating himself up for not flying home the day before like Claire had done. At the back of his mind he was thinking about the four years that Patti had wasted waiting for him while he was convincing himself that school was all important. He replayed their hospital scene over and over again in his mind remembering the feeling he'd had that their relationship was over then. Now he had a sick, sinking feeling flowing over him that maybe *they* weren't meant to be.

When the power went out, plunging Rose's home into semidarkness, he ended their conversation and helped Rose scurry around lighting candles in the dingy, afternoon light.

"I was watching the news channel just as the lights went out," Rose said as her living room filled up with flickering candlelight. "They were telling everyone to stay off the streets if at all possible. I'm so sorry, Dear. I don't think you're going to be able to fly out tonight. Maybe if things let up you can catch a flight tomorrow."

"Did the news say how long they expected this storm to last?"

"From what I saw before the power went out, this is just the leading edge. Chicago is getting hammered right now and it's headed this way!"

Dave flipped his cell phone to the weather and read basically all the bad news that Rose had just given him.

"I guess it's a good thing that your cell phone still works without the power being on."

"I think the cell towers all have emergency backups."

"This old house isn't very well insulated," Rose said after a few moments. "Those windows give off a terrible draft. The last time this happened, I had to use my woodstove to keep from freezing."

"Do you have any firewood?"

"There's some in the old mower shed out back."

"Should I bring some in before it gets too bad out?"

She laughed. "It's already bad out there, but if you need something to do to take your mind off your girl I suppose you could bundle up and haul some wood up on the covered porch out back. There's also some lump coal out there and a couple of buckets to haul the coal in."

She guided him out to the back porch and he stood watching for awhile waiting for the blowing snow to let up enough so that he could see the shed she was talking about.

"I hate to send you out in this!" Rose exclaimed softly. "I've been meaning to bring some of that wood and coal up on the porch all fall. You just never know when you're going to need it but I didn't want to clutter up the back porch. Maybe we should wait for awhile to see if the power comes back on."

"I doubt anything's going to happen soon. If you were a lineman would you want to be out there in this weather?"

"No. I suppose not. It's still early in the day though. Let's leave that as sort of a last resort. If it hasn't come back on by the time it starts to get dark, I may have to send you out there. I'd help but I don't think that would be too wise. I don't get around as well as I once did."

"No, and if you fall down and break something that would be a disaster!"

"It's a good thing I had them deliver groceries yesterday. I hadn't planned on having guests for Christmas dinner but I sort of splurged. I bought a turkey breast and all the trimmings for a right nice Christmas dinner. Problem is, my kitchen range is electric."

"Do you have tinfoil?"

"I do."

"I remember as a Boy Scout cooking hobo dinners in a campfire. We could do those in your woodstove. I don't know how we'd manage a whole turkey breast though. Just sawing off frozen slabs might prove to be an issue."

"Oh that's not a problem. I can thaw it first in cold water."

She smiled. "I remember making hobo dinners in tinfoil as a young girl. We might just be able to make do."

"I think I'll see about getting some wood in here right now. The way that wind is howling, your house might cool down pretty fast. If we get a fire started right away it'll slow the process down."

"I saved my husband's heavy wool coat and overshoes. I always wondered why. Now I suppose they'll come in handy. He's also got an old wool cloth faceguard that will help too. Nowadays they make them out of knitted wool but the wind blows right through them."

She led the way to a battered, old armoire sitting in a corner of her back porch. "All of his gear is in there. I do hope it'll all fit. I think you're about his same build."

110

A few minutes later, Dave began the first of what proved to be a number of stumbling trips out to her so-called *mower shed*. Her husband's ancient but still sound outerwear worked wonders, even protecting his face from the stinging, snow-filled wind.

A look came over Rose just as he closed the door behind him for what he thought was the last time. "I hate to even mention this," she said, "but Hershel, my next-door neighbor, is nearly ninety and none of his kids live nearby. He lives alone and I just saw him outside yesterday. Would you mind slipping over there to see if he's okay while you're still all dressed up?"

***

A skinny, stooped, mostly-balding old man answered his front door after Dave had knocked on it long enough that he'd almost given up and left.

"What can I do for you?" the old man asked as he opened the door a couple of inches.

"Rose sent me over to see if you're okay?" Dave said.

"Huh?" Hershel asked, inclining his left ear forward.

"Rose sent me!" Dave shouted.

"Oh, come on in here!" the old man shouted back. "I can hardly hear you over the wind!"

From what Dave could see the moment he stepped inside and closed the heavy wooden door behind him, Hershel's home wasn't nearly as nice or ornate as Rose's.

"Hello, Hershel. I'm Dave Tolman, one of Rose's renters. Rose sent me over to see if you're okay?"

"Doin' well for now, but I can't reach my candles. It's gonna be dark in here pretty soon."

"Can I help you get them?"

"Sure thing," Hershel said as he turned toward a darker, inner room. "Thank you. The candles and my matches are out here in the kitchen above the fridge. I'm not too sure-footed anymore. I'd use a step stool but I'm afraid I might fall."

Dave followed closely behind him as he slowly shuffled into the kitchen. He smiled as he spotted Hershel's refrigerator. He hadn't seen one like it since he was a kid. He was amazed that it still worked. The word *Frigidaire* was scrawled in cursive, chrome letters across the front of the antique, round-topped door. A couple of tall, fat candles sat just inside the cabinet door above the fridge, along with a familiar-looking, short, cardboard container of *strike-anywhere* matches.

"Just light one of those candles and set it on the stove," the old man wheezed. "That way I can see to cook my dinner. You know I've got a couple of old kerosene lanterns down in my cellar that would really come in handy if the power stays off very long. I can't go down those stairs, though. I don't think I'd ever make it back up. Would you mind fetching them up here for me?"

Dave lit both candles, set one down on a glass plate atop an ancient, wood-burning range to catch the candlewax, and then handed the other one to the old man so he could see ahead of him. He followed Hershel to the back of the house where the stooped, old man pointed at a door.

"The cellar's down there. Mind those steps though. They're pretty tricky."

Dave turned on his cell phone light and carefully climbed down the steep, narrow, concrete stairway. The old man's cellar looked like something right out of the eighteen hundreds. Two, dust-covered, antique lanterns hung from heavy wires attached to the bottom of the floor joists. An old red can labeled Kerosene sat against a concrete wall beneath the lanterns. A ponderous, ancient, coal-fired furnace sat near the middle of a small room that smelled heavily of coal. Alongside the old coal furnace stood a more modern gas fixture. A galvanized, steel heat duct protruded out of the top of the newer furnace and turned at nearly a right angle under the floor joists to join another much larger duct still attached to the top of the coal furnace. A flue handle formed from a steel coil to protect the user from burns was attached to the flue that separated the two ducts.

"You okay down there?" the old man shouted.

"Yes, I'm coming. Should I bring up your extra kerosene?"

"The lanterns should be full but I may need the extra later on. Don't try to carry everything up here all at once though. If ya break one of those globes the lantern is ruined. They don't make them like that anymore."

Compromising, Dave took down one lantern. He couldn't carry his lighted cell phone and more than one lantern at the same time anyway.

"That's a pretty unique, old furnace you've got down there," Dave said as he joined the old man at the top of the stairs.

"Yeah, it's an old beauty. I used to use that all the time until the do-gooders decided it wasn't proper to burn coal in the city anymore."

"Does it still work?"

"Last time I tried it, it did. It takes a little doing to get it fired up but once you get it going you only have to stoke it up a couple of times a day. It doesn't need electricity to work. Convection sends the hot air up through the heat ducts. About all I'd have to do to make it work would be to flip that flue over from one furnace to the other."

"I could smell coal. Is there a coal room down there?"

"Uh huh. The coal is in a room to itself off to the left of the old furnace, and it's chuck full. I used to top it off every fall when I could still buy coal. I'll bet it's been forty years now since I bought a load. Carry that lantern in here and set it up on the stove. I'll trim the wick and see if that old fuel will still burn."

Dave watched as Hershel carefully dusted off the large globe, lifted it and turned a small knob that raised a cloth wick, charred along the upper edge.

"Looks like the wick is still soaked up," Hershel said. "Strike one of those matches and see if it'll light."

As a lazy, smoky flame caught on the cloth the old man turned the wick down and lowered the globe back into place. A welcome yellowish glow filled the kitchen.

"That's quite amazing," Hershel chuckled to himself, "I bet I haven't touched that lantern in fifty years."

"Rose told me you guys had a big power outage a few years ago. Didn't you use it then?"

"No, I'd been in the hospital that winter and I was staying with one of my sons while I recuperated. Luckily with that open, dirt-floor cellar, the house stayed warm enough down there that my old plumbing didn't break in the cold. This old house has cast iron plumbing and I was afraid I'd have to replumb everything."

"Does this range still work?" Dave asked nodding at the antique, wood-burning range currently acting as a base for the old man's lantern and a single, burning candle.

"Oh yes. You can't be in a hurry though. It's so heavy that it takes a bit to get it heated up. I can burn either coal or wood in it. I use it every time I want to bake something. Where I'm all alone, I don't fix many big meals anymore. The microwave works great for most of my old-guy dinners."

"You know, Hershel, I just happen to know that Rose bought a turkey breast for Christmas dinner and doesn't have any way of cooking it now if the power doesn't come back on. How would you feel about having a couple of guests over for Christmas dinner? We'd bring all the food. All you'd have to do is share a little light and maybe some heat."

"I'd like that! Rose and I jaw over the garden fence most of the summer. She still tends a mean garden and I've got a couple of fruit trees. She trades me vegetables during the summer for fruit in the fall."

"I'll call her and see what she thinks," Dave offered, punching a button on his cell phone.

To his horror, the phone screen lit up but there was no service.

"It looks like the cell towers might be down," he mused mostly to himself.

"I don't have one of those things. I still have an old landline. I'll call her on it if that's okay? In the meantime why don't you go back down there and bring up that other lantern. If I'm going to have company, it'd be nice to be able to see what we're doing."

"The phone's dead," Hershel said as Dave clamored back up out of the basement with the other lantern. "Looks like we'll have to walk over there and talk to her."

"I'll go. I don't want you to fall."

Outside the storm raged on, and when Dave could see more than a few yards ahead of him, he could see that large snowdrifts had already filled the streets. No cars moved. There were no tracks in the street and no other soul in sight.

"This is going to be a bad one," Rose greeted him as he stomped the snow off of her husband's galoshes on the porch and pushed through her front door. "How's Herschel?"

"He's amazing, actually! I carried a couple of kerosene lanterns up out of the cellar for him. Did you know he has an old, coal-burning furnace down there that he claims still works?"

"Oh that's right! And I know for a fact that he's got an old, wood-fired kitchen range. When he decides to cook something besides microwave food, I can smell the wood smoke."

"I sort of invited ourselves over there for dinner," Dave added hesitantly. "I'm hoping with that coal furnace and that old kitchen range we'd be warm and well fed."

"And he was okay with that?"

"I offered your turkey breast, was that okay?"

"Yes that seems like a fair trade. He's ordinarily a very private person."

"He told me that you two share vegetables and fruit over the back fence."

"Oh we do that all the time and he's friendly enough with me but I think he feels awkward about having a woman in his home when he's all alone. I've only been in his house half a dozen times over the years."

"If the power stays off for very long it only makes sense to heat one home instead of two and if that coal furnace still works, like he claims it does, I'd bet his home would be the better choice."

"It might be. I'll have to run the water in my sinks to keep the pipes from freezing. That doesn't worry me as much as the sleeping arrangements. I know he has three bedrooms but two of them are upstairs. I'll bet they're unheated. I've never been in them. I don't know how clean he is, either, if you know what I mean."

"Better to be a little uncomfortable than freeze."

She smiled. "I haven't had a great adventure in a lot of years. This might be fun."

"We tried to call you but there's no cell phone service and Hershel's landline is dead."

"Oh dear!" she exclaimed as she hurried to an old dial phone hanging on the wall. "I've never had that happen before. There must be trees down across the wires."

"Anything?" he asked as she held up the receiver.

"No, and now that I think about it, what you said a little while ago about the linemen not wanting to go out in this storm makes sense. If there are trees down we're in for a long night without power – maybe even a few days like the last time."

"Maybe I should go ask Hershel if he'd mind having guests tonight. If he's okay with that, I can help him get his furnace going. He told me it takes a while to get it all stoked up – whatever that means."

"Before you do that, would you mind going upstairs and turning on a trickle of water in your bathroom sink and shower? I don't climb stairs too well anymore."

***

Hershel seemed more than happy to have them share his home and by dark they were all set up at his place and the two old neighbors were carrying on an animated discussion as they cooked beef stew and biscuits on his wood-fired range. The storm showed no signs of slowing down and in fact the wind had increased from a snow-driving nuisance to a low, moaning howl that rattled the windows and caused the old house to creak.

Just before they sat down to dinner, Hershel produced an old transistor radio that sprang instantly to life after Dave changed out the acid-swelled batteries. The news that came pouring in over the radio was dismal. O'Hare International was closed. The freeways were snarled. Traffic in town was at a standstill. The widespread power outages could last through Christmas and everyone was being warned to shelter in place. The outside temperatures with the windchill were subzero.

Dave glanced at his phone screen for the hundredth time as he sat down at the kitchen table – still no service!

"I'll bet your sweetheart is beside herself with worry," Rose said sadly as she watched him pocket his phone. "Even if the airport was open, you couldn't get there now and she's sitting at home not knowing if you're coming or not."

"I can't believe there's no cell service! What do people do if they have an emergency?"

"I don't think the first responders could get to us even if we had an emergency," Rose said. "I suppose we'd be on our own."

"A lot of people used to die in blizzards when I was young," Hershel said, "before we had all those newfangled phones. Course back then we had coal and wood to heat our houses with. If this goes on for very long, most folks are going to be in trouble."

"What do I have to do with that furnace downstairs besides keeping the firebox stoked full of coal?" Dave asked.

"Once a day you have to haul out the clinkers."

"Clinkers?"

Hershel chuckled. "Yes, clinkers. When the coal burns it melts down a lot of the impurities into something that looks kinda like hot, porous, lava rock. You probably didn't notice but there's a poker and a long-handled, claw-like device standing in an old, galvanized bucket alongside the furnace. You have to break up the clinkers with the poker without hitting the firebrick and then fish 'em out in pieces with that claw and put 'em in the bucket. I have a lidless concrete box by the back door where I used to empty the bucket of hot clinkers. The box will keep the clinkers contained until they cool down so they don't start a fire."

"This reminds me of my girlhood days," Ruth joined in. "Back in the day my family had something my dad called a *Stokermatic*. It burned crushed coal and had a built-in coal bin. It was my job to carry the coal in from the back shed in buckets and keep that bin full. It fed coal from the bin into the firebox automatically. I remember my mom wouldn't let me deal with the clinkers. She was afraid I'd get burned. Dad did that."

"We used to burn heating oil when I was a kid," Dave joined in. "We had a big tank behind the house that fed a line through the wall into the furnace. I remember my dad complaining when the oil man came because he'd always leave us a big bill."

"Lots of folks around here still burn heating oil," Hershel said, "but the do-gooders are trying to get them to switch over to propane or natural gas. My boys saw to it that I got a gas furnace installed a few years ago. I couldn't have afforded to do it on my own but they're both pretty well-to-do."

"Why don't you go live with one of them?" Rose asked. "I'll bet they worry about you being up here all alone. Where do your boys live now?"

"Lance lives in Michigan. Karl lives in Ohio. My daughter Charlotte and her husband move around a lot. Right now she's living in Oregon. Besides, I like being my own man. I'd probably just make trouble if I moved in with any of them. I figure as long as I still remember who I am and can dress and feed myself, I'll stay here with my memories."

"How long has your wife been gone now?" Ruth asked reverently.

"Not that I'm keeping track," Hershel offered a smile, "but it'll be nine years in January."

Dave's phone suddenly chimed, and continued chiming for awhile as message after message displayed on his screen.

"Looks like they got the cell phone towers working," Dave smiled as he glanced at his messages. Every one, of course, was from Patti. He looked at his voicemails. There were six!

"You haven't finished your dinner yet," Rose winked at him, "but under the circumstances I think you need to take your stew and slip into the living room where you two can talk without us eavesdropping. I'll bet she's beside herself with worry!"

***

"Hello!" Patti answered eagerly.

"Hi Love," Dave answered.

"I'm going crazy out here!" she cried. "We've been watching the news. O'Hare is closed."

"It is," he said sadly, "we're having a blizzard here. The power is out. The roads are all closed. Cell service has been down all afternoon."

"I finally figured that out when the phone started telling me that your message box was full. So I guess this means you won't be flying in tonight?"

"I hate to say this but the way things look, I may not even be able to get home for Christmas."

A long pause settled between them.

"We should FaceTime," Dave suggested.

"No. I'm a mess. I've been crying for an hour."

"Sorry."

"How long has the power been out?"

"All afternoon."

"Is your phone charged up?"

"It's about half, but worst case I can fight my way out to my car. I have a phone charger in there."

"The weather reports on TV look really bad. How are you staying warm without power?"

"The old man who lives next door to my apartment has an old home with a coal-fired furnace. It's old school but it works. I'm holed up here with him and my landlady. My roomie left yesterday to fly home for Christmas."

"Lucky her!"

"That's just what I was thinking this morning. The campus called early and told me they'd canceled my meetings because of the weather. If I'd known what was coming I'd be home already."

"We just can't catch a break, can we?" she said, her voice dripping with emotion.

"I'm so sorry, Patti!"

"I'm sitting here in my room twisting your new ring around my finger. I was really looking forward to putting it on you tonight."

"FaceTime me. I want to see it!"

"I'm not ready to do that yet."

"Hey I've seen you without makeup before. Do you plan to be made up all the time when we're married?"

"Of course not silly, but this is different. I'm ghastly!"

"No you're not. No matter how bad it gets, you could never look ghastly."

She didn't answer for a few moments.

"Let's have this discussion tomorrow or the next day when we see what's happening with this storm."

"I've been watching the weather forecasts. They're not expecting O'Hare to open until after Christmas. I guess thousands are stranded."

"At least I'm not stuck in the airport."

"Yes, there's that, I suppose."

Another pause passed between them.

"What are you wearing?" he joked.

"Nothing at all."

"Hang up and FaceTime me!"

"How come you've changed your mind? You didn't even want to see me in my naughty robe last time."

"Did I mention it's really cold here? I need something to warm me up."

"While two old people look on?"

"Well there's that, I suppose."

"Mom has dinner on. I should go. Can I call you back after a while?"

"Sure."

"What are you and your old neighbors going to do to pass the time?"

"I heard Rose say something to Hershel about Gin Rummy."

"I haven't played that in years."

"I don't know how," he laughed.

"Well I'm an expert so you'd better have them teach you well. I think as struggling students we may be playing a lot of cards for entertainment."

"I can think of something else we can do for entertainment."

"And what else do you plan to do with the other 23 ½ hours a day?"

"That's rude."

She laughed.

"I miss you."

"Please don't even start!" she cried. "I just sorta got control of myself."

"I do though," he insisted, "and you already know that I love you."

She didn't answer for a moment.

"I'm sorry," he finally continued. "I am sitting here kicking myself for being such a fool. We should be married with one kid already and another on the way."

"Let's not talk about spilled milk," she suggested. "I think I finally got your attention. Let's just go on from here."

"Call me when you finish dinner."

"I'm an emotional wreck, Dave. Now that I know what's happening or not happening and have heard your voice, maybe I should just curl up by the fire and feel sorry for myself. I don't want to waste your phone battery and I need to quit crying sometime tonight so I can sleep. Let's just say goodnight now. We'll talk tomorrow."

Chapter 14

"**J**s everything okay at home?" Rose asked as Dave walked back into the kitchen to join them.

"Not really, but we seem to have a little time on our hands here, so if you don't mind I'll tell you the whole long story."

A little over a half hour later, Rose reached out and touched the back of Dave's hand. "I'm really sorry to hear all of that," she said softly.

"I hate to change the subject," Rose said haltingly, "but it appears that we'll be spending some time here. What should we do about sleeping arrangements?"

"I've got two bedrooms upstairs," Hershel offered, "but they're not heated. My kids used to bundle up in a feather tick during the winter to stay warm. I've still got a couple of those hanging around but those stairs are too treacherous for either Rose or me to hike up."

Hershel glanced at his living room. "Rose, I think you should have a little privacy. I've got clean sheets that I'll put on my bed for you and I'll bundle up in one of those feather ticks on the couch. Dave, it looks like you'll be batching it upstairs in the other one."

"It's a good thing I brought a bag with my pajamas and face creams," Rose chuckled. "This is his house so I'm sure Hershel has all he needs. Dave, it looks like you're going to have to get all bundled up again and make a trip back to my house for your stuff. You can double check my house for me while you're over there if you would please. Be sure I've got water dripping from all the faucets."

"I can do that. In fact, I'm going to dig my car out while I'm outside so I can plug in my phone. My phone battery is getting low and right now it's our only contact with the outside world."

"You mean it's your only contact with Patti, don't you?"

"Yeah, well there's that too."

Knowing he didn't need to worry about anyone stealing his car in the storm, Dave just dug his driver side door out of the large drift that had swallowed it so he could start the engine and let it warm up while his phone charged. After he checked Rose's house, he left his car running until the heater started blowing warm air and then he shut it off and fought his way back to Hershel's house.

"Both of my feather ticks are upstairs in my kids' rooms," Hershel said as soon as Dave had shucked off his snow-plastered coat and had time to warm up a little. "Each room has a chest at the foot of the bed. The ticks are crammed into those chests, if you'd be so kind as to dig them out. I'll need one down here. You can toss the other one out on the bed of your choice and fluff it up a little so it'll keep you warm. I hope they haven't been crammed in those chests too long. If they've lost their loft they'll be cold to sleep in."

Dave laughed. "I've never even seen a feather bed before. I remember John Denver singing a song about one once. As I recall the song said it was *nine feet high and six feet wide and soft as a downy chick*, or something like that."

Rose chuckled. "That's probably not far from the truth. They're pretty big. I remember that song, too. It goes on to say that it was *made from the feathers of forty 'leven geese*. This is really going to date me, but I remember helping my mom make a couple of those when I was young and I'm here to tell you that's probably pretty accurate. We raised a few tame geese and in addition my dad and brothers hunted waterfowl every fall. We had to pluck all the feathers to make pillows or feather ticks. I know it took a lot of critters to fill up one of those mattresses and they weren't feather proof! We always had stray feathers in our hair in the morning and a few drifting around our bedrooms most of the winter."

When Dave opened the big chest at the foot of the first bed it seemed to take forever to pull the feather-filled sack up out of the chest. As it fluffed up, it was hard to wrap his arms around so he could carry it downstairs. In fact, when he got to the top of the stairs, he just launched it down the stairway. Hershel and Rose teamed up on it at the bottom of the stairs and roughly folded it in half so they could drag it into the living room.

"My gosh!" Dave exclaimed as he helped them spread it out and fluff it up. "Now I know what John Denver meant when he said *it'd hold eight kids and four hound dogs.*"

"*And a piggy we stole from the shed.*" Rose laughed. "You know I don't know who got away with my feather ticks but now that I see this one, I wish I still had mine."

"Did it really take a whole bolt of cloth to make the sack like John Denver sang in his song?"

"I don't recall," Rose said, "but as you'll notice, this is flannel. The cloth helps make it warmer but the weave is so open it lets some of the feathers escape."

"How on earth do you sleep in one of these?" Dave asked.

"You just sort of lay down in it and it folds up around you," Ruth explained. "The first time you do that you'll swear you're going to smother to death but there's so much air in between the feathers that you never will."

"Yeah," Hershel mused, "folks nowadays wouldn't know how to keep warm like we did in the winter. Dad never ran the heat overnight. He'd get up early and get the old kitchen range stoked up for breakfast and we'd all hustle down the stairs in the morning in our underwear and stand next to it to get dressed. He'd stoke up the coal furnace in the morning before he went off to work and Mom would shove another load of coal in it from time to time during the day. When he came home at night, I'd haul out the clinkers and then he'd restoke it. It'd burn hot until midnight and then stay sorta warm the rest of the night."

"You and I had a similar upbringing," Ruth mused. "As I recall, though, we switched over to fuel oil in the late fifties and they broke up our old cast-iron furnace for scrap."

Dave left the two to talk trivia and went upstairs with one of the lanterns to get his own bed ready. As he held the lantern up next to the only window in his room, the glass panes were already mostly iced over and he could see his breath when he breathed out through his mouth. He hoped that what his two friends were saying about the feather bed being warm was right!

"If you'll leave your bedroom door open!" Hershel called up the stairs to him, "a little warm air will drift up the stairway. I'd pull on a pair of socks before you go to bed, though, so your feet don't stick to the floor on the way down in the morning!"

***

The blizzard raged on the next day, showing no signs of abating. Dave learned to play Gin Rummy with his two old friends and listened to their friendly banter as they spent the day together reminiscing, cooking over Hershel's antique range, and listening to the impossible weather reports over the radio.

Dave called Patti on Christmas Eve morning. She still didn't want to FaceTime. He wondered about that, worrying that he'd see anger in her eyes, not loneliness or anguish. The spark was gone from her voice. After less than an hour, she made an excuse that she had to help her mom and dad with the tree and hung up. He didn't know when they put their tree up. He knew that to some families, decorating the tree on Christmas Eve was a tradition, but in their busy, modern lives, he hardly believed that was the case. He ached inside, wondering if he had recognized too late how much she meant to him.

127

Hershel and Rose decided to make Christmas candy once they got the stove fired up and Dave eagerly joined in. His grandma had always made divinity, peanut brittle, fudge and taffy. Although it meant sending Dave over to Rose's house a few times in the storm, between the two old people they had all the *fixings* they needed for the candy. He made notes on his phone and took photos of the whole process so someday; maybe, he could repeat it when he had a family of his own.

Hershel didn't have a tree, but Rose had an old, artificial one stashed away in a big cardboard box in her cellar. Dave made enough trips back and forth to bring up the tree, the lights, and a box of antique ornaments that he'd remembered having seen something similar to on his grandmother's tree. About halfway through the day, between the candy making and the tree trimming, Dave noticed the obvious spark between the two old people. As fun as it was to watch, it only made the ache in his heart worse.

The activities wound down after a hot soup and homemade bread supper and in order to give his friends a little *together* time, he went up to his room to phone Patti.

"Hi!" Patti answered brightly. "I'm ready to FaceTime now, if you want to."

"I'd love that! I'm feeling really bad about myself right now."

"If you're going to cry, maybe you won't want me to watch," she teased.

"I don't really care if I do. I just want to be able to see you when we talk."

When the phone rang again, Patti was sitting cross-legged on her bed. Dave was folded up in his feather tick with candlelight illuminating his face from the side.

"Where are you?" she laughed. "You look like something out of a Hallmark Christmas movie."

"Actually, I'm all wrapped up in a feather bed in Hershel's upstairs bedroom. If you notice fog coming out of my mouth when I talk it's because it's probably nearly zero in this room and there's no electricity so I'm coming to you by candlelight."

"How romantic."

"It would be if you were here. We could wrap up together in this old bed and nobody would ever find us."

"Is it warm?"

"Toasty – but lonely."

"Where are your friends?"

"Downstairs sparking," he laughed. "You know what they say about cold weather, don't you?"

"No, what?"

"It breeds togetherness."

"That sounds sort of nasty the way you say it. Is that why you're hiding upstairs?"

"No Patti, it isn't. I wanted to talk to you alone and there's not much privacy downstairs. By the way, I'm an expert now in Gin Rummy. I can't wait to trounce you!"

"That's not going to happen!"

"We'll see!"

"Dave, I really miss you!" she said after a short pause. "And I mean I *really* miss you! My mom gave me a tongue lashing this morning after you and I talked and I realized how selfish I was being. If you're as heartbroken as I am, all I was doing was adding to your misery. I'm so sorry."

The breath caught in his throat and his eyes teared up.

"I can see that Mom was right," Patti managed through a few tears of her own.

"I was worried."

"Why?"

"Because I kept thinking about what happened in the hospital. I guess I'm afraid I'm losing you!"

"No, you aren't! Like I just told you, I was being selfish. All I could think about was how this weather and all was ruining *my* plans. I wanted you here for four glorious days. I wanted to look into your eyes, cuddle up and talk about our wedding plans. I really was being selfish. I'm here with my folks. You don't have anyone."

"I've got Rose and Hershel," he teased.

"Are you serious?"

"They taught me how to make Christmas candy, stoke up the old coal furnace and carry out the clinkers."

"Clinkers?"

"Never mind. When the power comes back on, I'll send you a long, short story. The time with those two has been fun but horribly lonely. Right now, I just want to talk about us."

"Okay," she said softly, "but first let me get into bed too. You look so comfy lying there in your feather bed. Maybe I'll light a candle and pretend we're lying here in bed together looking into each other's eyes, spending our first Christmas Eve together as engaged people."

"Too bad we're not married."

"Don't get my engine running," she said as she lit a candle and set it on her lamp table. "This is going to be hard enough as it is."

They talked for long hours as the flickering candlelight reflected off of her soft features. They talked about all the trivia they'd forgotten about each other—all those little things that had been so important to her that Dave had somehow missed. When she finally paused unwittingly between thoughts and her eyes drifted shut, Dave ached to hold her and kiss her eyelids. He'd never felt so much love for anyone, ever. As sleep claimed him too, his last thought was, maybe it was going to work out for them after all.

***

When Dave awoke with a start, natural light was filling his room. He glanced quickly at the window. All four panes were iced over with a thick, intricate ice painting that resembled white stained glass. His candle had burned down to a puddle of red wax punctuated in the center by a small charred nub. He quickly fumbled around in the folds of the feather bed for his phone. It was dead – Its battery exhausted from having been left on in FaceTime mode.

He drew a deep, cold breath, unwilling to pull himself up out of the warm, clutching bed. Then he noticed that the wind was no longer howling outside his window. The light pressing through the frozen window pane denoted a clear, sunny sky. It was Christmas morning! He needed to charge his phone and call Patti.

An instant after his stocking-covered feet touched the icy floor, Dave realized how very cold it was in his room. His first thought was to grab up his frigid clothes and race downstairs to hover around the wood-burning kitchen range. Then he thought better of that and forced his legs into the nearly frozen fabric of his Levis, wishing as he hurriedly got dressed that he'd taken his clothes to bed with him. Moments later as he navigated the steep stairway down into Hershel's kitchen, he felt a welcome hint of warmth and knew that Hershel had been up before him.

"Good morning!" the old man sang out, "and a very Merry Christmas to you. Rose and I have been up for hours."

"We have not." Rose laughed. "If we had, you'd smell breakfast cooking. We've been huddling around the range reminiscing about the good old days while it warms up."

131

"I'm glad you remember them that way," Dave laughed. "Frankly, I'd just as soon roll out of bed into a warm room."

"That's what's wrong with you young people today," Hershel laughed, "you lack character."

"Good news," Rose chimed in, "the radio just said that most of the freeways and the airport are open. I just looked outside, though, and nobody's plowed our street yet. It might take several days to dig us out. I doubt we'll get power before the end of the day, if then."

"I don't think the airport being open will make much difference for me then," Dave mused as he joined his friends around the warm kitchen range. "I'm sure that with all the people stranded at the airport I won't be able to get a flight to Colorado Springs today anyway. I'll go to the cellar and get the furnace stoked up and then I need to go out and get my car started. I fell asleep last night and left my phone on while I was talking to Patti. The battery is dead."

"I hope your car will start," Hershel chimed in, "the weather report said it's minus five this morning."

Outside, the drift that Dave had hacked through the night before to get into his car had been reformed by the wind and had frozen solid in the cold. The icy snow beneath his feet was so cold that it squeaked as he walked on it. He had to cut the drift away in blocks with a shovel before he could get his car door open. Thankfully, in spite of the cold, the car started without complaint. He quickly plugged in his phone and dialed Patti's number.

"Good morning!" Patti exclaimed happily as she answered his FaceTime call, "and even though it really isn't, Merry Christmas!"

"Good morning, Love. Did you sleep well?"

"You should know. You watched me fall asleep."

"Actually I didn't watch you very long before I fell asleep too. I woke up a little while ago with a dead phone battery. I'm outside in the car right now talking to you while I let it charge. The sky is clear, and the wind has quit blowing but it's icy cold."

"I can see that you're all bundled up. Are you freezing?"

"Nope, I'm talking to you. That's keeping me warm."

"Liar!"

"The heater is almost blowing warm air now. I'm good."

"Can you fly out today?"

"I doubt it. The airport is open as are the freeways, but the power is still out and my street is sitting under four and five foot snowdrifts. My landlady tells me it might be a couple of days before they plow us out."

"Sorry," she sighed. "You still have to be at Raytheon on Tuesday morning, don't you?"

"Yes, and if things don't work out so I can get to Colorado Springs, I'll have to call the company and have them switch my flight from Chicago instead."

"As much as I hate to say this, wouldn't it be a waste to fly down here now? We'd only have a couple of days together."

"No it wouldn't be a waste! Even if I could just spend a single day with you it'd be worth the effort and the expense. I'm packed up and waiting for the plows. I haven't called for a flight yet though. Unless I can get to the airport that would be a waste of time and effort. When we hang up I'll go online and look to see if there are even any flights available to Colorado Springs. Because the blizzard shut the airport down there are probably a bunch of stranded people waiting in line for flights."

"From what you're telling me, I shouldn't get my hopes up. Should I?"

"Probably not."

"Have you had breakfast yet?" she asked solemnly.

"No. Rose and Hershel were just starting it when I came outside. I think I already told you this but we're cooking over an antique, wood-burning range. It takes a while to get it up to temperature."

"I should let you go then. Mom called down to me a little while ago. She's got breakfast ready too. Call me back when you can."

"Love you," Dave answered.

"Love you too," she said. "Thank you for calling. You've made my morning."

"And you, mine."

Before Dave went inside he looked for flights to Colorado Springs. There weren't any out of Chicago for two days. Discouraged, he called his contact at Raytheon and told him the situation. They'd try to book him on a flight out of Chicago on Monday afternoon. His contact promised to call him back as soon as he could make the changes in his flight.

They'd just gathered around Hershel's kitchen table for breakfast when the lights flickered back on.

"Oh good," Rose mused. "I guess we can cook that turkey in my range after all."

"Why?" Hershel asked with a twinkle in his eye. "My old stove is already nearly up to temp. It'd be a shame to waste all that heat."

"You've got a point there," Rose grinned. "Well Hershel, what do you think we ought to do? You know if I was younger, I could shack up over here until my renters get back."

"I'd love to have you!"

"I'll move back into my room next door," Dave laughed, "so you two can have your privacy."

"I don't think there's going to be anything going on over here that we'll need our privacy for," Rose grinned, reaching across the breakfast table to take Hershel's hand.

Chapter 15

Dave started school at Purdue on January 4th. The New Year's holiday had been a fiasco. Because of the bad weather he'd barely made his flight out of Chicago to Raytheon just after Christmas. The visits with his new company had been the highlight of his week – at least they'd been productive. He'd met with a quorum of people over four days and came away feeling like he was part of their engineering team.

The new scholarship they offered him was a reviewable contract of sorts – depending on his scholastic performance. It was nothing short of amazing. As long as he kept his grades up, they paid everything – including a $500.00 a month stipend while he was in school for incidentals. They would pay him a competitive starting salary during the summer with his internship. When he told them about his marriage plans, they told him that his summer internship in New Jersey wasn't set to begin for two weeks after his last day of school, so that would leave them a little time for a honeymoon. When Dave passed along dates and details, Patti was ecstatic.

On New Year's Eve, Dave and Patti spent hours on FaceTime celebrating – as well as they could under the circumstances. In the end, though, in spite of Dave's good news it left them both feeling lonely and hollow. Phone calls – even using FaceTime – were a poor substitute for *cuddling*. It was going to be a long winter.

Raytheon more or less directed Dave's selection of classes for spring semester. They filled up his curriculum with a lot of upper division classes that left him very little time for anything more than study. A week into the semester, Dave was already beginning to seriously question his decision. In retrospect he began wishing he'd stayed at Colorado State, where he and Patti could have started their lives together in February under far less pressure.

When Dave answered Patti's FaceTime call on Friday night, he could tell that she was feeling the strain as well.

"You're not smiling," he teased.

"Even though it's great to see you, I don't have much to smile about," Patti answered after a short pause. "I'm trying to take classes this semester that will help me fill in the gap between what I've already taken and what Purdue claims I need to have to make an effective transfer."

"Are you having second thoughts?"

"About school? Yes. It would be so much better for me to just finish my degree here at Colorado State. I wouldn't lose any credits in the transfer process, it'd be cheaper, and I wouldn't have to take a year off. That's going to be the hard part – even if we don't start a family right away."

"Sorry."

"Don't be. We've already talked this through. I'm just feeling a little overwhelmed right now. I'm sure it'll look better a week or two from now when I've settled back into a routine. The long holiday break between semesters is never kind to me."

"I wish summer was closer. In fact I wish I was closer!"

"So do I Dave."

"We both have a spring break coming up. If they coincide let's plan something."

"Like what?"

"A warm beach in Florida."

"We both know how that would end and then what we *didn't* do before Christmas wouldn't make much sense anymore. Besides, from what you've told me about your class schedule, you'll probably have to spend spring break trying to catch up. I know I will."

"This is going to be tougher than we thought."

"Yes it will be," she sniffed. "Hang on a minute while I try to pull myself together. You don't need a sniveling, needy woman making you feel bad."

They sat in their respective chairs, a thousand miles apart, saying nothing while tears traced their cheeks.

"I'm sorry, Dave," Patti finally began again, "I'm just feeling sorry for myself. Hey on a brighter note I've already cut June out of my calendar, glued ribbons all around it, stuck a pink balloon on it and hung it on the wall above my bed. It's the last thing I see every night before I turn off my lamp."

"Isn't your roomie giving you a ration of crap about that?"

"Nope. I'm the only one on our whole floor so far who has an actual promise. They're all unattached and jealous."

"A hotbed of female emotion?" Dave teased.

"You have no idea. We all realize that we're being silly but it's far better to be laughing and teasing about it than crying."

"I suppose I could do the calendar thing too."

"Do Rose or Claire come into your room?"

"No – not really."

"Then it'd be wasted effort. Besides that doesn't seem very manly if you know what I mean."

"I suppose you're right."

"Do you think Rose would mind us bunking up in your room when we get married?" she asked, not really meaning what she'd said.

"I haven't even brought up the subject. I guess I sort of thought we'd want our own place."

"Why?"

"Well, what if we make noise?"

She laughed. "I suppose I'd blush when I saw them."

"I think that'd be awkward, especially if I wanted to walk around naked. Did I tell you that I share a bathroom with Claire?"

"Yeah, there's that I suppose. I don't think Rose or Claire would mind if I walked around in the buff but I'm a girl. You on the other hand…"

Dave laughed and then turned serious. "You said you were having second thoughts. What about – us?"

"No second thoughts there!" she exclaimed, "every time I have thoughts like those, I change the subject!"

Chapter 16

Monday, Patti was just walking out of the library when a tall, blonde, somewhat-familiar-looking guy stopped her.

"Hi Patti. I haven't seen Dave yet this semester. How's he doing with his knee recovery?"

"I don't think I know you," she answered.

"I'm sorry. I'm James Baxter. Dave and I play football together. He's my competition. We're both receivers."

"Don't you mean you *played* football together?" Patti asked, her voice dripping with regret. "The team released him and when they did he lost his scholarship. He started spring semester at Purdue."

"Oh, I'm sorry!" James exclaimed. "I knew there was some question about all of that, and I knew he'd applied to Purdue for graduate school, but I didn't know that anything had been decided yet."

"It was all rather sudden," Patti answered, holding up her adorned ring finger. "They offered him a great scholarship out there. We got engaged over Christmas before he had to leave."

"Wow, I'm sorry. I'll bet you're missing him. It's quite a drive from here to Purdue."

The emotions that had been lying just beneath the surface of her eyes broke free and tears streamed down her cheeks.

"Oh, hey," James stammered, "I'm sorry. I didn't know."

"No problem," she managed after she gathered herself together, "and you're right. I *am* missing him. We've been together for more than four years."

"Really?" he forced an emotional response.

James already knew all that. Dave and he had often talked during football practice. If there was one thing that James had wanted worse than the recognition that Dave got on the football field, it was his girl. Patti was more than amazing. He didn't understand what Dave was waiting for. If he was with Patti, she'd have been wearing his ring for years. He'd always wanted to find an excuse to talk to her one-on-one, but Dave had been ever-present. Now he wasn't, and better yet, he was a thousand miles away. He'd have to work fast and be careful but with Dave being out of sight now, he hoped that with a little luck and a lot of charm he might be able to slip in between the two of them. A wave of excitement swept over him.

"I'll bet that's hard," he continued. "He's a lucky guy. When's the wedding?"

"We haven't actually set a date yet," she responded sadly. "Until he transferred to Purdue we were going to get married on Valentine's Day. Now all I know is he has a two-week break in June between when school gets out and when he has to be in New Jersey for his summer internship."

"Wow, that's exciting!" James exclaimed, putting as much emotion into his response as he could. "He's getting a beautiful wife, a scholarship *and* an internship. It doesn't get much better than that! You're a senior, aren't you? Do you plan to finish school here?"

"I haven't started my senior year yet. I'm just finishing up my junior year. We're planning on getting married in June and then I'll move to Indiana and live there for a year to establish residency. I'll finish my senior year at Purdue."

"How do you feel about taking a year off when you're this close to graduating? I think it'd be tough getting back in the swing of things."

She looked away. James was voicing all of her concerns.

"Sorry," he apologized, "I can tell that's a touchy subject. You've obviously already talked about that. Hey, well, congratulations on your engagement and tell Dave hi for me the next time you talk to him on the *phone*." He hadn't really meant the word phone to come out the way it did, but in retrospect he was glad it had. Maybe he could use that in the weapon chest he needed to put together to steal Patti away.

"Thank you James," she said, looking up at him. She'd already noticed that James was taller than Dave but until then she hadn't really noticed his pale blue eyes.

He offered a half smile and touched her on the shoulder. "I saw you a lot in the library last semester studying together. If you need a study buddy maybe I could fill in?"

"Thanks James," she replied, not really willing to commit to anything like that, "but there's a reason we studied in the library. We needed a place where we could go to study without being distracted."

"Oh that's right! You were both living in the dorms. I don't suppose you had a lot of privacy there."

"Aren't you living in the dorms?"

A little excitement swept through him as he responded. He had another advantage that Dave hadn't had.

"No. I live off campus with three other guys. We rent a house. We all have our own bedrooms but we live to a pretty strict set of rules. No loud music and no parties during the week. We can have friends over, though, as long as we're discrete."

"Why do you go to the library then?"

"I have an online class," he lied, "and the Wi-Fi in our house sucks. Besides my laptop screen is too small. I need a printer, too, and they have all that in the library."

She questioned his answer. Somehow his explanation seemed hurried, especially the side note about having friends over, but he really didn't have any reason to lie to her, and if he *was* lying he was really quick about it. Besides, his smile seemed genuine.

"Maybe I'll see you there," she said turning away. "Thanks for stopping."

"My pleasure," James said – and he meant it! His first face-to-face had seemed to be a success. She was even better looking at two feet than she'd been farther away. He didn't really have an online class – yet – but it wouldn't take much to sign up for one to cover his lie and he needed to do a little homework anyway, what better place than in the library with a great-looking *friend*.

He turned to walk away and counted his paces: one, two, three. Then he stopped and looked back over his shoulder. She hadn't stopped. He wished she had. If she was even remotely interested in him it would make this easier. He turned fully around to watch her walk away. She had it all, the talk, the walk, the beauty – and the body!

He turned back around and pulled out his cell phone as he walked.

"Hey Britt, it's James. I need your help. I just met this girl who knocked my socks off but she has a boyfriend who just left to go off to college in another state. This may sound awful but she's been dating this chump since high school—over four years now. I think there's an opportunity here. You've played a long-term-relationship game before so you know what that's like. What do you think it'll take for me to sweep her off her feet?"

"Flowers are instant attention getters."

"One flower or a bouquet?"

"One or two to start with."

"Then what?"

"You've dated before. What has worked for you?"

"I don't know, really."

"Whatever you do, don't talk football!"

"That's a given."

"What do you know about her?"

"Not a lot."

"Well that's where you start. As hard as this might be for you, everything has to center around *her.* Turn every conversation back to *her.* Take mental notes and then jot down the important stuff someplace where she won't inadvertently find your notes. Refer to your notes each time before you go meet her so she'll get the idea that you're interested in her. Most people like talking about themselves. Be sure you remember what she likes and dislikes. Does she like movies? If so, what kind? Does she read for entertainment? If so, what genre does she read? Most girls like candy but you should do samplers, not whole boxes – except maybe on special occasions. What are her political views – and be careful there. Stay neutral, even if you're not. If this works out between the two of you, you'll have years to discuss politics."

"What else?"

"Let her know you're interested, but be cool about it. Don't smother her. If you're in her face all the time she may push you away just to have some personal space."

Brittney paused. "Do you have any competition?"

"Yes. I already told you she has an absentee boyfriend."

"That makes it harder. Don't badmouth him, but be ready to give her everything he doesn't, or can't. Does that make sense? Where he's away, your simply being there for her will be a huge advantage. If she'll talk to you about him you need to pay close attention to his strengths and weaknesses. Don't battle his strengths. They may or may not be yours, just let her assume you're as good as he is without saying so, but be ready to demonstrate how good you are in areas where he might be lacking."

"Should I lie?"

"No! Not blatantly anyway. It's too easy to get caught in a lie. It's less obvious if you're just skirting around the truth a little."

"I really need this to work Sis." he said quietly.

"Wow, you must really be smitten. I know you, James, probably better than you do yourself. I hope you're doing this for all the right reasons. You already know you're good looking. That was your problem all through high school. You'd lead those wide-eyed, little teenyboppers along until they gave you what you wanted and then you'd just dump them. I was almost ashamed to call you my brother. I'm warning you, James, if this new girl is a keeper, don't break her heart. Don't treat her like a conquest."

"I don't do that!"

"Bullcrap James! I'm only a year older than you. I watched you play your little games. I saw the carnage you left behind. You've been at college long enough now, though, to know that popularity – like you used to get from being on the football team in high school is pretty fleeting. You need to seriously look at finding someone you can settle down with!"

"I think that this might be her."

"Then treat her that way. Keep in mind she's no high school chick. If she's anywhere near your age she's probably been around the block a time or two. Lose yourself in her. Be willing to do anything for her – even if in the end the best thing you can do for her means simply walking away."

A few long moments passed between them.

"James?" she finally asked. "Do you know what I'm trying to tell you?"

"I think so."

"Hey besides being your sister, I'm also a woman. Women are an emotional lot by nature. Until we've been trodden on a few times by unscrupulous men we're pretty gullible. Pretty boys like you destroy lives every day. Don't be one of those like you were in high school. If you're cool enough to woo her into falling in love with you, you're also cool enough to realize when you gain that power over her emotions, even if you really don't share her passion in some things. If she loves something that you don't, be willing to give her some space. You don't have to be joined at the hip to make a marriage work. It's okay to have and do your own things from time to time as long as what you want to do isn't abhorrent to her. Going out with your buds to strip joints is one of those. If you want to do something stupid like that then you may want to consider walking away now because I can tell you that won't appeal to her. Remember, James, marriage is supposed to be forever, not just until you get bored and need to move on like you did all the time in high school."

***

Long after James hung up, the things that Britt had told him consumed his thoughts. He began to make a plan. He had about five months – or less – to change Patti's mind about her engagement. The things Britt had said about his dating in high school was unfortunately spot-on. He'd found the high school chicks to be pretty simple. They wanted to date a cute boy. Better yet he'd been an athlete. They wanted to go to fun places and do fun things. A lot of the times, those so-called fun things walked on the shady side but that excitement often seemed to draw them in. He'd been very careful in that regard, though. He always used protection and he never told stories about his conquests.

James had had a job at a dude ranch every summer that had left him pretty flush with cash. He paused at that thought. That job had begun the summer after his sophomore year in high school and had followed him into college. He'd had a way with the *guests* and his bosses were appreciative. His bosses wanted everyone to have their best time ever so they'd come back the next summer – and maybe bring a friend or two with them. Most of the guests were wealthy so he often made big tips over and above his lucrative weekly salary.

He paused for a moment. If he'd had any conscience at all, it had begun to manifest itself back then. The programs were only a week long and he'd learned a lot about manipulation. If any of the two or three girls he'd picked from his assigned group weren't making out with him in the woods by Wednesday night, he'd simply moved on. There were literally hundreds to choose from and it hadn't taken him long to find out that most of the ones he'd *graced with his presence* were only all too eager to fulfill their wildest dreams while they were at camp. Even if the ones he jilted told stories to their friends, that often only piqued someone else's interest in him. He was very careful not to send any of them home with something that wouldn't wash off.

The problem with the dude ranch was it just whetted his appetite for the girls in high school. It took longer for him to get *there* with the high school chicks because they weren't together with him every day like the girls at the ranch had been but when he needed to let them go *free* he had mastered the sendoff. Just like the summer camp girls, he'd made sure they walked away with good memories, a smile on their face, and a promise that nobody else would ever know. He was at least smart enough to keep that one promise to them.

Patti came from a different part of the country so there was practically no way she'd ever find out about his prior conquests. He paused as that word rattled around in his thoughts again. Britt had called his behavior exactly that. What was it that Britt had told him? Oh, yeah, "remember, James," she'd said, "marriage is supposed to be forever, not just until you get bored and need to move on like you did all the time in high school." What she didn't know, of course, was his behavior hadn't changed in college. There were always parties! He'd had a lot of one-night stands but the girls he *victimized* here didn't seem to care. Neither of them had come to the party to build a long term relationship.

James had to think about that for awhile. Was he capable of doing the *forever* thing with Patti? He'd been with a lot of women. He knew what he liked in a woman, and Patti had it all! Maybe he could finally change if he had someone like her. He liked the idea of settling down with a wife, a job, a home, a kid or two. He wondered if he'd be able to make the adjustment. After two years in high school, followed by seemingly endless summers of short romances, he had polished his romantic skills. He didn't know why he'd called Britt. Maybe it was to convince himself that it was time to do something noteworthy. He suddenly felt confident that he could get Patti. She couldn't be that much different. She was far away from whatever emotional attachments she'd been tied to. She was lonely and probably feeling a little forsaken. She was wearing a ring, but he wondered how long it would take before he was able to get her to take it off? Britt was right. She was not a high school chick. She wasn't going to be easy, but he had a lot going for him besides his looks. If nothing else, he was here. Her fiancé wasn't. He had a little extra money to show her a few good times – away from the campus environment. Denver wasn't that far away. He wondered if she liked the theater.

As he locked his bedroom door behind him, he sat down with the new, hard-backed journal his mom had given him his freshman year that he'd never used. What he needed to do was going to take a lot of careful planning. He opened the first page, folded back the stiff pages a few times to limber them up and then wrote his first entry at the top of page one: *Patti 101*.

No sooner had he written the words than a thought crossed his mind. He could never let Patti see his plans. He scanned his room for a place to hide the journal. After all, somewhere in the back of his mind his ultimate plans called for getting Patti away from the library and into his bedroom. The only books he had in his room were text books. The journal would stick out in the midst of the fat text books. He didn't do any leisure reading. What spare time he had before or after homework, he spent in the gym sculpting his already nearly-perfect physique.

He smiled when he spotted his double bed. He'd opted for something a little larger than the typical single bed so often found in dorm rooms for several reasons. It fit nicely in a bedroom he shared with no one. He was a restless sleeper and often found himself flipping out of his single bunk at summer camp. He already had a great bed he'd brought with him from home, and finally it was easier to share a double bed with a *friend*. In fact, he wished he had room for a queen-sized bed. In either case, the journal would slip nicely between the mattress and box springs – shoved, of course, to the very middle of the mattress so in the rare event that Patti might happen to help him make up his bed afterward, she wouldn't inadvertently find it.

A slight grin raised the corners of his mouth. As a rule he normally didn't stock up on junk foods or soda, in spite of the fact that his mom had sent him off to school with a mini refrigerator. He'd remedy that, just as soon as he found out what Patti drank and snacked on. He didn't do snacks or soft drinks very often and he didn't drink beer. None of those were good for his physique, but he was sure he could learn to like anything that Patti did.

He glanced around his austere room. In anticipation of a visit from Patti, maybe he ought to get a couple of cool non-sports posters, maybe a decorative pillow or two for his bed. A fuzzy throw rug would protect her naked feet from the cool hardwood floors. The common bathroom would need some serious work. Neither he nor his roomie cleaned it very often. That would have to change. He'd have to keep up on his laundry and stow his dirty things out of sight as well.

Suddenly James grinned. He was already doing things that he thought Patti would like. Once he spent more time with her and discovered what she really liked, his room makeover would be easier. For the first time in a long time he started to actually think about what a woman might really want. A shiver of excitement coursed through him. Football practice didn't start until the first week in March. Until then he'd have a lot of time to find out all about Patti. This may very well prove to be his most challenging semester ever.

Chapter 17

James went to the on-campus, floral shop right after his last class and then took a seat in the library near the entrance where he could watch for Patti. He knew where she and Dave had often studied in the past but he wanted to make a grand entrance. He didn't want to appear as if he'd simply been hanging out waiting for her to appear.

He didn't have long to wait. He'd only been pretending to study a book on marketing for a few minutes when she walked in. Luckily, she didn't notice him as she walked straight to the back, took a table and turned her back to him.

He feasted his eyes on her as she walked. Her long auburn hair cascaded over her shoulders and swayed slightly as she walked. Even dressed in Levis and a casual pullover that mostly hid her figure she looked amazing!

He glanced quickly at his cell phone and set a timer. He'd give her five minutes. That was long enough for her to get settled without giving her time to get totally engrossed in her homework.

When the timer softly beeped, he got purposely to his feet and watched her as he approached. Thankfully she hadn't turned around. Surprise, for some reason, seemed appropriate.

"Hi Patti," he said softly as he stopped at her table, "I was hoping you'd be here."

He handed her the small flower vase holding one yellow and one white rose.

"I spotted your hair the instant I walked in. It's amazing."

He watched her soft facial features as several emotions swept over her. She seemed to like his comment about her hair, and when she allowed herself a moment or two to look at the flowers, the corners of her eyes raised a little in either excitement or appreciation. Either emotion was good. At least she hadn't seen right through him – yet.

"You seemed pretty down when I talked to you in the hall," he continued softly. "I thought these might help lift your spirits a little. I didn't know what kind of flowers you like so I just took a chance."

She finally smiled. "I love roses in any of their many colors, but yellow and white are perfect. Red seems too pretentious—even though they're beautiful."

"Mental note to self," a thought crossed James' mind. "She likes roses but nothing pretentious." He'd remember that the next time he brought her flowers, and he *would* bring her flowers again. She seemed appreciative. He wondered if Dave had done that very often?

"Mind if I join you?" he asked. "I know this might seem awkward, though, so if you'd rather not I'll understand."

More subtle but quick emotions swept across her face. "I really appreciate your intent," she answered, "but I'd rather sit alone if that's okay?"

"I'm sorry Patti," he said her name softly, humbly, "I understand. I don't want to make things worse. I just thought you might need a bright spot in your day."

She half smiled. "Thank you James. Maybe some other time. I just got off the phone with Dave and I'm an emotional wreck."

"Is something wrong?"

"No," she answered looking down at her nails, "just the obvious."

"Sorry," he apologized again, "this was bad timing."

"It wasn't unappreciated though. I haven't had anyone give me flowers in awhile."

"Beauty for a beauty," he said – and then uncharacteristically he blushed. "Sorry, that was really corny. I meant well though."

A slight smile lifted the corners of her delicate mouth. "Thank you, James, for everything."

"I'll go find a computer," he hurried his offer, "I've got this…"

"Online class," she offered.

"Yeah. I don't know why I signed up for the stupid thing. It's just one of the fillers that I haven't taken yet. I'm sure I'll be bored to tears."

When she didn't answer, he turned and strode methodically away, taking the time to spot the rows of computers, but hoping at the same time that she was watching him walk away.

***

James went to the library a little later the next day, deciding instead to work out at the gym for an hour before he went to work off the butterflies. This time he wasn't armed with a mini-bouquet of flowers, or snacks – even if they'd been allowed in the library. He glanced quickly around the room looking for her red hair. Not seeing her he pulled all his *study* materials out of his backpack.

He actually cracked his marketing book and began reviewing the chapters the professor had covered that day in class. He didn't usually do this. He'd found that he could usually glean enough from the lectures to pass the class. He didn't get 'A' grades but he managed to keep his scholarship. He quickly found a few things in the book that he'd already forgotten from the lecture. He wasn't dumb by any means – probably just a little lazy. Until then he'd figured that as long as he got the BS degree when he graduated, nobody really looked at his individual grades in an interview anyway. The overall GPA probably meant something but he was satisfied with a 'B' average.

"Hi James," Patti's hesitant voice interrupted him. "I'm not coming right out of a sad phone call today, and there aren't a lot of vacant tables. Would you mind if I joined you?"

"Not at all! I really don't like studying but it's always worse doing it alone."

151

She pulled out a chair and seated herself across the table from him. "Is that why you came here instead of going home? I suppose you have a desk in your room?"

"I do," he answered.

"Note to self!" The thought rang through his head. She had been listening when you told her about renting a house and having your own bedroom.

"But sometimes I study better when there's a little distraction but a radio is too much. I catch myself following the lyrics of the song and not the concepts printed in my book. Besides, if my roomies are home sometimes random noises in the house are more disturbing than the low murmur I hear in here. I catch myself wondering what they're doing and if they're having more fun than I am."

She laughed softly. It looked good on her! Of course everything about her looked *so* good!

"There's probably a lot of truth to that," she admitted as she pulled a book out of her backpack.

"I guess I don't know what you're studying," he said as he looked for a title on her book.

"I'm studying to be a teacher. Eventually I want to have a family and teaching would go better with kids. I can be at home with them after school and during the summer."

"Smart choice. At least you put some thought into your major. I did well in accounting in high school so I figured it might be good to major in something I'm good at."

"Besides football?"

"Note to self." She obviously knows more than casual stuff about me. Maybe that's a good thing.

"Oh I'm not really that good at football," he countered half-heartedly, "Dave is better."

152

"He doesn't think so. He told me once that he felt bad the way they often called the plays. You were always getting pounded on the short passes because you have the physique to take it, where he got to grandstand with the longer-yardage gains. He said you'd never dropped a pass even in heavy traffic."

"He told you all that? I'm embarrassed. Here I always thought that what I did was unappreciated."

"I know he thought you were good. Dave told me that's just the way the game is played. You have to keep your opposition on their toes all the time if you expect to move the ball against them."

"Next time that subject comes up with you two, tell him thanks. I guess I never stopped to think about the game that way."

Her eyes smiled this time along with her lightly-painted lips. "I'll do that," she said softly. "He told me more than once that's why there are eleven guys on the field at any one time. It takes a team to win a game."

"Note to self." This girl is not only beautiful but she's smart!

"I don't want to pull you away from your studies, but how is Dave dealing with his new school? I mean until that bad hit, his whole college career was centered around football."

"I think he's doing okay. He told me once that his football scholarship was just a means to an end. His true love is engineering."

"Really? I know for a fact that he's been approached by NFL scouts."

"Yeah, he told me that but he never intended to go beyond college ball. He said there's too much physical risk in the game—and he found that out the hard way."

"Smart kid. Where you two are from Colorado, I suppose you do a lot of skiing? I'd think that bad knees would make that pretty hard."

"Yes we usually do a lot of skiing when we're home over the holidays. It's not just the knees, though, your arms, shoulders, and back are just as important."

She studied him for a moment. "I can see you keep yourself in great physical shape. You'd probably make a good skier."

He laughed. "I've tried my hand at it a few times. I'm originally from Idaho. We've got a lot of good resorts out there. My thing is summer though. I like the woods when they're green, warm, and beautiful. I've worked on a dude ranch for six summers. That's my idea of entertainment."

"Oh really? I've heard a lot of shady things about dude ranches."

"Must not have been our ranch. I don't think I ever heard complaints, other than having to get up at the crack of dawn if you wanted to eat breakfast."

"I'm not saying they're probably not a lot of fun, but I imagine there are a lot of *hungry* young women there in the summer, and they're only there for a week or so at a time, aren't they?"

"That's the fun of it," he chuckled, "a lot of them come there trying to get lucky in a week and I'm there to show them a good time without letting it get out of hand. I shamelessly flirt with them before I send them back to their cabins alone at night."

"I'm not stupid James. You can't tell me that you never took advantage of your tough cowboy/impressionable young girl relationships."

"We had strict rules," he lied, "the absolute worst thing we could have done was send an underage girl home from camp, pregnant."

"I'll bet you've had a lot of practice flirting though."

"Tons," he grinned, "but it's a little hard to take a relationship anywhere in a week."

"You're pushing me pretty hard. Are you still practicing? I don't think you need to, though, you're already pretty smooth."

"No Patti," he lied again, "I'm sorry that's the way you see me. That's not the reason I'm here, now. I'd be lying if I said I didn't find you attractive, but I'm not a jerk. I know how I'd feel if I were in Dave's shoes. He obviously thinks the world of you or he wouldn't have given you a ring."

He paused long enough to catch her eyes.

"I'm not here to woo the pants off of you Patti. I'm here because I'm a little lonely and like they say: *misery loves company*. That's all this is. I just need a friend."

"You've got a whole team of friends, don't you?"

"Not even. We get close as teammates because you need to have the other guy's back on the field so he'll have yours. You'll get hurt if you don't. Off the field most of them aren't really very interesting. They think all you want to talk about is football. To me, it's a means to an end like it was with Dave, but there's a whole other world beyond the stadium. I guess I saw a little of that on the dude ranch. People came there from all walks of life. Most were rich. I'd like to be rich, but unless I win the lotto I don't see that happening. In the meantime, I'd just like to have friends."

155

Chapter 18

*I*t wasn't until James got home and began jotting a few things down in his 'Patti 101 journal' that he realized he'd missed the point. He'd told her a lot about himself without really gleaning much of anything from her. Other than the fact that he knew she wanted to be a teacher, she liked to ski, and she liked pale roses, he didn't really know much about her. She, on the other hand, knew about his dude ranch experience — at least what he'd lied to her about — and she knew all about the insecurity he felt on the football field.

He glanced at the calendar over his desk. Time was ticking away and in this case time was his enemy. He jotted a note in his journal: *must get her to quit wearing her ring by Valentine's Day, (even if Dave doesn't know she isn't).*

He counted the weeks. There were less than six short weeks between now and then.

Thoughts of Denver flashed through his mind and he went online to look for engagements. "Les Miserables" was in its first week. He'd read the book in high school and watched the high school's rendition of the screenplay. He remembered liking it. It was Friday, the 13th , tomorrow. He wondered if it was too late to ask her on a Saturday *date*? Worse yet, the tickets were $300.00 a pop and they might already be sold out this late. According to the ad, the production was still playing through the 22nd but he didn't want to waste a week if he didn't have to.

A few clicks later he had tickets for an upper balcony. They weren't the best seats in the house, but hey, they were in the theater. Then he nearly panicked. That was a dress up joint, and he didn't even have a suit. She may not have a dress either. One didn't ordinarily pack frilly things for college — unless, of course, you were planning on attending one of the on-campus, formal dances.

He'd call her, but didn't have her cell phone number. What he'd just done was foolhardy. He might as well have opened his bedroom window and thrown $600.00 out on the snow.

Next he needed a lie. He thought about Britt. Patti didn't know his sister. He could explain it to Britt later so she could cover his lie, in case the subject ever came up.

He went online to look for a tuxedo. There were several places in Fort Collins. He hoped they'd have what he'd need on such short notice. The real problem was tomorrow was Friday. He was more than out of time. He'd made a terrible tactical error. She'd need time – even if she had a dress. He'd need a corsage. He wondered if he could get her class schedule from the registrar.

***

James found himself standing outside an empty window at the registrar's office at 7:50 a.m. the next morning, waiting impatiently for the office to open at eight. His first class started at eight but he'd already decided to sluff if he could find out where Patti was. As the minutes ticked painfully by he became more agitated. What he'd done was straight up stupid.

Then another thought crossed his mind. Because of the short notice, at least Patti couldn't accuse of him of *planning* a night away with an engaged woman.

"Can I help you?" a young woman asked as she appeared at an opening in the glassed-in office. The *window closed* sign still sat on the counter in front of him.

James instantly recognized her as one of the girls he'd spent a night with after a party a year or so ago. Their relationship hadn't gone anywhere but she wasn't at all bad looking – with or without clothes!

He offered his best smile and she blushed. "I know you ordinarily don't give out information on students," he said in his best flirtatious voice, "but I need to find where Patti Carlson's first class is. I have an important message for her."

She caught his eye for a moment, seemingly undecided, and then she looked away. "Hang on a minute. My computer hasn't booted up yet."

James tried not to fidget as he watched the girl stare at her computer screen.

"Oh here she is. She has an English class at 8 a.m. in wing 'C' room 215. That's pretty close. If you hurry you might be able to catch her before class starts."

"Thank you so much," he beamed at her. "While you have her information up, do you think I could get the rest of her class schedule for today in case I miss her first class?"

The girl punched a button and moments later handed him a printed sheet of paper. "I'm not supposed to do this," she added quietly as he took the paper, "so if anybody asks where you got this, play dumb."

***

James caught a flash of Patti's auburn hair just as he streaked down the hall toward her room. She had already taken a seat by the time he hurried inside.

"Patti!" he gasped, clearly out of breath, "can I see you in the hall for a second?"

She looked concerned for a moment and then left her backpack on her chair and followed him out into the hallway.

"Hey this is going to sound totally nuts but my sister called me late last night. She has tickets to *Les Misérables* in Denver on Saturday night and can't use them. They're just going to go to waste if I don't want them. I know I'm putting you on the spot here, but would you like to go?"

She hesitated. "I've always wanted to see that," she finally answered, "but…"

"Do you have a dress? I imagine that the dress code is pretty formal. I'm going to have to see if I can rent a tux. I don't even have a suit with me at school."

Still unsure, she answered his second question first. "I do have a dress but it's kind of special…"

"Oh, sorry! I know I'm putting you on the spot. I'd have called you last night but I don't have your number."

"Maybe you could take someone else."

"No, never mind. Thanks anyway. It was just a thought."

"Wait! Did you say it's this Saturday?"

"Yeah, tomorrow, the fourteenth."

"Do you think you can find a tux?"

"There are half a dozen places in town that rent tuxedos. I checked online last night but I needed to talk to you first before I started calling. I don't think there are any other formal events this early in the month so I imagine they'll have something in my size."

"I really would like to see it."

"Are you okay with the last-minute thing and all – especially where we're really not friends – yet?"

She pursed her lips and then a slight smile smoothed them out. "I'd love to, actually. I think it might help me get my mind off of other things for a night."

"What color is your dress? I need to find you a corsage."

"Red."

"Bright or pale?"

"Bright red."

"Wrist or shoulder corsage?"

"Wrist, actually. I have a light jacket that goes over my dress but the dress has really narrow straps."

"Thanks Patti!" he exclaimed. "I'll let you get back to class."

"What's your phone number?"

James spouted off his number.

"I'll text you from class so you'll have my number. When does your first class start?"

"Five minutes ago, but I'll never make it now. I'm going to skip it and go look for a tux."

"Aren't those tickets pretty pricey?"

"They aren't box seats or anything like that but my sis tells me they were still $600.00."

"Wow! That would really be a waste not to use them then."

"That's what I was thinking. Thank you Patti. This should be fun."

"You're welcome. Thanks for asking."

With that she stepped back into her classroom and closed the door behind her.

James' mind was running rampant. He'd pulled it off. Now he'd have hours alone with her. The play would get out late. He should take her someplace nice to eat beforehand. Then he paused. On the other hand if they didn't eat until after the play, maybe she'd agree that it was too late to drive home…

Her text interrupted his lurid train of thought. "I'm excited," the text read. "What time do we need to leave tomorrow?"

"Depends on whether we eat dinner before or after?"

"Afterward would be too late, maybe before?"

His less than stellar thoughts were dashed, but she was right. He was moving too fast. This wasn't the dude ranch. He still had a few more weeks – but not many.

***

She was standing on the sidewalk outside her dorm at 3:20 p.m. on Saturday afternoon when he pulled up, and hurried around to help her in.

"Wow!" he exclaimed as he opened her car door. "You look amazing."

She blushed through her tastefully done makeup.

"Sorry, I didn't mean to put you on the spot."

She slid inside without answering him.

"I don't know if I told you already but we have dinner reservations at five." James said after closing his door behind him. "My google says it's a little over an hour and a half to Denver, and the roads aren't bad so we should make dinner in plenty of time."

"You're right. I've driven that freeway lots of times on my way to and from Colorado Springs. It's an easy drive if it's not snowing. If it gets stormy it can be a challenge."

"How do you like Colorado Springs?"

"It's okay. How is Idaho? You didn't ever tell me where you live?"

"I live in Boise and like you just said, it's okay. I grew up there so until I came out here to school I didn't have much to compare it to."

"Where is your dude ranch?"

"It isn't my ranch but it's farther north in the panhandle of Idaho near Coeur d'Alene."

161

"What did you do up there?"

"We offer a little of everything. We ride horses, hike, swim, eat like pigs, hold awesome campfire programs, do crafty things – pretty much whatever our rich guests want to do."

Suddenly, James realized he wasn't following his own plan, again. He needed to know about *her* not vice versa.

"My life is rather boring, actually," he tried to change the subject. "What do you like to do when you're not studying your guts out?"

"I ski, and I like backpacking."

"Where do you like to ski?"

"We've got a ton of resorts, around here, actually. When I was younger and had a lot of time on my hands, I'd buy a season pass to Vail just because it seemed like the place to go. It's famous and so a lot of celebrities go there. When I started college and didn't have a lot of time or money, I'd just look for places with discounts."

"Too bad school and winter go hand in hand," he chuckled. "Where do you spend your summers?"

"I'm usually working so I ordinarily pick someplace close to home. When I get a three-day weekend I love to go backpacking or drive through the mountains from Colorado Springs to Silverton. You won't find better scenery."

"Do you go hiking a lot?"

"Whenever I can. I've got my own light-weight, backpacking gear," she said with an element of pride. "It's taken me a few years to afford good equipment but I've got it down now to where my pack only weighs 35 pounds with a week's worth of dehydrated food. Water is extra weight, of course, but I usually hike where there are streams and I carry a filter."

"That's pretty impressive! I think the last pack I lugged around on the dude ranch was somewhere around sixty pounds or more. Of course I try to start out light because invariably I end up carrying some of our guests' gear for them before I'm done. I think they figure just because I look all buff that I can carry anything."

She laughed. "I used to belong to a Girl Scout group so I know what you're saying."

"So did you learn how to start and then put out a fire?"

"Yes I did! I even learned to start a fire with flint and steel."

"That's an art form that even a lot of serious backpackers have never mastered."

"It's all in the prep," she said. "If you've got good tinder you can build a fire."

"So tell me about your dress," he ventured.

She turned her head to look out the window.

"Sorry!" he apologized. "I should have known that when you told me it was special that there is a lot of emotion tied to it."

"There shouldn't be, I suppose," she continued after a few moments. "I sorta knew that Dave was going to propose to me so I spent something like four days before Thanksgiving with my mom, looking for the perfect dress."

"Ouch, and now here I come stumbling all over your sweet memories."

"That's okay," she said quietly.

"You do look awesome in it though. Pardon me if I say so but I think the time and effort was well spent. I suppose Dave was blown away by it?"

"Yeah, it's too bad we didn't have the time to go out someplace nice where I could flaunt it."

"Like to a playhouse?"

"Well, there's that I suppose. When he got hurt, that cut out any dances and the like. I sprung the dress on him at Thanksgiving, then we had finals and he had to go out to Purdue to get enrolled and get things out there set up before Christmas. We were planning on spending Christmas and New Year's together. But he got snowed in at Christmas and then he had to fly out to Raytheon right afterward for four days."

"So when did you get engaged?"

"Over Thanksgiving actually. That's a story all itself," she began, and then suddenly stopped.

"Sorry. I don't mean to pry."

She was silent for awhile. Just as he was about to ask his next set of questions, she continued.

"Do you remember the big storm that shut down all the power for four days after Thanksgiving? We decided rather than stay stranded in a cold dorm room, we'd drive home. They had power in Denver and Colorado Springs. We stopped in Denver on the way home and picked out my ring."

She paused for a moment.

"We hadn't planned on telling our folks until Christmas, but after we went home for Thanksgiving and I put this red dress on it sort of speeded things up a little. He proposed and we were going to do the big ring exchange thing for the folks over Christmas. It didn't happen. I already had mine so I'm wearing it and I still have his ring."

He laughed. "I don't doubt for a minute that dress changed his mind. I think I've already told you this, but you look awesome. Dave is a lucky man."

James carefully directed the rest of the conversation toward her all of the way into Denver. When he figured out what to ask, she was quite willing to talk about herself. Britt had told him that she would be. He kept making mental notes and in fact after they arrived a little early at the restaurant and they both scurried off to their respective restrooms, James punched all of his mental notes into his cell phone notebook. He was getting there, but he still had a long way to go. Knowing things about her and knowing things to do for her were two very different exercises. He needed both.

They only had to wait for a few minutes to be seated and when he held her chair and she removed her light jacket as he pushed her chair closer to the table he involuntarily took a deep breath. She'd told him that her dress had small straps and she wasn't kidding. What straps there were, barely kept the bodice of her dress from sliding off of her ample breasts. If she was wearing a bra underneath, he couldn't see one. The dress' silky fabric clung to her every curve. He had to maintain eye contact once he sat down across the table from her for fear she'd catch him staring. He couldn't concentrate on much of anything else.

***

"I'm sorry about the dress," she said softly as they drove to the playhouse after dinner.

"Why apologize? It's fabulous."

"I'm not naïve James. You tried not to stare but I caught you looking a few times. Don't get me wrong. I know how men think. This was my fault for wearing it in the first place but I didn't have anything else dressy enough. It's even worse because I didn't have a bra to go under it. I have one that works but I must have left it home when I packed for school."

"I'm surprised you even brought that dress with you to school. There aren't many school functions that call for formal wear."

"I was hoping Dave could come home for spring break."

"Is there any question?"

"Yes, actually there is. We just found out a couple of days ago that Purdue's break only overlaps ours by two days. It's too far to drive and he won't have much money until after he goes to work for Raytheon this summer, so he can't afford to fly. We talked and he's going to try to save up enough money over the summer to cover the difference between Purdue's resident and non-resident tuition. If he can, I won't have to take a year off when I go out there."

"That's great news," James lied. "I know I'd hate to finish my junior year and then have to quit for a year. How soon will you know?"

"We already know approximately how much money he's going to make and my parents will still help with my tuition even after we're married. We both think that if we're careful and I work during the summer too, that we'll be able to make it."

James concentrated on the road for a few moments.

"This is so sweet of you," Patti mused after their conversation dried up. "I've been an emotional wreck lately. It's really good to get away for awhile."

"You're welcome Patti. I won't lie to you, though, I'm having a hard time keeping this date strictly on a *just friends* basis. Dave has probably already told you this but you're a beautiful, amazing woman! Do you believe in love at first sight?"

"I think I know where this is going," she said, quietly, "maybe we ought to turn around and drive back to campus. I'm engaged James. I love Dave. Just because he's not here to speak up for himself doesn't mean I'm ready to jump ship."

"Okay, you're right." James answered quickly. "Let's just forget I said that. I'm a simple person, Patti. I'll admit that. I say what I'm thinking sometimes even when, like now, I create havoc. We don't want to waste these tickets, and you told me you really wanted to see the play. Just let me back up a couple of minutes."

"You mean to when I was scolding you for ogling me over dinner?"

"I wasn't ogling you and you weren't scolding. I think you were warning me and I heard you loud and clear. I won't take back a word I said about you or your dress though. It's amazing and you look awesome wearing it, and just for the record I wasn't the only man in the room who noticed."

A sly smile stole across her face. "I know. I noticed."

"Then why are you beating me up?"

"Like you just said, I wasn't scolding you, I was just warning you. My dress may not leave much to the imagination but it's not coming off anytime soon. Just as long as we understand each other, I'll still go."

"I can live with that," he said eagerly – perhaps a little too eagerly. In his mind he had already undressed her. He'd been around. He'd seen a lot of bodies, and frankly, Patti appeared to have one of the best. He'd have to use all the tools in his box, and maybe even borrow a few. Valentine's Day was coming up and his goal for that day wasn't necessarily to get Patti in the sack by then but he wanted that ring off her finger.

Patti slipped off her light jacket when they found their seats in the theater and they made small talk while they waited for the play to start. From the seat beside her, and from his slightly elevated position due to his stature, he could watch her body without being noticed, and he took full advantage of that. When she looked up, he stared only at her eyes. When she looked away, he'd look back down. By the time intermission rolled around his motor was roaring.

As they walked to the lobby for a potty break and snacks, he softly touched her every time he got the chance without making it seem obvious. He had already undressed her a dozen times in his imagination. Then a few non-random thoughts crossed his mind. He had her phone number. That was a giant plus. He couldn't call her all of the time without her feeling overwhelmed but he could text.

She'd been so wrapped up with Dave that James didn't think she had a lot of friends on campus. Isolating her wouldn't be hard – except maybe from her dormmates. He wondered what it would take to talk her into moving off campus with him? He didn't know what she paid to stay in the dorms but maybe he could offer to let her live with him rent free, to save money for her senior year at Purdue. He didn't know how often she called Dave, but he guessed it was every day. He wondered if she called him at a regular time or randomly? He needed to find out when and then do his best to interrupt their calls. As long as she was seeing Dave's pining face on FaceTime, she wouldn't be lonely enough or be feeling forsaken enough.

The next part of his plan – that of being there with her all the time would take some concentrated effort. He'd already gotten a printout of her class schedule. She had regular back-to-back classes until 1 p.m. every day. Then she had a break until two, meaning she probably ate lunch then. Luckily, he didn't have a class conflict. Eating lunch together should seem to her to be rather innocuous, unless she was seeing right through his duplicity. He'd have to be careful. If she suspected that he was stalking her, it was over! If ever he needed charm it was now. He'd been able to turn it off and on at will with the women at the dude ranch, and just as easily with the girls in high school.

He drew a deep breath. There was so much to do, and so little time to do it in! She'd already told him that she'd been with Dave for four years. If they were really childhood sweethearts why hadn't Dave taken their relationship to the next level? That suddenly didn't ring true. Why would any reasonable-thinking man leave a fabulous woman like her on the lamb for so long? Were they really that committed to one another or just *comfortable*? He'd play that card as soon as he could. He needed to put doubt in Patti's mind and then be there to pick up the pieces when and if she decided to move on.

"Hey James," her sweet voice cut through the audience milling around them. "I think they're about ready to start."

"Do you want a drink or a snack?"

"I could use a Diet Coke and a bag of salted peanuts."

He grinned. "Let me guess, you stuff the peanuts in your drink, don't you?"

A puzzled look swept over her face. "No, why would I do that?"

"The peanuts enhance the flavor of the Coke. It's even better if you're a Pepsi drinker but the process is the same. I wouldn't even suggest it if they only had drinks in cans. It's a lot easier to get the peanuts back out of a bottle. Tell you what; I'll get you a Diet Coke and me a Pepsi. You can try mine and if you don't like it, no harm – right? I'll finish it."

James waited until they were seated and then did his peanuts-in-a-Pepsi thing and handed the bottle to her.

An anxious look passed over her. "This is so not-formal," she whispered. "I feel like I just got on the school bus in my underwear."

"Don't fret." he teased. "What are they going to do, ask us to leave? They sold me the drinks. If you don't like it, I'll take over. I'm not afraid of your mouth!"

She laughed and took a sip.

"Well?"

She grinned. "It's really quite good. I've never been a Pepsi person but I could get used to this."

"So are we going to share or do I need to go get another drink? Diet Coke really isn't my thing. I think it sort of tastes like battery acid."

"Battery acid! How would you know that?" she whispered.

"I've been around my share of mechanical contrivances and I may have inadvertently touched an acidy old battery and then licked my fingers afterward."

"That's gross!"

"So now you know why I don't like Diet Coke."

"Never mind. You've proven your point. I'll share."

For the rest of the performance every time he shared her drink he couldn't help but think about where the mouth of his bottle had been. He longed to taste her lips.

***

As they milled around in the entrance after the performance, the chilly outside breeze swept over them every time the doors opened and James instantly saw gooseflesh on Patti's arms. She hadn't brought a coat. He swept off his jacket and draped it over her shoulders.

"Thank you James," she said with a small pout, "I should have brought a coat but I didn't have anything that matched my dress."

"Hey the sun was up when we left, and you looked so good that I couldn't bear the thoughts of covering all that up with a coat or I would have suggested one."

He grinned down at her. This time she didn't seem to be offended by his mention – again – of how good she looked.

She tried pulling his jacket around her at first as they walked outside but the cold breeze pushed its way right through.

"Here," he insisted as he gently tugged his coat away from her and held up an arm hole. "Wear this thing like it was meant to be worn. It'll help."

She pulled the coat on and then tugged it tightly together in front of her.

"Thanks again James," she murmured, "you're a real gentleman."

The way she said the word gentleman, warmed him from the inside even though he was shivering on the outside. He wondered again how Dave could have let their relationship drift on for so long. If she said the word today, he'd marry her tomorrow!

James' car was as cold inside as the air was outside, so after helping Patti inside, he stopped to pop open the rear hatch on the way around to the driver's side. He always carried a sleeping bag in the back for emergencies.

She glanced up at him with questioning eyes when he reopened her car door, unzipped the bag, and held it out to her.

"Fold this around you," he said, "It should help a little until the heater warms up."

He didn't wait for a response. He was shivering now as well. He'd thought about bringing his parka but it didn't go with formal wear either.

"This was so fun!" Patti said, her teeth chattering a little as she spoke. "Thank you James! I haven't done anything like this in a long time."

"Well don't tell Dave what you did!" he insisted as he started the car and moved out into traffic. "I know if I were him, I'd be livid just thinking about you spending time with somebody else."

"He's not the jealous type."

"Then he's either blind or he's a better man than me!"

"Are you the jealous type?"

"Define jealous? Would that mean I get raging mad when someone touches something of mine or would that mean that I feel uncomfortable in a situation like that?"

"I don't know. You say."

"I don't see myself losing my temper if that's what you're getting at. I would be uncomfortable if someone else was honing in on my girl and I'd try to talk them both out of it. I don't see it ending in violence if that's what you're asking. After all, a relationship takes two people. As a man, I can offer, but as a woman it would be your decision to accept my advances or turn me away."

"Is that what you're doing – offering?" she asked.

"Hey, please don't turn this around on me. I like you, Patti. I've had a great time tonight. I've loved having you share this with me, but I'm not here to beat Dave's time."

"I almost believe you," she said, looking over at him.

"Almost?" he asked.

"You may not realize it but you're sending out a lot of vibes here."

"Of course I am. I'm a normal, red-blooded American male in the presence of true beauty. Why wouldn't I be sending off vibes, as you so aptly put it, but that doesn't mean I want to kick Dave to the curb. You two have a lot of history – both ancient and modern. How could I ever compete with that?"

She stared out the windshield for a moment before she answered.

"I followed him to Colorado State," she began after a few moments. "It seemed to be the right thing to do. We've been dating since we were in high school."

She stopped for a few long moments.

"College wasn't what I expected it would be," she finally continued. "We were both busy – he with football and me with my studies. There never seemed to be time for just us. Do you know what I mean?"

"Pardon me for saying so, Patti, but in my opinion that's just a matter of priorities. I can't speak for Dave but I can't help but think you'd be top priority in my book. Sure he was busy with football, trying to keep up his scholarship and all that but you said yourself that he never fully intended on making football a career. I know that first hand. I saw him talking to the NFL Scouts. They seemed interested. He didn't. I'd think with your folks helping you with your tuition and the school paying his, you two would have had the means to get married and double up somewhere. It's got to be cheaper to support two people in one place than paying double everything."

172

"We actually talked about that a little — but not until after he got hurt and I found out he'd applied to Purdue."

She hesitated.

"Now everything seems to be in a tailspin. I really don't want to take a year off but I can't afford out-of-state tuition at Purdue."

"You just told me that he should be able to work on his internship for a summer and make up the difference."

"That's what he says, but what if…"

"I'm sure it'll work out," James interrupted. "Love always finds a way."

"I've heard people say that," she mused, "but that doesn't mean it won't be hard."

"Nothing worth having comes without a price."

She looked up at him. "I'm confused James. At the beginning of our evening, I could have sworn you were in attack mode. Now it's like you're defending Dave."

"I'm just trying to give the guy the benefit of the doubt. I know if the tables were turned, I'd want that. He's probably sitting out there in his apartment going nuts without you. How often do you two talk on the phone?"

She pouted and glanced at the clock on his dashboard. "Every day at ten, just before I ordinarily go to bed."

"You're late. It's nearly 10:40."

"I know!"

"He's going to be going nuts, you know. We won't get home until nearly midnight. How are you going to explain that?"

She looked away and James slowed down.

"What are you doing?" she asked.

173

"I'm going to take the next exit, find a place to pull over where you can talk, and then I'm going to go take a walk and give you a little privacy."

"You don't need to do that."

"Yes I do. It's really the right thing to do. I wouldn't FaceTime him, though, if that's what you ordinarily do. How will you explain being in a car in a sleeping bag, with your face and hair all made up, wearing your sexy red dress? He'd probably fly home tomorrow if he sees that."

She laughed. "Are you sure James?"

***

James pulled the car into a truck stop and pulled to a stop in front of the convenience store.

"Here," he said handing Patti his keys. "Flash the lights when you're done. I'll go get me a Pepsi and a bag of peanuts and hang around inside until you're done."

She smiled warmly, handed him his jacket and touched his arm. "Thank you James. Bring me one when you come back."

***

James wandered aimlessly up and down the aisles in his tuxedo looking at nothing in particular as people gave him side-glances. It was nearly eleven now. He was sure they all suspected that he was doing more than waiting for his date to come out of the restroom. After a while he even caught the eye of a wary clerk. That's when he picked up two Pepsi's in plastic bottles, two bags of salted peanuts, and walked to the front counter.

"Sorry," he apologized to the clerk as he paid for his merchandise. "My date got a call from her mom and I really didn't want to sit in the car with her and listen to all that. Do you mind if I just hang around near the front windows and wait for her to finish?"

The clerk smiled. "No, not at all. Thank you for explaining though. We often get shoplifters."

"I understand. That's why I came up here."

***

James had nearly finished his Pepsi when his car's lights flashed on.

"Thank you James," Patti said quietly as he slipped behind the wheel. "We usually FaceTime but I told him that I left the library late and my roommate was home and still awake so I couldn't."

"Did it go okay?"

"I think he believed me."

He handed her the other Pepsi. "Would you rather have something else?"

"No, this will hold me over until I get home. I can't believe I'm drinking peanuts."

"So is that a good thing or a bad thing?"

"It's something different—sort of like this night."

"So it's just different?"

"The nuts are."

She paused.

"But this night has been good."

She leaned across the console. James didn't need to wonder what she wanted and he rejoiced. The stop at the truck stop had tipped the scales in his favor! He slipped his hand behind her neck and gently pulled her close as their lips met.

Suddenly he felt her fingers around the back of his neck as well as their kiss lingered and her lips relaxed and folded against his. Adrenaline coursed through him, causing an involuntary gasp.

She pulled gently away and giggled.

"Sorry," he apologized, "I've never felt anything quite like that before."

"With all the women you've kissed in your life, I can hardly believe that."

"You're not anything like those other women. That was totally unexpected and electrifying."

"So now you probably think I'm a tramp."

"You're not naked yet, so no, I could never put you in that box."

"It's a good thing we're in a car in a parking lot under a lot of area lights or I could be."

"Don't do that." James said.

"Do what?" she grinned.

"Lead me on. You're engaged. I hardly know you. I know you're not the type. This can't go anywhere beyond the front seat of my car. After what just happened I'd suggest we stop somewhere on the way home but we'd both feel horrible afterward. Let's just call it what it is, a great night out between friends and go home before I change my mind."

She sat upright in her seat and pulled the sleeping bag up around her neck.

"I'm sorry James. I guess I'm a little confused right now."

"And you just got off of the phone with the man you love and are engaged to. Don't feel bad – really! This will not go beyond the front seat of my car."

He started the engine and backed out of the parking stall.

She was quiet for a while as they pulled back on the freeway.

"Thank you James," she finally broke the silence. "I'm sure you can tell that I'm feeling really vulnerable right now. Thanks for not taking advantage of me."

"You're welcome Patti."

He looked over at her and grinned. "I could use a cold shower right now though. I hope you know that!"

She laughed. "You're not the only one."

Chapter 19

*D*ave was sitting in bed reading a textbook when Patti called. He glanced at his alarm clock. It was nearly midnight, his time.

It had been a rough first week at school. The university, in conjunction with Raytheon, had *strongly suggested* that he take a few classes at Purdue that hadn't been offered at Colorado State. More specifically, those classes were steering him toward the study of missile structure and dynamics. That wasn't really out of the ordinary, though, because in his interviews with Raytheon he'd declared that that was his intention for his graduate study.

The excitement he felt when he saw her phone number pop up on his caller ID quickly faded when he saw that she wasn't using FaceTime. His daily dose of *Patti* was what had kept him motivated. He bought her excuse for not using FaceTime at first but after their abbreviated conversation had ended, he had a nagging suspicion that something was amiss. For one thing, even though she claimed she was in her dorm with her roommate and didn't want her roomie to be able to hear their confidential conversation, the background noise – or lack thereof – didn't seem right.

Their conversation had wiped away the study cobwebs that had begun to obscure the bright, receptive corners of his mind and now as he sat alone once again, he had the sudden urge to call her back.

He paused at that thought. What if he caught her out with another man? On the one hand what if he didn't? He didn't want her to think he didn't trust her – but then on the other hand they were engaged. He should be able to trust her – but what if he couldn't?

His mind rewound to the conversation they'd had in the hospital. Just as he began to feel the anguish and fear he'd felt then, the memories of their time together at Thanksgiving and later the memories of the night of the storm in Greeley, flooded away that fear.

A dark thought crowded out those warm memories. Was she having second thoughts? He knew that she'd been heartbroken and frustrated when they'd had to move their wedding from February to June. Worse yet, now they both knew that if they couldn't work out their finances, she'd have to take a year off of school and he knew that she hated that idea. It didn't make good sense from the point of the continuity of her study habits, and what if they decided to start a family? She may never finish.

A nagging fear crowded its way into the corners of his mind. She'd almost been ready to walk away that night in the hospital and when he looked back on their relationship – or the lack thereof – he was worried. His mom was right. He'd taken advantage of her patience. She'd taken a back seat to football and his educational goals for four long years. Yes, they seemed to have reconciled those glaring differences around Thanksgiving, but once again because of his educational choices, Christmas and New Year's had been a disaster!

He fingered his cell phone, clicking on her phone number. Then before he could press the send button, he switched it off. Now though, he was wide awake.

Dave climbed off his bed, quietly opened his bedroom door and crept down the creaky, ancient stairway. He kept a six-pack of Dr. Pepper in Rose's refrigerator. He doubted that the caffeine would add any more *awakeness*, to his frazzled mind than was already there.

"Can't sleep?" Claire's soft voice reached out to him in the semidarkness as he walked into the living room.

"I just got off the phone with Patti," he said quietly. "She called late tonight and now I'm wide awake."

"Problems?"

"Not that I can tell."

"You don't sound too convinced."

He slumped down on the opposite end of the sofa from Claire and took a sip of his drink.

"I don't know what to think anymore," he answered after a short pause. "I think I already told you that we've been seeing each other since high school. I wasn't very smart, though, and I guess I was just treating her like a friend. It wasn't until after I got injured that she let me know how she really felt. I suppose it was a combination of emotions over seeing me hurt and feeling neglected but she nearly walked away that night."

"I didn't know that."

"It put me in a tailspin. I thought we reconciled at Thanksgiving but then I got snowed in here over Christmas and had to travel straight from here to Raytheon, so we couldn't spend either Christmas or New Year's together."

"And?"

"And something was different when she called me tonight. For one thing she always tries to call me at ten her time – eleven our time – so she won't keep me up too late. Tonight, she didn't call me until nearly midnight and then she just called. We usually FaceTime."

"Did she say why?"

"She said she was at the library late. I sort of believe that because since she started school, she's been complaining about the bad classes she's had to take so her credits would transfer out here. Anyway, then she said her roommate was home and she didn't want her to know our business."

"That all sounds plausible."

"Maybe, but I've talked to her in the dorm before and there's always background noise. There was a little tonight but it was different. Maybe that's because it was later than usual."

"It's late and even though it's Saturday night, I don't imagine a dorm room is a very conducive spot for a party."

"I could swear I heard car noises – you know, something you'd hear alongside a busy highway or something. Her dorm is a long way from a major road."

"So do you worry that she's cheating on you?"

"I don't want to think that."

"It happens."

"I suppose you're right, but that would kill me!"

"Sorry."

"Hey, why are you up so late?" he asked.

"I've been studying and couldn't get my mind to shut down. It looks like you use Dr. Pepper. I use warm milk but the process is probably the same. I sorta funnel my thoughts into my olfactory senses – mouth, nose, throat! When I concentrate on them it helps drain all the random technical thoughts out of my head."

He chuckled. "I'd never thought of it quite that way. I sometimes shut my eyes tightly and concentrate on the flashes of light that occur as my optic nerve slows down."

"I've never heard of that but I suppose the process is the same. We both use sensory input to funnel away cognitive thought."

They sat in silence for a few moments.

"You know, Claire, we haven't had much time to chat. Would you mind?"

"No actually, as long as I'm not thinking about compound chemical concoctions, I think it might help."

"Where did you tell me you hail from?" he asked.

"Duluth, Minnesota."

"Cold country!"

"It can be, but it can be fairly pleasant – especially during the summertime."

"What brings you here?"

"Engineering school and research projects."

"Are you in a graduate program then?"

"Yes. When I finished my master's program last year. I was *invited* to join their doctorate program here to do research."

"Are they paying your way?"

"Yes actually, but only because I qualified to join their research team."

"What do you do when you need to get away?"

"I used to go home for the summers, but our summer research program is being funded by some big pharmaceutical firms and it pays enough to make staying here worthwhile."

"Any siblings?"

She chuckled. "Yeah, my dad was married three times and had children with all of them so I have people scattered all over. I'm his youngest. All of my other siblings went off to live with their respective mothers. My mother was his last and youngest wife. In fact, she was what a lot of folks would call a trophy wife."

"That's sad."

"We lived out of town then, so when I was little it was just me and my mom. I was the only child in the house at the time so my dad tried to take me under his wing whenever he was home. We became good buddies – especially when I took a liking to football. Because we lived in a rural area we did lots of weekend campouts and sleepovers. I learned to love the woods."

She paused for a few moments.

"And then Dad changed jobs and moved us into the city," she continued. "That was tougher. People weren't as trusting so sleepovers became a thing of the past and building campfires was frowned upon."

"I'll bet."

"What about you?" Claire asked. "What was your boyhood like?"

"Pretty happy from what I can remember of it. I have a brother. He's only a year younger and we became good friends. We both got involved in sports. He loved baseball. I loved football but Dad taught us how to throw and catch both. Team sports were sort of like a second family to us. We also belonged to a Boy Scout troop and because they were always short of leaders, my dad ended up being our Scout Master. I loved that. When we weren't playing sports on the weekends, we were camping out in the hills somewhere, so I know what you mean about loving the woods."

"I envy you. I really don't like my mom much. She was mean to me and to Dad. I don't know why he put up with her. Maybe he was tired of being divorced. Maybe she kept him happy in other ways. I won't even go there. I enrolled in summer semester at junior college right out of high school just to get out of the house. It lessened the friction between me and his trophy wife so that was good."

"I'm sorry."

"Don't be. That's just them. I couldn't live like that – you know with a partner like her."

"Not all relationships are like that."

She stared at him in the semidarkness for a few moments.

"No, I suppose you're right," she agreed quietly, "but from what I've seen in my short lifetime, guys like your dad are the exception rather than the rule."

"Wow, that's hard. I guess I never saw that in our community."

"The operative word there is *saw*," she answered curtly. "I think you might change your mind about people if you could really *see* what goes on behind their closed front doors. My mother was very friendly and well-liked by the women in whatever neighborhood we lived in. As a result she heard a lot of gossip and passed a lot of it on to me when she felt like I was old enough to understand it. I think she only did that so she'd have somebody to vent to. My dad didn't want to hear any of the local gossip."

"So what you're telling me then is that you think all men are pigs?"

She laughed. "No, not all. And don't get me wrong, there are a lot of *fishwives* out there too."

"Fishwives?"

"Yes, I think you know what I'm talking about: coarse, loud, abusive, obnoxious."

"I think I get the picture. I'm thankful my parents weren't like that."

"You should be. Having been around you a little I can tell you were raised better than that."

"Even if I pushed away the best thing I've ever had in my life for football?"

"That's just an error in judgement in my way of thinking. It's not a personality flaw. The bright spot on your stage is you can learn a new act. You just need to rewrite your script to include Patti in everything you can."

"I hope it's not too late."

"Are you having those feelings?"

"Maybe. That's why I'm sitting here in the dark after midnight on a Saturday night, unable to sleep."

"Too bad she's so far away."

"That's exactly what I'm worried about. You know what they say about being out of sight."

"You mean out of mind?"

"Uh huh. Until tonight we've been using FaceTime for all of our calls back and forth so I could see her emotions—and she mine. I hope she wasn't lying tonight but I wonder. I don't think women have the market on intuition."

She studied his eyes for a moment.

"No we don't," she finally answered, "and I wish I had an answer for you. If it means anything, I feel your anguish."

"Thanks Claire," he said as he twisted the plastic cap back on his half-finished Dr. Pepper and got to his feet. "Maybe I'd better go lie down and try to sleep. Sometime tomorrow I need to go back to the library."

"Maybe you need to take a day off."

"I probably need to, but it can't be tomorrow. One of my idiot professors is giving us a comprehensive exam on Monday to see where our learning base is. If I blow that, it'll undoubtedly give him the wrong impression and my GPA at this point is all important. If I fall down the last semesters of my undergrad work, I may lose it all."

"You need to be careful with your sanity though," Clair countered softly. "Maybe this weekend is different because of that test you've got coming up but can I offer you a little advice from someone who's been there?"

"Sure."

"You need to take at least one day a week away from that grind to cleanse your mind. I don't know if you're a religious type or not, but in the Bible, God talks about resting on the Sabbath. I didn't take much stock in that at first but I soon found out that if I just left my books in my room and spent time going to church or wandering the woods, my Monday was always a lot more productive."

"I think there's some truth to that," Dave said as he put his drink away. "Maybe I should do that. I've got so many other things on my mind right now, I don't know if I could study anyway."

She smiled. "Besides if that professor is trying to determine where his students' knowledge base is, I don't think that trying to bone up on nearly four years of college engineering will be very productive."

He looked down. "You're right. There's a lot of wisdom in what you just said. I guess I'm just too stirred up emotionally right now. Maybe I *could* use a break. I'll bet you could show me a couple of your favorite spots," he said with a slight smile. "What are you doing tomorrow?"

"Actually I have church at ten. You're welcome to come with me."

"I don't have a suit."

"You don't need a suit. The group I meet with are pretty casual. Do you have a nice pair of slacks and a shirt with a collar?"

"I do."

"Then you're set. I promise you won't feel uncomfortable. There's no hellfire and damnation preached at our meetings."

"Thank you. I used to attend church meetings often but I've sort of gotten out of the habit at school. With football demands, I always had to use Sunday to catch up."

"And now you don't have football so you really don't have an excuse."

He grinned. "You're beginning to sound like my mother."

"I'm honored. I just told you that it looks like you came from a good home. I'd be honored to serve as your surrogate mother."

Chapter 20

Patti's phone rang early Sunday morning.

"Good morning Patti!" James said as she answered. "Do you have plans for today?"

"I just woke up," she complained, "you kept me out way too late last night."

"So that means you haven't had breakfast yet. I'm famished! Throw on some sweats and I'll take you to IHOP for breakfast."

"I can't just leap out of bed and rush out the door like you guys can! It takes me a little time to put on my face and fix my hair."

"You don't need makeup to look beautiful," he argued. "Just wash the sleepers out of your eyes and run a brush through that fabulous hair of yours. You'll look better than any other woman in the place. I promise."

"I haven't even had time to take a shower."

"Unless you slept in a pigsty last night, I'm sure you don't stink. Come on. Haven't you ever done anything spontaneous before?"

She glanced at the mirror on her bureau. Sleep hadn't done her much damage. Still, she was a little annoyed. It was Sunday. It was her only day to just chill.

"Come on," he prodded, "you have to eat sometime and I'm offering you a great breakfast. It's got to be better than Cheerios and toast."

"I prefer bagels."

"They serve those at IHOP too, and they'll be fresh, not days old like the ones you haul home from the grocery store."

"Oh okay," she surrendered, "give me ten minutes."

"You've got five. I'll be waiting outside in front of your dorm."

Patti dropped her phone on her bed and pulled a matching pair of sweats out of her bureau. She was agitated. Couldn't James take no for an answer?

Then memories of their kiss in the car the night before colored up her cheeks. She hadn't kissed Dave since Thanksgiving, and yet she'd somewhat willingly allowed herself to do that with James on their first date – and it really wasn't an official date. Or was it? All the events of the prior two days swept over her in a torrent.

She stood in front of her mirror and ran a hairbrush through her hair. She wasn't wearing a hint of makeup. She would never have met Dave like this…

She even wore makeup when they just hung out together in the library. She hesitated. Why did it matter if James saw her without makeup or not? They weren't even friends.

She stopped at that thought. What were they if not friends? You didn't just kiss people who weren't your friends… at least not on the lips. She'd often kissed her mom and dad but not on the lips and…

She blushed at the memory of the night before. Maybe she'd just been missing Dave. Maybe she'd just been lonely.

She paused as another thought crossed her mind. Maybe she was a tramp.

No, she wasn't that. She could never be like that. It had to be the loneliness. She ached to wrap Dave up in her arms. The passion she'd felt the night before with James raised her heart rate. Was it his raw good looks? Was she attracted to him or just…

She couldn't force herself to even think the word. The gentler word for what she was feeling was *needy*.

She spun away from the mirror before she could look herself in the eyes. This was wrong. Dave would be furious – or heartbroken. She picked up her phone and looked for James' recent call. Somehow she couldn't bring herself to click his number. What would she tell him? It was just breakfast for Pete's sake.

She snatched her purse off the bureau and angrily shoved her phone inside. What was she doing? Didn't James have any manners – any regard at all for Dave?

She turned back to the bureau and picked her engagement ring up out of a small glass dish. As she slipped it on her finger, she vowed to herself that she'd flash it at James every chance she got. She needed to share the guilt she was feeling with him. If James was an honorable man he should get the hint.

***

James kept Patti laughing from the time he hurried her into his car that was double parked in front of her dorm until they were mostly done with their meal. It felt so very good to laugh for a change. As she thought back over the past two months, she hadn't really had much to laugh about. James had something awkwardly wise and silly or insightful to say about nearly everything. He joked happily with the waitress. He made fun of the way Patti cut her French toast into uniform strips before she ate it. He leaned forward a few times to quietly say nasty things about people seated nearby. Even though he joked unashamedly with their waitress – he quietly made fun of her makeup and the way she walked – when she turned away, but in tones that only Patti could hear.

All too soon it seemed, they had finished their meal, turned down dessert, and walked outside into a stinging, cold wind.

"Yuck!" James fumed as he shut the weather outside of his car door and started the engine. "Sometimes I hate winter!"

"I like it!" Patti countered.

"Only because you ski." he argued. "Tell me what's so attractive about winter to the rest of us who don't bundle up in so many layers we can hardly walk?"

"Winter's beautiful!'

"Really?" he stared at her with a slight grin still gracing the corners of his mouth. "I'll call your bleached white, dead landscape – punctuated by dark, leafless tress – and raise you a vibrant, green hillside, graced by a warm, gentle breeze. In fact, I'll even toss in the fragrance of a million wildflowers and the ripple of a nearby brook."

She laughed. "Did you just plagiarize that from a passage in a book?"

"Nope. That's just the way I see the world."

"Didn't you tell me you live in Boise? You have winter in Idaho too."

"Yes we do, but we also have three other glorious seasons. Winter to me is full of dreariness, cold and death."

"That's depressing."

"Only if you don't dribble the season with bright, colored sprinkles like on a birthday cake."

"I'm having a hard time picturing you as a philosopher."

"Just because I'm a jock doesn't mean I'm dumb. I can see and enjoy the finer things in life. Take you for example. You're like those brightly colored sprinkles I was just talking about."

She recoiled a little mentally. She hadn't seen it for what it was until now but James was really hitting on her! He was serious! Not knowing what else to do she raised her left hand to her chin, pretending to scratch an itch.

"I hate it when you lead with your ring finger!" James exclaimed softly. "I'm well aware that you're engaged and frankly that pains me. You're the most exciting woman I've ever met!"

She blushed.

"I won't play games with you Patti. To be totally blunt, I find you fascinating. I'm in this for the long haul. I'm sure that Dave is a great guy but let's be honest shall we? He's had four years to make his move. Have you ever wondered what's taken him so long? Is he serious or are you just one of those items on his checklist of things to do. You know: Get an education, check. Get a job, check. Get married, check. Raise a family, check. I'm offering you a different choice. I won't be so stupid as to argue whether or not I'm better than him. That's poor form and he's not here to defend himself. I'd just like to hang around with you for awhile and let you decide."

He smiled.

"Will you let me do that?" he asked softly after a moment. "No strings. I promise. You're a wise woman. What have you got to lose? He'll never have to know that we're seeing each other. If I don't measure up just tell me so and I'll walk away."

"Maybe I don't want to make that choice."

James frowned. "That's fair I suppose. After all, you've got a good thing going here. You obviously have strong feelings for Dave. You're wearing his ring. That means he has certain expectations of you. You've probably both told your respective parents about your engagement. I'm sure you've spent some time making plans and thinking about what life with him will be like. All I'm asking is that you keep an open mind and give me two weeks."

He opened his cell phone and glanced at the screen. "Today's the 15th of January. Can you give me until the end of the month?"

"I don't know James. This is really sudden. I'm not unhappy. I'm just a little lonely."

"Okay, I understand that. I'm not seeing anyone either. I'm lonely like you. I feel great when I'm with you. I don't think I've ever felt this way before. I love the feeling. I'm excited. I'm motivated."

He paused for a few moments.

"I'm hopeful," he finished.

She studied his eyes for a few moments but didn't answer.

"What could it hurt?" he prodded. "It's not like I'm going to tie you up in my basement or anything like that. I won't even take you to do cool stuff like we did last night to try to sweep you off your feet."

He smiled. "Let's just hang out together."

She hesitated.

"Did you like breakfast?"

"What's not to like," Patti responded, "IHOP always serves a great breakfast."

"That's not what I meant."

"I know what you meant," she responded, "and yes I had fun this morning."

"Even without makeup?" he teased.

She laughed. "Yes, even without makeup and wearing my frumpy sweats in public. That's something I've never done before."

"It looks good on you – freedom, I mean."

"And I'm wracked with guilt."

"Why? You mean about last night? That was just a buddy date to a concert."

"Come on James, I kissed you!"

"We kissed each other and it was warm and wonderful, but that doesn't mean we have to pack our bags for the honeymoon."

"Maybe kissing someone doesn't mean the same for you as it does for me."

"That's fair, but I only think it's different for you because you've attached a little guilt to it. To me that kiss was warm, erotic, and very personal. It gave me hope."

"I'm afraid I sent you the wrong message."

"Maybe, so help me understand. How was it for you?"

She looked away.

"Don't do that," he said softly as he touched her chin and gently moved her face back so he could see the emotion in her eyes. "Look me in the eyes and tell me it wasn't the same for you."

She looked down to avoid his eyes.

He lifted her chin slightly and leaned across the console to kiss her. She didn't pull away.

Chapter 21

Dave was worried. The first time that Patti had *ghosted* him by phoning rather than using FaceTime had been on Saturday, the 14th of January. Since then, that had happened four more times in less than two weeks. She always had a good excuse, though, so based on her explanations, he shouldn't be worried, but he was.

Dave had just talked to Patti on the phone and walked down into Rose's living room to pop open a Dr. Pepper and stew in his juices a little when Claire joined him on the sofa.

"Who kicked your trike in the ditch?" she laughed.

"Is it that obvious?"

"You've got gloom hanging all over you like ivy on a wall."

"I'm sure it's nothing. I just got off the phone with Patti."

"And?"

"And she called again instead of using FaceTime."

"Maybe she looked a wreck."

"Patti never looks a wreck."

"Maybe she's let herself go since you left."

"I doubt it. She's not the type."

"You mean like me?" Claire asked pointedly.

"I never said that."

"It's true though. I'm certainly no raving beauty. I cut my hair short so it's easier to manage. In case you haven't noticed my hair is really thin so I added a little radiant color to it for contrast. It makes it look thicker."

"I hadn't noticed."

"No, I don't suppose you would have."

"What do you mean by that?" he asked, recognizing by the tone of her voice that he'd somehow offended her.

"Oh nothing."

"Are we still friends?" he asked hesitantly, "I'm afraid I've done something to offend you."

"I didn't know that we were friends. We're roommates."

"That hurts! I' consider you to be a friend."

"So why do you think she's not using FaceTime?" she asked, changing the subject.

"I don't know for sure. She told me tonight that she was still in the library studying and didn't want to make noise so she stepped into the lady's room."

"I don't think I could talk on the phone in the restroom. That has to echo a lot and what if someone came in?"

"I didn't think that sounded very plausible, either. I walked into a men's room once and a guy was sitting in a closed stall talking on the phone. It was really awkward."

"Did you hear any echoes over the phone?" Claire asked.

"No."

"What did you hear in the background?"

Dave considered her question. "I guess I really didn't pay any attention to what was going on around her. I only wanted to hear her voice."

"Was it quiet? Was there traffic?"

"It was quiet."

"Maybe she was in one of those smaller unisex bathrooms – the ones where you have to lock the door behind you. They're small enough that there might not have been an echo. I think you need to give her the benefit of the doubt."

"I would but…"

"Man's intuition?" she asked.

"Maybe."

"I think you're just feeling alone and jealous."

"Jealous of whom?"

"Maybe nobody. Maybe you're just jealous because she's there and you're here and you can't be there."

"That's no reason to feel jealous."

"No? Did she sound happy?"

"Sort of, yeah."

"Then I think you're jealous that she's happy and you're not."

She paused for a few moments.

"How long did you say you've been together?"

"Four years."

"Do you trust her?"

"I think so. Maybe who I don't trust is the thousand other men on campus."

She laughed. "You need to get over that. She accepted your ring. If she loves you, she'll fend them all off."

A moment of silence passed between them.

"And if she doesn't, she doesn't deserve you. You're attractive, upwardly mobile and from what little I know of you, you have a great personality. Can I offer you a little advice?"

"Please."

"Short of quitting school here and running back to Colorado State, there's nothing you can do about her anyway. She's free to do anything she wants until you exchange your vows. Next time you need to pump yourself up a little before you call her. Keep your conversation light and hopeful. Seem happy, even if you're having doubts. That'll keep your personality ringing true in her ears and even if somebody else is hustling her, she'll remember the real you. As busy as you both are, six months is going to fly by."

"Thanks Claire. This helps. You're wise beyond your years."

"No, I'm an independent third party sitting here unaffected by the high emotions you're feeling. It's easy for me to look at things logically."

"That's true enough."

"Besides Dave, I'm just enough of a romantic to believe that *if* this thing you've got going on is the real deal you'll both survive any distractions that might come along."

"And if it's not?"

"Did you hear what you just said?" Claire asked. "Are you having second thoughts about your engagement?"

"No. I know how I feel. I just worry about her. I already told you about that night in the hospital. I'm afraid she might have already made up her mind and is just waiting for the chance to let me down easy."

"Then if that happens, you'll eventually pick up the pieces of your shattered heart and move on. Years later when you look back, you'll know that you both made the right decision."

She hesitated for a moment.

"Don't get me wrong!" she exclaimed as she saw the shadow slide across his countenance. "I'm not trying to gloss this over, but I really think it's too soon to get all stirred up. This may sound strange, Dave, but you're grieving. You've temporarily lost your best friend. The big difference is you can talk to her every day."

She continued after a short pause. "Have you ever stopped to think that maybe the reason she doesn't want you to see her on FaceTime is because she's as lonely as you are? Women's feelings lie closer to the surface. You don't know but maybe she's been crying and doesn't want you to feel bad about making her cry. She knows you've got a tough schedule. She knows how much this semester means to your scholastic success. I think what she's doing is simply a way to help you keep your mind on your studies. That's why I just told you that the next time you call, be sure you're all pumped up and excited. Make notes if you have to so you can carry on with all the *fun* you're having here. That will help lighten her load."

"Thank you Claire. You have an uncanny knack for putting things in perspective."

"Yeah, I'm a wise old sage. Maybe I need to change my major and study psychology."

***

The next night Claire was already propped up on the couch, waiting, when Dave paced down the squeaky, old staircase.

"Well?" she asked before he spoke, "how did it go tonight?"

"No FaceTime again but I think we ended on a high note. I made notes like you told me to and happily rattled from one positive note to another."

"And when she responded?"

"She sounded a lot more like herself. Thank you. Can I take you out to dinner or something to get even?"

"No, but thanks. I'm not a gregarious person by nature. I like structure. My research classes at the U give me structure. Quiet dinners here with you and Rose give me structure. I know, I'm weird but I've become accustomed to my weirdness. I'd like to think it becomes me."

"You wouldn't have to dress up, if that's what's worrying you."

Something crossed over Claire's countenance that he didn't understand. He didn't think she was angry.

"I'm sorry," he quickly apologized, "have I offended you?"

"No, not at all. It takes a lot to ruffle my feathers."

"Speaking of feathers," Dave changed the subject, "are you still seeing feathers from Christmas?"

"I am," she laughed. "I know that feather pillows and the like, lose a few feathers but there are enough feathers drifting around this house that I could swear somebody plucked a goose and just threw all the feathers around the room. You three must have had a pretty wild party over at Hershel's place. The only reason I should see feathers is if you carried them in here on your clothes, or in your hair."

"I swear I had them everywhere." Dave laughed, "I'm surprised there were any feathers left in the bed."

"Rose told me you guys had quite an experience. I wish I'd have been here to see it for myself."

"How was your Christmas at home, by the way?" Dave asked.

She looked down at her milk for a moment before she answered. "Nothing's changed. My dad still thinks I'm his football buddy. Mom and I respected each other's feelings but didn't say much of anything substantial to one another."

"Ouch!"

"I don't know if I told you already but she's one of those high society babes," Claire grumbled. "She refuses to age gracefully for fear she won't be part of her little troupe of groupies. As a result, she has a bureau dresser full of all the latest wigs. She cuts her hair short so her wigs will fit. She paints herself up like a gypsy, wears clothes that only a model would wear, and struts herself around the house in spiky heels like we're buying all of her false pretenses."

"Wow! I can sense your hatred."

"I don't know if I really hate her or not. She's almost like the evil Cinderella stepmom if you catch my drift. The only difference is my dad pretty much shelters me from her."

"I'm sorry I asked how your holiday was."

"No, don't get me wrong. I love my dad. He loves me and he pampers me. I think I already told you that he's paying all of my school expenses. He bought me a fancy, new car for my high school graduation and I promptly wrecked it. I think that was the only time in my life when I was afraid he was going to smack me. After he cooled down for a week or so, he bought me another car—a used, bent-up, pickup truck this time."

She grinned. "Buying me that truck was actually a good move on his part. I had a few more scrapes before I learned to concentrate when I drive. The new dents were pretty much indistinguishable from the ones my old truck already had. And," she continued without a breath, "I could drive it over the dusty backroads without feeling bad about not constantly washing it. Mom pitched a fit every time I parked it out front so I had my own designated parking spot in an equipment shed at the back of the property."

"You like the backroads?"

"Yes, but not for the reason you're probably thinking. We have something like a million lakes in Minnesota and I think I've paddled my kayak across most of them."

"So you fish?"

"Nah. I don't eat fish. I love birds, though, and I take pictures – lots of pictures."

"You need to show me sometime."

"I'd have to haul you all the way to Duluth to do that. Dad built me a room in the house to display my work. Mom refuses to set foot in there. When I'm not home to keep ahead of the dust, the room gets to looking pretty shabby."

"What does your dad say?"

"Our monster football TV is in that room. Does that give you a clue? Like I already told you, I'm his little football buddy. He's never hunted waterfowl and he appreciates fine things so he's as much at home in that room as I am."

"I take it your mom doesn't do the football thing?"

"Nope. In fact as soon as Christmas dinner was over this year she fled with her troupe of groupies to who knows where and left Dad and me home alone to run amok."

"So your folks aren't close anymore?"

"Nah. I suppose she keeps him happy enough in the bedroom to keep him from throwing her out. For that he keeps her bank account full. They sleep in separate rooms because he snores."

She chuckled.

"He always sneaks down the hall to her room for awhile whenever he comes home but before long, he's back in his own room snoring the rafters off."

"He sounds fun. I'd like to meet him sometime."

"Oh, I promise you'd like him. He's big, over 6'6". He's like a big teddy bear. He's the CEO of a pharmaceutical firm."

"So that's what got you into Biochemical Engineering?"

"Bingo!"

Dave glanced at his cell phone. "Oh, my heck! It's after midnight and I have an early class."

"Nice talking to you," Claire said as he got to his feet.

"I enjoyed it! Maybe you should send me a bill. I think psychologists get something like $150.00 an hour."

"Friends don't charge friends."

"So we're friends now?" he grinned.

"I'd like to think so," she said. "I don't have many."

"Neither do I."

Chapter 22

$\mathcal{P}$atti quit trying to avoid James. It was almost impossible. He bought her lunch every day. He joined her at their quasi-assigned study table in the library every afternoon. He drove her to her dorm at the end of the day. He brought her flowers nearly every day, and if he didn't bring her flowers, he brought her a few chocolates he'd bought from a specialty shop downtown. She kept looking for the chink in his armor but even though the end of the month was fast approaching, she hadn't seen one yet. From what she saw and felt he was exactly what he said he was, lonely – and maybe infatuated with her.

Her mind drifted away from the book she held in front of her. And, like it or not, he had raised emotions in her that she hadn't…

She stopped at the thought. No, Dave hadn't ever been overly affectionate, but she'd felt plenty of passion with him the few times he'd lowered his guard.

She smiled. Dave was always such a gentleman. She remembered the afternoon in her room at Thanksgiving. They'd both been on the verge. Dave had pulled the plug before…

She could tell that just beneath his eyes he'd wanted her as badly as she'd wanted him…

"Hey Patti," James said brightly as he joined her in the library. "What have you got going tomorrow?"

"It's Saturday. I need to do some laundry and clean my room."

"That's boring."

"Maybe so but I'm running out of things to wear and my roommate informed me it's my turn to scour out our bathroom."

She studied him for a moment.

"So what's lurking in that devious mind of yours?"

"I thought it might be fun to go skiing tomorrow. The weather forecast calls for light overcast but no snow."

"I didn't think you skied."

"I've never told you that I don't ski. I just told you that winter wasn't my favorite season. I've spent my share of time on the slopes."

"I don't have any equipment with me."

"Neither do I, but there's a ski shop downtown that rents or there are always rentals at the resort but if it's busy we might not find what we need at the resort – especially outerwear. It'd be better to get what we need here in town."

"I can't afford…"

"My treat," he cut her off. "We don't have to spend all day. Let's just go up about noon when it's warmer and ski until it gets cold. Afterward we can warm up in the lodge and eat dinner before we come home."

She hesitated. Library visits, lunches together, and drives home were innocuous enough. They hadn't really gone anywhere significant together since *the thing* in Denver. When she thought about that night in Denver she worried. Things had gotten a little out of hand right after the play but…

She paused at that thought. That was over three weeks ago. They'd shared a few passionate, but brief kisses since then. And as much as she tried to tell herself otherwise, she had liked them. She'd begun to let her guard down a little.

"Oh, okay," she said with a smile. "I'll promise my roomie that I'll clean the bathroom on Sunday."

He grinned. "You make me a happy man, Patti."

She tried to look away but couldn't. There was something about his eyes that just drew her in.

"By the way," he said softly after glancing around them to be sure nobody was listening in on their conversation, "bring your swimsuit. The lodge has a hot tub. There's nothing better after a hard day on the slopes than a hot soak. It helps you warm back up and loosens your muscles so you won't be sore the next day."

An alarm went off in her brain. The only swimsuit she had was a bikini and the only one who'd seen her in it was Dave – other than the few hundred other people at the lake of course – but that was different. Bikinis were common at the beach.

"I'm not sure about the hot tub thing," she said. "Don't you have to rent a room or something to use it?"

"No. I've been there before. It's pretty cool actually. It's outside, completely surrounded by a wooden deck that looks out over the mountain. I've sat in it before when it was snowing like crazy. It's a really cool experience."

She still wasn't comfortable with the thought.

James smiled. "I don't want to put you on the spot. We don't have to use the tub if that's a deal breaker. I just thought it'd be fun to get away for awhile."

"I'd love to go skiing. I haven't been in forever."

***

Their day on the slopes was fabulous. The lifts weren't overly busy and there hadn't been snow for a few days so the trails were all well-groomed. She hadn't been skiing in so long, though, that by 3 p.m. she'd had enough.

"Are you done for the day then?" James asked as they coasted to a stop at the bottom of the hill near the lodge.

"I think so. My legs were getting a little wobbly on that last run."

"We shouldn't push it then. You'll be sore for a week. Did you bring a suit, or would you rather just go straight to the restaurant?"

"I brought it, but I want to have a look at that hot tub before I commit. I don't want to be on display for everyone in the restaurant."

He laughed. "It's in the back. There might be a few other people in the tub but it's early in the day so we might have it to ourselves. I promise you won't regret it. Like I told you before, I've never been sore the day after if I spend some time in the tub before I go home. Come on, we'll leave our skis in the rack and I'll show you."

***

The hot tub was everything that James had told her it would be. The resort charged a modest fee that gave you an hour in the pool and a fluffy towel. The dressing room was near the tub so she wasn't exposed to James' stares for long before she was able to slip beneath the bubbling surface, out of sight from the neck down.

"Oh, it's hot!" she exclaimed as she eased her way down into the steaming water.

"It's only supposed to be 105 degrees," James laughed as he watched her, "but I think it's a little hotter than that."

Knowing she was uncomfortable being nearly naked in front of him, James maintained eye contact as much as he could while she climbed in and kept the comments about how good she looked to himself.

A wave of dizziness swept over her as her body reacted to the stinging, hot water. She instantly felt her tired muscles relax as a sort of euphoria rippled through her from head to foot.

"Ahh!" she gasped as she settled back into a molded seat along the edge. "You're right. This feels *soo* good."

He slid over next to her, leaned back and closed his eyes. "Told you," he murmured, "I'm glad we came early. It looks like we'll have the tub to ourselves for awhile. It's more fun at night, though, especially if it's snowing."

"As hot as it is, I don't think I'll be able to stay in very long."

He found her hand beneath the water. "I can tell you don't hot tub very often. You're supposed to soak until you're all heated up and then get out and sit on the edge to cool down. When the dizziness goes away you slip back in."

"The view off the deck is spectacular." Patti said a few moments later. "How often do you come here?"

He sat up and looked at her. "Two or three times a winter."

"Who else have you come up here with?"

James laughed. "You probably won't believe me but this is the first time I've come with a date. Most of the time I just come with a few guys from the team."

"I suppose alcohol was involved?"

"No, actually it wasn't. We come here to ski not to party. Besides somebody has to drive home and the road to get up here is pretty unforgiving."

"Thank you for coming with me today," James said a while later. "I needed a little break."

"How are your classes going?" she asked.

"Let's not spoil this by talking about school. I came here to get away from that."

"Sorry."

"Let's talk about us," he ventured as he gently gripped her hand.

"There is no *us*!" she said, pulling her hand away, not really believing her own words. "I'm still engaged, James!"

"You didn't wear your ring today."

"I didn't want to risk losing it. I'm surprised you noticed."

He smiled. "Of course I noticed. You usually make sure I see it several times every time we're together."

"Am I that obvious?"

"Sometimes. When you flaunt it like that and yet keep seeing me it makes me wonder if you're having second thoughts? Do you have to keep flaunting it to remind *yourself* that you're engaged?"

"I feel like I have to flaunt it, like you so aptly put it, because it seems like you're ever present. I think I've spent more time with you in the past three weeks than I have with Dave in months."

"And is that a bad thing Patti?" he asked as he studied her eyes, "I don't think I need to say it to your face but I know you can tell that I love you. I know you probably don't feel the same way about me, yet, but I keep hoping."

His words sent a shock wave through her. She didn't really know why though. He'd made his feelings very obvious by the way he looked at her, fawned over her, tried to do everything he could to please her.

"James please," she said softly. "I knew this was a mistake."

"Coming here, or coming here with me?"

"The latter."

"I don't think it is," he countered softly as he took her hand again. "Look me in the eyes and tell me you don't feel anything at all for me."

She turned her head.

"That's what I thought," he whispered softly.

Then his hand was on her chin. Their lips met and his hand slipped lower, pulling her body gently against him. She tried to see Dave's face in her mind but she saw only the darkness behind her closed eyes, felt only James' lips and his hand as it moved to her breast.

"I need to get out!" she gasped as she pushed him away and hoisted her hips up on the edge of the pool.

"I'm sorry," James mumbled as he watched her get to her feet and wrap her towel around her.

"I'm getting dressed!" she hissed angrily down at him as she turned and hurried toward the dressing room.

James was already dressed and waiting on a chair near the exit by the time Patti finished in the dressing room.

"Take me home!" she said angrily as she approached.

James studied her with sad eyes. "Please Patti. I'm so sorry. I just got caught up in the moment. Let's at least have dinner before we leave. It's a long drive back to campus."

She quickly weighed her options. She was upset, but she was famished. It was at least an hour's drive back to campus and she hadn't eaten since breakfast – and that had been little more than half a bagel with cream cheese.

She studied her hands for a moment.

"I promise I'll keep my hands to myself," he added.

"That was wrong in so many ways!" she chided him, still angry.

"Yes, I admit it was. I've already apologized. Give me a break here Patti. I'm a guy and you – well, you look fabulous."

"And I'm engaged," she added for emphasis, "you know that!"

"I won't argue that fact. You're right. Maybe this was a mistake but I'm trying to salvage the day. Let's at least get something to eat before we leave. I don't know about you but it's easier to be angry when I'm hungry."

"I believe they call that being *hangry*," she said through a pout, "and you're right. I'm starving."

***

They were stiffly cautious around each other over dinner, keeping their conversation light and away from anything to do with their personal feelings. It wasn't until they were in James' car and heading back down the canyon that James raised the issue.

"I really am sorry about what happened," he said. "I didn't really mean for that to turn sexual. I mean really, Patti, what could have possibly happened in a public hot tub in the middle of the afternoon?"

"So what were you trying to do, just cop a feel?"

"It didn't feel like that at the time. I love to kiss you and we were sitting side-by-side."

"That didn't mean you had to grope me."

"I didn't mean for it to seem that way. I just got caught up in the heat of the moment and wanted to hold you."

"Maybe it wouldn't have been so bad but I was nearly naked."

"I could tell you were pretty uncomfortable. When I asked you to bring your swimsuit. I didn't know you'd wear a bikini."

"That's what I wear to the beach. A hot tub filled with just the two of us is a little different."

He didn't answer for a while.

"Maybe I overreacted," she eventually mused.

"No, I don't think you did. I know what I did seemed to be off limits, but seriously Patti, what I did was spontaneous, not planned."

"Does that spontaneity come from all those girls you kiss when you're at your dude ranch?"

"I don't even want to go there."

"No James, I suppose you don't, but you can't sit here and tell me it didn't happen."

"I won't lie and tell you it hasn't, but I don't make a habit of it, and it never went any further than a little light petting. Like I already told you, the worst thing that could happen at the ranch is if we sent one of our underage girls home pregnant."

"So tell me James," she asked, not willing to let the subject die, "what did these little romances in the woods look like?"

He chuckled. "Nothing more than a lot of flirting, a little kissing now and again, and occasionally a brief make out session hidden away in the trees. I wanted them to go home a little titillated but without regrets."

"Is that what you're doing with me?"

"No, Patti, it's not. I'm not playing you. Let me be perfectly honest here. I love you. I know you think you love Dave and are willing to wait for him but I'm hoping I can change your mind."

She wasn't at all surprised by James' response. In spite of his attempts to keep their interaction light, she knew deep down that he was aggressively pursuing her. She tried to tell herself that she was put off by it but she wasn't. She'd seen nothing in his behavior until today to indicate that he was anything but honorable. He was right. He'd told her on more than one occasion that he loved her. Although she'd been put off by that at first, now what he was telling her didn't seem so objectionable anymore. If Dave and his ring weren't always on her mind, things would be different. She was attracted to James, what woman wouldn't be? He was good looking, sensitive, generous, and always eager to please.

"What's racing through that gorgeous mind of yours right now?" he prodded. "Am I scaring you?"

"No. I'm not worried. The last time I checked I was still free to make my own decisions."

"So are you having doubts then?"

"About us or about Dave?"

"Dave, of course. I know you've had doubts about me all along but I hope now that you've gotten to know me better that those doubts are dwindling a little. I mean I feel bad for Dave. I really do, but the way I look at this, he's had his chance and in my way of thinking he's kind of blown it. If I were in his shoes I'd have married you years ago."

"Is this some sort of a proposal?"

"I won't go there until you decide. I think you know how I feel about you. I keep hoping you're feeling a little that same way about me. If you give me the nod, I'll propose tomorrow. I'm that sure about how I feel about you. I know we could be happy. We're both nearly done with school. If you wouldn't mind living in a house with three male roommates, we already have a place we could live until we graduate."

"This is all way too sudden!" she protested lightly. "We've only known each other for something like three weeks."

"I guess I'm just naïve enough to believe that if I find the right person I don't need six months or a year to convince me whether or not I love them."

"I can't just jump into something like this."

"What's it going to take to convince you that I'm serious?"

"How can you ask me that? You're asking me to act on a few dates and blind faith that you're really who you seem to be."

"Do you think I'm lying to you?"

"I don't know, James, are you?"

"No! I'd never lie to you."

"That's easy to say but harder to prove. Anyone can put on a front for a while."

"Is that what you think this is – a front?" he argued. "I wish you could see how I really feel inside. You didn't ask me in so many words, but yes, I've known a lot of women in my life. That's why I'm so gung-ho about you. You're different. You're everything I've ever wanted in a woman. If you say the word, I'm done looking."

She turned to look at him. "I need some time, James. You can't ask me to make up my mind like this."

"Okay," he said quietly. "I hear you. Just how much time do you think you need?"

"I don't know. I can't quantify that right now. I know that you think you're sure, but I'm not."

"How about Valentine's Day?" he mused.

Another shock raced through her. Valentine's Day had originally been her intended wedding day.

"I can't give you a day."

"Okay," he answered softly, a hint of frustration coloring his reply, "then if you can't give me a specific day can you just do one thing for me while you're trying to make up your mind?"

"What's that?"

"You're not wearing your ring today and I'm sorry but that ring is to me like Kryptonite is to Superman. Nobody but you and I will know if you don't wear it, so maybe you could just leave it in your jewelry box for awhile. Then when we're together you won't be constantly fiddling with it, making both of us think about Dave."

"I'll think about it, James, but you've got to realize that I have years of history with Dave. That just doesn't go away overnight."

"No it won't, but I want a fair shot. I've said my piece. The decision is yours. I promise I won't bug you about it again."

Chapter 23

$\mathcal{P}$atti used FaceTime to call Dave from the common's room in the dorm just after 10 p.m. She would have called from her room but her roomie was home and would hear everything.

She tried to collect her thoughts before she dialed Dave's number. She'd just spent nearly the whole day with James. It was only right that she spent some quality time with Dave so she needed to keep their conversation light and happy.

"Hey girl," Dave answered happily. "You're looking good. How was your Saturday?"

"It was good. I was supposed to do laundry and clean my bathroom but at the last minute I decided to go skiing with a friend."

"I'm jealous. Who did you go with?"

"My roomie," she lied. "We both decided we needed a little break. School this semester sucks so far. Maybe I was stupid for taking those extra classes that will transfer to Purdue."

"How was the weather?"

"Partly sunny. The snow was in great shape."

"I'm jealous. I haven't been on skis in years."

"Neither had I. My legs are going to be sore for a week."

"You should have got in the hot tub before you came home," he said, "that always helps me."

A wave of guilt swept over her. Those were nearly James' words verbatim. "I didn't think to take a swimsuit. My friend said nearly the same thing."

"I wish I could have been there. I could use a break."

"Are your classes really bad?"

"Not so bad really, just a little different. I've got a couple that are focused on specifics rather than theory. I'm sure my postgraduate classes will do that too but I wasn't ready for that quite yet."

"How's Rose?"

Dave laughed. "Ever since Christmas, she and Hershel have been spending a lot of time together. She's so cute for an old lady. I think she's embarrassed by us thinking that she, at her age, has a boyfriend. Even though her house is a lot more comfortable than his, she has been going over to Hershel's place a lot. Just recently, though, she's enlisted him to help her cut out fabric blocks. They spend a lot of time in her quilting room together. She still does breakfast and dinner for us here, but recently Hershel has been coming over to eat with us."

"At least you're getting fed. I was worried about what you were going to do where you weren't living on campus anymore. You're not that great in the kitchen. I figured you'd eat fast food – but then maybe you wouldn't where you're trying to save money."

An incoming call flashed across Patti's phone. It was James. She rejected the call.

"Did you just get a call?" Dave asked, "I heard some clicks in the background."

"It was just my mom. I'll call her back."

"Isn't it a little late for her to be calling?" Dave asked. "Maybe you should call her back. What if something's wrong at home?"

"No, I'm good. She usually calls me on Sunday. Maybe they've got something going tomorrow."

"You can call me back when you're done."

"No that's okay. She can wait."

Another incoming call flashed on her screen. It was James again.

"It sounds like she must really need to talk to you," Dave said as he heard her reject the call again. "Call her back. I'll wait."

"Oh, okay. I'll call you back in a few."

Patti angrily disconnected their FaceTime call and clicked on James' number.

"What do you want?" Patti asked gruffly.

"Hey, I just wanted to talk to you and be sure we're still okay after today," James answered.

"I was in the middle of a FaceTime call with Dave!"

"Sorry."

"I thought you'd get the hint when I rejected your first call," she answered, annoyance coloring her reply. "What's so important that you can't wait for a few minutes? I would have returned your call!"

"Wow, I'm sorry! I must have called at a bad time. Are things okay between you and Dave?"

"They're fine! He heard your calls clicking through. I told him my mom was calling. That was a mistake because when you called again, he was afraid something might be wrong at home and insisted that I call her back."

"Well now that you did, let's chat a little."

"No James! You had your time with me today. I'm calling him back right now, so quit calling!"

She hung up before he could respond and dialed Dave's number.

"Is everything okay?" Dave asked as his worried face appeared on Patti's screen.

"Yes, she didn't know I called you at this time of night and when my first call disconnected, she thought she'd try again. She'll call me tomorrow."

"I didn't mean to take time away from your mom."

"I don't get that much time to talk to you, Dave. My mom can wait."

"You're frowning. Are you sure everything's okay?"

"I'm fine, really," she lied. "I don't get to talk to you very often and I get annoyed when something interferes."

"I'm happy to know I'm still a priority."

"Why wouldn't you be?"

"I don't know. You've seemed distracted lately and you often phone instead of FaceTime."

"It's just school," she lied, "I have to spend a lot more time studying. It's disrupting my routine."

A bad feeling intruded as she thought about what she'd just told Dave. She didn't count how many lies she'd already told him but there had been several. She hated that. A good relationship couldn't be founded on lies and yet…

"I went online today and started looking for apartments," Dave said.

"Why? Won't they be more expensive than Rose's place?"

"Right now my scholarship is paying rent. I thought if I could find something in that same price range they wouldn't care and I could move now and start getting the place ready for us. My spring break starts March 20th. Even though our breaks only overlap by a couple of days, I was thinking you could fly out here and spend your break with me."

Guilt swept over her. She wondered what that would cost? She wondered what James would say? Then she paused in her thoughts. Did it really matter what James thought? She wasn't engaged to James!

"We couldn't go anyplace exotic or far away," Dave continued, "but your plane ticket out here would be cheaper in the long run than it would be for two plane tickets to somewhere else—and we would save the motel room costs. Food would be cheaper, too, if we cooked at home."

She didn't answer right away. She was still mulling the thoughts over in her mind.

"You're frowning again," Dave said quietly. "Is something wrong?"

"No, no," she lied, forcing a smile. "Sorry. I'm just a little distracted."

"So I've noticed," he returned. "Is there something you're not telling me?"

"No Dave!" she exclaimed, perhaps a little too forcefully, "I'm just tired from today. My wardrobe is down to sweats. I'm going to have to stay up late tonight and do laundry so I'll have something to wear tomorrow and I still need to clean my room. I shouldn't have gone skiing."

"Didn't you have a good time on the slopes?"

"Yes of course I did."

"Then don't sweat it. You wouldn't have gone if you didn't need a break."

James' words swept over her. He'd nearly begged her to go skiing with him. In normal fashion, he had refused to take no for an answer. She didn't really need the break from schoolwork and laundry. She wouldn't have gone at all if… Yeah, there was that other factor that she didn't want to face right now. In spite of herself, she liked being with James. It seemed like there was never a dull moment around him.

"I suppose you're right," she admitted, looking straight into the camera. "I miss you Dave. You always have a way of calming me down."

"I wish I'd been there. I'd have gotten you in the hot tub afterward and I'm sure you'd feel better now. You should take an anti-inflammatory tonight if you have one. It might help with the soreness tomorrow."

Her thoughts flashed to the hot tub. Yes, she wished he'd been there. If he had been, the kiss and the touch would have been so much better!

She involuntarily smiled at the thought. Things might have gotten out of hand if he had been though. What if someone had happened upon them?

"You're blushing," Dave laughed, "what are you thinking about?"

She knew she had to lie again, but she had to be careful.

She giggled. "I was just thinking about what might have happened if we'd been alone in a hot tub together. Somebody might have gotten their eyes full."

"That's an erotic thought," Dave laughed. "I'm going to stuff that in my dream bank for later tonight."

***

Their telephone call went longer than usual and by the time they finally disconnected their call, Patti was torn. The call had refreshed her feelings for Dave and left her feeling guilty about the day she'd just spent with James. Worse yet, she hated lying to Dave, but if he knew the truth, the thoughts he'd have stuffed in his dream bank for the night would be more nightmarish than comforting, especially knowing that his rival on the football field was competing for his fiancée's attention.

She'd barely ended her call with Dave when her phone rang again. She hurriedly snatched it up and answered it before she looked at the caller ID.

"Hi Patti," James' voice shook her. She had supposed it was Dave, calling back to wish her one more *goodnight* and one more *I love you*, before bedtime.

"It's late James!" she grumbled.

"I know, and I'm sorry but I've been sitting here alone in my bedroom wondering what sweet things you two were talking about."

"That's none of your business James! Like it or not he's my fiancé! Did you call just so you'd have the last word at the end of the night?"

"Calm down Patti," he insisted. "No, I didn't call with the intent of beating his time. I love you. I just wanted to call to thank you again for going with me today. That's why I called in the first place. I had no idea you were talking to him."

He paused for a moment.

"I had a great time today. I hope you did," he mused.

"I already told you that I did, but your calling right after you knew that I'd been talking with Dave is bad form! You had your time today. I was trying to give Dave some time – even if it wasn't equal time. I'm engaged to him, James. I love him, and you being in my face every waking minute is not going to change that!"

James didn't answer for a few moments for fear she'd sense the anger in his reply. Yes he had tried to be in her face every waking minute. That's the way he worked. He knew that was what it was going to take to get her to break away from Dave. He just didn't want her to see it like that, but now that it seemed she had. He was speechless.

"I'm sorry," he finally responded after furiously searching his thoughts for something to tell her, "I thought you liked being with me. If you don't then either I've been reading more into our relationship than there really is or else you've been sending me signals that I've somehow misread. If you want to talk about bad form, then you're just as guilty as I am. I think you've been purposely leading me on."

"No I haven't!" she countered angrily. "Look back James. I didn't go looking for you in the library every day. I haven't been calling you every day – sometimes half a dozen times a day. In fact I've never actually called you, James, not until tonight to tell you to back off! I feel like you're smothering me!"

"I'm sorry you feel that way!" James answered curtly. "I'll admit I'm infatuated with you. I feel amazing every time I'm with you or when I hear your voice on the phone. I've already told you that I love you. I can't help that. You're the best thing that has ever happened to me. That's why I asked you not to wear your ring when you're with me. I don't want to have to compete with Dave every second we're together! You kissed me Patti! Am I misreading you? Doesn't that mean you feel something for me? If you're just kissing me for the excitement of it then you're no different than those little dude-ranch groupies I dealt with every summer. I thought you were more mature than that!"

She was stunned. Maybe he was right. Maybe all she was feeling was the excitement, the titillation that came with his kisses. His face flashed through her thoughts. She couldn't deny that she felt excitement when she was with him but if she was being honest with herself there was something else as well. She felt at ease with James— actually more so than she did with Dave.

She was shocked by that admission. Why didn't she feel at ease with Dave? Was it the frustration she'd felt from having their relationship drag on for so long without going anywhere? Did she just feel obligated now after all their years together to push him to the next step? The feelings that had flowed over her that night in the hospital swept over her again. For whatever reason, that night she'd reached her breaking point. Their relationship had been stale for so long that she'd almost decided to end it.

A little anger prodded her. Why had it taken something like that to make Dave take her seriously? Now she wondered if he'd suddenly snapped out of it only out of guilt? Were the emotions involved with suddenly reaching the end of his football career the only thing that had pushed him out of his comfort zone? Did Dave really want what they had or was he just moving on – checking a box?

"I don't know what to say," she finally answered James. "Accusing me of just being a member of your little troupe of groupies is pretty harsh!"

"What then?" he prodded. "What am I supposed to be feeling here? Are you single-handedly ending us? Don't I even have a say?"

Now she was speechless. She wasn't sure she wanted to end this onslaught of attention from James but she, in good conscience, simply couldn't let it go on like it had either.

"I think I have my answer!" James angrily answered his own question after a few long moments of silence. "Have a nice life Patti!"

Tears trickled down her cheeks when her phone went silent. She was torn. She was confused. The last thing she wanted to do at this point was go crawling back to James. Dave was still there – like he had been all along. Thankfully, he hadn't had to sit in on James' and her conversation. If he even suspected what was going on between them that would probably have spelled the end of their engagement. He'd never seemed to be the jealous type, but then she'd never given him reason to be.

Patti took a deep breath. In a way she had her answer. She thought about what Dave had suggested for spring break and clicked on the airline app on her smartphone. What he'd said made perfect sense. If nothing else, she needed to be sure that what she still felt for Dave – and he for her – was real. A week together away from school and parents and any other distractions would do that. A roundtrip flight to Indiana in March couldn't cost that much. She knew if she and Dave together couldn't afford it, that she could ask her parents to help. She was sure they'd understand.

She paused as the cell phone app opened up. Was going out to spend the week in an apartment with Dave very smart? They'd barely survived being alone in her bedroom on Thanksgiving. What would a week alone in his apartment look like? Things they had not done on purpose now teased her. But would that be so bad? They were mature adults. Surely they could be careful with each other for a few days – if they set the ground rules beforehand. If they could have afforded going somewhere else for spring break it wouldn't be any different – but spending it with him in Indiana would be a lot cheaper.

When a tear dripped on her cell phone she realized she was emotionally out of control. She had two very different decisions to make. In a way she'd already made a decision about James. She'd lost him but she knew based on what he'd told her that she could rekindle their relationship in a heartbeat – if that's the decision she made. He was frustrated. He was angry, but she thought his recent emotions would be fleeting. The other decision – staying with Dave – seemed easier, and yet it wasn't. If she went to Indiana over spring break and spent a week alone with Dave it would obviously lead to intimacy that would only further cloud both of their decisions.

No longer sure of anything, she decided she needed a good night's sleep and careful consideration of her own emotions. Thankfully, Sunday wasn't spoken for – except for laundry and a good scour of her bathroom. She might even go to church. She always made better decisions after a good spiritual boost. She knew in her heart that either decision at this point was entirely hers to make. It wasn't a decision she should take lightly. Whatever she did would color the rest of her life.

Chapter 24

James threw his cell phone on his bed and violently kicked his trash can across the room! He raged at the thoughts of all the money he'd spent on Patti – the little slut! Including flowers, candy, the tickets to the play, his tux rental, the expensive dinner before and now a day of skiing with all the amenities! And all for what – a few kisses and a quick feel in the hot tub? Pursuing Patti had seemed so simple in his mind. It had worked so well for him before. None of his prior conquests had seen through his façade. He was always the one who had decided when it would end – and how.

He snatched the new throw pillows off his bed in one hand and hurled them at his open closet door. One missed completely. The one that did penetrate the closet blasted half of the hangers off the closet rod, sending his clothes tumbling into a heap. That only further enraged him! He'd been so sure that she was buying what he was selling that now all he could do was stand flat-footed and fume, knowing she'd seen right through him!

He spotted his cell phone and snatched it up. He'd get even! She was so smug and sure of her relationship with *Dear Dave*! What would Dear Dave do when James told him all about their dates, and the kissing? She'd just gotten off the phone with Dave. James was betting she'd told him about going skiing. If she had, he was sure she'd lied to him about who she'd been with. Well, Dear Dave was about to get an earful. By the time James finished, he was sure Dave would call off their engagement.

He grinned evilly to himself as he found Dave's number in his cell phone contacts list. If Dave only believed half of what he was about to tell him, the engagement would be off, especially if he embellished his relationship with Patti a little to include some casual sex! She'd deny it, of course, but even if Dave didn't believe James, seeds of doubt would have been sown. That's all he needed at the moment.

James lifted his finger to make the call and then he hesitated. If he called Dave it might end Patti's engagement but it might also kill any chance he had with her as well—and that was unacceptable. As angry as he was with her, he still had a little hope. He was obsessed! He couldn't imagine himself with anyone else… and after all, he still had the advantage. He was here. Dave was there. It had worked admirably well so far.

He turned off his phone and tossed it back on the bed. Sure they'd had a little setback but he'd only been pursuing her for less than a month. He'd simply made a tactical error. Guessing that she would call Dave sometime before ten, he had deliberately called right in the middle of their phone call. When she'd declined his call the first time, he'd known for sure that she was on the phone with Dave. She'd always answered his calls before. In fact after she declined his call the second time and before she returned his call to tell him to back off, he'd been planning on redialing her at least one more time just to make a statement. What he hadn't expected was her angry response. Unfortunately, he'd allowed himself to feed off her anger and lost his poise. That was bad. Now he'd shown her a chink in his otherwise spotless, shiny armor.

He sat on his bed and studied his hands as he slowly calmed himself down and thought back over the last of their heated conversation. What he'd done was so uncool. An apology would have gone so much further. Now he wondered if he could salvage anything. He knew that calling her back right away would be another tactical error. He needed to give her some time – actually he needed to give himself some time as well to plan his next steps. He'd give her all day Sunday to stew about what *she'd* done. Then rather than call, he'd go see her. He was always better in person than he was on the phone. He knew she loved flowers… She couldn't read his body language over the phone and his body was his best asset.

***

Sandra, her roommate wasn't home when Patti keyed the door and walked inside. She hurriedly gathered up her dirty laundry and hustled back downstairs to the laundry room. She'd planned on going back upstairs while her things washed but there was nobody else in the laundry room and there were chairs so she took a seat and spent time checking her emails instead, thinking about what had happened between James and her and trying to decide what her options were, going forward.

Her day with James on the mountain and then their phone conversation afterward tumbled through her mind almost in rhythm with the rumbling drum on the nearby clothes dryer. His unexpected angry response grated on her nerves. It had seemed so out of character for him… But then maybe it wasn't out of character. What did she really know about James? In reality she'd only known him a few short weeks. In that time, he'd seemed flawless. But was it all an act? Had she just seen a small piece of his real self, tonight – the real self that he kept hidden?

On the other hand, she felt so safe with Dave. James was an unknown – good looking and exciting, but an unknown. She tried to give him the benefit of the doubt. Maybe he'd just been tired too. She knew her emotions were always closer to the surface when she was tired.

***

Sunday dawned dismal – overcast and snowing. At first Patti rolled back over in her bed and pretended to sleep.

"I know you're awake," Sandy teased from across the room. "It's nearly nine. If we're going to make church you need to get up."

"How can you be so wide awake? I know *you* were out late too," Patti responded without rolling over. "I know you weren't home before midnight."

"Actually I was in bed early," Sandra laughed. "I just didn't get up and come home until this morning."

Patti sat bolt upright in bed and swung her legs over the side. "Oh my heck! I didn't think you and Fred…"

"Don't go jumping to conclusions!" Sandra laughed. "I drove to Greeley yesterday to visit my aunt and I was too tired to drive home. She insisted that I stay over. I only got home a few minutes ago. By the way, I saw James picking you up yesterday."

"Yeah, we went skiing."

"How was that?"

"Fun but I'll be sore today. I haven't done that in a couple of years."

"You seem to be spending a lot of time with him lately. I thought you were engaged?"

"I am. James is just a friend."

"I'd be careful with that. You may not know this but he has quite a reputation."

"Yeah, he told me about the dude ranch."

"I don't know anything about a dude ranch. I'm talking about Colorado State. You were probably too wrapped up with Dave to keep up on the gossip but he's a heartbreaker."

"Really?"

"Do you want names?"

"I probably wouldn't know them anyway. Are there a lot?"

"Enough that nearly everyone in the dorm has blacklisted him. I was really surprised to see you hanging out with him."

"I wish I'd known all this a month ago."

"You're not involved with him, are you?"

Patti hesitated. She wanted to say no but after yesterday…

"Oh my heck!" Sandra exclaimed. "You are, aren't you?"

"Not really. It's just a casual thing. We study together at the library. He took me to a play in Denver though. His sister had tickets to *Les Misérables* that she couldn't use."

"And then he took you skiing yesterday? I'd say that pretty much qualifies as seeing him."

"It's not like that."

"Hey, it's not my place to badmouth the guy. Everything I've heard is third or fourth hand and you know how the gossip train around here gathers momentum."

"He seems okay to me. He's fun to be with."

"And it doesn't hurt that he's drop-dead gorgeous either, but you're engaged. What does James think about that?"

"He doesn't want me to wear my ring."

"I'd say that's a warning signal. I don't know you very well, Patti, but please be careful. I hear he's a lady killer."

"A lady killer?"

Sandra laughed. "Sorry, that's a term my mom used to use. That means he's a slick character and leaves a lot of used-up women in his wake. Are you and Dave on the outs?"

"No not really. I'm just lonely. He's at Purdue. We talk or FaceTime almost every day."

"But he's not here to defend himself, right? How do you really feel about him? In your mind is the engagement still on?"

"Yes."

"Are you sure? I know if I were engaged, I wouldn't be dating around."

"I'm not…"

"Okay, never mind. I don't want to make you mad. I'm just saying…"

"You're probably right. That's okay though. James and I had words last night and I think it's over anyway."

***

Patti and Sandra hurried off to church together. Even though the speakers in church were good, Patti couldn't concentrate. If James was a so-called lady killer like Sandra had said he was then she'd escaped in the nick of time. But what if he wasn't? People could change. He'd admitted to his flirtations at the dude ranch. What if all his relationships at college had been more of the same? He certainly had charm. The James she knew seemed okay. At least what he'd shown her seemed honest enough.

"You were a million miles away during church," Sandra said with a smile as they left the building. "Who's on your mind, James or Dave?"

"Both really."

"And?"

"I don't know."

Sandra looked over at her. "I told you this morning that if I were engaged, I wouldn't be dating. I don't want to make you mad but it looks to me like you've just been leading James on. I'd say if you're not sure about Dave then maybe you should break off your engagement. There's nothing worse than getting stuck in a marriage you hate."

"I can't do that. Not yet anyway. Maybe I'm just lonely. Maybe I'm confused."

"And maybe this thing with James isn't all it's cracked up to be," Sandra finished for her.

229

Patti didn't answer for a few moments as they walked on in the gently falling snow.

"I've been thinking about going out to see Dave over spring break," Patti finally continued.

"Do you think that's a good idea?" Sandra asked. "Going out there means staying with him, doesn't it? Are you ready to add a few more complications to your relationship?"

"I've been thinking about that. Dave and I have been celibate so far – not that I really wanted to."

"Well I'd say if you wanted to and he wanted to, but you didn't, when you get together for a week at his place you won't come home the same. Pardon me if I say so, but once you go to that next step it clouds your reason."

"You really think so?"

"It's a fact, Jack! All you'll be able to think about is how great that all felt, not necessarily what you really think about him. Once you do that, the next step is marriage and what if you get into that six months and find out you messed up?"

"What should I do?"

"I can't tell you that, Patti, but if you're even considering that you better go get on the pill. Spring break is only a little over a month away and it takes a little time for your body to react."

Patti recoiled at the thought. If she did that, there would be nothing holding them back.

"From what I can see," Sandy continued, "you've got a lot of deciding to do. The problem as I see it is James isn't one to let any grass grow on his dating shoes, if you catch my drift. If he's already taken you to a downtown play and now skiing, I'd say he's pretty serious."

"But what if he isn't? What if he's just been playing me? You told me before we went to church that he's a lady killer. How can I decide if he's really interested?"

"Use your common sense, not your emotions Patti. In the finance world they tell you that if something sounds too good to be true, it usually is."

Sandra waited for a few moments before she continued. "What are your impressions of James so far?"

"I'm in a tailspin. I'm lonely with Dave gone, and James hardly lets my feet touch the ground. He wants to be with me all the time."

"That can be good or bad. I've heard about guys that swarm you to try to drive away all of the competition, but if he's seeing the real you, like I do, he's got to know that you're an amazing person. If he's been around a lot maybe he knows that you're the real deal and just wants to be around you all the time. Do you know if he's seeing anyone else?"

"I've only been hanging around with him for a few weeks but I don't think so. He's with me all of the time."

"You told me you had words. How bad was that?"

"I was mad. He called when I was talking to Dave on FaceTime. I rejected his call and he called right back. Dave heard the clicks so I told him my mom was calling. Dave insisted I call back so I called James and jumped his case. He didn't like it much. He told me to have a good life and hung up."

"I can't say that's a good thing but it's not bad either. If you decide to end it, it's already over. If you decide to break off your engagement, I'll bet James would take you back in a heartbeat."

Neither of them said anything for a few more moments.

"You've got to know, though Patti, that the ball is in your court now. You'd better be ready to live with whatever decision you make."

***

Patti decided to take a walk by herself after dinner. She had a lot of things on her mind and walking outside in the gently falling snow seemed to be a good choice. Her meandering walk eventually took her a couple of miles from her dorm. When the wind picked up a little, driving the cold through her light coat, she stopped at a diner to get out of the storm and warm up a little.

She found an empty booth in the corner, settled in with a hot chocolate and an apple fritter and glanced at her phone. She'd planned on calling Dave around nine. It was early but it was Sunday. She doubted he'd put off homework until that late. Instead of using FaceTime there in the diner where people could eavesdrop, she phoned him.

"I've been thinking more about flying out there over spring break," Patti told Dave a couple of minutes into their conversation, "but I'm a little nervous about that."

"Because of the sleeping accommodations?" Dave asked.

"Yes."

"I've been thinking the same thing but maybe that wouldn't be so bad."

"It would be great," she said softly, "but…"

"I know what you're thinking. You already told me you didn't want to feel guilty about wearing white."

"There's more to it than that."

"What?"

"I think it'll cloud our judgement."

"Are you having second thoughts Patti?"

She *was* having second thoughts but the last thing she wanted to do was blurt out all of the reasons why. She knew if she told him

232

about James, Dave would probably end it in a flash of anger. She didn't want it to end that way – if it did. She needed more time before she made that decision.

"Not really," she answered after a pause.

"Have you been seeing someone else?"

"No," she lied. "I'm just frustrated and lonely."

"I'm sorry Patti. I've made a mess of this, haven't I? I can't believe I was so blind."

"Are you sure it was blindness," she ventured, "or were you just comfortable with things the way they were?"

"I don't know how to answer that. I've loved you since high school. You've always been my best friend. Maybe I was too comfortable with you. You obviously wanted things to progress in our relationship and all I could see were all the reasons why getting married would be hard."

"And now?"

"I don't think things will be any easier, but I think I'm ready to face the challenges."

"Is that the way you see me – a challenge?"

"Not you, our relationship! This can't be any easier for you."

"I guess I'm seeing this a little differently than you are," she answered. "I was frankly really looking forward to doing all this – school, marriage, etc. – together. To me it's exciting, not something to be afraid of."

"I think we're saying the same thing."

"No, I really don't think we are. Right now, I'm feeling like I'm something that's just going to add more stress to your life. Be honest with me, Dave. If I hadn't walked away that night after your injury would anything have changed? I feel like I forced your hand. In fact,

I'll take it a step further. If you hadn't gotten hurt, where do you think our relationship would be right now?"

"I'd still be at Colorado State," he answered quickly. "I'd be playing football next year. I'd still have an athletic scholarship."

"That's not what I asked. I didn't ask where *your* life would be. I asked where *our* lives would be. There's a difference Dave. Do you think we'd be engaged?"

Dave didn't answer.

"That's what I thought," Patti said after a few moments. "Did you plan to give me a diamond for Christmas before all this happened?"

He was dumfounded. No, he hadn't planned on doing that—not that he regretted doing it now, though.

"Your silence is shouting out your answer," she said quietly. "I think we need to take a break from all this for awhile, Dave. I'll mail your ring to you. Maybe after we've both had some time to consider our priorities, we can try this again."

Patti ended the call before Dave could respond. Tears flooded down her cheeks. Her breath came in soft sobs. She just felt like she'd ripped her heart out and thrown it under the table.

Her phone buzzed. It was Dave calling back. She declined his call. She was hemorrhaging the love that she had so carefully stowed away in her heart for nearly four years. There was no going back now. In her mind what she'd just done to their relationship was fatal.

She turned to peer out into the storm. Heavy swirls of snowbands, driven by a moderate wind, played under the streetlights.

She softly cursed herself for walking. She was a couple of miles from the campus. She'd be frozen and wet by the time she got back. Sandra didn't have a car – but James did.

Somewhat desperate she found James' number in her phone.

"Hi Patti," James answered somewhat irritably, "what's up?"

"What are you doing?"

"Watching TV."

"Feel like some company?"

"I thought we said all we had to say last night."

"I was angry, James, you called me right in the middle of my phone call with Dave."

A long pause passed between them.

"Where are you?" James finally asked.

"At a diner a couple of miles from campus."

"What are you doing there?"

"I had a lot on my mind. I went for a walk."

"It's awful outside. Why would you walk in this?"

"It wasn't so awful when I left."

"I could pick you up, if you'd like."

"Would you please? I'd like to talk."

James launched into a flurry of activity. She said she wanted company – that she wanted to talk. It would be too cold to sit outside in the car for any length of time. He knew she had a roommate. Talking in her dorm would be awkward. He wondered if she'd agree to come to his house instead? He hurriedly cleaned up the clutter he'd let accumulate and replaced the pillows he'd hurled across the room the night before. By the time he scraped the snow off his car and drove to the diner, over fifteen minutes had passed. He saw her watching from a booth as he drove up. He jumped out and started in but she slipped outside before he could get to the door.

"Hey James," she said as he held the car door open for her, "thanks for coming to my rescue. It was dumb going out in this."

He didn't answer until he climbed in beside her.

"Sorry it took me so long," he finally answered as he shut the storm outside his door. "I had to scrape the windows. It's still cold in here. The heater has just barely started blowing warm air."

"We could go to your place," she suggested.

Her words broadsided him. He'd wondered ever since they met how he could get her into his room. "Are you sure you want to do that?" he asked.

"I'm not afraid of you James. It's too cold to sit in the car for long and I don't want all the women in my dorm knowing my business so we can't go there."

"It looks like you've been crying."

"That's another reason why I don't want to go back to my dorm."

"My fault?" he asked quietly.

"No, it's mine actually. I just broke up with Dave."

"Really? I'm so sorry to hear that."

"Be honest James. Are you really?"

"Okay if I'm being honest, I'd say no. You know how I feel about you."

"Even after last night?"

"I was angry and frustrated last night. I've been kicking myself ever since I hung up the phone."

"I'm sorry for what I said," Patti answered. "I was angry and frustrated too."

"Are you sure you want to go to my place?"

"Yes. It's not even midnight. I've been bawling and I don't want to have to talk to my roommate about it. You know how women are. It'd be all over campus by morning."

"Your coming to my house would be worse."

"I don't plan to spend the night, James. I just want to have some time to calm down and talk. Can I trust you to not spread this all around campus?"

"I don't talk about things like that and my roommates were all in their rooms when I left," James said. "If we're quiet, they'll never even know you're there. The bedrooms are pretty spread out. There are two upstairs and two down. Mine is on the main floor. I don't think anyone will see you come in and even if they do, we'll just make sure we make a bunch of noise when you leave so they will know you didn't sleep over."

She was looking at him through tear-stained eyes, considering his reply.

"Yes you can trust me," he finished earnestly. "I won't do anything you don't want me to."

"That might be a problem then," she replied.

"Oh wow! I don't know how to answer that. You're really putting me on the spot. Being who I am I'm over the moon with that insinuation, but considering that you just went through a breakup I'm worried. I don't want to take advantage of you."

"Let's just go and see where this leads us."

Chapter 25

Daylight found Patti lying naked on her back under the blankets, listening to James' deep, even breathing beside her. She'd been lying awake for awhile. What they'd done had driven a stake through her heart that she'd already thrown under the table at the diner the night before. There was no going back now. She was embarrassed! She hadn't meant for this to happen! First, they'd just talked. Then he'd held her while she cried. The rest was just a blur.

Anxiety swept over her. It had to be nearly 7 a.m. She had a class at eight. How could she discretely get out of bed, get dressed, and get back to the dorm without…

"You awake?" James asked quietly.

"Yes."

"You have class this morning."

"At eight."

"Do you want to shower before I take you home?"

"No. I need to change before I go to school and everything's in my room."

"Your clothes are on the chair."

"Are you going to watch?"

"I won't if you're uncomfortable, but after last night…"

"It was dark last night."

"Outside maybe."

"Please just turn your back."

James turned his back just long enough for her to throw off the covers and step out of bed and then he sat straight up in bed and watched with hungry eyes while she walked over to the chair.

"I told you to turn your back James!" Patti shouted as she tried to hold her shirt up to cover herself.

"Why? It's not like I didn't see it all last night. Why don't you just skip school today and come back to bed?" he asked, passion coloring his reply.

"What happened last night was a mistake James. Are you going to drive me, or are you going to make we walk?"

"It's too far to walk. I'll buy you breakfast on the way back to your dorm."

"I don't have time. Please James. Don't make this any harder than it already is."

"It didn't feel to me like a mistake last night."

"I was out of my mind last night. Are you going to look away or not?"

"No. I don't know what the big deal is. You've got a beautiful body Patti. You've got nothing to be ashamed of."

"That's not the issue James. I'm embarrassed. Nobody's ever seen me naked before."

"Not even Dave?"

"No, not even Dave!"

"Then he missed out. Are you telling me that I'm your first?"

"Yes but don't get a big head about it. I already told you that this was a huge mistake!"

Not wanting to argue, Patti turned her back and hurriedly threw on her clothes. Her face felt like it was on fire.

***

Sandra was gone when Patti walked into her dorm room so she decided to skip her first class. She cried for awhile as she stood in the shower and then walked across the street to the cafeteria. James was there. The last thing she wanted to do right then was talk to him but he'd seen her first and motioned her to his table.

"I didn't know you ate at the cafeteria," she said as she picked a couple of items off the serving line and joined him.

"Sorry about this morning," he replied quietly so nobody else could hear him. "I couldn't help myself. You are the most fantastic-looking woman I've ever met."

"I was naked, James, I don't think you were being very judgmental."

"You already know I've been around, Patti. I'm not lying to you. I wish you would have stayed."

"What we did last night was a mistake, James, a huge one! You knew I was an emotional wreck. I'd just broken off my engagement. The last thing I needed was to end up in bed with you!"

"Hold it down a little," James whispered. "You're getting loud."

"I feel like screaming at you!" she hissed. "All you did was add another notch in your belt!"

"It's not that way!" he said earnestly, trying to keep his voice down. "I've already told you a dozen times that I love you. What we did last night was beautiful!"

"How can you really say that? How can you love a person you only met three weeks ago?"

"It doesn't take me four years to decide whether or not I love someone."

"That's poor form!" she hissed. "You leave Dave out of this!"

"I'd love nothing more! I need you Patti. Marry me!"

"Are you insane? You barely know me!"

"I know you well enough to know that I want to spend the rest of my life with you."

She wanted to look away but she couldn't. His eyes seemed to be drawing her in.

He reached across the table and took her hand. Her first reaction was to jerk it away, but somehow, she couldn't.

"I know you're confused after last night," he said quietly, "and I'm really sorry it happened that way. Maybe you were upset and vulnerable, but I wasn't. Give me a chance Patti. I know I can make you happy. How many ways can I tell you that I love you?"

She looked down at her hand captured by his. Even though she was still embarrassed, a chill passed through her. Maybe he was a lady killer and she'd just become his latest victim – but what if in her case he wasn't? She couldn't honestly tell herself that she was repulsed by him – quite the opposite was true in fact. She did know one thing for sure, though, if this was going to happen between them she needed time – not four years, of course, but time.

"I need to slow down," she heard herself whispering to him as she looked up. "I need to be able to get my feet back under me."

James smiled, not a lustful, evil smile that she expected, but a warm, understanding smile that seemed to stop some of the hemorrhage going on in her chest where her heart had once been.

"I'll give you all the time you need," he muttered. "I need this to work between us. I really do. You accused me Saturday night of smothering you. I'm sorry you saw it that way. That certainly wasn't my intent. I can back off a little if you want me to but I'll tell you right now, that's not going to be easy. My heart explodes inside me whenever I'm near you. To coin an old, overused cliché: *I'm drawn to you like a moth to the flame.* All I can see is you."

She felt the passion in his eyes, blushed and looked down at their entwined hands.

"I really wanted you to spend the day with me," he began, "but in lieu of what's happened, I guess we both need a cooling off period. Can I call you tonight?"

"No. I need a couple of days."

"That's fair enough. How about Wednesday? Is that too soon? I'll even go one step further; I won't go to the library to study in the meantime."

"I don't know. I'll call you."

"Will you really, or is this just a way to let me down easy?"

"Yes, I'll call you. By then maybe I'll be able to wrap my head around all this."

Chapter 26

Dave sat dumbfounded on the edge of his bed after Patti hung up and simply stared at his phone. He had been a little worried the past couple of weeks because of Patti's lack of enthusiasm when she called, instead of using FaceTime, but he'd been blindsided by how quickly their call had gone south.

He racked his brain. What had he said to set her off?

Then their years-old relationship drifted through his mind and he finally saw the truth. Everything had been about *him*, not *them*. He ached inside. Yes he'd lost his best friend but now he realized that he'd lost infinitely more. He felt nauseous. He thought back over the time they'd spent together around Thanksgiving. Maybe for the first time in their relationship he'd seen her as a desirable woman and not just his best friend.

He silently cursed the weather and school and …

Then he realized those were just tiny moments in all the time they'd known each other. He hated to admit it but maybe she was right to have stepped away. She'd had expectations all through their high school days together or she wouldn't have followed him to Colorado State. He'd been so blind – so selfish!

He softly made his way downstairs to the refrigerator.

"Hey," Claire said from the semidarkness of the living room, "how did your phone call go?"

"Not well," he said as emotion choked him. "I think we just broke up."

"Oh wow! What happened?"

Dave took his customary seat on the far end of Rose's sofa and took a drink before he answered.

"When I look at what happened, I realized that this has been coming for a long time. I was just too blind to see it."

"You told me that you've been dating for something like four years. Did she get tired of waiting?"

"In a word, yes, and that's all my fault. She was the best thing that ever happened in my life and I guess I got too comfortable with just being friends. She wanted more."

"That's understandable. Her biological clock is ticking. She probably wanted a home and a family."

"I couldn't give her that right now."

"Sure you could have. Tons of your peers suffer through the early years together. Sacrifice can bond you and build character."

"Yeah, I suppose you're right. We actually talked about that – but not until it was too late. And there again that's all my fault. I didn't have to take this stupid offer at Purdue this winter and walk out on her. If I'd just finished my junior year there, we'd have been married. Now that I look back, that was the final straw. We had a great time together at Thanksgiving and I was finally seeing her for the woman that she is."

"And then you came here, got snarled in a snowstorm, and went off to Raytheon."

"Uh huh. You know the story."

"Are you sure it's over?"

"I think so. She told me she was going to mail her ring to me."

"Maybe if you try to keep in touch and then go out there over spring break you can rekindle your relationship. If she loves you I think she'll be just as heartbroken over this breakup as you are. You need to show her that you're serious."

"A long distance relationship might have worked if we were both passionate about it."

"You seem pretty passionate."

"But from what I heard on the phone tonight, she isn't. The fire I sensed in her at Thanksgiving is gone. What I heard was the same sadness that I heard that night in the hospital. After she hung up tonight, I tried to call her right back but she wouldn't answer."

"That's understandable. I'm sure she was pretty emotional. Give her a few days and then try calling her back again, but when you do, you better have a speech all prepared."

"I can't do that."

"Yes you can, and even if she thinks you're reading from a sheet of paper you need to have a firm plan for getting together and then try to convince her why your relationship can thrive. I've been listening to your heart as you've been sitting here with me Dave. Yeah, you've got a lot of placid history to overcome but I can feel the passion behind what you've been telling me. I have no doubt that you love her but you need to convince her that you're a changed man. I don't know how you're going to do that over the phone but you need to be prepared to sweep her off her feet."

"I wish I could do that in person."

"Maybe you should."

"I'm in school."

"What's more important, a few catch-up study sessions after a week out there with her or…"

"I can't afford to let my GPA slip! My scholarship going forward depends on it."

Claire studied him for a few moments before she answered. "I think you just answered your own question," she finally continued, "I can clearly see what the priority is in your life, Dave, and in my opinion she made the right choice."

Without another word, Claire got to her feet and headed for the stairway.

Dave watched her walk away without saying a word. She was right. He was so blinded by visions of where he wanted to go that he was incapable of seeing anything else – including Patti.

He mulled those thoughts over and over in his mind as he slowly sipped his drink. Was he so indoctrinated by what he thought success looked like that he'd lost sight of the other things in his life? The real question, though, was he capable of changing? Worse yet did he want to change?

***

The next couple of weeks for Dave dragged slowly by. He dutifully pushed his emotions aside as he judiciously waded through his studies. There were a few instances as he exhaustedly got ready for bed at the end of the day when he picked up his phone and entered Patti's number – only to turn his phone off before he pressed the send button. He hadn't had the time to prepare a speech as Claire had suggested and he knew it would take something out of the ordinary to make Patti change her mind. Then suddenly he realized it'd been two weeks since their infamous last phone call. Now, by his seeming disinterest, he'd sent her a message far more impressive than any speech he might have made.

He thought about Valentine's Day and the plans they'd made at Thanksgiving. He wondered if Patti was thinking the same thing. He wondered if she'd been able to set their years together aside as easily as he had seemingly done? Truthfully, he had been able to think of little else lately. Thoughts of her constantly interrupted him at the most inopportune times. During a pop quiz, his mind had locked on the thoughts of her bedroom door and what hadn't happened behind it. He hadn't done well on the quiz simply because he'd spent too much time staring blankly at his test and run out of time.

***

Dave got a small package in the mail a couple of days later. He knew what was in it without opening it but he dutifully slit the tape and pulled out Patti's ring box. The glint of the diamond brought down the finality of it all. He'd hoped she'd reconsider – but he only had himself to blame. In spite of his good intentions he hadn't called her since their breakup.

***

"Claire tells me you've got problems at home," Rose brought up the subject over dinner. "I could tell that something was going on. You've been unusually quiet lately."

"Yeah, my girlfriend called off our engagement."

"Oh you poor dear," Rose said. "I don't suppose there's anything I can do for you is there?"

Dave glanced at Claire. "No Rose, there isn't. Claire gave me some really good advice the day after it happened but I haven't been able to force myself to face the reality of it."

"You mean you haven't called her?" Claire exclaimed. "Why not?"

"I just couldn't build that speech you suggested."

"I'm an old woman," Rose interjected, "and probably don't know the ways of the world these days, but it seems to me that your not calling to apologize or something sent her a clear message. What did you get in the mail today?"

"Her engagement ring."

"Oh my! I'm so sorry."

"Why didn't you call her?" Claire insisted.

"I don't know. I just couldn't go there. She broke it off, not me. I didn't feel like begging."

"Maybe she was looking for a little begging," Claire said. "I guess your silence speaks volumes."

"Yeah, I suppose it does."

"You're going to just flush four years of history without even trying?"

"You don't understand," Dave said.

"I'm a disinterested third party!" Claire argued, "and I think I understand just fine! It appears to me that she was right in breaking it off. I don't think you are as in love with her as you claim you are."

"And you don't know what you're talking about!" Dave growled as he got to his feet. "Sorry Rose, I just lost my appetite!"

Dave stormed out of the front door, got in his car and just drove. He didn't really pay any attention to where he was going, he just followed the road. A half hour later, he pulled into a Walmart parking lot and just sat there as a hundred thoughts flowed over him. He wasn't being very mature about all of this. The two women in his house were absolutely right. If he cared anything about his relationship with Patti he'd have at least tried calling her. If she'd rejected his call he'd have gotten the message. As it was, he hadn't even tried.

Dave's phone buzzed and he glanced down at the caller ID. It was Claire. He rejected the call and then as he went to slip his phone back into his pocket, he stopped and then punched Patti's phone number into his screen for the twentieth time since their breakup. As he studied those glowing digits his thumb involuntarily pressed the green call button. Patti answered before he could end the call.

"Dave?" came her soft voice. "Is everything okay?"

"No. It hasn't been okay since we talked last."

"I'm sorry."

"Don't be. This is all on me. Are you alright? I, uh, just needed to hear your voice."

A long pause passed between them.

"Did you get my ring?"

"Yes. I got it in the mail today. You could have kept it. You know where we bought it. You could have taken it back."

"I thought you may want it."

"Why? Even if I ever move on, I couldn't give it to anyone else."

"You never called."

"I figured you said all there was to say."

"So I guess that means you didn't want to argue?"

"I could tell by the sound of your voice that you had pretty well made up your mind."

"I was exhausted, and I wasn't in a good place. I kept hoping you'd call."

"You have *my* number."

"Yes I do, but under the circumstances I thought you may want to talk things out."

"I did but I couldn't face that again."

She didn't answer for awhile.

"I moved in with James," she finally continued softly.

"You what!" he screamed into the phone. "Of all people, why him? He's an asshole!"

"No Dave, he isn't. Maybe for the first time in my life I feel wanted and needed."

"So you went from not wanting to lock your bedroom door for fear of what we might do to jumping into the sack with James?"

"He was here when I needed him."

"Yeah I'll just bet he was, and I'll bet he has perma-grin plastered all over his face! You disgust me Patti!"

Before she could answer, Dave ended the call, stuffed his phone in his shirt pocket and slammed the palms of his hands over and over again into the steering wheel. Too angry to drive, he got out of the car and marched angrily around the expansive parking lot until exhaustion and cold drove him back to his car.

"Why him?" he shouted at nobody as he slammed the car door behind him. "He's the most self-centered, egotistical jerk I know!"

The shock of who he'd lost and who he'd lost her to, battered down the walls of disinterest and self-preservation that he'd been building up around himself ever since their last call. Hot tears streamed down his face as he screamed obscenities at nobody.

Chapter 27

James persuaded Patti to move out of the dorms and stay with him in his rented house, pointing out that she'd save the monthly rent. She didn't have much stuff and what she did have, they easily packed into James' room.

Two weeks later things were working well except for the fact that they had to share the bathroom on the main floor with his other roommate. There was really no room in the small bathroom for everyone's toiletries so James brought her a cardboard box that she could put all of her things in. It was inconvenient to pack it back and forth from his bedroom to the bathroom, but it worked.

She had locked herself in the bathroom a few mornings later to shower and do her hair when the roommate, Tony, tried the locked door and then knocked.

When she told him she'd be just a minute, he walked away grumbling. Moments later James kicked the door open, leaving her standing there naked!

"You're not the only one who lives here!" James bellowed. "You can't lock the door! People need to use the john!"

"In case you haven't noticed," she bellowed back, holding a towel up in front of her, "I'm a woman James! I need a little privacy!"

James grabbed her roughly by the arm and dragged her out of the bathroom in front of his roommate, ripping her towel away from her as he did.

"Now Tony has seen you, too, so you don't have anything to hide. If you're uncomfortable with that, shower when nobody else is home!"

She thrust out her hand. "Give me my towel back!" she screamed at him.

James grinned and threw her towel on the floor at Tony's feet. "Bend over and pick it up," he taunted her, "and while you're down on your knees, take care of Tony. I figure that's the least you can do where you're living here rent free."

Humiliated, she ran down the hall and slammed his bedroom door behind her.

A hundred thoughts screamed through her mind as she fumbled in the closet for something to wear. The first two weeks with James had been exciting and unreal! They'd done things that she'd never dreamed of doing before. And then, the last few days his requests had turned dark, even to the point of him hinting that he wanted to share her with Tony. This latest episode only shouted of that filthy request. She hadn't moved in here to play the house whore!

She pulled a sweatshirt over her head, picked up her cell phone and dialed Sandy's number.

"Hey Sandy!" she cried when her ex-roommate answered, "this is Patti. Do you have a new roomie yet?"

"Hey Patti. It's good hearing from you. Yes, I'm sorry, there's a waiting list for the dorms. A new girl moved in two days after you left. Aren't things working out between you and James?"

"No they're not!" she cried. "I can't live here!"

Suddenly James grabbed her phone away, ended the call and stuffed the phone in his pocket.

"You don't need to be telling your lies all over campus!" he roared.

"Give me my phone back!" she screeched. "I'm getting out of here even if I have to go live in a cardboard box!"

"Then you'll be walking!" he yelled back at her, holding up her car keys. "Good luck with all that! Oh and by the way, my house key is on this keyring. You walk out now and you'll be leaving everything behind!"

"What's wrong with you!" she screamed at him, lashing out with her fists.

James easily caught both of her arms and spun her around, shoving her face first down on the bed, wearing nothing but her sweatshirt.

"Knock it off!" she shrieked as he held both of her wrists with one hand as he yanked at his belt buckle with his other.

A few horrible minutes later he released her, backed away and stalked out of the room, leaving her crying and writhing in pain.

She cried alone in his room for what seemed like half of the morning. She was shocked and disgusted by what he'd done to her. She was missing classes but she had no choice. He had her phone and her car keys. He'd even taken her backpack with him when he left, leaving her without her laptop too. She couldn't even email her mom to tell her to come and get her. If she left and walked the four miles to campus she'd come back to a locked house.

When she finally had the presence of mind to get dressed and walk out into the kitchen, she found herself alone. Worse yet, it was snowing again! She wondered if it ever quit snowing in this godforsaken town?

Hungry, she rummaged through the mostly-empty refrigerator. There was no bread in the house so she had to settle for a few slices of cheese on bologna topped off with a couple of pickles.

***

James keyed the front door just before noon. She'd been sitting on the living room sofa watching television. When she saw him, she leapt to her feet, intending on running to their bedroom. Then she stopped. If she slammed the door and locked it behind her, James would just kick it in the way he'd done to the bathroom door. There was no place to hide. Instead she spun around to angrily glare at him.

"I'm so sorry for this morning," James said softly as he cautiously approached, holding out a bouquet of red roses in front of him. "I don't know what came over me Patti. When I saw you naked I couldn't help myself. You're beautiful! You pushed all my buttons!"

Gone was the evil scowl that she remembered seeing on his face that morning. Instead he wore an expression that reminded her of a sad, whipped puppy. Somehow, she couldn't look away. Tears stood in the corners of his eyes.

"Please Patti," he begged, "I'm so sorry for what happened. We hadn't done anything in a couple of days and I was… well, where you hardly had anything on I was so turned on seeing you like that, I couldn't help myself."

"You raped me, James!" she exclaimed, "and in the worst possible way!"

"No I didn't." he argued softly, "I thought you would like doing something different. We've done about everything else there is to do."

"You crossed the line James!" she argued. "There's nothing erotic or loving about being forced, especially from behind!"

"I was just playing," he countered. "You didn't seem to be put off by anything else we've done. Really Patti," he continued softly, "I'm terribly sorry. I didn't think it would be that big of a deal."

She didn't respond.

He reached into his pocket and held out her cell phone. "It was wrong for me to take your phone. I love you Patti! Can you forgive me? Nothing like this will ever happen again, I promise."

She took her phone and folded her arms petulantly in front of her but she still didn't respond.

"I realized right after class that I'd taken your car keys too and you didn't have any way of getting to school – or going to lunch. I'll bet you're starved!"

"There's nothing in this house to eat!" she fumed, "except bologna, cheese, and pickles!"

"What can I say?" he asked sheepishly, "this is a bachelor pad. We usually eat out – or in the cafeteria. We used to buy snacks but that just caused arguments over who was eating whose food. Let me take you to lunch."

"I've already eaten, such as it was."

"Do you have an afternoon class?"

"You know I do."

"It's snowing. Let me drive you. After class I'll take you to The Grill. They serve the best ribs!"

"Isn't that expensive?"

"It's not that bad, and besides I owe you."

"I don't know if I'm in the mood to go to school."

"I can't say as I blame you, and that's my bad. Please Patti, I'm trying really hard here. I'm sorry again for this morning. I promise nothing like that will ever happen again."

"What about Tony? I'm sure he thinks he can have me anytime he wants now. You totally humiliated me in front of him!"

"I'll apologize to him tonight. I think he was just as embarrassed as you were."

"Oh I don't think so! He wasn't naked!"

"No, he wasn't. Come on Patti! I'm trying really hard here. Won't you give me another chance?"

She didn't know why but she melted. He'd brought flowers. He'd apologized. He sounded sincere.

He must have noticed the change in her countenance because he stepped close and pulled her against him. Moments later their lips met and she felt like maybe he truly was sorry.

***

James' promise lasted about a week but she was still sore and in spite of his almost begging, she purposely hugged her side of the bed when they went to bed at night.

"What's wrong with you, you slut!" he raged after she turned him away for the fifth or sixth time, "I told you I was sorry!"

"I'm still sore, James. You made me bleed."

"Sorry," he answered sarcastically, "I forgot you were a whiny, little virgin!"

"I wasn't bleeding from the front, you ass! Of course you've probably had your share of virgins before, with you abusing all of those innocent, little girls at camp!"

James violently kicked her square in the back, sending her sprawling out of bed. As she struggled to her feet, he grabbed her by her hair and dragged her back up on the bed.

She struggled to fight him off, but the more she struggled, the harder he fought her. Finally, afraid he was going to slug her in the face, she simply went limp.

James didn't skip a beat. Seconds later she had to force herself to keep from vomiting in his face as he moved over her.

Long minutes later his deep breathing filled the room.

Patti slipped quietly out of bed, got dressed, dropped her phone in her purse, pulled on her coat, and walked numbly out into the cold. She needed to get away but she didn't know where to go! She should drive. James' co-rented house wasn't located in the best part of town but frankly, at that point she didn't care. Tears of frustration, rage, fear, shame, and loss streamed down her face as she turned and stomped down the sidewalk, gasping for breath as she walked. She probably couldn't see well enough to drive anyway! She'd been with James less than a month now and her greatest fears had begun to reveal themselves. In a matter of what seemed to be only days, he had transformed from an erotic, sensitive lover into something evil and loathsome. Sandy had been right. James was a lady killer and she, it seemed, had become his latest victim!

She stopped on the sidewalk a while later, bent over and vomited in the snow.

Suddenly her mind vaulted into shock. Along with being sore from being brutalized, she'd been sick to her stomach a couple of mornings in a row now. Worse yet, she was late – only a few days – but she'd never been late before.

The terror of what she was thinking now turned her around. There was a drugstore nearby and she needed to know!

***

Patti visited the ladies room in the Walgreens where she'd bought an EPT, followed the instructions and waited. Moments later she was fighting off a panic attack. Her life was over! She was pregnant by a man who she feared more every day. What options did she have? There were a few. She could count the days since their first unprotected encounter. Thoughts of abortion crossed her mind. She didn't want James' baby! She didn't want anybody's baby! But want it or not…

She walked numbly out into the cold crying the whole time and mulling over her options. Finally, freezing and barely in control of herself, she walked back to James' house.

"Where have you been?" James demanded the moment she opened their bedroom door.

"Walking."

"In this neighborhood? Are you insane?"

"I'm late, James," she blurted, "and worse yet, I picked up a test. I'm pregnant!"

"How can you be pregnant?" he bellowed. "I've been careful!"

"Not our first night together you weren't!" she countered angrily. "and think about what you just did!"

"Are you sure it's mine?"

"You're the only one I've *ever* been with James, and if you're going to try to point at Dave, you better get out your calendar. I haven't seen him since Thanksgiving!"

"I can't deal with a baby right now!" he yelled.

"Calm down! Do you want the whole house to know what's going on?"

"You need to do something about it!" he hissed angrily.

"I'm not having an abortion!"

"Then you're going to have to go home and deal with it!"

"I'm not dropping out of school before the end of the semester!"

"Then you need to move back into the dorm. I can't have some fat, pregnant cow living here!"

"I probably won't even be showing by the time we get out of school in May! Are you serious here, James? Are you just going to throw me out?"

James glared at her without answering.

"Besides, Sandra already has a new roommate. I couldn't go back to the dorm now even if I wanted to. There's a waiting list."

"You should have thought about that before you came crawling in here!"

"Is that what I was doing, James—crawling? I have an entirely different picture of what happened that first night. I came in here broken and you seduced me knowing full well that my emotions were out of control! It was your idea for me to move in with you!"

"Well now I've changed my mind!"

"You better carefully consider your next words, buster!" Patti shrieked. "I happen to know that the athletic department has a code of conduct. How do you think that will go when I tell them you seduced me, got me pregnant, and now want to kick me to the curb? How long do you think your fancy scholarship will last when I tell them that story?"

A look came over James that she'd never seen before. The corners of his mouth turned down in rage. His eyes turned dark and he lunged at her. She lost consciousness with his first blow.

Chapter 28

*P*atti regained consciousness in the hospital. She hurt everywhere. She was wrapped in an electric blanket, was wearing an oxygen mask and an IV had been inserted into her arm. A nurse stood nearby watching a couple of monitors near her bed.

"How are you feeling?" the nurse asked when she noticed that Patti was watching her.

"I feel terrible," she moaned through the mask. "I guess I'm in the hospital. How did I get here?"

"Two guys found you lying in the snow on the sidewalk nearly naked and called the ambulance. They thought you'd overdosed on something. They gave you Narcan. From the condition you were in they thought that somebody had mugged you."

"How bad am I?"

"It appears that you've had a methamphetamine overdose, you're mildly hypothermic, you've got a couple of broken ribs, a few deep lacerations on your face, and your oxygen content is low – probably a result of the meth and the rib injuries. Oh, and it appears you were raped."

"I don't do drugs!" Patti moaned through her oxygen mask. "You should also know that I'm pregnant. At least I was before my boyfriend beat the crap out of me!"

"Your boyfriend?"

"Yeah! I was in his apartment when I told him I was pregnant and he went berserk and slugged me!"

"I need to talk to the police!" Patti insisted as she pulled off her oxygen mask, "and the sooner the better! I'm scared to death that

James is going to come here looking for me. After all this I'm not sure what he's capable of."

"I'll be right back!" the nurse said as she hurried out.

***

The next hour brought a small army of people parading through Patti's hospital room. She gave statements to a police detective, and a female rape crisis officer. No sooner had the law officers done their thing and left, when the doctor on call revisited her.

"Our tests indicate that you're under the influence of methamphetamine. Are you a user?" he asked.

"No!" Patti yelled. "I've never used drugs in my life!"

"Your tests also confirm that you're pregnant," the doctor continued. "From what we've seen on your body it appears that you received several vicious kicks to your abdomen that broke two ribs. I suspect after listening in on your conversation with the law officers who were here, that whoever attacked you may have been trying to abort your fetus."

"Then if it dies, I want James charged with murder!" she spat.

"Hold on a moment. I think the detective is still at the front desk talking to our staff. I think you need to talk to him again."

***

The detective came back a few minutes later. "You told me earlier that you were knocked unconscious by your boyfriend," he said. "The two guys who found you on the street and called the ambulance thought you'd overdosed on something and they gave you a dose of Narcan. After we heard your story we sent a couple of officers to your boyfriend's house. He wasn't very happy about being rousted out of bed at 2 a.m.! I've got to tell you, though, that your alleged boyfriend and the other people living in that house are telling us a totally different story. They claim that you weren't living there, you are a drug user and you just went there for money. They said you were high, had sex with all of them and then you had an argument over money and left. Your boyfriend claims he didn't hit you."

"If I know James, he already cleaned up his bedroom and dumped all my clothes so I won't be able to prove that I was living with him!"

"Your medical tests indicate that you have enough methamphetamine in your system to have rendered you unconscious. Unfortunately, we can't get a search warrant for their DNA or for their house without being able to file charges and right now we don't have anything to formally charge them with. They claim there was no assault and that the sex was consensual."

"Call my ex-roommate, Sandy! She'll tell you that I'm not a druggie and that I've been living with James for weeks! I already told you that James knocked me unconscious."

"Do you have a number I can call?"

"It should be in my cell phone."

"I have a list of what little you had with you when you were admitted. You didn't have a cell phone."

"Or a purse, I suppose?"

"No."

"My purse, phone, and all of my clothes were in James' bedroom. Sandy lives in Dorm C, second floor, room 214."

"Okay, I'll see what I can do," the detective said. "Is there anything else I should know before I follow up on these leads?"

"Maybe you should know the reason James slugged me in the first place. When I told him I was pregnant, he tried to deny it was his, but he's the only one I've ever been with! I know if he hasn't killed my baby that you'll be able to match his DNA to my fetus. Anyway, when he told me to deal with it on my own. I threatened to get the university's athletic department involved for an honor code violation. He has a full-ride, football scholarship and something like this could get his scholarship yanked. When I told him that he knocked me out!"

The detective frowned and made a note in a small, wirebound notebook he'd been making notes in before.

"I can't promise you anything, Miss Carlson, but I think I'm finally seeing a few things that would substantiate your story."

"I hate to put this on you," Patti said, "but I'm freaking out here. I'm afraid he's going to come here and try to finish what he started. In the meantime, I'll bet you'll find all my stuff in a dumpster somewhere. I hope you can find my clothes. Other than this hospital gown and what few clothes they found on me, I evidently don't have a thing to wear."

***

A while later Sandy hurried into Patti's hospital room.

"You look awful!" she cried as she touched Patti's arm. "Did James do all of this to you?"

"I don't know. I can't see myself. All I know is he slugged me in the jaw. That knocked me out. Evidently a couple of guys found me lying in the street and called an ambulance. They told the cops they thought somebody had mugged me. Sometime between the time that James slugged me and a couple of hours later when I regained consciousness here and could tell them who I am, somebody injected me with meth, pounded my face pretty good, kicked me in the belly trying to kill my baby, and broke some ribs."

"Your baby?"

"Yes, that's what started all this. I found out today that I'm pregnant. When I told James about the baby, he lost it. We argued and when I threatened to get his scholarship yanked, he slugged me."

"I told the cops that you'd been living with him for nearly a month," Sandra said. "They also asked me if you used drugs. I told them no. Evidently that's not what James told them."

263

"I'm sure he purged his apartment of all my stuff. I don't have my purse or any identification, my phone is gone and I don't have anything to wear."

"We're close to the same size. I can loan you a few things until you can get back on your feet. Have you called your mom?"

"I couldn't! I don't have a phone!"

Sandy pulled her cell phone out of her purse and dialed a number. "Detective Oiler?" she asked as someone answered. "This is Sandy. I just talked with your people a little while ago about my friend Patti. I think she already told you that her cell phone is missing. I'm thinking if her boyfriend dumped her clothes and everything in a dumpster somewhere, you might be able to track her cell phone signal and find her stuff."

Patti started to say something but Sandy held up her finger to silence her. "Yes, I have her number. It's area code 719-555-7714. Could you please call me at this number if you find anything? She's pretty anxious to get her clothes and her cell phone back."

"Thank you," Patti said through her sobs. "You warned me about James. You told me he was a lady killer. Now it seems that term may be literal. I'm so sorry I didn't listen to you."

Sandy handed her phone to Patti. "I think you should call your mom before some well-meaning detective contacts them in the middle of the night to ask some inane questions."

"I don't know what to tell her!"

"Start with the truth, as painful as that may be."

"This may take a while."

"Hey it's after 3 a.m.! I'm already up in the night. I'll go hang out with the nurses and give you some privacy. This may be your only chance to clear the air. Scream, cry, do whatever. Your mom will understand, and if I'm not wrong, she'll be here with your dad by noon with a new wardrobe and a whole lot of love and support."

***

Telling her mom everything that had happened since Thanksgiving was probably the hardest thing Patti had ever done. Strangely, as she ended the call with her mom, she felt no shame, no remorse, only acceptance, love and concern. And yes, her mom and dad would be at the hospital by noon.

Patti had barely ended her call when Sandy's phone rang.

"Hello?" Patti answered.

"Is this Sandy?" a man asked.

"No this is Patti Carlson. I've been using Sandy's phone to call my mom."

"All the better. This is Detective Oiler. Thanks to the suggestions from your friend, Sandy, we found what we think are your personal belongings in a dumpster a few miles from the hospital. Your cell phone was among your belongings. If it's okay with you, we'd like to process your things to look for DNA evidence that might link your personal items back to your boyfriend. That might take a few days."

"That's okay," Patti said with a deep sigh. "My parents are driving up here from Colorado Springs later today to bring me something to wear. I'd like to get my cell phone back, though, if I can."

"We've already lifted some fingerprints off of it and swabbed it for DNA. I'll have an officer bring it by."

"Thank you detective."

"You're welcome, Miss Carlson. I'm so sorry about all of this. I'm going to alert hospital security so that nobody is allowed into your room without my permission, because we're about to bring the roof down on your boyfriend and his bunkmates and we don't want anyone coming here to threaten you."

"Thank you so very much."

"You're quite welcome. So sorry again about all of this."

***

Patti was doing better by the time her mom and dad found her in her hospital room around noon.

"Oh Patti!" her mom, Janet, cried when she saw her. "You look awful!"

"I feel awful, Mom. Thanks so much for coming."

"Your mom told me about Dave, James, and the baby on the way up here. I want to know what the police are doing? What else can you tell us, sweetheart?" Larry asked softly.

"I don't know," Patti muttered. "I told them everything I could remember about last night. I haven't seen anybody since then. The nurses have been trying to keep me awake until the effects of the meth overdose wear off."

"Do you know who I can talk to at the police department?" Larry asked.

"I remember a Detective Oiler. There were so many other people in and out of here I don't remember anybody else."

"Janet," her dad said softly, "I'll leave you here with Patti. I'm going to see if the police will talk to me."

"Your father is nearly going berserk," Janet said quietly after Larry left the room. He's been raging ever since I told him what happened."

"I'm so sorry Mom. This is all my fault. If I hadn't broken off my engagement with Dave none of this would have happened."

"Nonsense! You can't blame yourself for any of this."

Janet looked around the hospital room then put her coat and purse in an open cabinet and pulled a chair up next to Patti's bed.

"The nurses briefed us both on your condition before they let us come to see you so I think I know what your medical challenges are.

Would you mind telling me all of your emotional challenges or would that be too painful?"

"I think I told you most of that last night over the phone."

"There are a lot of questions I don't have answers to, though, sweetheart. Can we just talk?"

"I've ruined everything, Mom," Patti sobbed.

"I really don't think so. I think I know everything that happened until you came back up here to school. Why don't we start there?"

"What I have to tell you hurts more than what they did to me."

"But if you tell me everything you can start to heal mentally as your body heals."

"Did they tell you whether or not I'm going to lose the baby?"

"They wouldn't give us a lot of specifics. I guess HIPPA laws don't allow that unless you've signed paperwork and they told us you hadn't."

"Okay," Patti gasped slightly as she took a deep breath. "Here's the whole ugly story."

***

Patti's doctor interrupted her story a few minutes later.

"How are you feeling?" he asked kindly after he glanced at the computer near the foot of her bed.

"Pretty sore and groggy."

"Both are understandable," he answered.

"She wants to know if she's going to lose her baby," Janet interjected.

"Sorry, doctor, this is my mom, Janet Carlson. You can talk freely."

267

"I'm pleased to meet you, Mrs. Carlson. You may already know most of this but when they brought your daughter in early this morning, she was hypothermic, suffering from a methamphetamine overdose, and had suffered a lot of physical trauma. Her facial cuts and abrasions are fairly superficial. She has some deep abdominal bruising and two broken ribs but thankfully there's no sign of any internal bleeding."

He paused to glance at her chart for a moment before proceeding.

"She's responding well to treatment. Her body temperature, heart rate, and blood pressure are all about normal. At last check about an hour ago, when we took another blood test, most of the meth is out of her system. I'd say she is a very lucky woman. If someone hadn't found her when they did, she could have easily died from a combination of the meth overdose and hypothermia."

"Thank you doctor," Janet said. "Were you the doctor on call last night?"

"Yes. My name is Dr. Lowry. I'm a resident here."

He glanced at his watch. "I work twelves so I'm off duty about right now but I wanted to check in with Patti before I left. I'll pass this all on to my replacement. If you think of any questions that I haven't answered, the nurse can contact me."

"Thank you, Dr. Lowry," Patti answered. It appears that I owe you my life."

"Actually that fame should go to the two undercover narcotics agents who found you lying alongside the road in the snow at one in the morning. If they hadn't happened to spot you as they were driving past, you would probably be lying in the police morgue right now listed as a Jane Doe. Until you regained consciousness and could talk to us we had no idea even who you were."

Janet started crying the moment Dr. Lowry left.

"Oh Patti!" she sobbed. "This is so much worse than I thought!"

"Yes it is," Patti agreed softly, "Now where were we before we were interrupted?"

***

Nearly an hour later, Larry walked into Patti's hospital room carrying Patti's purse, a lunch sack, and a couple of drinks.

"Sorry girl," he apologized to Patti as he handed the purse to Janet. "The nurses told me that your lunch is on the way and you're on a restricted diet. I was starved. I picked up lunch for your mom and me."

"No, that's okay," Patti answered quickly. "Actually I'm rather nauseous. I don't know if that's because of the drugs or if it's morning sickness."

"Probably a little of both," her mom answered, patting her hand.

"What did you find out at the police station?" Janet asked, turning to Larry.

"Actually, I did more talking than they did," he answered sourly. "I was able to talk to Detective Oiler though. He told me that they're still gathering evidence right now that is most likely going to lead to several criminal arrests but he was unable to give me any specifics that might jeopardize their case."

They both looked at Patti.

"They told me last night that I'd been raped," Patti answered their unasked questions. "That's probably what he's talking about."

"I think it's more than that," Larry answered. "I think they're looking at assault charges at the very least and possibly attempted murder."

"He told you that?" Janet gasped.

"No, he didn't, but I was able to get another officer to fill in a few unofficial details."

"When will they know?" Janet asked earnestly.

"Oiler told me he didn't know. He did take my phone number, though, and told me that someone from the department would contact me as soon as they knew more."

Janet glanced at the wall clock. "You were gone a long time. Where else have you been?"

A solemn look crossed Larry's face. "When I came back here, you and Patti were still talking. I didn't want to interrupt you so I went for a walk to work off a little rage. It's a good thing I don't know where this James character lives or I'd have paid him a visit."

"Yeah, and then you'd have been in jail and he wouldn't be," Janet chided him. "I think that this is all out of our hands now. There's nothing more we can do but wait."

"What do you think I should do about school?" Patti asked softly. "I haven't seen myself but I'm sure I look terrible. I feel worse. The last thing I want to do right now is go back on campus."

"How far are you into the semester?" Larry asked.

"About five weeks. I started school on January 4th."

"Under the circumstances," he said, looking Patti in the eyes, "I'd suggest we contact the school and withdraw you for the rest of the semester. This early in the year they'll give you a *withdrawn passing* notation on all of your classes. That won't hurt your GPA and you can re-enroll in the fall."

"I'll be giant pregnant by then."

"Oh, that's right," Janet answered with a soft smile. "I'm going to be a grandma."

"Do you know when your baby is due?" her dad asked.

"If I go full term, I can probably tell you exactly when. It'll be due the first of November."

Her dad seemed to be deep in thought for a moment. "Dave's been at Purdue since the first of January," he replied.

"It's not Dave's baby. It's James' child. He's the only one I've ever been with. I barely found out that I'm pregnant. In fact I'm only about eight days late. I got an EPT and when I told James about the baby, he went crazy. That's what started all this."

"I'm so sorry," Janet said as tears filled her eyes. "This is just awful in so many ways. Please know that your dad and I will support you any way we can."

"I've got medical insurance through you that should cover the pregnancy."

"That's not the kind of support I was talking about," her mom smiled through her tears. "You've got to be an emotional wreck right now. We're here for you."

Patti's tears streaked down her face as she sobbed her reply. "Thanks Mom. I knew you'd understand."

Chapter 29

Detective Oiler dropped by Patti's hospital room just after nine on Wednesday morning and she introduced him to her parents.

"I'm sorry Patti, but I still can't discuss the case with your folks. Your doctor just told me that they're going to release you from the hospital this afternoon. What are your plans?"

"She's withdrawing from college," Larry interjected. "I talked to the admissions office yesterday. We're taking her back home to Colorado Springs."

Oiler's eyes narrowed a little. "I suppose that might be best under the circumstances, but I'll need an address and a phone number where I can contact you down there. I'm sure that if this results in legal action, Patti will be called upon to testify."

"What do you mean *if* it results in legal action?" Larry asked stiffly.

Oiler frowned and glanced around the room. "I can't really tell you much right now, but under the circumstances I'll give you an idea of what you're up against. Patti's alleged boyfriend, James, and all of his housemates claim that she went there that night and took money from them all for consensual sex so she could buy drugs. Then she left and they didn't know that anything had happened to her until the cops got them out of bed."

"That's a bunch of crap!" Patti yelled.

"Calm down," Oiler said quietly. "Their story has more holes in it than a sieve. We're still processing the evidence we have and are looking for more. We're also interviewing people, but your boyfriend and all of his buddies have lawyered up and aren't cooperating with our investigation. We've taken DNA evidence from your clothes, purse, and cell phone that we found in a dumpster that night—thanks to your girlfriend – but none of the four men have voluntarily agreed to give us DNA samples."

"What now?" Larry asked angrily.

Oiler vaguely smiled. "What they don't know is our people have already gone through their trash – which is legal, by the way, – and have a number of DNA samples – several of which indicate that Patti was in fact living there."

"How do you think this will go in court?" Janet asked quietly.

"Based on their combined testimonies it may be difficult to prove rape, but based on your testimony, Patti, I'm almost certain we can charge James with assault. That will get us official access to his house and car. Assuming what you've told us is true, he would have had to have transported you from his house nearly three miles to where the witnesses found you. Somewhere along that route, and near the dumpster that we found your things in, hopefully we can find security camera footage that will place his car at or near those two locations about the time you were found."

Oiler paused for a few moments. "I shouldn't be telling you all of this but I believe your story, Miss Carlson. I'm not buying what James and his buddies are telling us. I've been talking to the DA about the case and he's hoping we can find enough evidence to charge them with forcible sexual assault, possession of a controlled substance, tampering with evidence, and possibly even attempted murder. In my opinion those four did all they could to set you up so it would look like you simply overdosed on meth and then passed out in the snow and died of hypothermia. They didn't plan on anyone finding you in time to save your life."

Detective Oiler paused for a moment and then looked directly at Patti. "From what you've told us, Miss Carlson, your boyfriend, James, had motive. That's all I can tell you for now. I'm sure we'll be in touch. In the meantime, don't talk to James or any of his roommates, or for that matter please don't discuss this case with anyone except your attorney – should you decide to retain one – or to any of the other witnesses in your case – Including your friend Sandra. We don't want the defense to try to allege witness tampering on your behalf."

***

"Oh my gosh!" Janet exclaimed as Patti stood beside her bed and dropped her hospital gown so her mom could help her get dressed. "You're black and blue from your neck to your thighs. I knew you had cuts and bruises on your face but I didn't realize how badly he'd hurt you in other places. It's probably a miracle that you didn't lose your baby!"

"The doctor told me I'm not out of the woods there either," Patti answered sadly as she gingerly stepped into the underwear her mother was holding for her. The dose of meth they shot me up with may have harmed the fetus. I'm probably only three weeks pregnant. They won't know more until the baby is older and they can do blood and possibly tissue tests."

"Oh my," Janet exclaimed sadly, "and I overheard your doctor telling you that you may be addicted now. He said meth often alters brain chemistry even with just one incident. What are you supposed to do?"

"I need to check in with my family doctor when I get home," Patti answered. "He'll be able to monitor both me and the baby, and he told me to stay away from any opioids."

"Your father told me last night in the hotel room that it's all he can do to keep from going to find James."

"James is pretty buff. I wouldn't do that if I were him."

"Your dad was a brawler when he was younger. I wouldn't worry about him."

"But he's old now."

274

Janet laughed. "He's only forty-three and he's in great shape. He's been going to the gym several times a week for years. I think he can handle himself."

"But…"

"Don't worry. Your father may be very angry but he's not stupid. In fact when he went up to the university to check you out, he talked to the people in charge of athletic scholarships and told them what James was accused of doing. Based on what your father told them, they're planning on reviewing James' scholarship standing. Your dad told me they take a very dim view of their athletes abusing women. They've been sued for not taking action in cases like this before."

"James is going to be livid!" Patti exclaimed. "He didn't slug me until I threatened to get his scholarship yanked."

"Does he know where you live?"

"He knows that I live in Colorado Springs but it's not like he can waltz into town and ask people on the street how to find me."

"Nevertheless, that worries me. I think I'm going to tell your father that he needs to install a security system."

***

It seemed that nobody wanted to talk on the way back to Colorado Springs. They'd been on the road for nearly a half hour before her dad brought up the subject that Patti wanted to avoid.

"So, Patti, does Dave know about James?"

"Yes. He called me one night after I sent his ring back and I told him I'd moved in with James."

"And?"

"And he yelled at me and hung up. He hasn't called back."

"What are you going to do about him?"

"About Dave – nothing! I don't ever want him to know what happened!"

"It's not like you'll be inconspicuous."

"I'll probably never see him again. He's got a summer internship set up in New Jersey as soon as he gets out of school in the spring."

"Don't you think he'll want to come home before he starts that?" Janet asked.

"So what if he does? It's not like we live next door."

"We know his parents," Janet said.

"Not well."

"We've talked since your engagement. Do you know if Dave has talked to them since you broke up?"

"I don't know! Our whole telephone conversation took something like five minutes. I have no idea how often he talks to his parents. For all I know he's never even told them that we broke up."

"If he hasn't yet, he's going to have to tell them something. The last thing they knew, you two were still planning an early June wedding. I'm sure his mom will call him sometime."

"Well then it's up to him to give them the bad news."

"What if his mom calls me?"

"Unless she starts out with condolences about our breakup, play dumb. I don't want you to have to get in the middle of that and I don't want Dave to know what happened to me."

"Why not? It's not like you did anything wrong."

"Are you kidding me here, Mom?" Patti shouted. "I broke off our engagement and then promptly jumped into bed with James! How is what I did not wrong?"

"You must have had your reasons," Larry answered when Janet had nothing to say.

"For what?" Patti snapped. "For breaking off my engagement or for fornicating with James?"

"That sounds so ugly!" Janet snapped.

"It wasn't ugly until now, Mom. I'd been seeing James for awhile. That's why I broke up with Dave. The thing I'd had going with Dave was going nowhere and James made me feel – well he made me feel like he wanted me."

"And Dave wasn't around."

"So you think it *was* all my fault?"

"Was it?"

"No, Mom!" Patti fumed. "Dave just didn't *see* me anymore!"

"You seemed to be pretty excited at Thanksgiving. What changed?"

"This all started way before Thanksgiving! I'm not really in the mood to rehash all of that right now. I promise when I feel better I'll sit down with you and tell you all my reasons. For now, yes, I was stupid. I had decided my thing with Dave wasn't going anywhere but James took advantage of me. In fact, now that I think about the whole mess, I'm sure our meeting was no accident. He… well, never mind. I don't want to get into it until I have the time, courage, and emotional stability to tell you the whole story."

Chapter 30

Detective Oiler sat down in the DA's office on Friday morning.

"What have we got?" the DA asked. "Catch me up to speed here on what evidence we've got to date. I want to move on this case today if we're ready?"

"Do you want the overview or all the nitty gritty details?"

"I'm going to assume that you've got all of the backup for what you're going to tell me so I don't need to hear the details. I'll assume you can present them in court in a convincing manner."

"Okay then, I'll skip all the details about the victim. You already know that we've taken four different sets of DNA from in her or on her and that the DNA matches what we took from the garbage we found outside the accused's home."

"Was that garbage can up against the house or on the curb?"

"On the curb waiting to be picked up Monday morning."

"Good man! I don't want the defense team to be able to throw that out because it was obtained without a warrant. What else have you got?"

"We've got security camera footage showing two men carrying a body out to the back of the accused's Toyota RAV 4. Then we've got more footage showing that same vehicle only half a block from where the victim was found lying unconscious on the sidewalk. We also have security footage from a 7-Eleven showing the accused dumping clothing and other items into their dumpster."

"How did you find her property?"

"The victim's friend provided her phone number. We found her phone, her purse, and her clothing in the dumpster. We have DNA samples and fingerprints taken from the phone and her purse and we have DNA samples taken from the clothes hangers we found with her clothes."

"Anything else?"

"Yes, actually, we have camera footage showing a male leaving the accused's house and dropping something in a garbage can about half a block from their house. In that trashcan we found a syringe that tested positive for meth and we found DNA belonging to two of the men living in that home along with some DNA from the victim on the syringe."

"Did the meth traces match those found in the victim?"

"Yes."

The DA leaned back in his chair. "We'll start with assault charges against the accused based on the victim's testimony. With that, we can get a warrant to search their house and his car and legally obtain DNA on all four of the roommates. It'll be interesting to see whose DNA matches the results you found on the syringe. Frankly, I'm hoping one sample matches the boyfriend's."

"Where do you plan to take it from there?"

"Rape may be hard to prove because the victim doesn't remember the sexual assault and in spite of the bruising our people found on her that is consistent with rape, their defense attorney will undoubtedly play his *rough, consensual sex* card. I want to charge them with something that won't wash off in court. I want to nail these jerks for attempted murder because they left her unconscious, in a drug-induced state, alongside the road in subfreezing weather."

"What else do you want from me and my people?"

"I want witness testimony that she was living with the accused. I want a medical expert to testify that she's pregnant. I want the attending physician's statement describing her injuries. I want whoever's over the accused's athletic scholarship to sit on the stand and describe what happens to his athletic scholarship if the accused breaks the team's honor code and what that code entails."

"I can do all of that. In fact we've already started that process. In the meantime, a couple of the women we've talked to have painted a pretty consistent picture of this guy being an abuser. The women tell us he's left a trail of used-up women behind him at the university – some of their testimonies are pretty graphic."

"Those testimonies may not prove our case but they certainly won't hurt when we sit them on the witness stand in front of a jury to build a vivid picture of this jerk's character."

"The victim has withdrawn from the university and gone back to Colorado Springs. Are you going to want her to testify?" Oiler asked.

"Of course we will, but because of the way our judicial system moves that probably won't happen for some months. That may be in our favor, though, because by that time her fetus should be stable enough to get a DNA sample to prove its parentage."

"I think I can see where you're going with this, so you're planning the attempted murder charge to be your final trump card – even if we could charge him and his buddies with a raft of other things?"

"You've got it."

"Okay then, I'll slant our investigation in that direction and see what we can find to back up those charges."

***

James huddled his roommates around the kitchen table.

"Is everyone on board?" James asked as he looked at the other three. "I'm convinced that if we stick to our story the cops won't be able to prove squat."

"This is probably still going to go before the honor code board," Brad, one of James' roommates said. "Can you deal with the heat?"

"There are worse things afoot here than the loss of my scholarship," James growled. "I could kick the crap out of those two guys who found her. If they'd just driven on by, our plan would have worked. To coin a phrase: *dead men, or women in this case, tell no tales.*"

"The cops would have eventually figured out who she was and still brought the heat to our door," Seth, another one of James' roommates argued. "I knew moving her in here was a mistake, and I told you that, but no, you couldn't keep it in your pants!"

James scowled and tensed up. "Are you going to keep your mouth shut or not?"

"That depends," Seth answered. "You can go all bad on me if you want but I'm telling you right now, I won't go to jail for this!"

"You're an accessory!" James hissed.

"Only because I kept my mouth shut when the cops came here asking questions! I didn't knock her out and then shoot her up so it'd look like she'd overdosed and I didn't load her in your car and dump her on the street half naked!"

James' countenance stiffened and the corners of his mouth lifted a little into an almost grin. "Maybe not, but you took your shot at her after we drugged her up. You didn't use anything either. That means your junk is in her."

"That may be true but..."

"Yeah," James interrupted him, "but your story only holds water if we all keep our mouths shut. The story is, she came here wanting money for drugs. We all took our turn with her and gave her money. She was fine when she left here. We don't know who sold her the meth or beat her up for her money! What happened the second she stepped out of that door is on her, not us!"

"She'd have died if those guys hadn't found her!" Tony, the last of James' roommates, spoke up. "If that had happened, would you want that on your conscience?"

"That was the plan!" James raged, "and if you remember right you played along. Are you getting cold feet?"

"No." Tony answered, "but only because I'll go to jail with the rest of you guys if I say anything."

***

Patti went with her mother to the gynecologist the day after they got back to Colorado Springs. After listening to Patti's story, doing an exam and a blood test, Dr. Nielsen sat down opposite Patti behind her paper-cluttered desk.

"I won't tell you that I'm not concerned," the doctor began. "We have a number of unknowns here. The best news I can give you is that in spite of the battering you took to your abdomen, your organs and the fetus appear to be unaffected, but your fetus is too small at this point to really make that determination. If you don't spontaneously abort then we will begin to closely monitor its progress. What I can't tell you, yet, is whether or not the meth damaged your baby."

Dr. Nielsen paused, leaned back in her chair and stared at Patti for a moment. "All the cuts and bruises will eventually heal, Patti, but meth is an insidious drug. One exposure like you had can change your brain chemistry. Like it or not, you may be an addict. If you're not an active addict, you may very well have latent tendencies that will follow you the rest of your life."

"What can I do?" Patti asked.

"There's little you can do at this point except to be aware that may happen and stay away from any opioids. Then if or when it does happen, you'll need to seek help immediately. Will you promise me that?"

"Of course."

"Okay, I hate to be blunt, but there's one other thing we need to do. I want to see you back here in a week and we'll run tests for

STD's. I'm not accusing you of being promiscuous but anytime you've had sexual contact with someone, you've inadvertently had contact with anyone and everyone that person has been with. As prevalent as STDs are on today's campuses it's only wise to be proactive. An STD can also have consequences for your fetus."

***

Patti held it together until she and her mom got to the car. Then she dissolved. Janet held her in silence and stroked her hair for long minutes while Patti sobbed.

"Oh Patti," Janet finally broke the silence as Patti's sobs quieted. "I'm so very sorry."

"I was so stupid!" Patti fumed. "I can't believe I didn't see right through James!"

"Don't beat yourself up too badly," Janet answered softly. "What you did was understandable. You'd just lost your best friend, not to mention your fiancé. You weren't really in your right state of mind."

"Maybe not, but I felt justified at first. Dave just wasn't interested in me."

"I think he was in his own way. He's not a bad person. He just didn't have his priorities in the right place. I think at the back of his mind he was convinced that what he was doing, he was doing for both of you."

"I can't go there, Mom, I spent weeks, maybe months trying to decide before I finally broke it off."

"Are you ever going to tell Dave what happened to you?"

"Of course not!" Patti shouted. "This is none of his business, Mom! He's no longer a part of my life. Did you think now that I've been hurt I'd go running back to him?"

"Not right away, Patti, but who knows what your state of mind will be in a month or two."

"I'll never go back to him! I can't go back to him Mom! I'm pregnant! What do you want me to do, go begging him to take me back – and raise my big mistake as his own?"

"That's not what I'm saying, Patti. I'm just asking you to keep an open mind. Don't close him off completely. I think you two had a really good thing going for years."

"That's the problem Mom. I need a man – a husband and father – not a high school buddy!"

"I'm sorry, Patti, I just remember how happy you two seemed at Thanksgiving."

"Yeah, Mom, that was great! It was passionate. It was warm, but he chose school over me."

"Did he really?"

"I don't want to argue Mom."

"I'm not arguing with you Patti. I'm sorry you think I'm pushing you. That's not my intent. I just know you're going to need some help and support that your father and I can't provide. Don't get me wrong. We'll love having you stay here with us. You've nearly been a stranger to us ever since you went to Colorado State. It'll be fun sharing our home with you again. And if you decide to stay with us even until after the baby comes, we'll fawn over our first grandchild in spite of the circumstances."

"Then what?" Patti asked cautiously. "I think this conversation is heading somewhere but maybe you should spell out what you're thinking so I don't misinterpret."

"You went to college for a reason Patti. Your father and I have already talked about this. We think you should consider moving your credits back to the University of Colorado here in Colorado Springs so we can help with the baby until you graduate. You're so close now, Patti, we think it'd be a travesty if you didn't finish."

"I'm over a month into my classes at Colorado State and I just withdrew. I can't just jump back into…"

"That's not what I mean," Janet interrupted. "I don't really think you're in the state of mind right now to go back to school anyway. When did you say your baby is due again?"

"If it lives," Patti said softly, "I know exactly when it's due. I figure it'll be born around November 1st."

"Well that'll be a little inconvenient," Janet mused. "You should be able to do summer school but you probably shouldn't start fall semester because you'll just have to drop out when the baby comes. I think if you went to summer school and then spring semester next year, you might be able to finish up during the following summer."

"Sometimes they don't offer upper division classes during the summer."

"Maybe not, but at least that could be a goal. You don't want to just walk away now Patti."

"No, you're right Mom."

"I'm sorry," Janet apologized, "it's probably premature to be doing all of this planning, at least not for a few weeks."

"Until I find out if my baby will live and if I'm a meth addict?" Patti asked curtly.

"Please Patti, let's not dwell on the worst that could happen. Let's just take this one day at a time."

Janet paused.

"I hope you know that I'm just trying to help you through all this," she continued. "Can we just talk? I'm grieving Patti! You'll know how I feel when you have a child of your own. Everything that happens to you still happens to me, even if you're all grown up."

Tears filled Patti's eyes again and she pulled her mom into a tight embrace. "Thank you Mom!" she cried. "I don't know what I'd do right now without you and Dad. Yes I'd like to talk. It's like all of this has laid my soul bare. I no longer have any secrets. You know it all. I can really use your help."

Chapter 31

Dave's cell phone rang. He glanced at the number. It was listed as unknown caller. He ignored it and turned his attention back to the textbook he'd been studying. After a short pause another set of chimes indicated that someone had left a voice message.

Dave ignored the phone for awhile. Telemarketers sometimes left messages but he didn't often get messages from "unknown callers". Out of curiosity more than anything, Dave found the message and replayed it.

"Mr. Tolman, this is Detective Oiler with the Fort Collins Police Department. I understand that you're the former boyfriend of Patti Carlson. I need to ask you some questions about your relationship. Would you please call me at your earliest convenience?"

Dave replayed the message so he could jot down the detective's phone number. Anxiety gripped his chest. Why would a police detective be calling him if he didn't have bad news? Had she been in an accident – or worse? He fumbled the number into his cell phone keypad and waited impatiently as the number clicked through.

"Detective Oiler," came a male reply.

"Uh yes, this is Dave Tolman. You just left a message on my phone."

"Thanks for calling back, Dave."

"What's happened?" Dave blurted.

"How well do you know Patti Carlson?" the detective asked without answering Dave's question.

"We've dated since high school. Why?"

"Have you ever known her to use illicit drugs?"

"No! Neither of us has! I'm a … well I was on the Colorado State Football team. I don't touch drugs or alcohol."

"You *were* on the team?"

"Yeah, I got busted up at the end of the season and the team released me."

"I remember that game," Oiler said. "Did you go after the jerk that hit you?"

"I wanted to but it wouldn't have done any good. What's this about Patti?"

"I understand you were engaged."

"Was, being the operative word!" Dave answered angrily.

"May I ask why you broke it off?"

"She broke it off and I'd rather not get into it. Why are you asking me if Patti uses drugs?"

Oiler paused for a few moments.

"Have you heard from her in the past couple of weeks?"

"No," Dave answered anxiously. "Is she missing?"

"No, nothing like that. She was involved in an incident that my office is investigating. I can't go into details because this is an ongoing investigation."

"I'm going crazy here!" Dave exclaimed. "What's going on?"

"I'm not at liberty to discuss the case," Oiler repeated himself. "We've talked to her and her former roommate and both vehemently denied any involvement with illicit drugs, but, well, like I've already told you, she was involved in an incident and we found methamphetamines in a blood sample. That's all I'm at liberty to tell you at this time. I suggest you call her."

"I can't call her!" Dave answered angrily. "She broke off our engagement and hasn't been answering my phone calls!"

"I don't know what to tell you then, Mr. Tolman. Perhaps you should contact her parents?"

"Is that creep James Baxter involved?" Dave raged.

"I can't say that he isn't."

"He's the reason we broke up… or at least that's who she turned to when she ended our relationship!"

"How do you know him?"

"We were teammates on the football team… competitors more like it! I don't know him well off the football field but I've heard that he's a control freak."

"Could you be more specific?"

"I've just heard rumors," Dave answered carefully, "probably nothing that you could use in court, if this is where that's headed."

"What kind of rumors?"

"He fancies himself a ladies' man, if you know what I mean, and let's just say I hear he's left a lot of broken women in his wake. They fall for his good looks, and then he uses them up before he dumps them. Is that what he did to Patti?"

"Can you give me any names?"

"I can't. I don't follow the gossip, but I'll bet Patti's roommate, Sandy, could give you names."

"Okay thanks Dave. Do you know whether or not James used illegal substances?"

"I don't. But I doubt he did. He has an athletic scholarship. We have to undergo periodic drug tests. I doubt he'd risk that."

"I understand that James was living off campus with three other students. Do you know any of them?"

"No I don't. Like you may have already gathered, I don't particularly care for James. I don't know anything about him beyond the football field."

"Okay thank you Dave. I may want to talk to you more as this case evolves. Would you mind?"

"No. Are you sure you can't tell me anything else?"

"Sorry Dave. Not at this point. You have my number, though, so you may want to call me in a couple of weeks. Maybe I can tell you more then."

***

Dave stared down at his phone without moving until the screen went blank. He could barely breathe. From what he'd gathered from his conversation with Detective Oiler, Patti was probably in trouble, and James or his roommates were involved. As their conversation flowed back through his mind his thoughts slammed to a stop at the mention of meth. Everybody knew that once you were addicted to meth that you were always addicted to meth. Anger clenched his jaws. He wouldn't put anything past James – even drugging Patti to get her to do … whatever.

Dave brought up his phone contacts list, found James' number and pressed send.

"Hey Dave," James' smooth voice came over the phone as he answered. "How's Purdue?"

"I just got a call from a Detective Oiler from the Fort Collins Police Department!" Dave spat without answering James' question. "He asked me if Patti used drugs. What the hell is going on James?"

"I have no idea what you're talking about."

"You're lying! Detective Oiler wouldn't tell me much about the case but he asked me questions about you and your roommates. Why would he do that if you weren't involved?"

"Look, just because you're mad that Patti moved in with me for awhile, you have no right to call up and start accusing me of anything. Just for the record, Patti and I aren't together anymore. Our little fling didn't last long. I haven't seen her in a couple of weeks."

"If I called her would she tell me that?"

"She's so pissed at you I doubt she'd talk to you," James chuckled.

"You don't know a thing about her!" Dave raged as he lost his temper.

James laughed. "I do know that she looks great naked and she's a great lay! My roommates all think so too!"

Dave was speechless. He knew James wanted a reaction out of him and he wanted to scream obscenities into the phone, but he didn't want to give him that satisfaction. James had been jealous of him ever since they met. Instead of giving him what he wanted, Dave pressed the end button and leaned back in his desk chair as tears flowed down his face.

Knowing any further study for the afternoon was out of the question, Dave got shakily to his feet and walked downstairs to the refrigerator.

"What on earth is wrong?" Rose asked the moment she saw him.

Dave wanted to answer but his throat clenched shut the moment he tried to talk.

Rose hurried over to him and took the soda bottle out of his hand. "Talk to me, Dave!" she insisted. "What's wrong? Was there an accident? Did you lose someone?"

A moment later Claire joined them. He still couldn't talk.

"Come on Dave," Claire begged softly, "talk."

Rose took one elbow and Claire took the other. Together they guided him into Rose's living room where they seated him on the sofa and took a seat on either side of him.

For several endless minutes, all Dave could do was sob. Then finally he angrily took a deep breath. He was a grown man, for Pete's sake, not a five-year-old boy!

"Something's really wrong at Colorado State," he finally managed. "I just got a call from a detective with the Fort Collin's Police Department. He asked me if Patti used drugs, specifically meth. He wouldn't tell me anything else, really. He told me he was working on a case and couldn't divulge any details. Then he mentioned James Baxter and asked if I knew whether or not he or his roommates used illegal drugs. I put two and two together and called James."

"Then what happened?" Claire asked.

"He pulled all of my strings and I lost it!"

More tears streamed down his face and he couldn't go on. The two women waited patiently.

"Patti and I never... Well we were never intimate. Then James brags about seeing her naked and told me that he and all of his roommates think that Patti was a great lay!"

"Oh my!" Rose gasped, "how terrible!"

"Now I can't help but think that they got her hooked on meth and..."

"Have you tried calling her?" Claire asked.

"No. I just got off the phone with James. I was in no mood to talk to her. She wouldn't answer my calls after she broke off our engagement. I'm sure she wouldn't talk to me now about anything like that."

"Do you know her mom well enough to call *her*?" Rose asked.

"I doubt she'd talk to me either. I'll bet if something bad has happened that Patti has sworn her to secrecy."

"Were your parents friends with hers?" Claire asked.

"Yeah, sort of. They live close. We've done dinner together before."

"Then call your mom and see if she has heard anything."

"I don't think I can call her mom even if I get her number."

"Not right away," Claire answered, "but if we can get you calmed down a little, I think you can. I think you're right, though, if Patti's in some sort of trouble, especially involving that other guy, I'm sure she won't want to talk to you. Hey it's fairly nice out. Let's you and I go for a walk. I don't know any better way of working off a little anxiety."

The look in Claire's eyes was one of sympathy and understanding. He drew a deep breath. "From what I smelled when I came down the stairs, I'll bet Rose has dinner about ready – maybe after dinner."

"What you smelled was dessert," Rose quickly responded, "I just put a casserole in the oven and it won't be ready for an hour. I agree with Claire. I think you two ought to go get some fresh air."

***

"Let me talk first," Claire began after they'd been walking for a few minutes. "You're not the only one who needs to talk right now and I've been letting something build up inside of me for a long time and I need to vent. Maybe that'll make it easier for you."

"Okay," Dave managed. He'd finally gotten enough control of his emotions that he'd stifled his sobs but his throat was still constricted. He doubted he'd be able to talk much anyway.

"I've told you a little about the relationship between me and my dad," Claire began quietly. "I'm his football buddy and he dotes on

293

me all the time. We're not just father and daughter, we're best friends. Do you know what I mean?"

Dave nodded but didn't answer.

"My dad and I have had all the *talks* over the years. We can tell each other anything – and he has," she giggled. "I know all of the gritty details of his intimate relationship with my mom."

She paused for a few moments.

"At first I thought it was really off for him to tell me stuff like that but then I figured out what he was doing. I think in his own silly way he was trying to encourage me to go find a man."

Dave just listened.

"I have never been on a date, Dave," she continued after a poignant break. "Boys were really never interested in me. At first I figured that was just because I look a lot like my dad. Sadly enough I got his chunky genes. He's certainly not a girly man if you know what I mean. And then I realized something else, and this isn't easy to say, but I wasn't ever interested in boys."

"Oh," was all Dave could manage.

"Yeah," she continued after a moment. "That's when I chopped off my hair, dyed it two or three different colors, and started running with *that* crowd in college. I felt really bad about myself for awhile and then the kids that I was running with helped me change my attitude. I've never had any kind of a serious relationship. I guess I've never found anybody that I was passionate about."

"Does your dad know?"

"That's the cool part," she said. "He'd suspected it all along so he wasn't taken back when I came out to him. Our relationship hasn't ever changed and I love that I can tell him anything. It's just our little secret though. My mom would freak if she knew. She's one of those nose-in-the-air high society babes, if you catch my drift. My dad throws money at her, she keeps him happy at home, and lets him do his own thing."

"Doesn't she suspect anything?" Dave asked.

"She might but frankly, I don't care. She never asks about my social life and I've never brought a girlfriend home."

"Is that hard?"

"It hasn't been yet, but someday it might be. I asked my dad what he'd think if I did."

"And?"

"And he hugged me until I thought my head was going to pop off and then he told me that he would always love me no matter who or what I brought home – as long as it didn't come between us and football."

Dave laughed.

"There it is!" she laughed. "You have the most magical smile, Dave! I've loved you ever since we met!"

Dave reeled a little at her admission.

"Now don't go crazy on me Dave," she instantly responded. "I'm not putting the moves on you or anything but I love you as a person. I know that may be hard for somebody like you – all secure in your masculinity – to wrap your arms around, but love has nothing to do with sexuality. Love is love, Dave. You're a Christian, aren't you?"

"Yes."

"So am I and I read the scriptures all of the time. I think you know as well as I do that Christ was and is the epitome of true love, and you won't find a single reference in the bible that would tell you that his love was gender specific."

"I can't argue that."

"Nor would I want you to Dave. See, in my opinion there's a dark side in the world that tries to tell you that how I feel is wrong. Maybe it is. I've read all about Sodom and Gomorrah. I've read all of the scriptural passages that deal with that, but at the end of the day, Dave, I don't think there's anything wrong with me, or the people I run with. For whatever reason maybe we're just wired differently. I don't know why, but what I do know is that no matter how much preaching people do, they'll never change me – or us."

She paused for a few moments and then took Dave's hand.

"Do you feel threatened by me?" she asked as he stopped and looked down at her.

"No. Why should I be?"

"Thank you. That's the right answer. Even though I just told you that I love you, doesn't mean I want to be your girlfriend. I would like to be your dear friend, though. I think you're a wonderful individual and you have unlimited possibilities. My heart aches for you. I think I know what it means to lose someone you truly love so if nothing else I can empathize and maybe offer you a little comfort."

"That would be nice."

"Okay I can sense your hesitancy, Dave, and that's okay. I wouldn't have told you all this now except I think maybe I can help you heal. I've known grief and I've known – and know – love. I just wanted to clear the air in case you want to let me into your life a little. This way you won't have to feel guilty about not being physically attracted to me and you'll know that I don't have any expectations of you. Do you know what I'm talking about here?"

"Yes I think I do."

She smiled. "Okay then, sorry. Now that you can talk I want to hear your story. And don't leave out any of the nitty gritty details. I can tell that you need to vent and I'm a great listener."

***

296

Dave talked nonstop as they circled several blocks, finally finding their way back to Rose's home in time for dinner. Claire was right. He had needed to vent, and he did! It felt so good to be able to tell her his brightest hopes, his darkest fears, knowing that Claire wouldn't judge him or offer cures to questions that had no answers.

"This has been fun, Dave," Claire said softly as he opened Rose's door for her. "Let's do this more often. You're as easy to talk to as my dad—and that's saying tons!"

She glanced quickly inside to see if Rose was nearby. "Let's just keep my thing between us," she whispered. "Rose would never understand."

Chapter 32

*D*etective Oiler ended his call with Dave and jotted a few lines in his notebook.

"What did the boyfriend have to say?" one of Oiler's deputies asked.

"Just about what we suspected. He claims that neither he nor his ex-girlfriend are users."

"Yeah, we expected that. What would *you* say if a cop asked you if you were using?" the deputy replied.

"I'd deny it, of course, but the way I presented the questions to him, I believe he was telling me the truth. I could tell that the kid was blindsided by my line of questioning."

"What now?"

"I just had a thought," Oiler responded. "We've got a drug task force working the town, and more specifically the university. I want to know if they know who's dealing meth right now and if there's any connection between them and the accused or one of his buddies. Run that trap line and see what you can find out."

"Isn't the DA about to press charges?" the deputy asked. "Why don't we wait until he does and then run a blood test on all of them?"

"Because they may not be users, especially the accused. He's going to school on an athletic scholarship. If he burns the bottle, so to speak, even one time, he knows he's off the team. I don't think he's that stupid."

"So you're looking for a one-time buy then?"

"Yeah. By the way, have we got the results back from the lab yet on that syringe we found?"

"We've got fingerprints and DNA. What else do you want?"

"They were supposed to be analyzing the contents. None of the illegal meth labs are that consistent. We should be able to trace that sample back to a specific set of samples or to a supplier. If we've got anyone in custody for dealing meth and the product we took off them matches what we have, I want to lean on them hard – using a potential charge of attempted homicide to loosen their lips. It might be interesting to see where that leads us."

Oiler opened his phone and looked up a phone number. "This is Detective Oiler," he began as the other party answered the phone, "we spoke yesterday about one of your athletes and you were going to see what your university's policy is concerning the matters that we spoke about. Have you got any information for me yet?"

Oiler listened intently as the man on the other end spoke, making notes as he listened.

"Okay, what kind of a review board has to be convened, how long does that take, and who or what initiates it?"

Oiler jotted down a few more notes.

"No, we haven't pressed formal charges yet," the Detective answered, "but it's only a matter of a couple of days now, tops. We're still putting together our evidence and interviewing a few more people."

"I'd say the assault charge will stand, based on the victim's testimony. The sexual assault charges on the other hand are pretty nebulous. The DA doesn't think we can disprove consensual sex even though we're confident that all four men were participants."

"If you'd like, I can have the District Attorney call the Dean."

"I don't want to tell you your business," Oiler continued after a moment, "but I doubt that any of those kids are going anywhere in the near term. If you yank the accused's scholarship right away he may bolt and I don't want that to happen. I don't think he knows that we're pursuing legal charges, or that the University is reviewing his scholarship for that matter and for now I'd like that to remain our secret. We don't want to press formal charges until we've got all of our ducks in a row."

"I can't really tell you how long," Oiler continued patiently, "and I'm not at liberty to tell you anything more about the case. I just wanted to know the University's policy in the event we need to lean on the accused a little to see if he'll confess or plea out to a lesser charge hoping he can keep his good standing with the school. Thanks for your help."

"I think you may want to hear this first hand," Oiler's deputy said, holding up the receiver of his office phone as Oiler pocketed his cell phone.

"Put it on speaker."

The deputy punched a button, and laid the receiver on the table.

"We've got Captain Jackson on the phone," the deputy said. "He's in charge of the drug task force here in town."

"Hello Captain," Oiler said, leaning a little closer to the telephone on the desk. "Did my deputy explain what we're looking for?"

"Yes he did and I may have some good news for you. We have a couple of snitches working the campus and we were leaning on one of them just this morning. One of the local suppliers got a new shipment a few days ago and our snitch brought us a sample. We were aware of your case so we asked the kid if he'd had any new clients. He gave us a name and we just connected it to one of your boy's roomies. The snitch told us that he'd never sold to this guy before and he took him to the cleaners on the price. He charged him double and the guy seemed eager to pay so I suspect that he's not a regular user or he'd have pushed back on the price."

"We sent the syringe we recovered to the lab for analysis," Oiler responded. "If you have a sample, I'd like to have the lab compare the two products."

"I'm way ahead of you there, Detective. It's standard practice to test anything we get to make sure it's not poison. The batch we just tested is pretty potent – more so than usual. I assume you're using the same lab as we do. Do you have a sample and case number?"

Detective Oiler scanned his notes for a few moments and then read off the information.

"I'll get back to you in a few minutes," Jackson said.

"I have a question," Oiler said cautiously, "if you know your snitch is selling the stuff, why don't you bust him?"

"Because if we do, one of our sources of information dries up. We've made a deal with him. He buys just enough from his supplier to stay in good standing. For every five batches he buys, we buy four and he pedals the rest. That keeps us in the loop and it keeps his customer base happy – and surveilled – if you catch my drift."

"Pretty smart."

"We've been at this for awhile. It serves our purposes."

"Wow!" the deputy exclaimed softly as he put the receiver back in the phone cradle. "I had no idea any of that was going on around here."

"Just like a lot of the other stuff we deal with," Oiler said with a sad smile, "the public at large has no idea what's going on right under their noses."

"I believe that," the deputy said, "for instance I had no idea we had sex trafficking going on here."

"We don't at the University as far as we know," Oiler said, "but trafficking doesn't work without someone willing to buy and unfortunately a college town attracts the weirdos that are looking for that young stuff. We've known for a long time that there are a few pretty tight-lipped organizations running prostitution out of the university using coeds. Those people are careful though. There's always some sweet, young thing out there looking for a way of paying her rent or tuition. As long as what they do is consensual and nobody commits assault, it's almost impossible to bust."

Oiler's cell phone rang again a few moments later. "Okay," he said with a grin. "Will your snitch finger the guy he sold it to?"

"I understand your need for secrecy. Can he at least identify the kid from a mug shot? Wait, we don't have mug shots, yet. How about a discrete camera shot?"

"My deputy will email you the pictures. Let me know what you find."

"What's all that about?" Oiler's deputy asked.

"The drug samples are a perfect match. Now all we have to do is have their snitch identify one of the four guys in the house in question and we'll have another piece of our puzzle."

Chapter 33

*D*ave lay awake long into the night, his rampant thoughts driving away any semblance of sleep. He knew Patti had a roommate – or at least she'd had one before she moved in with James. If, like James had told him, Patti wasn't living with him anymore, had she gone back to the dorms? Was that even possible? There was usually a waiting list. She'd had a roommate before but he didn't know her name. He wondered if her ex-roomie would talk to him even if he was able to find her?

He rolled out of bed and rummaged through some of the paperwork he'd brought with him from Colorado State. He didn't know if the housing people would give him any information, but if they wouldn't, they could at least tell him if she was still staying in the dorms.

He found the information he was looking for and picked up his phone. Then he noticed the time. It was 3 a.m...

Lacking anything else to do in his insomnia, he pulled up his text message history with Patti. Knowing that the history was probably hundreds of pages long he thumbed back a year or so in time and started reading their exchanges. He hadn't read very far before reality began to crush him. Nearly everything they'd talked about had centered around him and his football or school schedule. There was none of the flirtatious talk that might have kept their relationship fresh.

He thumbed back another year, only to find more of the same. The only encouraging chats they'd had were during the summertime when on rare occasions there hadn't been football practice and they'd spent a few stolen hours alone.

Dave's heart ached. She'd always been there for him – patiently following – never demanding his time. In reality he wondered why it had taken her so long to give up on him. If the tables were turned, he would have never hung around.

He shut his phone down and lay back on his bed. He'd been such an idiot. Quick snippets of their Thanksgiving together rattled through his mind. Those few precious days had refired their relationship. He'd felt emotions that he hadn't felt since high school. He tried to analyze his feelings for her. Did he really love her?

That thought only gave him pain. Of course he did. He'd always loved her. How could he have been so blind?

Dave turned his phone back on and found the text message string he'd just been looking at. In turning his phone back on, it had returned him to their last conversation. A thought swept over him. He doubted she'd talk to him, but would she read a text? That was something she could do without her committing – or admitting.

He hated texting. It was so slow and clunky, but what if it was his only chance?

Word by word, phrase by phrase, Dave poured out his soul to her. In the back of his mind he wanted the facts – what had happened with James – where was she – did she still have any feelings at all for him? Instead, he concentrated on how he felt. He confessed again for being such an idiot. He recalled on his keyboard the special times he remembered when they'd been able to spend some precious time together. At last he wrote, and then rewrote a dozen times, a final paragraph telling her how much he loved and cherished her.

As he lifted his thumb to touch the *send* button, he added a few final words: "Patti, I know I've hurt you. I agonize every day over what I've done. I know it's probably everlastingly too late but even if your answer for us is still 'NO', would you please just let me know if you're okay? I will always love you, Dave."

He reread the entire text, changing a word here and there until it seemed to be as perfect as it could be under the circumstances, and then after praying a heart-felt wish, he pressed *send*.

Only after it was too late, he noticed the time. It was nearly 4 a.m. his time, that would be 3 a.m. her time! He wondered if she turned off her phone at night? If she didn't, she'd probably be so angry getting a text at that time of night that she'd probably just erase it without even looking at it. More remorse flowed over him. Texting had seemed like a great idea – an hour ago.

Still unable to sleep, Dave got up, got dressed, and quietly navigated Rose's squeaky stairs. He paused for a moment on the porch. It hadn't snowed in a few days but a light breeze was blowing, lowering the already frigid outside temperature a few more bitter degrees. He nearly turned around but knowing sleep would evade him, he plodded on down the ancient, tree-root-broken sidewalk.

As he walked, he thought about everything James and the detective had told him, and the words he'd used to pour out his soul to Patti. Somehow he knew things weren't right but unless she'd answer him, there was little or nothing he could do. He ached inside. If he was at Colorado State he could at least go to her dorm and talk to her roommate… A random thought crossed his mind. Thoughts planted in his mind by Detective Oiler – about meth – constricted his throat. Was Patti using? Was she addicted? Had she been kicked out of school? The registrar could tell him if she was still enrolled in school. He didn't think that information wasn't confidential.

Detective Oiler had refused to give Dave any specifics. Dave wondered if Patti's mom would talk to him? If Patti was in trouble with the law or with her standing at the university, her mom would know. If she refused to talk or was evasive, he had an answer of sorts. With that thought he had at least two phone numbers he could call. He assumed the registrar's office opened at eight – nine his time. He had a class at nine and others until noon.

Another thought crossed his mind. Records of arrests were public knowledge. Even if Oiler wouldn't talk to him, he should be able to find out if Patti, or James had been arrested.

***

Dave had a hard time concentrating in his classes. Not only was he dead tired after his sleepless night, but he kept sneaking looks at his text messages every few minutes, hoping Patti would have responded. She hadn't.

He hurried out of his last morning class, stepped outside where there wasn't any hallway noise and dialed the registrar's number.

A few minutes of anguish later Dave had an answer. Patti had withdrawn. In fact, the girl he'd talked to offered even more information that added to Dave's frantic thoughts. Patti's father had checked her out of school because she'd been in the hospital at the time!

Dave immediately punched in Detective Oiler's number.

"Detective Oiler," a man answered.

"Yeah, this is Dave Tolman, we spoke a couple of days ago about my friend, Patti Carlson. I just called the university registrar and they told me she was in the hospital and her father had checked her out of school. What's going on?"

"I'm sorry Dave!" Oiler answered curtly, "I told you when we last talked that I couldn't divulge any of that information."

"All I'm asking is if she's okay?" Dave fumed.

"I can tell you that she's no longer in the hospital and she evidently went home with her parents."

"Are there pending charges against her?"

"I'm not at liberty to divulge that information. I'm sorry."

"This is crap!" Dave yelled.

"Sorry sir," Oiler said, "I suggest you contact her or her parents. I can't tell you anything else about her case."

"Case?" Dave growled. "Then what you're telling me is that she was arrested?"

"I can't confirm or deny that at this point in time. Have a good day."

Angry almost beyond control, Dave glanced at the other phone number he'd written on a scrap of paper and called University Housing.

"Colorado State Student Housing, this is Denise," a woman answered.

"Hi, can you tell me if a friend of mine is still living in the women's dorms?"

"I can't give you any confidential information."

"I realize that, I just need to know if Patti Carlson is still living there."

"One moment please," Denise answered. Dave could hear a keyboard clicking in the background.

"Oh, here it is. No she's not. She moved out the first of February."

"Did she give a reason?"

"There's nothing in the record. I'm sorry."

"Thanks," Dave answered as he hung up. What he'd found out didn't tell him anything. He already knew she'd moved in with James around the first of the month.

Dave glanced at his text messages again, praying that Patti had responded. She hadn't. He found her mom's number in his contacts list and stared at the number for several long moments. Finally in desperation, he highlighted her number and pressed send.

"Hello Dave," Janet Carlson answered. "How are you?"

"I'm not good," Dave confessed. "Is Patti there?"

A long pause passed between them.

"She is," Janet finally answered quietly, "and I'm really sorry, Dave, but she won't talk to you."

"How do you know that? You just answered the phone. You didn't even have time to ask her!"

"She's been home for a few days, Dave, and we've had several long talks. In fact, she told me this morning that you'd sent her a long text in the middle of the night. She's not in a good place right now and doesn't want to talk to you. If and when she changes her mind, she has your number."

"Please Mrs. Carlson! Can't you tell me anything? I got a call yesterday from a Detective Oiler with the Fort Collins Police Department asking me if either Patti or I had ever been involved with drugs. I know she moved out of the dorms and moved in with an ex-teammate of mine and he called to flaunt that. In fact, he went further. He told me she'd moved out of his place. Worse yet, he told me some really ugly things about Patti, him and his roommates."

"I told you already!" Janet said, raising her voice, "I can't – I won't talk about any of that! I promised Patti I wouldn't!"

"I'm sorry Mrs. Carlson," Dave answered quietly. "Can you just tell me if she's okay?"

"She's having her challenges right now but nothing you need to worry about, Dave. Now I've got to go."

Dave's mind pinged out of control for long moments after their call ended. Then he slowly dialed yet another number.

"Hi Dave!" his mother answered brightly. "How are you?"

"I don't know right now, Mom. Have you heard anything about Patti lately?"

"No. Why? She's still at the university as far as I know."

"No, Mom, she isn't. I think I already told you that she broke off our engagement…"

"Yes, you told me that."

"What I didn't tell you is she moved in with a guy on the football squad right afterward and evidently something bad has happened to her because I got a call from a detective asking questions about drug use."

"Oh my!"

"And no he won't tell me anything. I'm a thousand miles away and I'm going crazy here! All I know for sure right now is that she moved out of the dorms, her dad withdrew her from school, she evidently spent some time in the hospital and now she's home. I tried to text Patti but she won't answer me. I just barely got off the phone with her mom and Patti has sworn her to secrecy. She wouldn't talk to me either."

"I can't say that's a good thing, Hon, but what do you want me to do?"

"I don't know, Mom. I'm sure if you called Mrs. Carlson right away, she'd know I put you up to something. I wonder if maybe you could give it a week or so and then make a casual call?"

"Do you think she got into drugs or something?"

"I don't know, but everything I've heard so far is pointing in that direction. If I can believe anything that James told me…"

"Who's James?"

"My ex-football teammate. That's who she moved in with after we split up. Anyway, if what he told me is true, she's had sex with him and all of his roommates. I can't believe she would have done that unless drugs were involved. I'm worried sick!"

"I'm sorry to say this, Dave, but it appears that Patti has made her choice. If that's all true then I doubt there's anything you can do – especially if that James guy told Patti that he'd talked to you. She's probably embarrassed if nothing else."

"Or addicted."

"Yes, that too."

"What can I do, Mom?" Dave asked, his voice cracking.

"Like I just told you, Dave, it appears to me that Patti has made her choice, and it evidently no longer includes you in her life. I know this is going to be terribly hard, but I think you need to walk away. As hard as this may be, I think you need to concentrate on your school work and let time heal your wounds."

"That's the problem Mom. For as long as I've known Patti all I've thought about was football and school. I blew it!"

"I'm sorry, Hon, but under the circumstances I don't think there's much you can do. You told me you've texted her. You've called her mom. She knows you're concerned. She knows you love her. The ball is clearly in her court now. Give her some space. It appears she may have some other complications in her life now that you may not want to get involved in. Did that detective tell you what kind of drugs she was involved with?"

"He didn't say she was involved, but he did mention meth."

"Oh wow!" she exclaimed softly, "that's really bad. I've heard that once you're addicted to meth that you're always addicted. I know how much you care for Patti, but in my opinion, you need to move on. After all, she broke it off with you and I hate to say this but you don't need a wife that's addicted to drugs. You've got your whole life ahead of you Dave. Don't throw it all away."

***

Dave went to his 1 p.m. class but he couldn't concentrate. The moment it ended, he left campus and walked back to his apartment.

Rose heard him come in and walked out of her quilting room to meet him.

"You're home early," she said.

"I couldn't concentrate so I came home."

"You were up wandering around late last night as well."

"I'm sorry I thought I was being quiet."

"Oh you were trying, my dear, but this old house squeaks something awful and I've become a light sleeper in my old age. You don't look well. What's going on?"

"Just silly girlfriend stuff."

"At your age you're not dating silly girls. I don't want to press you, but would you like to talk about it?"

Dave shrugged his shoulders and walked into her living room. He knew there was nothing Rose could do but Claire wasn't home and he needed to talk.

***

Dave talked and Rose listened for nearly an hour.

"That's heartbreaking," Rose offered when he finally finished and sat staring through her sheer curtains. "Do you have any plans?"

"Not really. I've done about everything I can. My mom told me that the ball is in her court and I just have to wait for her to call."

"That's probably wise advice."

"I can't just sit here and…"

"No you can't, Dave," Rose interrupted him, "you can't just sit here and torture yourself. From what you told me, she made her decision when she called off your engagement. Trying to hang on to something you once had won't do either one of you any good. I'm sorry to say this but I think you need to pull yourself together and move on. Your mother is wise in telling you that you don't want an addicted wife. I've seen too much heartache over the last few years brought on by drugs."

"Maybe I could help her."

"No, Dave, you can't. In fact, I'm going to offer you a little wise advice. From what I've seen of people involved in the drug culture, they have to hit rock bottom before they decide on their own to change. Sometimes that takes months, or years. You can't put your life on hold in the meantime. I had a young man staying here a little over a year ago who got caught up in all that. He appeared to be a real nice young man but before I called the cops and had him arrested he'd stolen from me and my other tenant, and I'm not just talking about money. He would steal anything that he thought he could pawn to support his habit. It about broke my heart but there was nothing else I could do."

"I can't just give up on her."

"That's not your decision to make. She knows who you are, what you had, and how you feel about her. You can't force yourself on her. She ended it, Dave. As painful as that may be, you need to accept her decision and give her some space."

Chapter 34

The District Attorney called Detective Oiler Thursday afternoon. "We're moving on your case," he began. "I finalized all the charges a few minutes ago and the local PD is on their way to their house as we speak to arrest them all."

"Are you sure they're all home? I'd hate to do something premature and have to chase one or more of them down."

"We have eyes on them. The last perp entered the house five minutes ago."

"What charges are you going forward with?"

"Our initial arrest warrant will charge James Baxter and his accomplice, Tony, with assault, possession of a controlled substance, evidence and witness tampering, and attempted homicide. From there we're hoping that one or more of the roomies may decide to turn states evidence against the other two."

"What's your plan there?"

"We'll offer the other two roomies a plea deal for a few misdemeanors rather than face felony evidence tampering charges. If they'll cave in and testify that it was James that beat the crap out of the victim to try to force a miscarriage – and the fetus doesn't survive – we can enhance the charges against him and whoever assisted in that brutal assault to premeditated murder."

"The fetus may die as a result of the meth injection."

"That's true, and I don't know if you know this or not, but they found bruising around a needle stick in the middle of her shoulder blade. There's no way she could have self-administered a drug in that location, and there were still traces of it in and around the needle stick. James' and Tony's fingerprints were both on the meth syringe so either one of them could be charged with injecting her, but we've got testimony from the drug cops that their snitch sold the meth to Tony. I think if we use that, and lean on Tony, he'll finger James for actually shooting her up."

***

Friday afternoon Claire was waiting for Dave when he came home from school.

"Have you seen the national news today?" she asked solemnly.

"I don't have time to follow the news."

She handed him her laptop; he settled down in the living room and rewound the news clip. The tension he'd been living with for weeks nearly strangled him as the news commentator flipped through the story. As the article finished, his emotions flew from rage to sorrow to concern and then back to rage again. No wonder Patti hadn't wanted to talk to him!

"I'm so sorry," Claire said as Dave closed her laptop and handed it back to her. "What are you going to do?"

"I don't know," he muttered, "what can I do?"

"I'm sure there's a lot more to that story than they showed on the news," she offered. "It said that two of the four men arrested have been charged with attempted murder. Didn't you tell me that your girlfriend was in the hospital?"

"Yeah, but nobody would tell me why."

"Maybe it's time to call Patti's mom again now that the story has hit the press. It's not like she'd be telling you any secrets."

"I think now it's more a matter of embarrassment. Patti broke off our engagement and then made some bad choices that put her feet on that path. Her not wanting to talk to me about what happened sends me a pretty clear picture."

"It's not her fault that they tried to kill her, Dave. Don't you think that changes things a little?"

"I don't know, Claire. She knows that I love her. I've told her that dozens of times. I think that if this is something that I can help her with she'll call. If she doesn't, I don't have any choice but to put it all behind me and move on."

"Aren't you a little curious? That news article screams more mystery than it explains."

"Of course I'm dying to know what happened, but I don't want to find out second or third hand. If Patti wants me to know and understand what happened she'll call me. If she doesn't, then it's none of my business."

"That's pretty harsh."

"I guess I'm feeling pretty harsh right now. If I was a thousand miles closer, I'd probably go looking for James."

"That wouldn't do you any good. He's in jail. Do you want to join him there?"

"Sorry, that was just wishful thinking on my part. I know how James works. I can't help but believe that the moment I stepped out of the picture he swooped down on her, and from the stories I've heard about him, Patti didn't stand a chance."

"I've known people like that," Claire said softly. "It's the *Little Red Riding Hood* story all over again but without a happy ending."

"I feel like I just watched a safari documentary where the lion jumps out of the heavy brush and grabs an innocent animal by the throat."

"Even if *you* don't want to know the rest of the story," Claire said, "I do! The problem is that article I just showed you is on the national news. That's why it didn't get any more airtime than it did. I really like you, Dave. You don't deserve this. I'm going to do some digging on my own. When I've put the story together, I'll let you decide whether or not you want to know the facts. If nothing else I'd think you'd want to know if that James guy gets his just desserts."

"Only because I don't want him to be able to hurt anyone else. At this point I don't really care what happens to him."

"I don't believe you. Two seconds ago, you were ready to drive to Colorado and shoot the guy."

Dave put his head in his hands and took a deep breath. "I feel like I just had a death in the family," he muttered.

"It sounds like you nearly did – literally!"

Dave picked up his backpack. "I need a little alone time," he said as he walked upstairs.

He'd just plunked down in his desk chair when his cell phone rang.

"Hi Mom," he answered.

"Can you talk?" she asked.

"Yeah."

"Have you seen the news?"

"My roommate just showed me a clip on the national news."

"I saw the same thing and called Janet. She wouldn't talk to me about it."

"I'm sure she wouldn't. That's Patti's place."

"I suppose you're right. I'm so sorry Dave."

"Frankly, Mom, I don't know how to feel. I wasn't finished grieving over losing her. Now this sort of slams and locks the door between us. It's going to take me some time to wrap my mind around all of this."

"We have friends in Fort Collins. I'm going to see what they've heard on the local news."

"Please keep anything you find out to yourself, Mom. I'm in a bad place right now and don't want to know any of the details."

"I thought where you and Patti…"

"If she wants me to know what happened, she'll tell me. At this point I suppose I'm happy that the charges are for attempted murder, not homicide."

"Yes, I suppose you're right. So sorry Hon."

"Yeah, me too."

Chapter 35

James' arraignment didn't take long. By the time he and his accomplices were called before the judge, the DA and his people had already worked plea deals with two of James' other roommates, Seth and Brad. They gave testimony that James had severely beaten and kicked Patti, then had perpetrated the drug injection and the sexual assault plot to cover his tracks.

James and Tony were bound over for trial without bail. The other two, as promised in their plea deals, were charged with various misdemeanors and released pending court appearances.

Claire briefly related to Dave what little she'd found out from her *sources*, but in order to preserve his sanity, Dave filed those facts in his mental vault and tried to get on with his life. He tried to tell himself that he could stay aloof, but he couldn't and his schoolwork suffered. In the end, spring semester proved to be a disaster. He finished the term with a 'B' average and had to meet with the Dean to discuss his scholastic standing. Thankfully the Dean was able to empathize when Dave bared his soul about why he had been distracted and the Dean convinced Raytheon that Dave was better than his GPA for the semester indicated.

Dave flew home and spent a week unwinding in Colorado Springs with his parents before he had to fly out to New Jersey to meet the Raytheon engineering team. Dave made his parents understand from the moment they picked him up at the airport that Patti was a forbidden subject. He was pretending to have moved on and needed to step away.

***

New Jersey and the frenetic work schedule that Raytheon immersed him in was exactly what Dave needed to get his feet back on the ground. He got along well with his assigned team of half a dozen seasoned engineers and was assigned to a cutting edge technology project that literally swept him away. Until then he'd dealt with a lot of engineering theory but having a hands-on approach further convinced him that he'd chosen his life's work well.

Midsummer, his intern program swept Dave and his team off to the Florida coast for three weeks for some practical hands-on rocket science applications. There he met Rebecca, a solid, no-nonsense graduate student assigned as the team chief on his project.

A tall, striking blonde, Rebecca came to the Raytheon team from Massachusetts, and had an interesting eastern accent. Unlike some of the other members of his team, Dave kept his hands, thoughts, and eyes to himself when they were working together.

"You're different," Rebecca told him one day as they were grabbing a quick, delivered lunch.

"Is that good or bad?" Dave responded.

"You intrigue me a little. You're not wearing a wedding ring. You don't talk about a girlfriend, and you don't gawk."

Dave grinned. "Sorry, I thought we were here to work on the project, not flirt."

"We are, of course, but sometimes your lack of *natural pursuit* makes me think there's something going on behind your eyes that I should be aware of. You don't seem gay."

"Let's just say I recently went through the painful breakup of a long-term relationship and I'm still pretty raw."

"Her idea or yours?"

"Hers… no, actually I can't blame her. I was an idiot."

"Let me guess. She could hear wedding bells and all you could see in your near future was a lot of gut-busting schoolwork."

"Are you clairvoyant?"

319

She laughed. "No but sometimes I can read people. You seem to walk around all day with this intense sense of mission on your brow that kinda tells me you're trying too hard to focus."

"I thought that was why I was here."

"Life is too short to be all about the daily grind. If you don't take time to enjoy the ride you're going to get ulcers. Worse yet, when you finish school and get a real job you'll end up taking your work home with you. That's bad! You need to learn to balance, Dave."

He frowned.

"Ah hah!" she exclaimed softly, "I thought so!"

"Am I that transparent?"

"Maybe. So tell me, Dave, how long did you date this person that threw you under the bus."

"Four years."

"Are you kidding me! Oh my gosh, are we talking about a high school sweetheart?"

"Yes."

"Someday when we have more time, I'd like to hear that story. I love gossip!"

"I may not want to talk about it."

"Your choice, of course, but if I was to invite you out for dinner and drinks, Friday after work, that might give us something interesting to talk about."

"Wouldn't that be a little awkward? Sometimes fraternizing with the boss is frowned upon."

"Nobody but us would know. It's not like we're going to be sneaking around while we're on the job. That would be poor form and would make everyone else feel uncomfortable. Frankly, I'd like to have someone to talk to that isn't always trying to look down my blouse."

She winked and he grinned.

Rebecca slipped him a note Friday afternoon. It read: "Dress casual and wear sandals. This may involve a walk on the beach after dinner."

She called moments after he got back to his hotel room. "Hi Dave. Sorry for all of the secrecy but I have an admirer on the team that's been trying to get me to go out with him ever since we got here. He's pretty persistent and I don't want to cause any tension. Do you like seafood?"

"Love it."

"Great! There's a place straight south, down the North Atlantic Highway called Q's Crackin' Crab & Seafood Kitchen. Watch for the California Avenue intersection. It's right on the corner on your left. If you put it in your phone, it should be easy to find. It's only about five minutes south of The Radisson. I'll meet you there in a half hour. That might seem a little early for dinner but they get really busy after six and I hate standing in line."

Dave thought he was going to be a little early but Rebecca saw him drive in and got out of her rental car to meet him.

"This place may not look like much from the outside but believe me they know how to do seafood. I've never had a bad dinner here."

"You come here often?"

"Yes, I love it. I live near the coast in Massachusetts. I was practically weaned on seafood. I've had good and bad elsewhere. I think you'll be pleased."

She wasn't lying when she told him to dress casual. She was wearing a light blue tank top over white shorts and was dressed in open-toed sandals. He hadn't really noticed before but her eyes were strikingly blue, not that they should have been any different with her naturally blonde hair. Dave followed her lead and a few minutes later they faced each other across a table by the south windows.

"Where this is your first time here," she said, "I suggest their sampler. It includes a little of all of their best sellers."

He glanced quickly at the menu anyway. There were so many things there that it didn't take him long to become confused. "Okay Rebecca," he surrendered after a few moments, "I'll trust you this time but if it's bad, I'll never come here again."

"It's Becca when we're away from work," she smiled, "but in the office it has to be Rebecca."

"Thank you. That's a lot easier to say."

"All my friends back home call me Becca. I don't know why my folks named me Rebecca. I think the only time I heard that word growing up was when I was in trouble. Is your given name David or Dave?"

"Dave. I think my parents wanted to avoid the formal name but believe me my mom knew just how to use that name to let me know when I was in trouble!"

She chuckled.

"Why engineering?" Dave asked.

"Uh-oh," she grinned, "is this where I have to listen to all the dumb, blonde jokes?"

"You may be blonde but you're hardly dumb. I find you fascinating."

"As compared to your ex?"

Dave nearly choked and quickly looked away.

"Oops, sorry! That was really poor form, especially where that's how you ended up here with me."

"How's that?"

"I can tell you're hurting. I have a sixth sense for that sort of thing. I was always hauling home strays – cats, dogs, turtles – you name it."

"Okay," she continued quietly. "I won't ask you anymore personal questions – yet. Instead I'll talk about me for awhile but after dinner we need to drive down to West Cocoa Beach Pier and go for a walk along the beach. It's not far. We could walk from here but there's a parking lot down there and I hate to take up parking in their parking lot here. Like you'll soon see, this place gets really busy."

***

True to her word, Becca filled the dinnertime conversation with her light banter. By the time they finished up and walked to their respective rental cars, he knew that she'd been raised in Salem, Massachusetts. Her father was independently wealthy, they owned a sailing yacht, and from the time she was little, she, her three brothers, and her parents had spent their summers sailing up and down the eastern seaboard. *Daddy* had insisted that she make something of herself and early on in her life he had thrown all sorts of opportunities her way to *help* her *choose* a line of work. In the end, her love of understanding what made things *tick* led her into engineering.

All too soon the easy part of the evening was over and he found himself walking beside her along the seashore listening to the rush of the breakers on the sand.

"I love this time of day," Becca said after a few moments. "The sun's not in your eyes, most of the tourists have worn themselves out in the surf or have gotten so sunburned that they've decided to call it a day. Now is when the deep thinkers come here. If you'll notice, there are a lot of people just sitting above the wet mark in the sand contemplating nature."

"I haven't spent much time along the coast," Dave answered. "I'm from Colorado but the surf seems so soothing to me."

"And with that Dave," Becca said as she stepped close and took his elbow, "it's your turn to purge. Even though I seem to have more

323

than enough to say, I had my say early so you wouldn't be tempted to break your train of thought to ask me any inane get-to-know-you questions. Why are you so sad?"

The way she asked the question instantly brought tears to Dave's eyes. There were so many things that he hadn't said to anyone…

"Wow," she said softly when she looked up at him. "I had no idea you were bottling so much up inside."

Dave took a deep breath and looked down into her eyes for a moment. "I suppose you're safe," he said carefully, "you hardly know me from Adam."

"Oh I know Adam," she snickered, "he's a dweeb. You're certainly not him."

Dave stared down the beach for a few long moments as they walked on, until he could finally control his emotions enough to begin.

She stopped him a while later and motioned toward the sand. "We should sit," she suggested. "With all you have to say if we keep walking we'll be in Miami and then we'll have to hire a taxi to bring us back."

"So you never found out what really happened to her then?" Becca asked later, after a long pause indicated that Dave had said all he could say.

"No. I didn't want to hear anything secondhand. I sent her that last long text, leaving everything in her court. I decided two things really. Either she didn't love me and it was over in spite of what happened, or else she …"

"Was too humiliated by what had happened to ever want to bare her soul to you."

"Yeah, I suppose I couldn't have said that any better."

They sat in silence for awhile, surrounded by emptiness, carried away in their own thoughts.

"I'm getting chilled," Becca finally said, getting to her feet. "That may sound strange. It's probably still in the 70's but there's something about the moist breeze…"

"Thank you Becca," Dave said as he faced her and brushed a strand of her long, blonde hair out of her eyes. "This has been really cleansing for me."

"You're welcome Dave. Like I told you at the first, I could tell that you were hurting."

They turned around and walked back toward the pier.

"Tell me about him," Dave asked quietly after a few minutes.

"Who?"

"Come on, Becca, you're beautiful inside and out and you're not wearing a wedding ring either. I think the only way you could have known I was hurting is because you've got a few unspoken sorrows of your own."

She didn't answer for a few long moments. "I don't know if I can be as brave as you," she finally said. "I could hardly breathe when you started talking about James. You see I was a victim of a man just like him. I swear when you were telling me about James that you were really talking about Blake. I'd had boyfriends all through school but I didn't really fall hard for anyone until my senior year in college. I thought by then I'd seen the best and the worst in men, but I really had no idea."

Dave gave her her space for a few moments, knowing she'd continue when she could.

"Blake, like James, was a pretty boy – worse yet he came from big money. He could afford to do all of the things that I thought were wild and exciting. He'd fly me to the Bahamas for the weekend. We'd go sailing and lobstering and gambling. There seemed to be no end to his bank account. He drove fancy cars. He got invited to all the fancy parties. He knew celebrities and he took me to all sorts of gala events. If he thought I needed a new outfit to flaunt myself with, he'd take me shopping."

"And then," Dave verbally nudged her after a long, poignant pause.

"And then I got an STD and my whole world fell apart. Before I accused him outright of infidelity, I used some of my dad's money and influence to hire a private detective. What I found out was beyond my worst nightmares. I don't know how he was juggling us all at the same time but when my detective started surveilling him he found out that I was one of eight women he was *dating* at the same time."

"What did you do?"

"My dad and I went sailing off the coast for a week where I could vent. My dad, of course, was livid and wanted to ruin Blake but how can you hurt an indestructible, gelatinous blob? It turned out that Blake has no morals, no backbone, no job, no conscience, and he has an unlimited stream of his daddy's money. He loves surrounding himself with shiny things and unfortunately I found out that I didn't mean any more to him than any one of his other shiny things. Do you know what he said when I called him up to accuse him of everything I'd found out?"

"No, what?"

"He laughed and said: *looks like you caught me then, do you need some penicillin?*"

"What did you do?"

"The only thing I thought I could do to get revenge. I flooded social media with hateful accusations."

"And?"

"And his father's million-dollar attorney called my father and threatened to sue us both for defamation if I didn't pull them all down."

"Did he ever call you again?"

"Of course not. I was just one of his shiny trinkets."

"How long ago was that?"

"It's been just over a year now."

"Wow, Becca, I am so sorry!"

She pulled his arm tightly against her and said nothing. Dave could feel soft shudders that wracked her body as they walked.

They reached the parking lot before the silence between them drifted away.

"Thank you Becca," Dave said softly as they paused beside her car. "This has been really good for me."

"It has for me as well, Dave," she said. "You're the only person I've ever told that story to, besides my dad, of course, and I couldn't even tell him everything. I was too embarrassed."

Dave gently took her in his arms and pulled her close. She laid her head on his shoulder and sobbed. He wondered for a few moments if he should kiss her but it didn't seem right. What they had shared was special and intimate but he knew a kiss would be inappropriate.

"Thank you Dave," she finally said, pushing herself gently away.

He took her chin in his fingers so he could look her in the eyes. "You're welcome Becca. I hope you know you can trust me."

Tears filled her eyes. "Yes, I know I can, and you can't believe how hard this is for me standing here in the arms of a strange man and being able to tell myself that I may have finally found trust again."

Chapter 36

Dave's last week in Florida was a time of healing – for both Becca and himself. Even though they would occasionally exchange a knowing glance in the company of the rest of the team, they were very careful not to let anyone else see. They spent every night after work and all day Saturday and Sunday together, far away from where anyone from the team would see them together. They built on the trust they'd shared but they were very careful with any physical touch.

"Man, I want to kiss you," Dave told her as they left the restaurant Saturday night, "but we're both flying out tomorrow and this has been so healing that I don't want to spoil it."

She laughed. "I was beginning to wonder if maybe you'd lost all faith in women – or maybe you were afraid I still had an STD or something."

"That was the last thing on my mind. It's been so very good to be able to talk to someone who understands what it's like to be eviscerated. I just didn't want any regrets."

"Nor do I, but I kiss the people I love all the time."

Dave was a little shaken by her statement. "I can't…"

"Can't what?" she demanded with a grin, "you can't kiss me?"

"Oh I can do that but I can't tell you that I love you."

"I can honestly tell you that I do love you, Dave – maybe not in a husband-wife sort of way but you're a great person. I've known that ever since we met. I'll always cherish this time we spent together. I finally think I'm brave enough to move on. Will you call me when you get back?"

"That can go both ways you know," he said.

"I'd like that a lot. I'm sure there'll be times when I'll need to call up and vent to someone I can trust."

"And love?"

She smiled and took him in her arms and kissed him. "Yeah, that too!"

***

Dave's summer intern program ended the middle of August. Classes at college were slated to begin the third Monday of the month. A couple of weeks later he had a three day break for the Labor Day holiday. He hadn't seen his folks in a while so he made plans to fly home before school started again after the holiday. Becca's call interrupted all that.

"Hey Dave," she began happily, "do you have big plans for the Labor Day holiday?"

"I thought I might fly home to visit my folks."

"That sounds like something a nice boy would do, but if you're going to spend a little of your hard-earned cash on a plane ticket anyway, why don't you fly to Boston with me and go sailing with my dad and me over the long weekend. My dad wants to go out lobstering and none of my brothers can go. It takes at least two sailors to man the boat and my mom is worthless on the water."

He hesitated. One of the things he'd thought about doing while he was home was dropping by Patti's place. She hadn't ever called and after speaking with his mom he found out that her parents had severed ties with his parents as well. He suspected something was seriously wrong. He wanted to know – no, he needed to know – if there was still anything between them. The deadly silence was an obvious indication but he wondered if what she was feeling was embarrassment over what had happened or if it was something more sinister. Was she addicted?

"Oh, okay. I won't beg," she said with a laugh. "I had a great time in Florida and I wanted my dad to meet you."

329

"Oh no!" he exclaimed in mock horror, "not the *meet my dad* thing!"

"It's not like that at all!" she laughed. "After the summer grind I needed a few days off and I thought you might like it. Have you ever been on a boat before?"

"Nope. What if I hate it? I don't want to be hanging over the railing all the time, or whatever you have to do when you're seasick."

"I won't admit this to my dad, but I have to wear Dramamine patches behind both ears whenever we go out. It's no big deal, really. We won't go out if it's really rough. I'm all stocked up with meds."

"Do I need to buy some seafaring clothes or something?"

She laughed. "Unlike Florida, Salem in September can be a bit nippy when you're out on the water. Just bring your Colorado clothes. We've got all of the foul weather gear you may need. I wouldn't bother with a swimsuit, though, unless you want to flaunt yourself. The water won't be conducive to a dip overboard."

He didn't answer for a few moments.

"You really are going to make me beg, aren't you?"

"No. I'm sorry. I've just got a lot of other things on my mind right now."

"Patti?"

"Yeah, her too."

"You can go home for Thanksgiving. You've got until then to mend those ties. It'll be too cold and rough to go sailing in November. Have you called her?"

"Not yet."

"Can I offer you a little advice? I think the silence from her end of the phone speaks volumes. Save that phone call until you're back in school. I don't think either one of you are up to trying to patch up a long-distance relationship over a long weekend anyway. You're hurting but you don't know what's going on behind her eyes. I really think if she wanted to go there she'd have called you by now. I know I would have."

"Okay," he answered quietly. "You're probably right. I guess the worst thing that could happen right now would be for me to fly home and find out face-to-face that she doesn't want to talk to me. Cauterizing my wounds over the phone will probably be less painful. The last thing I want to see is the darkness in her eyes when she has to tell me to my face that it's over."

"Great!" she exclaimed happily. "Can you be ready to go tonight? I'll make reservations on the redeye for both of us and have an Uber pick you up so you don't have to leave your car at the airport."

"Okay," he answered hesitantly, "Let me know how much the tickets are and I'll Venmo you the money."

"This is my treat!" she insisted. "I already told you that my dad is loaded and I have an open bank account. Seriously, all you have to do is bring your understanding self and help me spend a great weekend with my dad."

"Your paying my way makes me feel a little uncomfortable."

She laughed. "I'll tell my dad you said that. Seriously, the cost is nothing to him and if nothing else that should tell him that you're not another Blake, if you catch my drift. That little affair really made him gun-shy. I'm not saying they're all like that but sometimes rich boys have no real sense of value – for things or people."

***

Bryant, Becca's dad, met them at the airport.

"Hey Dad," Becca said as a short, balding, clean-shaven man stepped out of the crowd around the luggage claim area, "thanks for picking us up in the middle of the night. You know you didn't have to do that. I know my way home."

The man swept her into his arms and lifted her off her feet. "That's no problem at all!" he exclaimed after she kissed him full on the mouth and he set her back on her feet. "It's so good to see you Becca! And this must be Dave!"

"Bryant Lancaster," Becca said happily as her dad reached out a hand, "this is Dave Tolman from Colorado Springs. Dave, this is my dad, Bryant."

The moment Dave took Bryant's hand he realized a couple of things about Becca's dad. The man was fit and intense. The man's light brown eyes bore into him as if he was looking deep into his soul.

"I'm pleased to meet you, Dave!" her dad exclaimed. The grin that had graced his face only moments before had been instantly replaced by a more cautious, non-descript expression that reminded Dave of the expression he'd seen on the Dean's face when the man called him in to *discuss* his poor scholastic performance, after his first semester at Purdue. Dave couldn't tell if the man was skeptical of him and his motives or if he was just using the face he showed to all the strangers he met in the world in which he lived.

"Likewise," Dave managed. "Becca speaks highly of you."

Bryant chuckled. "She would do that. She has to treat me well or she knows I'll cut her off."

"Dad!" Becca protested. "It's not like that, and you know it. Don't you go putting on your pouty face. I like this guy and I'll not have you running him off before you even get to know him."

"I don't know whether or not you'll believe a stranger," Dave answered as he released the man's firm handshake, "but she really does speak highly of you."

"Yeah, I know," her dad said as his smile returned and he turned his attention back to his daughter. "She's the best daughter a man could have – and I've probably told her this before but second to her mom she's the best thing that has ever come into my life."

"What a great compliment," Dave replied, "there aren't many men who would admit that."

"And just so you'll know upfront Dad," Becca changed the subject, "Dave is here as my guest. He's uncomfortable with that, though. He's got backbone."

"Coming from Becca," Bryant replied, looking into Dave's eyes, "that's a real compliment. With one unfortunate exception, she has been a pretty good judge of character."

"And I've already told you about Blake," she interjected. "Dad told me that everyone needs a heartbreak or two in life so we can sort out the good things from the bad."

"Enough of all this political maneuvering," Bryant laughed. "In case you haven't noticed it's late and I'd like to be on the water early before the seas get choppy. I suspect Dave and I will get to know each other a lot better over the next couple of days. Being from Colorado, you probably haven't spent much time on the water, have you?"

"No," Dave replied humbly, "and frankly, I'm a little worried. I don't want to ruin this for you two. Becca is pretty excited about this outing."

"I like this kid," Bryant said warmly as he picked up Becca's suitcase, took her elbow, and led the way toward the exit. "He's not at all pretentious the way you described him."

"Dad, I never told you any such thing!"

Bryant offered a knowing grin and then turned his attention to Becca.

***

By 4 a.m. Bryant and Becca had given Dave a short tour of their small sailing yacht, assigned him a berth below deck and outfitted him in a weatherproof windbreaker and jacket – and a bright orange life vest.

"I won't try to teach you anything about sailing for now," Becca said as her *all business* face took over a few moments later. "I'd suggest you take a seat on the stern and stay out of our way for now. We'll run on auxiliary power until we get out past the breakwater and then we may put on some sail. I won't take the time to explain why for now. I think you'll get the gist of that all on your own."

Bryant was all business in the cabin as he watched a bank of glowing instruments and listened to a repetitive weather report as Becca scurried here and there around the deck. Dave did as he was told and stayed carefully unobtrusive. The rhythmic pitch and float of the deck beneath his padded deck chair began lulling him into a sort of semiconscious stupor as they moved on in the darkness. Exhausted and unneeded it seemed, he finally allowed himself to doze.

"Are you bored already?" Becca asked happily sometime later as she sat down beside him and folded her arm through his.

Somewhat startled, Dave roused. A light, cloudless, pale-blue sky stretched over them. He hurriedly glanced out at an open expanse of rolling water around them.

"Sorry!" he apologized. "I was pretty tired. What time is it? Don't you people ever sleep?"

"Not until we get the traps out," she said with a yawn. "The sun will be up in a few minutes and then we'll bait and drop the traps, sail off a little and drop a short anchor to keep the bow into the swells. Then we'll have a little something to eat and have a snooze."

"How far out do you go? I can't see land so I have to assume we're at least 12 miles out."

"Where did you learn that?"

"I don't know. Somewhere in my memory banks of useless practical knowledge I remember storing a snippet of information that talked about a 12-mile horizon. Am I anywhere close?"

She chuckled. "That's pretty tall talk for a landlubber, undergrad engineering student but in layman's terms that's probably about right. Like everyone else, Dad has his favorite fishing hole. We're headed to someplace about 35 miles off the coast."

"I thought a fishing hole was a discernable spot on a lake or a river where you can actually tell where you're standing."

"It's sort of the same thing out here. We just have to use instruments to tell us where it is. I won't pretend to know how it all works but Dad tells me the seabed varies a lot just like the dry land does as you drive across it. There are a lot of hills and gullies. Some places are just more conducive to sea life than others. He must know his stuff, though, because we always catch plenty of lobsters."

"I thought you said something about putting up some sails."

"Not this morning. Dad's all business today. He's got plenty of fuel aboard and he's anxious to get his pots in the water. This first day we'll all be tired enough that we'll probably just laze about, nap and eat. Tomorrow when we're all rested, if the sea and weather conditions are right, he'll probably put on some sail and go farther out. The worst thing we could do is get so far out that getting back in if a blow comes up would be bothersome."

"I'm not sure I like the sounds of that."

"Relax. Dad's been watching and we've got a clear forecast for the next two days anyway. We usually have plenty of warning if something's on the way. There are probably thousands of us out here at any one time. The weather boys do a fair job of keeping us informed so we won't get ourselves in trouble. They don't want to have to come out and rescue us any worse than we want to need to be rescued."

"Okay. This is all new to me. I feel like a brand-new Boy Scout on his first campout in the woods. The Scoutmaster can warn you about most of the things you shouldn't do, but he has no real control over what a meandering bear or protective momma moose might have in mind."

"That's a pretty good analogy, actually. We obviously don't expect any proverbial bears to come along but that doesn't mean it can't happen. Dad's seen a lot so I think he's prepared for most of those things."

"Have you ever been in rough weather?"

"You mean besides Blake?"

"I didn't think you liked talking about him."

"I don't, but like heavy weather, he's just something that happened along to ruin an otherwise great day of sailing."

"So …"

"So are you going to wax philosophic on me now and try to compare Blake to a nor'easter?"

"I don't really know what a nor'easter is, but I have to assume that's some sort of bad storm?"

"The worst! You don't want to be anywhere on the water when one of those blows in."

"Too bad you didn't have a weather forecaster hanging around when you met him."

"Oh, I did. That's part of the problem. My dad has a sort of sixth sense. He never liked Blake but he knew that trying to drive him away would just stiffen up my neck and make me more determined."

"So he just had to let you ride out the storm and then help recover the wreckage?"

"You got it!"

"And?"

She offered a shrewd smile. "And that's why you're here with him. I guess I don't trust my own judgement anymore."

"Then this is going to be an awful three days for me?"

"Not if you don't try to hide anything from him."

"What exactly does that mean?"

"That means that he'll know if you're trying to be someone you're not. After Blake, I've really learned to trust Dad in these matters. Does that make any sense at all?"

"Of course it does, but what if he just doesn't like my personality or the way I hold my mouth?"

"He can look past stuff like that to a point. Facial expressions can be faked but personality is generally the sum total of everything that you are inside."

She paused.

"The problem is, sometimes gullible little girls like me, can't see beyond the here and now. Dads don't get wrapped up in all of the emotional posturing. He's not here looking for a potential mate for me. He's here acting like the protective momma bear."

"Somehow that doesn't make me feel any better."

"You have absolutely nothing to worry about," she chuckled. "If you're anything like I think you are, he'll love you."

"And then?"

She caught his eyes and her facial features softened. "And then, maybe we can take this weekend to the next level."

***

Bryant kept everything on a mostly business level until after lunch, and then the inquisition that Becca had warned him about began. Even though Dave was watching for the man's technique, he was a half hour or more into a friendly talk when Becca slipped into some sun wear and announced that she was going to take a little nap on the bow while it was still warm. That's when he actually noticed the man's subtle attack. Rather than ask pointed questions, Bryant just acted like he wanted to chat. They talked about Dave's athletic scholarship, his love and hate of football and the reasons he'd decided to study engineering. Then their conversation shifted a little to weightier matters.

"Becca told me you recently went through a breakup," Bryant said, studying his countenance for a reaction, "I'm sorry to hear that Dave…"

And then Bryant told him a moving story of a relationship he'd had in college. Dave suspected that the man may have embellished the story at some point, but if he had it didn't matter because the man got his point across.

"Do you think you'll patch things up with Patti?" Bryant asked quietly after a pause in their conversation.

"I don't honestly know," Dave answered truthfully. "I don't know what Becca told you about that but I'm afraid I messed up pretty badly. It wasn't until after Patti spelled it all out for me that I realized that I was putting football and school ahead of everything else in my life. She got tired of waiting around."

"Do you think you've learned anything by that?"

A surge of anger flashed through Dave for a few moments and he had to look away, afraid the older man would see the tension in his face.

"If I haven't," Dave finally answered, turning back to look at her father, "then I'd say that I'm pretty stupid."

"Sorry to be so blunt," Bryant answered. "I can tell I offended you by asking you that but I honestly believe you're telling me the truth."

The man looked down at his hands for a few moments until he continued. "You know, Dave, I was born into wealth. I've never really wanted for anything in my life, but unlike a lot of guys in my somewhat envious position I think I've learned a lot about human nature. There are too many guys like me who use their wealth to lord over people and demand obeisance, if you catch my drift, rather than by gaining trust and respect among their peers or from those who work for them. Too often wealth doesn't build much character in a man. It's too easy to feel entitled."

He paused and studied Dave's eyes for a few moments.

"Do you know what I'm talking about?" he finally asked.

"Yes, I think so."

"I like you, Dave. You seem to be respectful. I can tell you've had a good upbringing."

He paused again, seeming to struggle for his next words.

"But," he finally continued, "I need to ask you some very probing man-to-man questions. I hope you'll seriously consider what I have to say without becoming angry or resentful. At the end of the day what I take from this conversation and talk to Becca about won't really influence her much. I really have no control over how either of you will react to what I have to say, so I'll just come right out with it. Becca is a strong-willed young woman – much like her mother. Her insight is really nothing like her mother's, at any rate. Her mom is pretty judgmental. Becca is often too trusting. She loves easily, as you probably gathered from the stories she may have told you about Blake. She fell hard for him. I'm sure after the Blake affair, she's put on some armor but she's still probably a little too naïve."

Bryant studied him for a moment.

"I don't want to play the wealth card, Dave, but I need to so you can make an informed decision. I understand she paid for your airline tickets out here. How did that make you feel?"

"Uncomfortable. I felt like I needed to pay my own way."

"That's good, Dave. That shows you have character. The problem is, because she's my daughter she's never wanted for anything and she and her brothers probably never will. If you were married to her, what would you imagine your life would be like?"

"I haven't known her for long. I've never taken the time to think about that."

"That's also admirable, Dave. I believe you. I'm not stupid, though. You're probably one in a thousand, maybe one in a million young men who might be able to look past that. I also sense a little turmoil so when you wonder what your lives together might look like. You're both engineering students. From what she tells me you've got a great future – and so does she – and not because I shelled out the cash or could have pulled strings to get her into Purdue. I didn't by the way."

Dave was instantly uncomfortable with the way the conversation was drifting, but powerless to stop that drift, instead, he just listened as Bryant continued.

"Do you think that you would expect Becca to change her lifestyle to fit into the one you and she can afford together? I know she has maternal instincts so she's going to want a family. Knowing her the way I do I think she may want to step away from her career and become a fulltime mom when that happens – which would be great! The problem is, Dave, what then? Will she become resentful if you can't provide for her in the way she's become accustomed? Would your pride allow me and/or her mother to help when and where you can't? Will you be angry if we give things to your kids that you can't afford?"

Dave considered the questions for a few moments before he answered.

"You know, Bryant, I can honestly say that I've never even considered anything like that, but what you're telling me has a lot of merit. On the one hand I can say that I'd never step between you and Becca, or our children if we should have any. But on the other hand, I don't know Becca well enough yet to know how she'd react to that either – especially if she considers what you're doing to be an intrusion into our lives. I think that I consider myself to be self-sufficient enough that I'd always try to provide a good living for her. I guess what it all boils down to are expectations. If, as you've told me, she's used to living a millionaire's lifestyle and I can't provide that for her, then she has to make a decision. Will she be willing to lower her expectations and be satisfied with what I can provide for her or will she end up resenting me when I can't do more?"

Bryant nodded as if he agreed.

"I guess my take on all that would be I'd have to defer those matters to her. I wouldn't be above accepting your help if and when she needs it – or when you would like to freely give us something without any expectations. If I were in your shoes I'd want to help my kids out all I could. What I couldn't live with is her thinking that I'm less of a man because I can't match giving her what her father can."

Bryant smiled. "I hope you can see where I'm coming from Dave. And assuming you're being straight with me I really like your answers. There are a lot of men who envy my wealth. You may not think it does, but having wealth comes with a very heavy burden. If you empower your kids the way Blake's parents did him, you'll ruin their lives. Someday he's going to wake up and realize that his youth is gone and he's surrounded himself with parasites with no natural affection for him – vermin that will walk away the moment the money quits flowing. Unless he does something truly out of the ordinary, he will probably never spend all of his parent's fortune. I'm just old fashioned enough to believe that true happiness comes through the love of people. My prediction is he will never find that and will turn to vice until it destroys him way before his time."

Bryant stopped for a moment to gather his thoughts, and then he continued. "I've met a lot of younger men who would like nothing better than to be able to do what Blake does. He doesn't see the need to go to school, he's never worked a day in his life, he has taken his folks for everything they're willing to give him and sometimes demands things that they aren't willing to give. He's a waste of a life, a moral degenerate – the worst kind of a man!"

Neither men spoke for awhile.

"I guess I don't know what you want from me," Dave finally answered. "I can sit here and nod dumbly and agree with everything you've just told me. It's easy when I don't have to make those decisions to play armchair quarterback and suppose I'd take all the right steps. But I think we both know I'd be lying if I said I'd never be tempted by any of that. I'd never considered this before but you're absolutely right when you tell me that wealth is a heavy burden. I can't say whether or not I'm up to the challenge. In fact at this point I'm not even sure I want to consider it. I've only known Becca for a few short weeks. I like her. I respect her. She's an amazing woman and like you just told me she has a good heart. She's easy to love."

Their eyes met and held for a few long moments.

"I think at the end of the day it's way too early for either me or her to look very far beyond the preliminary feelings we have for each other. I understand what you're trying to tell me and I appreciate why you've done this but you've just met me. You have no idea what's going on behind my eyes."

A genuine smile crept across Bryant's face. "No Dave you're right. I don't know you, but sitting here in this chair I can honestly say I feel you. I'm not infallible but I think I have a fair grasp of people and I sense that you're a good man. From what Becca has told me you may be prone to tunnel vision but I can tell you've learned a lot from that mistake – maybe hard things like Becca learned from Blake."

Bryant offered his hand. "Thank you Dave," he said as Dave firmly grasped his hand. "This has been a good conversation. Now let's put this behind us and enjoy that wonderful young woman we came out here with. I'll bet by now we should have a few lobsters in the traps. There's nothing quite like the taste of a fresh lobster right out of the ocean!"

Chapter 37

*D*ave's first night on the open ocean under the stars with Bryant and Becca left him filled with both awe and apprehension. Sometime between the time when he finished his little talk with Bryant and when they all sat around the table in the evening to gorge themselves on seafood, Becca had obviously had *the talk* with her dad. Any reservations she may have shown on their brief dates in Florida fell away and he instantly saw the Becca that was so easy to love. It frightened him. On the one hand he was still raw and bleeding from what had happened between him and Patti. On the other hand the sea was placid, the sea breezes were light and fresh. The billions of stars coming out of a gray-blue sky overhead weren't impeded by either clouds or by any hint of a moon. As Becca lay down beside him on a wide cushion on the bow of the yacht and tugged a light blanket over them, he could hardly breathe.

"*A penny for your thoughts,*" she asked quietly a few moments later.

"I'm speechless."

"Because Dad is listening?"

"Is he?"

"Probably not. He went downstairs to his berth ten minutes ago. He's tired and he was young once. He knows what forces are afoot here."

"I'm afraid," he whispered.

"Of what?"

"Isn't this when Jaws jumps up out of the water, crashes down on us leaving us screaming, knowing that at any second he's going to chomp us in half?"

She laughed and pulled him close. "That only happens in the movies. We're perfectly safe here."

"I wish I was so certain."

"Are you afraid of me?"

"Not really afraid of you, but of what you represent."

"Okay, and just what might that be?"

"Your dad told me you're easy to love. You are, and that's what really scares me."

"Why, because maybe it means closing the chapters of your life that has Patti's name scribed on every heading?"

"Like it or not I think I've already done that."

"Then what?"

"Do I need to spell it out? This couldn't be any more romantic if an orchestra suddenly floated up out of the ocean complete with fireflies and fairies floating all around us."

She giggled. "You really do watch too many movies."

"Tell me I'm wrong."

"I can't," she said after a few moments.

"I think I'm too vulnerable."

"I know the feeling."

"You shouldn't be. How long ago did you say you broke it off with Blake?"

"Please don't say that name," she whispered. "You just threw a bucket of ice water on me. Besides it's not the breakup with him that's haunting me."

"What then?"

"Now I suppose you want me to spell it out, so I will. I think you already know that I love easily and you might think this is dumb to say because we barely know each other, but I really do think I love you Dave. I've never felt this way with anyone else before and I've had a lot of boyfriends, if you know what I mean."

"I think it's just the setting."

"No it's not, and quit throwing cold water on me! I've felt this way ever since we sat on the beach together in Florida and poured our hearts out to each other. I feel like we're kindred spirits."

"If only that were true."

"Why are you doubting?"

"Probably because of the little talk your dad and I had today about wealth and responsibility."

"Did he throw ice water on you?"

"I think he hit me with the bucket instead."

She laughed. "You've got such a way with words but really, is that why you're afraid of me?"

"I don't think I'm afraid of you, but your dad made a good point. Will we both be the same people we are now in twenty or thirty years? Will you get tired of me when we have to deal with real life on a daily basis?"

"You could ask the same question of any couple," she countered. "Wealth may add complications but I think in order to stay together you need to grow together. No we won't be the same people that we are right now or even a year from now, or longer. The important thing is that if we decide to do something beyond this night—this weekend – we need to do it together in open and total honesty. My mom was a pauper when she met and married my dad and they're still together."

"But you told me they don't get along."

"I didn't tell you that! What I told you in effect is that she's very different than my dad. She's strong-willed, hard to love, hard to live with. That's just her. The interesting part is, she's been that way ever since I've known her. I don't think she ever really changed. That's what drew my dad to her in the first place. He loves her for who she is. He never tries to change her. They trust each other enough that they can live their own separate lives as individuals and yet they still trust each other to only share themselves with each other. Does that make any sense?"

"I think it does, actually. My folks are a little different in that they try to share interests and support one another."

"So if I decided I was totally interested in ceramic pot making and you wanted to go on safari in Africa, how would that work? Does that mean we should both give up what we love doing and find a second interest together that's more compatible?"

"Do you think our interests would be that varied?"

"They could be. Can you tell me what your likes might be in twenty years?"

"Good point."

"Okay," she said softly as she raised herself up on one elbow, "are we going to talk all night or is there something else you'd rather do?"

He cupped the back of her neck softly in his hand as she moved up over him to kiss him.

A few minutes later, Dave gently turned his head away and then folded her up in a tight embrace. "I can't go there," he managed.

"I can," she said, "but I'll understand if you don't want to."

"It's not a matter of not wanting to."

"I know. It's complicated. I totally understand."

"Maybe we should go below deck where we can sleep," Dave chuckled, "there's something about this night air that's keeping me awake."

***

When Becca woke him up, light was flooding through the porthole just over his bed.

"Breakfast is on, sleepyhead," she said as she bent over and kissed him, "and the wind has come up a little. Dad suggested we put on some canvas and go for a sail. He knows some cool islands just off the coast that might be fun to visit."

"What about the lobster traps?"

"We'll pull them up before we leave in case we decide to go back another way."

"Good morning," Bryant offered enthusiastically as Dave made his way into the crowded galley. "Not knowing what you eat for breakfast, I just cooked for myself. If you're not into a traditional French toast sort of thing I have sweet rolls or yogurt. I believe there's also some chilled lobster left over from last night if you'd rather."

"I'm not picky," Dave said, "whatever you've got going on smells great to me."

"You hear that Becca?" her dad laughed, "he's not picky. I think he'll be easy to satisfy at the table – or elsewhere."

"Dad!" she protested.

"I noticed you came downstairs early last night," Bryant teased, "somebody turn out the lights on deck?"

"No," Dave grinned. "It was too hot on deck. I needed to get closer to the water level to cool off."

"And in case you're wondering, Dad, Dave was a perfect gentleman. I liked the heat. I was afraid he was going to jump overboard when I told him we didn't have enough fresh water for a cold shower."

Bryant laughed merrily. "Ah Becca you tease, now you've turned his face all red."

Dave sat down at the cramped table across from Bryant and reached for a slice of toast. "You're really easy to talk to," he said.

"Funny thing about carrying on a great conversation," Bryant said as he passed the butter, "it helps when you're talking about things of mutual interest."

"In this case, I assume you're talking about your daughter?" Dave laughed.

"I believe that's the topic of discussion."

***

Regretfully, Dave and Rebecca had to catch an early Monday afternoon flight out of Boston.

"I had a great time!" Dave said quietly as they settled down into their aircraft seats. "My only regret is that it was way too short!"

"Yeah, but short as it was it's going to be especially hard to go back to classes."

The flight attendant interrupted them for awhile and then other than superficial chatter, they didn't address the subject that seemed to be on both of their minds until after their flight had reached altitude and all of the cabin chatter had faded.

"Where do we go from here?" Becca finally asked.

"I'm open to suggestions."

"We could find a place together," she whispered in Dave's ear so the man sitting in the aisle seat couldn't hear her.

Dave glanced at the stranger and then quietly whispered back, "later."

She nodded and busied herself with a magazine.

Sitting in the window seat, Dave stared out at the world floating along far beneath them. He'd been wanting to ask Becca that very question for the past few hours. Indeed, where *did* they go from here? He honestly didn't know. In spite of the long weekend he'd just spent with Becca, Patti still hung heavy on his mind. What had happened to her after the James incident? Why hadn't she called or answered his text? Was she really done with him or just embarrassed because he knew about what had happened between her and James? The real question in his mind, of course, was did *he* still love her? His thoughts drifted to the time they had spent together during Thanksgiving. He began trying to compare those feelings with the ones he'd had during those few precious times he'd spent with Becca on the beach in Florida. More recently he thought about the time he'd spent with her crammed together aboard her father's yacht.

He drew a deep breath as he thought about the conversation he'd had with Becca's dad that first night on the yacht. What Bryant had said still weighed heavily on his mind. What if Becca couldn't, or didn't want to live a more ordinary life – a life he could afford? Could they really build a marriage and a life together having varied interests? Having wealth helped precipitate any kind of lifestyle you could imagine – but what did it mean for the bonds that it would take to hold their marriage together?

Another related thought interceded. Would it bother him if his in-laws were constantly interjecting themselves into their lives? He could imagine them inviting them on lavish all-expense-paid vacations to exotic places – or sailing excursions off the coast. Things, of course, that he could never afford on his own. What would things like that do to their relationship with *his* parents? If they had children, which set of parents would see more of them, his parents or hers?

As he spotted a checkerboard pattern of houses far below him he wondered where they'd live? Would her parents insist on funding a lavish place for them to live, complete with maids to keep Becca from having to keep up on all the attending house chores? Would they take no for an answer if Becca and he decided on something more rustic – something where they could live as man and wife without having others invade their privacy?

Serious doubts began flooding his mind. Neither relationship at this point was a go, but either one still had possibilities. He tried to compare the two women. They weren't as different as night and day of course. Both were beautiful in their own unique ways. Both were, or had been loving...

He drew a deep breath and closed his eyes. Both relationships were too complicated. He didn't know if the thing with Becca would go beyond the next few weeks. Even though they were both studying to be aeronautical engineers, she was in her second year of graduate school. He, on the other hand, still had nearly a year to go to get his undergraduate degree. What would she want to do when she graduated? Both of them were being sponsored by Raytheon. She would have a guaranteed job waiting for her the instant she graduated. What would she do for four years while he struggled through the rest of his studies? Would she want children or postpone them or put them off entirely in favor of a career? You just didn't go to all the work it was taking to finish a graduate engineering degree and then just walk away.

His head hurt as he forced even more unknowns into the equation. Then suddenly he had his answer to at least one of his questions. Before he trod another step down the path with Becca, he had to know where he stood with Patti. He didn't know how he was going to find out, but he was convinced by the time the Labor Day week was finished, he would know, even if that meant flying to Colorado Springs, renting a car, and driving out to Patti's house and beating on her door. He wouldn't be put off another week! It wasn't fair to Becca, to him, or to Patti.

***

Rose and Claire cornered him around the dinner table one evening. "Did you ever find out what happened to Patti?" Claire asked.

"No. Raytheon kept me pretty busy during the summer," he answered quickly, and then he stopped and answered her question honestly. "Actually, I've been waiting for her to call me."

"It's been nearly seven months!" Claire exclaimed. "I think if she was going to call you she'd have already done that. Dave, you need to get on with your life!"

"I suppose so," he answered quietly. "I decided that on the way home from the coast today."

"What are your plans?" Claire insisted.

"I thought I'd start by trying again to call her and her mom and then I thought I'd try calling my mom."

"Have you tried to find out what happened to that James guy at Colorado State?"

"No. I don't know who to call."

"You had that detective's number. You told me he wouldn't give you any information on the case before because it was still under investigation. I'd start there."

Not really wanting to talk to the detective and yet knowing that he owed Becca some sort of answer, he pulled out his cell phone and walked up the long staircase to his bedroom.

"Oiler", the detective answered on the second ring.

"Yes, Detective. This is Dave Tolman. I was Patti Carlson's boyfriend before James Baxter got involved. The last time we talked, the case was under investigation and you couldn't divulge any information."

"Where have you been Dave? That case was settled the middle of the summer. James and his buddy, Tony, were convicted of attempted murder and several other lesser charges and are either already in prison or soon will be."

"I've been living at Purdue University in Indiana and more recently in New Jersey working for Raytheon on a summer internship. What can you tell me about the case?"

"What do you want to know?"

"Specifically, what happened to Patti?"

"You can read all of this on the official case files but I'll give you the highlights. The official case file indicates that she was physically and sexually assaulted by James and the other three men living in his house. Evidently when she told James she was pregnant with his child he went nuts and tried to beat it out of her. When James realized what he'd done, he knew he'd be going to jail for assault and probably lose his scholarship. He convinced his roomies to help him inject her with meth to make it appear as if she'd overdosed. Then he and one other guy tossed her in a snowbank alongside the road, figuring that by the time somebody found her she'd be dead. That got him and his accomplice charged with first degree attempted homicide. Two of the roomies turned state's evidence and fingered James and Tony. Both James and Tony were sentenced to eight-to-twenty-four years in the state penitentiary."

"What happened to Patti?"

"I don't know that. Due to the circumstances, the judge allowed her to testify via remote camera and because of HIPPA laws whatever happened to her or the fetus was not entered on the court documents. Evidently the fetus survived, though, or the charges would have been enhanced to first degree murder."

"Thank you," Dave said quietly. "Thanks for your work on the case. From what you just told me I'm sure that took some good police work to prove."

"You're welcome, Dave. Is there anything else I can do for you?"

"No. I suppose not."

Dave sat staring at his phone for several long minutes after he ended the call. No wonder Patti wouldn't talk to him. Not only had she gone through a horrific experience but now she was carrying James' child. He finally glanced up at the calendar on his wall. The month still read May. He stood and rifled through the pages until September stood exposed. Then he turned back the pages of his memory to their last conversation. She'd told him in February that she'd moved in with James. He counted forward nine months. If the child had lived – which Oiler had indicated it had – she'd be due sometime near the first of November. If he flew home that next weekend, she'd be heavy with child.

He stopped at the thought and tried to decide on his next move. If he just showed up at her door neither she nor her mother may let him in the house.

That was only part of the problem. If she agreed to talk to him what would he say? They hadn't spoken to each other in over seven months! Did they still have anything to say to one another? He tried to imagine what was going through her mind. He could imagine her crying every time she saw her reflection in a mirror, and thought about their last words – and then the horrific beating and attempted murder at James' hands.

He turned his phone on again and found Patti's number. Maybe she'd talk to him on the phone first. He hated to go to all the time and expense to fly there only to be rejected at the door.

Instead of dialing Patti's number, he called his mom.

"Hi Dave," Karen answered cheerily. "I haven't heard from you in a while. How are you?"

"I'm okay. I just got back from Raytheon a couple of weeks ago and I've started fall semester here at Purdue."

"How did that go?"

"Mom, as much as I'd like to catch up, I've got more serious matters on my mind. I just spoke with the detective in Fort Collins who investigated Patti's case. Did you know that she was pregnant with James' child when he beat and drugged her and left her to die in the snow?"

"No!" Karen gasped. "I didn't know any of that!"

"So I suppose you haven't talked to Mrs. Carlson since then?"

"No. I'm sorry. I know I should have called but…"

"Never mind. She probably wouldn't have talked to you about that anyway. I tried to call them both right after it all happened. Patti wouldn't answer her phone and her mom just told me that Patti wouldn't talk to me."

"That is just so sad. I'm sorry Dave. I sense that there's something else on your mind. What are you thinking?"

"Mom I met someone in Florida this summer and I just got back from spending the Labor Day weekend with her and her father on a yacht off the coast of Massachusetts."

"Oh!"

"Yeah, and now I'm literally on the horns of dilemma. I've never stopped loving Patti but under the circumstances I don't know first if she'd even talk to me, and second if she would if I'd just be wasting my breath. I just can't move on without knowing. If I only knew how she felt, I could make a decision."

"I really don't think you'll be able to do that over the phone, Son."

"I know. That's why I was thinking about catching a flight home Friday night or early Saturday morning, but even if I do there's no guarantee that she'll even talk to me."

"No, maybe not, but if she won't then at least you'll have your answer."

"What would you do Mom?"

"I think you're right. If I were you I'd fly home. I really think she owes you an answer."

A long pause passed between them.

"You may want to try calling her first though – no, on second thought I'm thinking that maybe you should take some time and compose a long text message to her first, explaining what you know, how you feel, and that you need to see her on Saturday. If she doesn't want you to meet at her parent's house, you could take her for a short drive somewhere. The autumn leaves have started turning in the canyons. That might be nice."

"That's great advice, Mom."

"Oh, and Dave, do you want me to get flowers or do you want to do that?"

"You've got great taste in flowers, Mom, would you do that for me?"

"I'd love to Dave."

Dave thought about the conversation he'd just had with his mom for awhile, convincing himself that in spite of the pain he was probably going to cause in everyone's lives, going to see Patti was the best solution.

Then as he went to get back on his feet he thought about Becca and he turned on his phone again.

"Hi, lover," Becca answered. "Do you miss me already?"

"You know I do," he answered quietly.

"Okay," she continued hesitantly, "why aren't I feeling any happiness in this call? What's going on, Dave?"

"I've decided to fly to Colorado Springs this weekend."

"Oh."

"I'm going crazy here, Becca. You know the whole story and you know how I feel about you…"

"But?"

"But I just can't let us go any further until I settle things with Patti once and for all."

"Are there complications?"

"Are you clairvoyant?"

"You asked me that before. There are, aren't there?"

"Evidently she's pregnant by the guy who tried to murder her."

"Wow! That's heavy!"

"Yes, it is."

"I just had a Blake flashback when you said that. I wonder what I'd have done if I had gotten more from him than an STD?"

"Would you have aborted it? I'm sure your dad…"

"No!" she exclaimed. "In my mind that child would have been conceived in love – at least from my standpoint. There hadn't been any force or ugliness involved. I couldn't have lived with that on my conscience."

"Even with everything you've got going for you in school?"

"Oh, I'd have finished school. It just may have been a lot rougher, and I'd have had to depend on my dad to help out."

"So do you think I'm nuts?"

"No Dave. You're an honorable man. I've already told you that. Don't think for a minute, though, that I won't be sitting on pins and needles and crying all the time you're gone. Do you think you'll have an answer by the time you're ready to fly back here or do you think this is going to take some time to decide even if you can talk to her?"

"I wish I knew."

"Me too!"

Dave could tell by the change in the pitch of her voice that she was crying.

"I'm so sorry, Becca!"

"Me too, but you know what, Dave? This only makes me love you more. Any other guy would have just let the dead dogs lie and then worried about what might have been for the rest of his life. If you don't clear this up and get closure it'll haunt you – and us if we get together – for the rest of our lives."

"Can I call you after school tomorrow afternoon?" he asked.

She hesitated for a moment before she answered. "No Dave, please don't. I'm going to start my grieving process tonight, and then if you call me with good news on Sunday, I'm going to meet your plane at the airport and celebrate by taking you to a suite at the Hilton. To coin an old war phrase: *damn the torpedos, full speed ahead!*"

***

Dave sat down at his desk for the next hour and carefully composed a text message to Patti. He almost called instead but he wanted to have everything he wanted to say rehearsed first in case he simply got too choked up to continue. After he read through the entire manuscript five times, correcting a few nits, he hesitated for a few moments and then pressed the send button. He half expected his text to be returned as undeliverable but a few seconds later, he received the notice that his text had been delivered.

Dave sat silently for a few more long minutes carefully watching his screen, waiting for a reply. None came. Finally, he opened up the airline app on his phone, made flight reservations for early Saturday morning and then called his mom back to let her know what he'd done. She promised she'd pick up flowers on Friday before the florist shop closed.

357

Chapter 38

James' first week in prison was an exercise in frustration, reflection, and self-loathing. Here behind bars he had no freedom and no individuality. He dressed the same as all of the other inmates. He ate the same thing as all of the other inmates. He had an hour a day to exercise like all of the other inmates, and he spent at least 18 hours a day in his cell, like all of the other inmates. He had to share his open-fronted, barred room with another inmate – Arturo, a Hispanic inmate serving time for murder.

Arturo didn't say much, and when he did speak, he did so with such a heavy Spanish accent that James had a hard time understanding what he said, so they pretty much ignored one another.

The August weather was too hot outside to spend much time in the yard so when his scheduled exercise time came he crowded into the air conditioned gym along with everyone else. He'd come through college football training thinking he was pretty buff. But it only took a few minutes the first day to realize a lot of the other inmates were heavier built and stronger. Many of them had spent infinitely more time with the weights than he had.

The inmates had established a pecking order in nearly everything that took place behind the barred walls. Some ate first – leaving him the dregs. Others were assigned to the good jobs – leaving him cleaning toilets and showers. Still others had been assigned cellmates they could communicate with. He had Arturo.

He did notice one thing, though, it wasn't impossible to challenge the pecking order. If nothing else, he had honed his communications skills. Tales of his years at the dude ranch got others listening to him and before long he had a little clique of groupies who seemed to hang on his every word. They didn't know if what he told them was true, of course, so in order to build himself up in their eyes he often embellished the truth. If there was one thing the inmates seemed to like was the tales of his exploits with the young women who came to the dude ranch.

One large man in particular – Spencer – seemed to take more notice than the others. What Spencer didn't do, though, was get involved in the catcalls and crude comments the others did as they listened to his tales. That didn't bother James at first; he knew nothing about any of the inmates and for all he knew, Spencer may not be overly intelligent.

James was halfway through a story a few days later, describing in detail a particularly titillating story about a buxom brunette he remembered from his first year at the ranch. Connie had challenged him from the first day. She was amazingly beautiful, easy to talk to, and even though she had a great body and loved to flirt, by the third day in camp he hadn't gotten past first base with her.

"Did she have a dime-sized birthmark under her left ear?" Spencer suddenly interjected.

James should have known something was afoot when his audience went silent, but thinking the man was just exercising one of his own fantasies, James eagerly continued.

"Yes, as a matter of fact, she did," he said. "And I found out later that she had another one just like it under her left nipple."

"You better shut your pie hole!" Spencer suddenly raved. "I knew her! She was a nice girl, not one of the whores you're always talking about!"

Not willing to lose face with his audience, James instantly countered. "How do you know her? Are you from Oregon?"

"Yes I am, and I knew Connie. She was never the same after she came home from her week at that dude ranch of yours. You ruined her!"

"I didn't do anything she didn't want me to do," James countered, showing his best grin.

Spencer stepped forward and got right in James' face. "And I told you to shut your pie hole!"

"Leave it alone, Spencer!" one of the other inmates said, stepping forward. "You know what'll happen if you touch the newbie. Come on man, you've only got three weeks left in this shithole. You don't want to do this!"

Spencer slowly stepped back half a pace, raised a hand and stabbed his index finger against James' chest. "You don't know who you're messing with you little freak!" he growled. "And for that reason, I'll let you live. But I've heard enough of this bullshit. You tell one more story and I promise it'll be your last."

James quickly sized the man up. He shaved his head, was probably half an inch shorter and not nearly as buff, and had a single small tattoo of a tear under his right eye. The man scowled at him through grey eyes as his threat hung heavily on James' mind. No, he didn't know who he was dealing with. Until Spencer had joined his little story group he'd never seen the man before. From what the other inmate had just said, Spencer was evidently a seasoned inmate if he only had three weeks left. The thing that worried him was from their silence, the other inmates obviously knew who he was and what he was capable of.

"Sorry man," James answered humbly. "I didn't know she was a friend of yours."

"That's the problem you maggot!" Spencer hissed. "Every one of those young women you victimized was somebody's sister or daughter. If I'd have known what was going on up there in those woods, I'd have brought a few of my boys with me and we'd have hung every one of you pigs up by your nuts."

"Okay man. You made your point!"

"No, I don't think I did!" Spencer shouted, stepping forward again. "Connie was there with some other girls that she thought were her friends. When they found out what you were doing to her, they all came home with stories to tell. Her boyfriend dumped her, the other girls started bullying her on social media, her parents found out what had happened and she blew her brains out with her brother's shotgun!"

"Oh wow!" was all James could say.

"So, how do you feel about yourself now, pretty boy?"

"Guard's coming!" someone shouted and all of the other men moved a step away.

"This ain't over, slime ball!" Spencer grumbled as he took a step backward. "It ain't over by a long shot. I promised her brother that if I ever found out who'd done her I'd even the score!"

"Break it up!" someone bellowed.

James turned to look. A guard was bearing down on him, a nightstick thrust out in front of him.

"The newbie started it all!" a man yelled as the rest of the crowd pulled back, leaving James alone to face the guard.

"Turn around!" the guard yelled, "and put your hands behind your back!"

James did as he was told and an instant later handcuffs snapped around both of his wrists.

***

"You screwed up big time," Arturo said in heavily accented English as the guard removed the handcuffs and slammed the cell door behind him.

"Who is that Spencer guy?" James asked.

"He's trouble. He coulda killed you with his bare hands."

"I didn't know that."

"He been here 'bout two years for poundin' somebody. Nobody messes with him!"

"What should I do?"

"Watch your back!"

"How do I do that? I've only been here a week. I don't know how all this stuff works!"

"Don't go nowhere alone. Fact is soon as ya do your chores you'd best come back here and tell 'em to lock you up!"

"I didn't mean any harm. I was just trying to fit in. How was I supposed to know I was telling stories about somebody he knew?"

"Don't matter. You already said what ya said. If ya get lucky for three more weeks he be gone."

***

As Spencer moved to the end of the dinner line that afternoon he glanced up at the man serving desserts. "Give the newbie my pudding," he mumbled as he held out a pudding cup. "Make sure nobody else gets it."

The other inmate nodded without replying, took Spencer's cup and sat it down at the back of the serving line.

As usual, by the time James was able to take his turn in the line, the food had been pretty well picked over. The inmate serving desserts pushed a pudding cup to the front of the display case and winked at him. James recognized the man as being one of the men who had gathered around him to hear his stories every day and smiled. At least somebody appreciated what he was trying to do to fit in.

"You made it," Arturo said as James pulled off his orange jump suit and slumped down on his bunk. "I seen you been staying away from people. That's good."

"Do you think he was bluffing?" James asked. "Nobody messed with me today."

"No. He don't bluff. Just watch yourself. Maybe not shower. Too easy to jump somebody in the shower."

"I can't go three weeks without showering!"

"Better stinking than bleeding man."

With that Arturo laid down on his bunk and turned his back.

***

Arturo began banging on the cell bars early the next morning.

"What's all the ruckus!" A guard yelled as he walked down along the hallway.

"This man no breathing!" Arturo yelled.

The guard hurried to the cell. "Hold your hands up here!" he demanded.

Arturo thrust his hands through the bars and waited as the guard handcuffed his wrists together outside the bars, then keyed the lock and hurried inside.

"This man's cold!" the guard shouted. "When did he quit breathing?"

"Don't know!" Arturo answered. "I just woke up."

***

The medical officer walked into the warden's office later in the day.

"Well?" the warden asked.

"Fentanyl."

"How much?"

363

"Doesn't matter. Enough to kill him."

"Looks like we're going to have to have a lock down this afternoon and bring in the dogs. Somebody's going to be seeing the judge for murder one."

"I think the newbie just overdosed," the med tech offered.

"That may be, but if he did, he had to have gotten it from somebody."

"Word in the house is Spencer and he had words."

"Check Spencer's cell first then."

"I think that's a waste of time. He's not stupid."

"Yeah, you're probably right but that's protocol," the warden muttered under his breath. "Here's where we start interviewing all Spencer's friends and enemies too. I'm sure somebody saw something."

"I suppose so, but we both know that'll go nowhere."

"Damn, I'll be glad when they let that guy out of here. I've been doing this a long time and I was never really afraid of anyone before he came in here."

"Yeah, I know what you mean."

***

Later that day, Spencer moved through the dinner line as usual. When he reached the dessert line he made quick eye contact with the inmate standing behind the sneeze shield.

"We okay?" Spencer asked quietly.

The other inmate thrust a pudding cup to where Spencer could touch it and carefully nodded without looking up. Spencer took the pudding cup and moved on.

Chapter 39

*P*atti was watching TV in her parent's living room when her cell phone dinged. When she saw that the message was from Dave, she lifted her finger to the delete key, and then she paused. It had been months since he'd last tried to contact her. Until then, he'd honored her request and stayed away. Why now? She shut her phone down and laid it across her extended abdomen. She felt so ugly! She couldn't see her feet without bending far over her non-existent waist. Her feet and lower legs were swollen almost every day. Her pediatrician had warned her about her weight gain and insisted that she start walking to help with her circulation and her muscle tone. The problem was, she didn't want to walk anywhere in her neighborhood. In desperation, she'd finally talked her mom into driving her to a gym across town where she'd spent an hour on the treadmill every day.

"Did I hear your phone ding?" Janet asked, looking over at her.

"Yes, I just got a text message from Dave."

"What did he say?"

"I don't want to look at it."

"Patti!" her mom insisted angrily as she got to her feet and walked over to stand in front of her. "You at least owe him an explanation – as difficult as that might be. It's not really his fault that all of this happened to you. If you don't want to ever see him or talk to him again, you at least need to tell him that so he can get on with his life."

"What makes you think he hasn't already?"

"I don't know, and that's the travesty of this whole mess Patti! It's not fair that you let this hang over him so long!"

"You don't know that I'm doing that! For all we know he may have just sent me a wedding invitation!"

"Then if he did you should at least have the decency to text or call him back and congratulate him. You're a mental wreck, Patti! You've let yourself go. You cry all the time. I've tried to get you to go to that counselor and you won't. Patti you can't let that bastard, James, ruin your life!"

"Maybe it would have been better if those guys hadn't found me in time!"

"Patti!" Janet screamed as she reached down and shook Patti's shoulders. "You take that back! I thank God every day for you and for the life of that little girl you're carrying inside of you. You're bigger than this Patti! You really are!"

Janet burst into tears and ran out of the room, leaving Patti to stare numbly at the message notification on her phone.

She missed Dave. She thought at first that she'd made the right decision, but she'd been such a fool. Walking away from Dave may have been the right decision at the time, but not seeing right through James had been a serious mistake. And now she was stuck. The only bright light shining through the whole sordid affair was that James was going to prison for what he'd done. The instant she thought about that, though, she realized that she'd never be free of him. She was carrying a child that someday he may want to include in his life. She'd seen the news stories. In her mind it was wrong to allow parental rights to someone who had… Worse yet, he wouldn't be in prison forever – and then what?

She touched her cell phone screen again, bringing it back to life. The message was still sitting there in her inbox, along with the one that Dave had sent months before. She'd already read the first one and at the time it had filled her with shame and regret. She highlighted the old text and raised her thumb to the delete key. Then she paused. It had been so long since she'd read it she wondered now if she should re-read it first before she opened the latest. After all she'd been in such a dark frame of mind maybe she had read more into that old text than had really been there.

Finally, she gently touched the glass and his old text filled the screen. The message was so long that she had to scroll up to find the beginning. Tears trickled down her cheeks as she read it. Emotions she had nearly forgotten swelled her chest and a slim smile crossed her lips. Dave wasn't the most flowery writer. It was obvious as she read on that what he had written must have taken him a lot of time and thought to do.

She drew a deep breath as she finished the first message and her thoughts flowed back over their relationship for the hundredth time. The first sentence of his new text lay open to view. Somehow, she couldn't bring herself to scroll down to read it. What if it *was* a wedding invitation – or something just as bad?

Sweet memories floated through her mind. She'd been drawn to Dave from the moment they first met. They just seemed to complete one another. It wasn't as if when she'd start a sentence, he'd finish it or anything like that, but when they'd spent time together she'd just felt natural and comfortable around him. They could talk about nearly anything – and they had.

The memories of their college days together weren't nearly as exhilarating. They'd both been challenged by the academics – he more than she. He was so obsessed over his grades that about all he wanted to do after school was study. She wanted good grades too, but she wasn't obsessed like he was. If he wasn't studying, he was running or training – even in the off season. She could only remember a few fleeting times when they had broken away and spent an unencumbered day together – often in the mountains. They both loved the mountains.

Anger began to push its ugly head into her memories, and then recent history back-flowed through her old memories and she faced an awful truth. Nearly every outing they'd gone on, she'd initiated. She'd had the power all along to nudge him in her direction. She'd heaped the blame for their split-up on his head – but now she realized it wasn't entirely his fault. She'd never insisted on being the dominant figure in their relationship. She'd sort of followed his lead, wanting him to be happy. Too late, she realized that she could have easily guided him in her direction. Thanksgiving had been a shining example of that fact. He'd probably have done anything that she asked that day.

A chill swept over her as she poised her thumb on the following text. The past months had been awful. What if his message was something she didn't want to see? Could she sink any lower?

She turned the phone screen down and set it back on her belly. Her daughter kicked at the pressure. A smile pushed through her frown. Early on she'd hated the idea of carrying James' child. She was afraid it'd be defective and the nightmare would follow her the rest of her life. The pain and deep bruising after the beating had taken weeks to subside. Her ribs still hurt. She'd hoped every day that she'd lose the baby. She'd had nightmares of it being born with James' striking features! She was sick for nearly three months! And then it had gotten better – much better – for awhile. Now that the final weeks were ticking away and she was facing the reality that would soon be thrust upon her she had drifted into depression.

Needing to break out of those thoughts, she picked up the phone and scrolled through the first few lines of Dave's new text. She smiled. It was obvious that he'd agonized over every line – again. Nothing he said followed his usual conversational style. It was as if he had tried to write a love letter.

Then she realized that was exactly what he'd done. She hung on his every phrase. She had to wipe her eyes over and over again so she could read on. When she finished, she let her tears run freely down her face until they dripped off her chin.

Long minutes passed as she read and reread his text. Then the reality of what he'd written swept over her and she panicked! He was flying into Colorado Springs tomorrow! She was a mess!

"Mom!" Patti yelled as she struggled up off the sofa. "Mom, I need some help!"

Janet flew into the room, a look of alarm gripping her face.

"What's wrong?" she exclaimed.

"Dave's flying in tomorrow! He's coming here! I'm a mess!"

The panic gripping Janet's face smoothed and then turned into a slight smile. "We have some work to do then, don't we? I'll call Betty."

"Her shop is closed!" Patti cried. "She can't possibly do my hair tonight – and besides, she doesn't even know about…"

"Yes, she does, Patti. She's my best friend and I needed a confidant through all of this – besides your father of course."

"Oh that's just great! Of all the women in town, you choose to confide in your hair dresser! Mom what were you thinking?"

"Betty and I have been friends for longer than you have been alive. I'm sure she hasn't told a soul."

Not looking convinced, Patti looked down. "What will I wear?"

"You have several nice new tops to choose from. You're not going dancing for Pete's sake. You're…"

"Meeting Dave!" Patti interrupted. "We haven't seen each other for months!"

"Calm down, Patti! You're the same woman he knew and loved months ago." Then she stopped and smiled, "just a little extra is all."

Patti burst into tears. "I can't do this! I'm going to call him and tell him not to come!"

"You'll do no such thing Patti! You'll do your hair, wash your face, put on a little makeup for the first time in months, and then you'll open that front door when he comes and sweep him off his

369

feet just like you did years ago! If he still loves you – and I suspect he does – then this…" Janet gently poked her belly… "won't be a deal breaker."

Patti rubbed her eyes and looked down.

"Unless you want it to be," Janet added quietly. "Do you want him back?"

"Of course I do!" Patti exclaimed. "I've lived with self-loathing ever since…"

"Ever since you tried to force his hand?"

"Is that what I did?"

"Sort of. It's not your fault that circumstances got in the way. I think he had good intentions. It wasn't his fault that a blizzard kept him from flying home over Christmas."

"I was *so* stupid!"

"You were on the rebound, you were lonely and upset – you were vulnerable, Patti. You didn't know that a wolf was stalking you."

"Am I reading too much into this text message?" Patti asked as she turned on her phone and thrust it at her mother.

Janet carefully read what Dave had written, and then a warm glow filled her countenance. "I'd say after reading that, that the ball is firmly in your court, Patti. You need to decide tonight how you want this to go. Dave didn't say so in his text, but if my women's intuition is speaking to me correctly, I think he may have met someone new and he's reaching out to you one last time before he finally moves on. The question to you is do you still love the man?"

"What about the baby?"

"He already knows about the baby. It's not like he's going to be surprised when you open the door."

"That's not what I mean."

"What you're asking is will he want both you and the baby? I'd say he has no choice. If he still loves and wants you, he'll take you for better or for worse."

"What if James..."

"You don't want to cloud up this decision with questions that neither one of you have answers to right now. If that idiot wants to try to claim parental rights sometime down the road, then you'll have to deal with it then. But I don't think any judge in the country will grant him rights. He tried to kill the baby in your womb. Worse yet, he tried to murder you because of it!"

Janet took Patti's phone, punched a phone number into it and waited for Betty to answer.

"Hey girl!" Janet answered brightly. "I need a fairy godmother and I need one tonight. You know that thing I told you about Patti? Well, Prince Charming is flying in tomorrow to see her and she's sort of let herself go. Would you like to come here?"

Janet laughed. "Okay, we'll see you in about ten minutes at your salon. Thank you so much Betty. I owe you one!"

Chapter 40

Dave's dad picked him up at the airport at 8 a.m. Saturday morning. "I'll drive you home," Frank said as Dave stowed his suitcase in the trunk and climbed in. "Mom has your flowers. You can take our car to go see Patti. If we need to go somewhere in the meantime, we can use my pickup truck."

"Thanks Dad," Dave said quietly as he fastened his seat belt and looked down at his hands.

"You nervous?" his dad asked as he pulled away from the curb.

"I really am."

"What are your plans?"

"I don't have any. I'm playing this by ear."

"Your mom and I have been talking about this ever since you called and told her what was going on. Are you okay with raising that other man's baby if you two decide to get back together?"

"Why wouldn't I be? It's not the baby's fault."

"Do you love Patti?"

"I always have, Dad. I wouldn't be here today doing this if I didn't."

"Why did it take you so long to decide? Why now?"

"It's complicated, Dad. There's a lot you don't know. I told Mom a little of this already but when I couldn't come home for Christmas this guy on my team made a move on her. Turns out he was a freak but Patti didn't see through him until it was too late. It nearly cost her her life."

"You already told your mother all that and now that guy is going to prison and Patti's having his baby. I think I understand. What I want to know is why did it take you all these months to decide to do this?"

"I tried to reach out to Patti and her mom right after it all happened but neither one of them would talk to me. I was a thousand miles away and after she'd told me that she'd moved in with James I figured she'd already made up her mind. I didn't find out what happened until I got back from Raytheon and called Detective Oiler."

"Do you think she's changed her mind now?"

"I don't know, Dad. That's what I'm here to find out."

"Just out of the clear blue?"

"No. There's more to it than that. I told Mom that during the summer when I was doing my internship with Raytheon I met someone."

"So now there's another woman involved?"

"Yes and no. I mean Becca is great and I think I'm falling in love with her but…"

"But your first love is Patti and you need to know if there's still anything there?"

"Exactly."

"Okay, Son. I understand, and you know what, I admire you. Most guys would have slammed the door on Patti the moment they found out what happened, especially because she made the first move. Are you sure you can live with that?"

"I don't know, Dad. I've been agonizing over that question for months. Maybe she's already made the decision for me. She may have been done with me months ago when she moved in with James. I just can't in good conscience let my relationship with Becca go another step forward until I know. If I found out years further down the road that Patti just shut the door between us out of embarrassment over what happened with James, I don't think I could live with that."

"How far has this relationship with Becca gone?"

"We haven't known each other that long, but I really like her. There are complications though. Her father is wealthy and she has grown up as an entitled child. She's cool because she doesn't flaunt it. She's rich but she doesn't act like she is. Does that make any sense?"

"It does."

"She's also way ahead of me in school. We're both studying engineering but she's starting her third year of graduate school at Purdue this fall and I've still got a year of undergrad work left. She's great looking but really down to earth. She's had a few hard knocks in life and has grown from them. I think she's attracted to me because I'm pretty transparent and she likes what she sees."

"So what's the problem, besides the wealth thing?"

"The wealth thing is really the elephant in the room. I met her dad over Labor Day. They took me on a cruise off the coast of Massachusetts. While we were out there, he took me aside and we had a really down-to-earth discussion about wealth and expectations. He described wealth as being a heavy burden. Anyway, it planted a few doubts in my mind. For one thing, I don't see her parents being overly intrusive in our relationship but neither do I see them stepping away. I don't know how I'd respond to having his wealth hanging over my head all the time. I've always tried to be self-sufficient."

"That could be an issue for sure but that would depend on how you and Becca handled it."

"Exactly," Dave agreed. "For example if we have kids I'd want to give you and Mom equal time as grandparents but what if Becca's folks think that a great way of spending time with us would be a two week all-expense-paid vacation to Hawaii or something? How could a simple camping trip in the Colorado back country with you compete with that? I think Becca and I could deal with that but what about our kids?"

"You said *if* you have kids. Is there a problem there?"

"I don't know," Dave answered quietly. "What little we've talked about a family I think she wants kids but I'm wondering how that would look. She's really good at what she does and where she's in graduate school, I can't see her setting a career aside to raise kids."

"That might be tough. I've seen a few people do that, though. It might mean splitting time with the kids between you two. Depending on how her career goes, you might end up being a stay-at-home dad. How would you feel about that?"

"I've always wanted a family, and I think she does too. I think it would work, but that's definitely an unknown. It's easy to talk the talk, but …"

"I get it," Frank said quietly.

They drove in silence for a few moments.

"Any advice?" Dave finally broke the silence.

"I think you're on the right path Dave. I'm really glad that you made the decision to bring this thing with Patti to a head before you step away. What if Patti breaks your heart again?"

Dave drew a deep breath. "Then I have my answer and I'll move on. Maybe this thing with Becca won't work but I can't let that go any further until I know."

***

Dave's mom was standing in the doorway when he and his dad drove up. She took him gently in her arms and held him, refusing to let go for long moments.

"Are you ready for this?" she finally asked quietly.

"Ready or not," Dave responded.

"What time did you tell her you'd come by?"

"Ten."

"Oh good! Then you've got time to comb your hair and have some breakfast."

"Do I really need to comb my hair?"

"That's just an expression. You look fine, Dave – worried and a little thinner than I've seen you in a while, but you look fine. Have you been eating?"

Dave grinned. "Yes Mom. I've been eating – maybe not a balanced diet all the time, but I've been eating. I think the difference is I'm not working out for football anymore and I'm not as buff as I once was."

"I think you look great," Frank added. "How's that fake knee treating you?"

"I haven't had any trouble with it at all. When I talked to the doctor after the surgery, he told me that he thought I'd get along well with it, and he was right. Thanks to a lot of physical therapy its doing fine."

"Dave isn't here to talk about his knee or sports," Karen chided him.

"I know that, dear, but if you haven't noticed, the boy is a little nervous and he has about an hour and a half to kill. I was just trying to help him relax and think about something else."

"Sorry," Karen apologized, "your dad is right of course. But speaking of all that have you decided what you're going to say?"

"No, Mom. I thought I'd lead off with the flowers and whatever compliments I can think of and then let things go where they go."

"I think I know how you feel about Patti," Karen said softly. "How do you think you'll handle it if she has decided to end it?"

"I've actually been thinking a lot about that," Dave began.

"Come in the kitchen," Karen stopped him. "I'll make some French toast while we talk. There's no sense in standing around here in the foyer like a bunch of strangers."

"Like I started to say," Dave continued a few moments later as he settled into a kitchen chair and laid his elbows on the table, "I've had a hard time thinking about anything else lately. I've run both scenarios around in my mind until my thinker is raw. I finally came to the conclusion that if she has decided to end it that I'll try not to cry, I'll wish her well, and try to escape with my dignity."

"Well spoken," Frank said.

"What if she still wants you?" Karen asked quietly.

"Then that's when we talk about marriage and logistics and finances – all of that important stuff."

"We haven't had to help you with school," Frank offered, "we'd be happy to help you with finances."

"That's generous of you Dad, but I think once we get the medical expenses behind us, we should be okay. I made a lot of money this summer as an intern. They put me up in a subsidized apartment, paid me entry-level engineering wages, and gave me per diem while I was there so I was able to save most of what I made. They acted like they really were interested in having me join their team."

"Well just know that the offer stands. You may not know this yet but it costs money to raise a child."

"I hope I get the chance."

"Her baby has to be due soon," his mom said, "will you move her to Indiana before she gives birth?"

"Mom, you're getting the cart before the horse. I don't even know yet if I'll be welcome in her home."

"No doubt," Karen mused, "she's been through a lot. She's had months to think about it but until you told her you were flying out here, she probably figured she'd be doing it all alone."

"I need to ask you both a question that's been nagging at me ever since I decided to do this," Dave said. "If you were to put yourselves in her situation what do you think you'd do? I can think of several scenarios. What if she really wants me but is worried that the baby and everything that happened between her and James will come between us?"

"That's something I think you need to talk about right up front Son," Frank answered. "Both of your emotions are going to be really raw. Neither one of you are going to want to say anything to ruin this, but I think you owe it to each other to ask all the heavy questions up front. This is the time for total and complete honesty. If you don't address those things until later, you may live to regret it."

"I agree," Karen said, reaching out to touch Dave's forearm, "and please don't just tell her what you think she wants to hear just so you won't hurt her feelings."

"I think I know how I feel Mom. I won't lie to her. I love her, but I won't beg. This has to be her choice."

"No Dave," Frank countered, "like we say in the business world, it has to be a consensus. Both of you need to agree."

***

Patti's cellphone rang while she was sitting on pins and needles in her living room waiting for Dave's appearance. When she looked down at the number her heart skipped a beat. It was Detective Oiler!

"Hello?" she asked apprehensively.

"Are you kidding me?" Patti answered after listening in silence for a few moments.

She continued to listen without answering as the detective talked on. Her mom watched silently from across the room until Patti ended the call and dropped her phone in her lap.

"What on earth is wrong?" her mother asked, seeing fresh tears streaming down Patti's face.

"That was Detective Oiler," Patti managed. "He called to tell me that James overdosed in prison and died."

"Oh my hell!" the older woman swore. "Can this day get any worse? Come with me, Patti! You're undoing everything we've spent an hour fixing. I know this probably seems impossible at this point but you need to pull yourself together!"

"These aren't tears of sorrow, Mom!" Patti said getting to her feet so she could follow her mother into the bathroom, "these are tears of relief! I've been worried sick that James was somehow going to get out of prison early on good behavior and come looking for me! It's like a giant weight has just been lifted off my chest!"

***

All too soon, it seemed, Dave parked the car in Patti's driveway and walked the seemingly endless walkway up to her front door. He hadn't been this nervous since their first formal date – the one where he'd had to meet her father for the first time! He had to concentrate to breathe in and breathe out rather than hold his breath or hyperventilate.

As he reached for her doorbell he wondered if she would let her mom answer the door or if she'd be standing there, waiting.

Inside the house a slow, melodious chime sounded and he held the flowers a little higher in front of him.

He resisted the urge to bolt.

What seemed like an eternity later the inner, wooden door opened and the only thing that separated him from Patti was a single-paned, glass storm door. His breath caught in his throat! He'd always thought she was beautiful but what he saw standing there now was beyond beautiful. Her shoulder-length auburn hair glowed in the early morning sunlight. She wore a hesitant half frown – nothing warm and wonderful like he'd expected.

His heart sank! This did not look good – not good at all!

Everything seemed to happen in slow motion. As she reached for the door handle, he noticed her slender fingers and a flash of memory streaked across his mind as he remembered those fingers lightly caressing his cheek. He stepped back a half pace to allow the storm door to swing open. She hesitated.

He studied the look on her face. He saw hesitancy – fear – and something else that he didn't recognize. His heart nearly stopped.

Then she pushed the door all the way open and he held out the flowers.

"Red and white," she said quietly as she took them from him, "just like at Thanksgiving. They're beautiful Dave. Thank you!"

He instantly sensed the hesitancy in her voice. She was telling him what he wanted to hear and yet at the same time the way she said the words sounded almost sarcastic.

"Mom's choice. I had to trust her again."

Patti glanced over her shoulder. "Mom told me she couldn't bear to watch," she said solemnly. "She didn't know how this was going to go."

"That's what I'm here to talk about."

An awkward silence settled between them.

"Wow!" he finally managed, "you look so good!"

"Don't look down," she mused.

He couldn't help but glance quickly down. He couldn't say he was put off by what he saw but a quick ache passed through him, an ache knowing that the child she was carrying wasn't his.

"That's my little girl," she said as she noticed his glance.

She laid the flowers on a short table in the entryway and then took his hand and led him to the stairway leading down into the basement. "You already know where my room is. I think we need some privacy."

Dave noticed as Patti closed her bedroom door behind them that like so many months before, she had already staged her room. Two padded folding chairs again stood facing each other at the foot of her bed. A box of tissues sat on the bed between the two chairs. She motioned to one chair and then turned and sat facing him on the other.

Not wanting the awkward silence to overwhelm them, Dave began. "You really do look great, Patti. How are you feeling?"

"Pregnant."

"I've never experienced that, could you be a little more specific?"

A slow, sad smile pressed up the corners of her lightly painted lips. "It's awful and yet wonderful. I don't think my body will ever be the same. My feet and legs swell. I get indigestion at the drop of a hat. I can't even see my feet anymore."

"Okay," Dave said, staring into her pale green eyes, "but what I really want to know is how are *you*, Patti? How are you really?"

Tears broke free and streamed down her face. He reached out a knuckle and caught them before they dripped off her chin. She reached for the tissue box.

"It's a good thing you've got those," Dave said softly, "I think we're both going to need them."

Patti dabbed away the tears and then reached out and took both of his hands and took a deep, cleansing breath.

"Okay, buster," she said softly, "I think we've tiptoed all around that artfully enough, so here's where we talk about the elephant under my blouse."

"That's no elephant. That's a child," he tried to make a joke. "The elephant is in the room and I agree with you. We need to clear the air, or bare our souls, or whatever else we have to do. I want honesty, Patti. Do you want me to start or do you want to?"

"I think I know how you feel, Dave, or you wouldn't be here, so if you want honesty, here it is. When our Christmas turned into a disaster and I moved in with James I was angry. I was hurt. I was lonely ..."

"I'm so sorry I wasn't there for you."

"Don't interrupt me," she insisted. "I need to vent a little here."

"Okay. Sorry."

"After that night you and I spent together in Greeley and our Thanksgiving together I was convinced that I loved you and that it would work between us. But then I guess I started thinking about all the years we'd spent together doing basically nothing and I began to doubt. I didn't know James then like I know him now. I know now that he was ruthless. I was weak..."

"Patti," Dave answered quietly as he touched her on the chin. "You don't owe me an explanation."

"Yes I do!" she insisted angrily, touching her belly. "I feel horrible about this. You and I were always so careful..."

"I'm not your priest," he said quietly. "I'm not here to hear a confession."

"Then why are you here?" she insisted.

"I'm here because I love you, Patti. I'm here because I need to know that in spite of everything that's happened if you still love me too. That's all that matters right now."

"That's easy to say, Dave, but there's more involved now than you and me!"

"None of this is your child's fault. If I was to lay blame on anyone I'd point at James. I'm sorry he took advantage of your loneliness. I'm sorry I let school come between us – again. I didn't have to go to Purdue when I did. This is all my fault, not yours."

She began to speak and then stopped herself and just stared at him for a few long moments, and then tears welled up in her eyes again.

"Yes I still love you Dave. I never really stopped loving you. I guess I just got impatient. I was frustrated. I couldn't see us moving on together. I wanted more and I didn't think you could give me what I needed."

"And now?"

"I don't know Dave. You're here. I suppose that means something but maybe it's not enough."

"I think I've grown up a little," he added hastily, "my life has been hollow and meaningless. I've been going through the motions but not a day goes by without me thinking about you, wondering how you're doing, worrying about you."

He stopped for a moment and looked down.

"I wish so badly that you'd have answered my first text. I tried to get the cops to tell me what happened but I was a thousand miles away and they wouldn't talk to me. They told me there was an ongoing investigation. I was worried sick! I knew something bad had happened between you and James but nobody would talk to me about it. In fact, I didn't know about the baby until I got back from my summer internship and called Detective Oiler. Because the case had been settled by then he would finally talk to me. I've been going crazy ever since worrying about how you were doing, how you were coping, feeling totally useless because I hadn't been there to help you through all this."

"I'm sorry, Dave. I didn't know any of that. I figured you knew it all and was so disgusted with me that you didn't want anything more to do with me. I thought that's why you never texted me again."

"Wait a minute Patti! I tried to call you several times before. You wouldn't answer my calls. You didn't respond to my voice mails! In desperation I sent you that last text. When you didn't respond I finally decided that you were done. That's when I quit trying and tried to get on with my life."

"I was in a dark place Dave. What did the detective finally tell you?"

"Not all of the gritty details, but enough to know that when James found out you were pregnant, they brutalized you, shot you up with meth and left you alongside the road in the snow to die."

"That about sums it up. I was broken physically and mentally. I didn't know if the baby would survive after my beating and the drug thing. Dad checked me out of school and moved me home. They've been supporting me in all of this ever since."

"Are you still in a dark place?" he asked softly.

A slight frown darkened her face. "I was until I got your last text. Since then Mom has been working me over. I'd really let myself go."

"You'd never know that from looking at you," Dave smiled. "Maybe it's motherhood, I don't know, but there's a certain radiance about you."

"That's just the new hairdo and an hour's worth of work on my face."

Dave got to his feet and reached out his hands.

"Wait," she said, lowering her hands to her sides. "There's other stuff we need to talk about."

Dave sat back down and waited.

"I don't know if you've heard yet but James just died in prison."

"Really! How?"

"Detective Oiler just called me a few minutes ago to tell me. He claims it was a drug overdose."

"I shouldn't be happy that a man's dead but in his case I am."

"There's more," she said quietly. "Because this is his child, it's possible that his parents may sue for grandparent's rights sometime down the road."

"Can they do that?"

"I don't know. We never got an attorney to represent us. I'd think under the circumstances that we could block their request but you know the way the courts work anymore. They don't often care what's morally right. All they look at is the letter of the law and the long and the short of this is James is the father and as such his parents may have rights."

"How do you feel about that?"

She looked down at her hands. "Right now I hated the very thought of ever having to see or have anything to do with him or his family again. I hate him – but I don't hate my child."

Dave wanted to scream accusations. He wanted to curse James' name, but under the circumstances it appeared that karma may have interfered. Anyway he could tell that she had more to say so he held his peace.

"James was really good to me at first. He saw me. I thought he loved me for who I am," she continued quietly.

"He was just beguiling you!" Dave growled. "I can't believe you can't look back at that and see what he was doing!"

"You weren't there, Dave!"

"No I wasn't! But if I had been, I'd have broken his jaw!"

"You might have tried."

"So now this comes down to physicality, not love? Just because he was your first I suppose that must mean something in spite of the fact that he tried to murder you?"

"You make it sound so ugly!"

"It was, Patti! It is! I wasn't there. I don't know what you did!"

"You had your chance, you know."

"Really Patti? After all *we've* been through—after all *you've* been through – this is coming down to sex?"

"No, it's not just that! It's our whole relationship! You looked at me but you never really saw me!"

"I think that's all changed now!"

"Has it, Dave? Has it really?

"If you're talking about intimacy I was trying to make our wedding night something special."

"I'm not talking about our wedding night! I'm talking about four long years of you ignoring me. I'm talking about a real *you-me* relationship! Do you really think that will change overnight? I think I understand your emotions right now – why you're here – but do you think anything has really changed?"

"Yes I do! The time we spent together around Thanksgiving was amazing!"

"I can't say it wasn't but then you immediately went right off to school."

"I didn't have a choice, Patti! If I didn't take that opportunity…"

"What Dave? What? Do you really think they would have pulled your acceptance to their graduate program? There's no reason why you couldn't have finished your undergrad at Colorado State. We could have gotten married on Valentine's Day like we'd planned to do. I could have finished *my* degree too. Then when we finally went off to Purdue, we'd have gone there together."

"Financially it was…"

"Is that all that's important in your life – money?"

"You're turning this all around!"

"No I don't think I am. I've had months to sit here and think about everything that's happened. It wouldn't have been easy but you could have gotten loans. It could have been different. If you'd stayed at Colorado State, James would have never been in the picture!"

Suddenly Dave couldn't answer.

"I made some *really* bad decisions," Patti continued after a few poignant moments, "I'll admit that! But I wasn't alone in the decisions I made. For the first time since we met, Dave, somebody gave me what I needed, and I'm not talking about sex! He made me feel special and wanted. You never did that, Dave, and I don't think that'll ever change!"

"Please Patti! I'm trying to pour out my soul here! I know I hurt you. Like you just said, I guess I really didn't really see you at first and then when I finally did, circumstances beyond our control ruined things. If only I could have come home for Christmas!"

"Do you really think that would have made any difference?"

"Yes, Patti! Yes I do! I had decided that I was going to ask you to run away with me over Christmas so I could take you to Indiana with me! We would have been pressed for time and we wouldn't have had the big fancy wedding but we'd have had each other! It may have taken me a few days to find someplace for us to live but I'm sure that

Rose and Claire wouldn't have cared if you stayed with them until I could."

"You never told me that."

"No I didn't! When I got stuck in that blizzard, I didn't want to make you feel any worse than you already did so I kept it to myself. I thought everything would work out. We were planning on getting married in June anyway. If I'd have known James had designs on you I'd have flown home after my first week of school and taken you back with me! I was that sure that I wanted and needed you!"

She looked away as tears ran down her cheeks.

Dave gently turned her face back to look at him, took a tissue from the box and gently wiped away her tears.

"What about the baby, Dave?" she asked.

"What about her? She's part of you. In fact she's a bigger part of you than she is of James. I'll raise her as my own and love her as much as I do you."

"What if she looks like James?"

"She's a girl. I'm sure she won't look like James."

"What if she has problems? What if I have problems, Dave? They shot me up with meth. My doctor told me I would always have a tendency toward addiction, and my pediatrician told me that there's always a chance that my baby will be addicted, too."

Dave put his hand gently behind her neck and pulled her a little closer as he studied her eyes.

"Then we'll face those all of those things when we come to them. I'm here for you Patti. I don't want you to have to face any of this alone."

"What about us?"

Dave slipped off his folding chair and knelt in front of her.

"I brought your ring with me Patti. Will you marry me?"

She smiled. "I'd say that was a little presumptuous of you. You had no idea that I'd say yes."

"So will you marry me? I love you as much today as I ever have."

"In spite of everything?"

"Yes, in spite of everything! None of that matters now."

She closed her eyes and bent forward to kiss him. He stood, pulled her to her feet, and then wrapped her up in a long embrace.

Soft sobs shook her as she clung to him like a small child and cried.

"Yes," she finally managed between her tears. "Yes, I'll marry you."

She paused.

"When?"

"Today. Right now."

"That's not practical Dave. Where are we going to find a justice of the peace on a Saturday morning? When do you have to fly back?"

"I have a ticket for Sunday night but if you'll come with me, I'll cash it in and buy new ones for both of us."

"I don't know if they'll let me fly right now. I'm due November first. That's just less than two months away. Besides, my pediatrician is here and she wants to follow through with the birth and check out the baby when she's born."

He kissed her again. "Okay then, speaking from a practical standpoint, how about if I come back at Christmas and we do the whole thing – big wedding, white dress, and something white for our little girl."

She pulled back a little and studied his eyes. "Maybe you should be watch the weather this time," she teased. "Are you so very sure of this, Dave? I feel…"

"Do you still love me?" he interrupted her.

Fresh tears sprang into her eyes. "Yes," she whispered. "You know I do. In spite of everything else, I've never quit loving you."

Dave reached in his pocket, pulled her engagement ring out of a small box and then gently took her finger and slipped the ring on it. She looked down at her hand for a moment and then took him in her arms again.

After a while, she released him and turned around to glance into the mirror on her bureau.

"I'm a mess!" she giggled.

"No you're a redhead and you're gorgeous!" he whispered in her ear as he gathered her in his arms and hugged her from behind.

She laughed. "We fit together a little better this way."

"Was that what I thought it was?" Dave asked softly, adjusting his hand a little on her tummy.

"Yeah, that's our little girl," Patti said as she put her hand over his. "She doesn't like being messed with."

"I think she's just saying hi," Dave laughed.

Patti turned around and pulled him close. "You make me so happy, Dave. Let's go upstairs and blow my momma's socks off!"

Author, Mike Nelson

Mike grew up on a farm where he learned the value of dedication and hard work. He is the proud father of six children, numerous grandchildren, and great-grandchildren. He is an active member of his church. He and his wife, the love of his life, have been married for over fifty years and live in Brigham City, Utah. He served in the United States Air Force in Communications Intelligence and was stationed near Istanbul, Turkey for over three years. After his honorable discharge in 1974, he attended Weber State University and graduated with a Bachelor of Science Degree in Accounting. He worked for thirty-eight years for an aerospace firm as a cost analyst, retiring in 2014.

Although Mike has been writing for most of his life, he didn't seek publication until after his retirement. He is an active member of the League of Utah Writers and his third novel, "Clairvoyant", was awarded The League's Silver Quill award for adult literature in 2019.

In Mike's own words:

Undone Innocence is my fifteenth published novel.

In addition to my novels, I have contributed numerous short stories published in League-sponsored anthologies.

I love most things out-of-doors and in my younger days I backpacked, hunted, and fished the mountains of Utah, Idaho and Wyoming. Even though I have hung up my hiking boots and backpack, I still enjoy exploring the great out-of-doors with my wife, from the seat of our side-by-side UTV.

My Publications:

Thorns of Avarice

Treehouse in the Hood

Clairvoyant

Clairvoyant Book 2

Clairvoyant Book 3

Broken Cowboy

Broken Cowboy – The Homecoming

The Highwayman

Mike's Shorts

Arrowhead Gulch

Vanish

Silent Watcher

The Invitation

The Stick Maker

Undone Innocence

These works are all available on Amazon in various formats. (Type in "books, mike nelson, Thorns of Avarice—or any novels listed above" in the Amazon.com search block.) When the book pops up, click on my name in blue to take you to my author page.

If you have comments or questions, Contact me on my e-mail account at dittybopper1074@gmail.com. I would love your input.

Get an author-signed copy by contacting me via e-mail.